OTHER NOVELS BY

BART SCHNEIDER

Blue Bossa, 1998

Secret Love, 2001

Beautiful Inez, 2005

The Man in the Blizzard, 2008

NAMELESS DAME

MURDER on the RUSSIAN RIVER

A NOVEL BY

BART SCHNEIDER

SOFT SKULL PRESS | BERKELEY
AN IMPRINT OF COUNTERPOINT

MAIN LIBRARY
Champaign Public Library
200 West Green Street
Champaign, Illinois 61820-5193

For George Rabasa, brother in fiction.
Long live the Fiction Factory.

Copyright © 2012 by Bart Schneider.
All rights reserved under International and Pan-American Copyright Conventions.

This is a work of fiction. Names, characters, places, and incidents are the product of the author's imagination or are used fictitiously. Any resemblance to actual persons, living or dead, is entirely coincidental.

Library of Congress Cataloging-in-Publication Data is available.

ISBN: 978-1-59376-435-7

Cover designed by Jeff Miller, Faceout Studio
Interior designed by Neuwirth & Associates, Inc.

Map design by Chester Arnold and Kat Bennett

Soft Skull Press
An imprint of COUNTERPOINT
1919 Fifth Street
Berkeley, CA 94710

www.softskullpress.com
www.counterpointpress.com
Distributed by Publishers Group West

10 9 8 7 6 5 4 3 2 1

In the first canto of the final canticle,
Too conscious of too many things at once,
Our man beheld the naked, nameless dame . . .

—Wallace Stevens

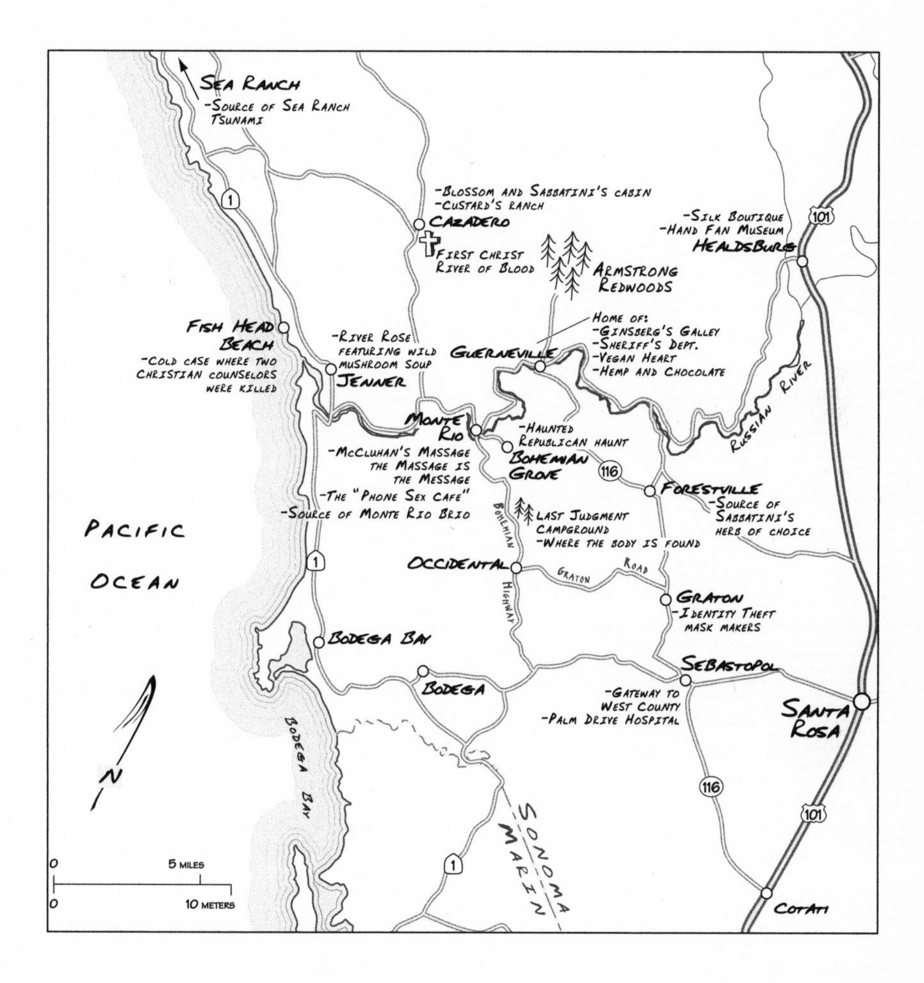

Sea Ranch
-Source of Sea Ranch Tsunami
1
-Blossom and Sabbatini's cabin
-Custard's ranch
Cazadero
First Christ River of Blood
Armstrong Redwoods
-Silk Boutique
-Hand Fan Museum
Healdsburg
101
Fish Head Beach
-Cold case where two Christian counselors were killed
-River Rose featuring wild mushroom soup
Jenner
Guerneville
Home of:
-Ginsberg's Galley
-Sheriff's Dept.
-Vegan Heart
-Hemp and Chocolate
Russian River
Monte Rio
-McCluhan's Massage the Massage is the Message
-The "Phone Sex Cafe"
-Source of Monte Rio Brio
-Haunted Republican haunt
Bohemian Grove
116
Forestville
-Source of Sabbatini's herb of choice
Pacific Ocean
Bohemian Highway
Last Judgment Campground
-Where the body is found
Occidental
Graton Road
Graton
-Identity Theft mask makers
Bodega Bay
Bodega
Sebastopol
-Gateway to West County
-Palm Drive Hospital
Santa Rosa
N
Bodega Bay
Sonoma
Marin
0
5 miles
0
10 meters
Cotati

CHAPTER ONE

The Detective Who Found Poetry

I'D BEEN RESISTING this trip for some time.

It was one degree when I flew out of Minneapolis early in the morning, but fifty-nine a few hours later in San Francisco.

My buddy Bobby Sabbatini had been trying for some time to get me to visit him and the family out in Sonoma County, near the Russian River. It was Bobby and Blossom, and baby Milosz. They'd left behind an upscale condo along the Mississippi River in Minneapolis and moved to an off-the-grid cottage outside the town of Cazadero.

I wondered which of them favored the seclusion more. Sabbatini, the former homicide detective who'd found poetry, or his wife, the wily Blossom, who'd once been my assistant and whose wayward twenties had included a formidable stint in prison.

Clearly, this was Sabbatini's adventure. Blossom loved the man madly, and if following his bliss meant opening a poetry karaoke bar in the town of Guerneville, she wasn't going to stand in his way.

Every Sunday morning, Sabbatini called from California and recited a new poem. They were never his, but I feared those might be lurking.

"Check out this gem, Augie," he'd say, "from the Monte Rio poet Gail King."

I will always have
boxes and chairs
boxes like I never
moved in
chairs like where
are all the people.

"That describes our life, the simple glory of it. We have giant redwoods, a gorgeous river, the sweet salt air from the ocean. If there ever was a place made for poetry, it's the West County of Sonoma."

I wasn't having it. I'd come from Northern California and wasn't anxious to return. Not even for a visit. I had no family left, and my youth and early twenties in the Bay Area had faded into a charmless daguerreotype, blurred at the edges. All my adult life I'd struggled to find a work ethic, and I was afraid that even a short visit to California would turn me back to a full-time slacker.

I'd also been pissed at Sabbatini and Blossom for leaving me alone in Minnesota, with my P.I. business floundering, my meager investments disappearing, and my head filled with verse from that damn poetry-rabid detective.

Sabbatini had surprised everybody, a couple of years earlier, bailing from a career gig with the St. Paul Police Department. I thought he'd gone mad. Newly married, with a baby on the way, he gave up a way of life along with the paycheck. He'd inherited the Cazadero cabin of an old aunt and claimed he had some money set aside. "I'm fifty-five years old, Augie, and I've got a dream." That's how he described his bonkers notion of the poetry bar.

The night he came over to break the news, he tried sounding reasonable.

"Of course, we won't be doing poetry all the time. I'll have to cultivate the neighborhood. But the beauty of it, Augie, is that the folks out there aren't interested in being socially networked. They'd rather sit down, smoke a doob with you, drink a good local. I'm going to get them breathing poetry. Memorizing it. Living it."

Sabbatini had become a poetry charismatic once he discovered it after 9/11, but now he'd truly gone crazy.

A year and a half after arriving in Sonoma County, Sabbatini was actually opening the poetry tavern and wanted me there for the gala. Broke, depressed, and clearly in need of some sort of vacation, I gave in, bought a cheap airline ticket to San Francisco, and signed up to bunk with Sabbatini and family for a couple of weeks.

Doubling Down

Although I was starved by the time I picked up the rental car, I pushed on a little past the town of Petaluma, where I found an In-N-Out Burger. At an outdoor table, I roared through a Double-Double so quickly that I had to order another, along with a pouch of fries. I told myself that this was a strategic move—I was heading out to the wilds of West County. Who knew when I'd find my next meal?

On the drive up from Petaluma, I composed a haiku about my meal.

Famished in late winter,
a pair of Double-Doubles
crunched at an outside table.

The haiku had become a recent habit. After years of listening to Sabbatini spout poetry, I'd gotten with the program and had begun memorizing poems. Casting around for some new stuff to memorize after Sabbatini left town, I discovered the haiku, an ideal form for the lazy man. I read a couple of collections of them and pretty soon I was writing them. The little poems issued from me as reflexively as small farts. It became an instant way of digesting my experiences. Always looking to make things easier, I decided to forgo the syllable count. As the rest of the world twittered, I tweeted myself with haiku.

Cul-de-Sac

I made it without trouble up the gracious, redwood-lined road from Highway 116 to Cazadero, but that's when things got crazy. Sabbatini had sent me a hand-drawn cardboard map highlighting the unmarked dirt roads beyond Cazadero that led to his cabin. Big red arrows showed all the turns—right, left, left, right—and I thought I was pretty much on it. But once I turned off onto the first dirt road, indicated by a dotted line on the map, I lost myself in a spiraling maze that led nowhere. I didn't see the red traffic cones Sabbatini said he'd set out to mark their road. I didn't see the base of the steep hill, marked by two good-size madrones. And I sure as hell didn't see a cabin painted the color of Dijon mustard.

I cursed myself for not picking up a GPS device when I'd rented the car. My cell phone had no service out in the wilds and I couldn't even find my way back to town. After a good hour of going in circles, without another car in sight, I pulled over and got out. It was four in the afternoon and I had half a tank of gas left. Time to regroup.

The web of roads might have been my life in the last few years—a labyrinthine gloom that I'd been unable to shake since my wife left me. Every time I thought I'd steered myself clear, I'd slip back into the muck.

Despite a full tummy
and a nice piss in the woods,
our hero is lost again.

The Church of Derelict Poetry

After I stood in the middle of the road, leaning against my chartreuse Neon for half an hour, a colossal candy-apple-green pickup roared around a curve and pulled up beside me. The windows were tinted dark, and as soon as the driver whizzed one down, I noticed the rifle in his rack.

The man appeared like an apparition in the opened square of window, as the sun bounced off his dark glasses.

"You know you're on a private ranch," he said, beckoning me over.

The news bewildered me. I hadn't driven onto a ranch. I'd just been going around in circles. "I think I'm lost."

"I know you're lost. But that's alright because I can probably get you found. Where are you trying to go?"

"I have a map." I reached through the window and grabbed Sabbatini's drawing. Sketched in colored pencil on shirt cardboard, the curious artifact looked more like a third-grader's treasure map than anything a lummox could follow. I figured that Sabbatini had probably been righteously stoned when he made the map.

By the time I retrieved it, the big dude had gotten out of his pickup. In his late forties or early fifties, he wore a tan Stetson and a string tie with a shiny agate. He jiggled a plastic quart of pop in his right hand. The yellow cup had the words *First Christ River of Blood* emblazoned in red on its side.

I handed him Sabbatini's sketch.

"What's this, a fucking treasure map?" The big man chuckled. I could see that he wanted me to join him, but I pulled out a handkerchief and blew my nose instead. He looked me up and down. "Hey, are you Jewish?" he asked.

"No." I was surprised by the question.

"Funny, you remind me of a Jewish fella I used to know." The rancher squirted a nasty line of tobacco between us. I wondered if this was a commentary about his onetime Jewish acquaintance or a message to me. In any case, the dude gave me the creeps.

"You trying to get to somebody's cabin or something?"

I had little hope that Sabbatini would be known by such a local. "Yeah. Guy named Bobby Sabbatini."

The man chortled. "Sabbatini, the High Priest of Poetry?"

"You know him?"

"Everybody knows Sabbatini. We call him Poesy."

"Poesy?"

"Yeah, it's another word for poetry or something."

"Wow. I can't believe you know him."

"Oh, yeah. I'll get you over there. No, Poesy's much loved around here. Much loved. Don't get me wrong, there's those he makes uneasy. Some see Poesy posing a threat," he said with a cackle.

"A threat?"

"Well, he's getting everybody in West County to memorize poetry. Some people think he's taking it too far. That'd be the religious extremists. A couple of the churches . . . they're frightened."

"Of what?"

"The poetry virus."

I laughed hard, but the big dude kept going.

"That's what they call it. They see it as a strategy for building his congregation and stealing from theirs."

"What congregation?"

The rancher spit another tobacco stripe in the dirt. "It's really spread. People you wouldn't expect. I mean, I'm working on an e. e. cummings poem. It's not as easy as it looks at first."

"I know," I said, silly with glee at the thought of Sabbatini spreading a virus of poetry out West.

The rancher smiled at me. "He got you memorizing the shit, too?"

I nodded.

"Well, I'm almost there with my poem. I hope to have it nailed by the end of next week when he opens the poetry tavern."

The rancher spit out a nasty plug of tobacco and rinsed his mouth with his soda, spewing a fat ounce of it onto the dirt road. Then he pulled an exotic chocolate bar out of his pocket, peeled back the iridescent lavender foil, and took a big bite of it.

"Excuse me," he said, "my medicine. No, there are folks who think Poesy's the Antichrist and that he's establishing a church of derelict poetry out here for all the deadbeats and faggots. My view is I don't care if he is. Live and let live. If a man wants to memorize poems, let him."

"Wow." I found everything the big hombre was saying incredible. I watched him snap up the rest of his chocolate bar and then pull another, this one with a pistachio-green wrapper, from the pocket of his jean jacket.

"I can never get the dosing quite right," he said, sticking half of the second chocolate bar in his mouth. "Yep, Ginsberg's Galley's opening at the end of next week."

"That's what he's calling it?" I asked. "I didn't know that Sabbatini was that into Ginsberg's work."

The rancher shrugged, swallowed the rest of his "medicine," and then took a few pinches of tobacco from a round tin and wedged them into tight spots between his lips and gums. Then he looked at me seriously for a moment.

"You sure you aren't Jewish?" he asked, grinning.

"Yeah," I lied, "what of it?"

The rancher chuckled. "Oh, nothing, I just sort of pride myself on being able to tell the races."

"Yeah, and what race are you?"

"Me? I'm All-American. Yep, American through and through. You know those Paul Revere brand frankfurters? I'm like their motto, 'All Meat and All American.'"

The All-American frankfurter reached his meaty hand out toward me. "I'm Gordon Cust. Folks call me Custard."

I didn't want to shake his hand, but did. "Augie Boyer."

"Augie," he said, grinning, "I know about you. You're the Minnesota detective, took a couple of bullets in the butt."

As usual, my notoriety had preceded me.

Intuition

It was campaign season back in 2008. Republicans were stinking up St. Paul as they came in for the convention. To add to the circus, the Republican governor granted right of assembly on the state capitol grounds to an anti-abortion group. Women at full term came from all over the country to give birth in medical tents on the capitol grounds.

Meanwhile my daughter Rose, who the rest of the world knows as the iconic singer-songwriter Minnesota Rose, was appearing across the capitol grounds at the pro-choice rally. I didn't like the idea of her playing in the shadow of all those anti-abortion evangelicals, knowing there had to be rabid and violent ones among so big a crowd. Rose, with her fame and her attitude, was too easy a target.

I went to the capitol grounds to hear my daughter perform, hoping that somehow my presence would keep her safe. But I was messed up that day. A client had gone missing on me and I feared she was in danger. On top of that, the birthing circus, with all the giant crucifixes and the blood-soaked signs on the capitol grounds, made me ill. I arrived late for Rose's set. I could hear her singing as I got close, but snuck into the bushes first, just like a sixteen-year-old, and smoked a fatty.

My talent as a detective is quite limited. Tracking an individual in a car, I'm as likely to get lost in a cul-de-sac as to keep up. My breaking-and-entering skills, never a highlight, have become negligible. But I possess two prized attributes: a stinker that can distinguish Gorgonzola from Maytag Blue, and an intuition for impending doom that kicks in just before the doom impends.

As I sucked on my roach, I sensed that sweet Rose was in danger, and burst out of the bushes, hurling myself onstage like the athlete I'd never been. I took two bullets in the butt shielding my girl. Two slugs in the gluteus maximus and I became a hero.

CHAPTER TWO

Custard, Blossom, and Poesy

BLOSSOM CAME OUT of the cabin as soon as we pulled up the drive. I was thrilled to see her.

"Look who I found stranded out on my place," Custard hollered, as he climbed out of his truck. "Poesy here?"

Blossom ran over to the car and practically yanked me out. She grinned. "Lost again, huh, Augie?"

She looked terrific and much changed since I'd seen her last. She wasn't wearing any makeup and she'd grown her hair out, letting it go back to its original color, a rich chestnut. No more of the spiked ruby hair of her Minneapolis days.

"You look great, Blossom."

"Doesn't she?" Custard said, his tongue making a show of licking his lip.

Blossom sneered at him. "Yeah, just like a hillbilly woman."

Once I stood in front of her, Blossom winked at me. "Looks like you stopped on the way up for something to eat."

"What are you talking about?"

She nodded toward my chest and I noticed a thin feather of a French fry somehow knit into the wool of my sweater—an emblem of my gluttony.

"Looks like an In-N-Out fry. So, you had a Double-Double, I s'pose."

"Right," I said, too fast.

"Oh, Augie," she said, grinning again, "you put down two Double-Doubles, didn't you?!"

I never could keep a secret from Blossom. She and Custard laughed. I already disliked the all-meat frankfurter, having decided that he was an anti-Semite and a probable chauvinist pig, but when he pointed to me and said, "You better watch this big boy, Blossom, he'll eat you out of house and home," I truly detested him.

Before I could get worked up, Sabbatini came to the door. He was dressed in a pair of orange drawstring pants and a Guatemalan shirt, with a string of old ivory beads hanging around his neck. Sabbatini's hair was bundled at the back of his neck in something approaching a chignon, and his feet were saddled in a pair of Tibetan monk thongs. The old police detective had acquired a shamanistic aspect. I wondered if he'd traded in his fancy linen suits and tweed coats when he went native.

Bobby was stooped over, holding the hand of his toddling son Milosz. When he looked up and noticed me for the first time, he shouted, "Augie!"

We gave each other a hug and I bent down to shake Milosz's hand. The boy looked into my face and started laughing.

"Am I supposed to be offended?"

Sabbatini shrugged. "If you must take offense, Augie, take it."

"Hey, Poesy," Custard said, "I've almost got the e. e. cummings." He smiled at Blossom, giving her a little wink. Then he started reciting "Rain or Hail."

When he finished with what he had of the cummings, Sabbatini nodded and said, "You're impressing me, man. Imagine what you'll be able to do with a full karaoke machine worth of poems. I can see you performing a big, ripe Robinson Jeffers' narrative like 'Roan Stallion.'"

Custard took in the praise and loosened his string tie. He winked at Sabbatini. "I suppose it would be fitting for me to embody a stallion, Poesy."

The Francophone

The knotty pine cabin was built as a summer retreat, which is to say it had zilch insulation. I noticed an enormous woodpile covered in creative tarping along the side of the cabin. Sabbatini had built some nice nook-and-cranny shelving into the place, and thin poetry volumes were stuffed everywhere. The place had a handsome stone fireplace with a slow fire burning in it. I stood warming myself as Blossom and Sabbatini got into a sparring match about Gordon Cust, now that the rancher had left. It reminded me of the days when they were courting in Minnesota.

"How come that man gives me the creeps?" Blossom asked, with her hands on her hips.

"Aside from the fact that he is a creep," Sabbatini said, "I couldn't tell you. But you have a particular sensitivity to guys like that."

"Creeps?"

I felt like chirping in and offering my two cents about Custard as an anti-Semite, but decided to be the fly on the wall.

"I think you're being a little rough on him," Sabbatini said. "He's just a redneck. He can't really help that."

"He's a creep; you just said so yourself. And the way he looks at me like he's undressing me."

"So, the guy's got good taste in women," Sabbatini said with a grin.

"You're as bad as he is, Bobby."

"Come on, the guy's memorizing a poem."

"Like that means jack."

Sabbatini turned toward me. "Sometimes you can't reason with her."

"Don't talk about me like I'm not here."

"But in this case, I think it's a matter of *le chat échaudé craint l'eau froide*."

"Do not patronize me with your fucking Frenchie phrases, you prick," Blossom shouted.

"All I'm saying, is once bitten, twice shy, or if you prefer the literal, which is always a bit more colorful, a scalded cat fears cold water."

Blossom walked over and kicked Sabbatini in the shin.

"Ow."

Milosz broke up laughing at the exchange.

Sabbatini lifted a leg of his dervish pants and showed off the rising red blotch. "The woman's trying to maim me."

"If that's what I wanted to do," Blossom said, "you'd be maimed." She smiled at me and then at Sabbatini before picking Milosz up off the floor and gurgling with him.

"Hey, I warned you guys about each other," I said, as I strolled over to my bag to get the small gifts I had brought along.

"You didn't have to do that, Augie," Sabbatini said, as I handed a package to each of them.

Milosz sat on the floor with his mom and started chewing on the airplane wrapping paper, before Blossom helped him open it. She pulled out the crocheted tam o' shanter and fitted it on Milosz's head.

"If that isn't the cutest thing," she said.

Milosz managed to quickly knock it off his head. Meanwhile, Sabbatini pulled out the black beret I'd bought for him at Hymie's Haberdashery in St. Paul. He couldn't have been happier. Once he'd settled the beret sideways on his head, it looked as if it had always been there.

"You shouldn't encourage him with his damn Frenchie routine," Blossom said. "He thinks he's some sort of Francophone."

Sabbatini bent over, rubbing his bruised shin, and said, "*Je vous t'ai demandé l'heure?*"

"What are you saying to me?" she demanded.

"Did I ask you the time of day?"

Blossom glared at her husband.

"Open your gift, Blossom," I said.

I'd found a splendid pair of deerskin gloves at Bibelot for Blossom. She used to wear gloves all through the year to cover the homemade tattoos she'd acquired in prison. I looked at her scarred hands now as she unwrapped the gloves.

"Nice, Augie," she said, pulling them on. "You know, I've evolved a little bit on this front. I'm not wearing anything to cover my tats anymore. I've gone au naturel."

"You'd think she was talking about her tits," Sabbatini said.

Again, she glared at Sabbatini. "You bastard," she hissed.

Milosz began to whimper and Blossom petted the boy until he quieted. Then she regarded the gloves once more and said to me, "But I'll wear these to the opening. That is, if I go."

Mutual Admiration

The last thing I wanted was to go out. But Blossom and Sabbatini insisted that we drive into Guerneville to have a look at Ginsberg's Galley. Five minutes after Blossom had hissed at her husband, she was kissing him.

"I'll get Milosz ready for a ride," she said.

I did my best to bow out. "I'm pretty bushed. Maybe I'll stay here."

Sabbatini wasn't having it. "Come on, Augie, I want you to see the joint. You can sleep until noon tomorrow."

"Yeah," said Blossom, "and we'll take you to the Vegan Heart for dinner. They've got the best macaroni and faux cheese in West County. After those Double-Doubles, it might be time for you to go faux."

"Have you guys become vegans?" I asked.

Sabbatini looked at me seriously. "Nope, we're still carnivores, but we like the atmosphere of the Vegan Heart."

"And you know what tonight is?" Blossom said.

"What's tonight?"

Sabbatini grinned at me. "It's belly-dancing night at the Vegan Heart."

"It's not like it's a real belly-dancing show," Blossom cautioned. "It's only the waitresses."

"Are they vegans?" I asked.

Blossom stuck out her tongue. "Don't ask stupid questions, Augie."

"Hey, just being my inquisitive self," I said, studying my old assistant for a moment. Beside growing out her hair and letting it assume its natural color, the woman had put on a few pounds.

She dropped a hand onto her hip. "What you looking at, Augie?"

"Lovely Blossom."

She winked at me. "You've gotten pretty cute yourself in your old age, Augie."

As Blossom and I stood admiring each other, Sabbatini waddled in a crouch after the toddling Milosz, who gurgled with pleasure.

"Hey, Augie, Blossom confessed to me that you always had a crush on her."

"Think you got that wrong, Poesy, it was the other way around."

Blossom blushed, shaking her head. "We're going to have to find a nice girl for this old man, don't you think, Bobby?"

"Just as long as she's legal," Sabbatini said.

"I think I have just the beauty in mind," she said.

"Who?" Sabbatini asked.

"Tell you later."

"Hey guys, I'm just visiting," I said, wondering if two weeks in the outback might be more than I could survive.

To Town We Go

Next thing I knew I was in sitting in the backseat of Sabbatini's Volvo, beside chunky Milosz in his car seat. The kid was eighteen months old and seemed to do nothing but gurgle with pleasure. He looked like a little Buddha, amused by the human comedy.

"Milosz loves the belly dancing," Blossom said.

"Milosz looks like he loves everything," I said.

Sabbatini eyed me in the rearview mirror. "You provide the right environment, that's what you get, Augie."

Blossom pointed out the highlights as we made our way through the tiny town of Cazadero. The general store, the post office, the sawmill, closed now for a generation. "There's a really nice swimming hole, right down there on the river," she said. Then she pointed out the two churches, side by side. "That one there's Presbyterian, and the other one's our born-again creep show, First Christ River of Blood."

"That's what it's called?" I asked, incredulous.

"You bet," Blossom said. "It's a real bleeder."

Then I remembered. "That's what Custard's cup had on it!"

"Surprise, surprise," said Blossom.

Sabbatini pulled up in front of the church. "They've got some great signage. We get a real kick out of the place." It was a simple, white, wood-frame church, but damned if *First Christ River of Blood* wasn't spelled out in large red gothic letters. To the right of the building was an old school signboard, with red plastic letters that read: "He who guards his mouth and his tongue keeps himself from calamity."

"They're kind of phobic about the work Bobby does," Blossom said, "and more and more they tailor sayings to him."

I caught the prophet's eye in the rearview mirror. "I take it you haven't been guarding your mouth and tongue, Mr. Sabbatini."

"Makes me feel like I'm on the right track," Sabbatini said. "I like it especially when they go biblical. Last week they had that gem from Matthew: 'Ye shall know them by their fruits. Do men gather grapes of thorns, or figs of thistles?' You know me, Augie, I'm all about thorns and thistles."

Ginsberg's Galley turned out to be directly across the street from the Vegan Heart. Sabbatini found a parking spot in front of the Galley. The low-slung building had been painted a bright persimmon, and the lettering looked to be in the same stark, spacious font as the title of Ginsberg's *Howl* in the City Lights Pocket Poets series.

"Nice," I said, "this place will be easy to find."

"My sentiment exactly," Sabbatini said.

"It's time for Augie to bond with Milosz," Blossom said, before proposing that I carry the boy in a Snugli. I didn't resist, and was pleased to watch Blossom's hands, with their savage tattoos, tenderly adjusting the straps of the Snugli.

It had been more than a generation since I'd worn a baby on my belly. My daughter Rose, who'd been that baby, would get a kick out of me now. Milosz, sleeping now, melted into my chest.

Deep into middle age,
with a baby on his chest,
his own child reappears.

CHAPTER THREE

Coolican

JUST AS SABBATINI was working the locks of the Galley's front door, a sheriff's car roared up Guerneville's main drag and screeched to a halt behind the parked Volvo.

A tall, sleek, Indian deputy sheriff in his thirties leapt from the car and hollered to Sabbatini: "Poesy, they found her."

Sabbatini left his keys in the door and hurried toward the deputy. "Dead?" he asked.

The deputy nodded.

"Aw, shit, Coolie. I'm sorry, man. Where'd they find her?"

The Indian took his cap off and ran a hand through his slicked-back hair. He had a tender face, but it was deeply pockmarked from ancient bouts with acne. "Found her in the redwoods off the Bohemian Highway. I was afraid it would turn out this way." The deputy dropped his head.

"Want me to run out there with you?"

"That's what I was hoping."

The deputy turned to greet Blossom and then extended a hand toward me. "Jesse Coolican," he said.

After I introduced myself, Sabbatini explained to the deputy that I was a P.I. who might be helpful.

Deputy Coolican gave me an amused look. "Might get in our way, too, since we're talking mights."

I'd have been happy taking a bye on this one, especially if the deputy wasn't wanting me along. *Just send me home with Blossom and Milosz,* I thought. *Let me get acquainted with the rollaway bed in the spare bedroom.* But I wasn't being consulted on the matter.

As Blossom and Sabbatini had a quick negotiation, I watched Deputy Coolican unzip his bomber and pull a toothpick from his shirt pocket. He worked for a second at something wedged between his molars, cleared a hunk of yellow matter, and said, "Corn. You'd think an Indian of my vintage would know how to eat corn by now."

Blossom dug the still-sleeping Milosz out of the Snugli and I felt strangely bereft as I watched Sabbatini slip the beautiful boy back into his car seat.

I sat in the back of the deputy's car, smothered in the unmistakable pong of marijuana. Behind the wheel, Jesse Coolican explained that the body of Ruthie Rosenberg had been discovered by some minister who happened to be hiking near the Last Judgment Campground. One of the Christian camps.

The deputy sneered, "I s'pose somebody was trying to give her a Christian burial."

"Was Ruthie a practicing Jew?" Sabbatini asked.

"No more than I'm a practicing Injun."

"Hey, you still smoke the peace pipe, Coolie."

"The pipe I smoke is nondenominational."

Coolican nodded toward me in the mirror. "Ruthie was a friend of mine, a bit of a wild child. Lots of partying, some heavy drug use. She didn't always keep the most savory company. A free spirit might be one way of describing her. Or you could say she lost her fucking way," Coolican added, fiercely.

"How old was she?" I asked.

"Thirty-three. Some of the kids who grow up on the river don't really grow up."

"Same as kids everywhere," Sabbatini said.

"Yes and no," the deputy said.

"Does Yevtushenko know?" Sabbatini asked.

"Yeah, the sheriff's department is dealing with him. They want me out of it. They think I'm too close to the victim."

"Who's Yevtushenko?" I asked.

I saw Coolican roll his eyes in the mirror. "Ruthie's on-again, off-again boyfriend."

"A Russian?"

"Right," Sabbatini said, "an actual Russian on the Russian River. Except that's not his name."

"Tell him how he got his name, Poesy," Coolican said.

"Well, the Rooskie's a bartender at the River Rose out in Jenner. Charming guy, really."

Coolican grunted.

"Coolie doesn't care for him, but the man's charming nonetheless."

I could see the deputy's smirk. "One man's charmer is another man's devil."

Sabbatini shrugged. "I met him when I first got out here and was scouting around for a place to open a poetry bar. Turns out that the dude has most of Yevtushenko's oeuvre memorized."

"And he ain't shy about laying it on you," Coolican added.

"You suspect Yevtushenko?" I asked the deputy.

He glanced at me in the mirror. "I don't *suspect* anybody. I don't *expect* anybody either. It's like my uncle used to tell me about the ponies: No horse should win, but one horse does, which was his way of saying, 'Bet your horses to place or show, not to win.' Of course, he only bet to win. Had his share of winners. He also ended up dead before he was fifty, without a tooth in his mouth or a dollar in his pocket. Richard L. L. Creek was his name. I once asked him what the L. L. was for and he said, 'Lucky Loser.' That's the way he saw himself."

In the mirror, I could see the deputy's eyes tearing up.

"He wasn't really my uncle," he said, "just an old Indian over in Monte Rio who was good to me. Anyway, I'm not a betting man. I'm just a little river town Indian deputy trying to keep my nose clean."

Sabbatini turned to face me. "And he's full of shit, too."

Now Coolican's grin filled the mirror. The dude switched on a dime. "Hey, Poesy's just pissed because his wife wants to run away with me. She's ready for a little native exotica."

"Could be, Coolie, but word's out that your little arrowhead barely rises."

"Yeah? I can dispel that motherfucker in a hurry," Coolican said, zipping down his fly.

"Keep it in your pants, Coolie."

I felt like I was driving with Cheech and Chong and tried to steer things back toward our purpose. "How long had Ruthie been missing?" I asked.

"Five days," the deputy answered. "Five sad and rainy days."

"Was it Yevtushenko who reported her missing?"

"Yeah."

"Who was seen with her last?"

"Hey, what's with the linear arc of questions?" Coolican groused.

Sabbatini turned to face me. "Don't mind Coolie; he just misses his literary theory classes at Stanford."

"Poesy, how many times do I have to tell you, I went to Cal?"

"Hey, I'm a Cal grad," I said.

Coolican met my eyes in the mirror. "Brother Bear." Then he turned back to Sabbatini. "Anyway, the problem with you old-school detectives is your mania for the linear. At this point in the history of the world, you should know that things don't happen step by step. Never have."

"He's talking out of his hat, Augie, kief-enhanced. He's never been a detective. He's a country deputy."

"You're still married to the status quo, aren't you, Poesy? Still living inside the box like a turtle. Me? I keep a stack of Foucault beside the toilet," Coolican boasted.

"The hell you do."

"Damn straight. I'm talking *The Archaeology of Knowledge*."

"Sure, Coolie, and you read *Death and the Labyrinth* while you're taking a crap."

"Damn right, wrestling with Foucault's discursive formations."

Sabbatini peeked around at me. "We're losing Augie."

"Maybe he wants to be lost," the deputy suggested. "Maybe that's the principal goal of his being."

That's the last thing I remember hearing. I fell off for a while just after we turned onto the Bohemian Highway, a twisting zipper through the redwoods.

The P.I. for Poets

I don't think I was out for long, but the mood had changed. It was quiet in the front seat. Deputy Coolican was in a world of his own, grieving, I supposed, over his dead friend. Sabbatini turned around to make conversation with me.

"So, tell me, Augie, how's the P.I. biz going in Minneapolis?"

"I'm barely keeping above water. I guess it's the economy. The attorneys who used to hire me aren't calling so often. I've become a fucking luxury item."

Sabbatini winked at me. "Some luxury."

"Even infidelity seems to have taken a vacation, with the result being I'm screwed."

"I'm sorry to hear that, buddy. Have you recalibrated the business plan lately?"

"What business plan?" I asked, incredulous.

"See. I've just been through all this of late with Ginsberg's Galley. A business, just like a man, needs to project a little intention."

"Yeah, well, I don't know what the hell I'm projecting, but all I'm getting back is bare subsistence." The last thing I wanted on my vacation was a dose of Sabbatini's musings as a Sufi entrepreneur, but the dude wasn't letting the subject go.

"Have you considered narrowing the focus of your practice?" he asked.

"If it got any narrower, it would disappear."

"But is it focused? How about you become a detective of distinction, say, the P.I. for the poetry-friendly?"

"What are you talking about?"

"You print that on the bottom of your business card. Augie Boyer—*Private investigator for the poetry-friendly.* You run a tag line: *Helping you solve the deeper questions.* Then you visit reading groups, go to poetry readings, and pass out your card. I'm telling you, Augie, this is an association that can save you and your business. The poetry-friendly are everywhere. Our numbers are growing, and the masses of poetry-phobic are dwindling. I can testify to that. The poetry-friendly are a people who favor investigations of both the body and the soul. Augie, my friend, you are in a position to be their guide and investigator."

I shook my head. "That's the craziest shit I've ever heard."

Deputy Coolican perked up and smiled at me in the mirror. "That's Poesy alright. He's had such success out here converting people to poetry that he's become a little delusional about its reach. He says it's not delusional. He claims that poetry is the spirit that moves us. I tell him he should open a church. Call it Sabbatini Salvation."

"Yeah," I said, touching Sabbatini on the shoulder. "Your creepy neighbor Custard told me there's some people a little freaked out about you starting a poetry church."

"He said that?" Sabbatini said, with a chuckle.

"He should know," Deputy Coolican said. "His wife's one of them, a born-again with a church bell in her throat."

"And Custard was walking around with a giant River of Blood cup, wondering if I was Jewish."

"Oh, don't get me started on Custard," the deputy said.

"Hey, let's not get off the track here," Sabbatini said. "We were talking about Augie, how there's a poetry-detective business out there waiting for him to turn the key. Rather than appealing to your client's basest instincts, you call out to their deepest ones. If you associate with poetry, you show that you're a dick with an imagination. Poets and their kind will come running to you."

"The only poets I've known have been broke and miserable."

"They need you, Augie."

"Well, I don't need them."

Disappointed, Sabbatini turned forward and mumbled, "That's a very narrow view, Augie."

Deputy Coolican caught my eye again in the mirror. "He's delusional, alright."

Herb of Choice

At this point, Sabbatini pulled out a joint and lit it. "Time for a little medicine," he said.

The deputy purred at the sight of the reefer. When Sabbatini offered the fatty to me, I declined. Bobby looked at me quizzically. I shrugged, not really interested in explaining my sobriety. Meanwhile, Coolican was sucking down the doob in great gulps. He even exhaled a beautiful trail of linked smoke rings.

"What are we smoking here," he asked, "River Rust or Forestville Fuck Face?"

"It's the Fuck Face," Sabbatini confirmed.

"Good," the deputy said, "I favor the *sativas*."

"Over the *indicas*?" Sabbatini asked.

"Absolutely."

"When did you guys start speaking Latin?" I asked.

Sabbatini turned and blew some smoke at me. "Hey, Augie, did I tell you I finally picked up my Medical Marijuana Certificate?"

"What's your condition?" I asked.

"I got mine for athlete's foot," Coolican chimed in.

"They give you medical marijuana for athlete's foot?"

Sabbatini grinned at me. "Welcome to California, Augie. I'm certificated for my hemorrhoids. River Rust really shrinks them."

"I don't want to hear about your hemorrhoids, Bobby."

"Ditto," said the deputy.

I buzzed down the window, trying to find some escape from the Fuck Face haze.

Big Sloppy Tears

What happened next surprised me. Maybe it was the dope that initiated the emotional cascade, but suddenly Deputy Coolican was crying big sloppy tears. He pulled a red handkerchief from his pocket, wiped his eyes, blew his nose, and finally pointed to the glove compartment with his hanky, asking Sabbatini for his sage pot.

"Mind lighting those sticks for me, Poesy?" he said sniffling.

Sabbatini flicked his lighter and a baby finger of flame lit the rope of sage twigs, imparting a stately breath of smoke, a sweet pungency that cut through the gaminess of the weed.

"I don't know if she ever recovered from her father's death," Coolican said. He took both his hands off the steering wheel and wafted the sage smoke upward. "He was a good man. It was cruel, the way the cancer ate him. Took out his mouth, his throat, headed straight down his gullet.

"I worked for him during high school. A Jewish deli in Guerneville. It did okay during the tourist season, but the locals never supported it. The river crowd's never been big on kugel and kreplach."

In the mirror, the deputy's eyes filled with memory.

"I fell in love with Ruthie during high school and never got over it. Can you believe this shit? More than fifteen years later. I figured when I went off to Cal, she'd fade. Pretty river girl always getting her ass in trouble."

"You knew her in high school?" Sabbatini asked. "You never told me that, Coolie."

"Plenty I haven't told you, pale face."

Coolican blew his nose and folded his handkerchief. "Damn girl always messed up. It didn't stop me from loving her. She had something down there, ready to flower. I touched her there and that scared her. She had a garden of demons. Probably bipolar or something. She'd go through these periods—all she wanted was to party. I couldn't keep up. Didn't really want to. A few years went by. I didn't see her much. Never even ran into her. I'd hear about guys she was seeing and try not to pay attention."

The deputy's eyes misted over again. "I gave her a hug at his funeral. I wanted to say something to her. Say, 'Come away with me. I'll take you anywhere you want to go.' She looked at me like that's exactly what she wanted me to say. But I didn't say a damn thing."

CHAPTER FOUR

The Heart

BOBBY SABBATINI HAD been smoking plenty of Forestville Fuck Face, and he was clearly fuck-faced when he got out of the car. He sucked a lungful of night air and blew it out slowly. Then he beelined toward a huddle of men. Despite the somberness of the occasion, everybody was glad to see Sabbatini. The men appeared to be making a fuss over his new beret, and he tilted it rakishly to the side. Sabbatini hadn't lived out here long, so I was surprised by how quickly he'd become a favorite.

I climbed out of the backseat and stood beside the deputy's squad car. Everybody was waiting on Coolican to make a move. Sabbatini and the others barely glanced my way. The Indian deputy hid inside the fogged-up car, skunky with weed and burnt sage.

My heart went out to Coolican. Unlike Sabbatini, who'd been a big-city homicide detective, Coolican was a country deputy. He probably hadn't seen too many dead bodies, surely not those of women he had once loved.

There were three sheriff's vehicles, along with a couple of unmarked cars, parked haphazardly in the gravel lot. The Last Judgment Campground had been closed. Blue police tape stretched from signage on the south end of the lot to a stand of redwoods. I couldn't see the tops of them.

Finally, Coolican stepped out of the car and nodded toward the men. I wanted to put my arm on his shoulder but couldn't presume such intimacy with somebody I'd just met. The deputy walked stiffly toward the others. I tailed behind.

"Coolie," the sheriff said, as they shook hands, "so sorry about this." He tried to meet Coolican's eyes until he realized that the Indian had his fixed on the ground.

Pretty soon everybody in the little gaggle of men was studying the ground.

"It's about a quarter mile out to Ruthie's body," the sheriff said, drawing on his cigarillo. A man in his late fifties, he sported a raw herpes blister on his upper lip. "No reason for you to go out there. We have her identified. Crime Scene did what it could do for the night. In a little bit we'll bring her in. Do a little more work out there in the morning."

Jesse Coolican didn't say anything at first. He walked a good twenty yards along a line of police tape and nodded toward a spot on the ground. "What's this?"

"Crime Scene found footprints out there," the sheriff said.

Coolican kicked at the ground a minute, lifting a cloud of dust ankle high. "You figure she was killed out here?"

"That's how it appears."

Turning back toward the men, Coolican asked who identified the body.

The sheriff nodded toward one of the deputies. "Mesker, here."

"Sorry, Coolie," Mesker said.

The deputy turned toward Sabbatini and explained, "We all went to high school together."

Coolican didn't seem to know what to do next. He walked back to the squad car slowly, but instead of getting in, draped himself over the hood and began sobbing.

Sabbatini glanced at me and motioned me forward. "Sheriff," he said, "this is my P.I. buddy from Minnesota, Augie . . ."

"Augie Boyer," the sheriff said, giving me a half smile before gliding his cigarillo back in his mouth,

We shook hands. I was surprised he knew my name.

"So," I asked, "when was the body found?"

The sheriff hadn't expected a question from me. He lifted an eyebrow, took a drag of cigarillo, and rubbed his left pointer over his herpes sore. "Late afternoon. I let Coolie know about five, when I got over here from Santa Rosa. I was expecting him earlier. We're putting a wrap on it for the night." He glanced toward Coolican. "Guess he doesn't have the stomach for this."

"The heart," Bobby Sabbatini corrected.

The sheriff nodded and puffed thoughtfully on the cigarillo. "Why don't you boys get him home? Somebody ought to stay with him. I can't read a guy like Coolican."

Sabbatini had his eyes trained on Deputy Coolican.

I turned toward the sheriff. "How was she killed?"

"Couple of bullets from a large-caliber rifle in the back of the head."

"Just like the two kids out by Jenner," Sabbatini said, and filled me in on that case, a nine-year-old unsolved double murder. A young couple found murdered in their sleeping bags on a beach north of Jenner, their packs filled with Bibles and other Christian literature.

"We don't want to jump to conclusions," the sheriff said.

"But we can't always keep ourselves from doing that," said Sabbatini.

The sheriff didn't seem to appreciate the comment and turned toward me. "It appears that Ruthie was found just in her panties. Barefoot in her panties."

"Molested?" I asked.

"Can't say for sure."

Coolican was still sobbing in the distance, and Sabbatini excused himself to go over to the deputy.

For some reason I asked to see the body. It seemed like one of us should. The sheriff regarded me for a moment. He bit off a piece of his cigarillo and sucked on it a moment before spitting it onto the toe of his left boot and shaking it off. "Sure, I'll take you out there."

Salamander

The sheriff asked one of the deputies to tell Sabbatini we'd be back in fifteen minutes. Then the sheriff and Deputy Mesker escorted me down a path through the redwoods. A breeze had come up and we could hear the sound of a blues harmonica.

"Damn Schoendeinst is playing his harmonica out there," the sheriff said.

The bent notes, tweeting in chorded clusters and singular wails through the redwoods, were quite moving.

"Well, he's sure got the mood right," I said.

My escorts nodded their agreement.

We surprised the harp-playing deputy when we arrived at the scene. He leapt up off a log and shoved the harp into his pocket. Twenty-five yards from him, at the foot of a blackened redwood trunk, I saw the body, covered in a green tarp.

"Schoendeinst," the sheriff said.

The deputy stiffened, expecting a rebuke.

"You've got a helluva sound."

"Thank you, Sir."

The sheriff, with Deputy Mesker tailing behind, led me over to the body.

"You ready for this?" he asked, crouching, about to lift the top of the tarp.

I nodded.

The two bullets had exploded the poor woman's head. Since the bullets entered the back of her head, they likely found her face-down. Whoever turned her over had a bit of a shock. Her face was gone. A hunk of charred and bloodied flesh clung to a mostly intact jaw that still held a tight row of pitifully small teeth.

"If Mesker hadn't been able to identify her," the sheriff said, "all we'd have here is a nameless dame."

Nameless dame. That struck me as a cruel way of referring to the dead. But it was the murder that had been cruel.

I turned back to Deputy Mesker. "How'd you identify her?"

"Her tattoo."

"I'll show you," the sheriff said. He folded the tarp down to reveal the body of a lovely young woman in her mid-thirties, clothed only in a pair of soiled panties. Small cantaloupe breasts, a flat belly, and beneath it a blue reptilian tail and some of the creature's body, tattooed on her navel.

"I told them to look for a salamander heading straight into her pussy."

In gloves now, the sheriff yanked the panties down toward the victim's knees. Her pubic hair was shaved so there was only a narrow thatch left. The head of the salamander extended all the way down.

"She always kept it shaved," Deputy Mesker offered.

"I'm not going to ask how you know that, Mesker," said the sheriff. He pulled her panties back up and then turned to me. "You think you've seen it all," he said, puffing on his cigarillo.

Back in the car, Coolican, wearing dark glasses now, was lighting some fresh faggots of sage. We sat in silence as he blew out the flame and the smoke rose in feathering drifts.

CHAPTER FIVE

For Some

I DIDN'T GET to sample the glories of the Sabbatinis' rollaway bed that night. Back from seeing the body with Deputy Mesker and the sheriff, I agreed to a bit of community service and bunked with Deputy Coolican at his cabin on the edge of Guerneville. It didn't really matter. I was limp with weariness and could have slept standing.

It turned out that Coolican's cabin was nice and cozy. Bookcases lined the walls. And there were several striking paintings, with bold, gestural stripes painted in shades of salmon. Although the stripes weren't black, the paintings were reminiscent of Franz Kline.

I also noticed a framed photograph of a large-eyed young woman with a creamy complexion atop a side table. Rose petals were scattered around the base of the frame. I walked up and studied the photograph. The woman looked fresh and hopeful. Or was I just imagining that? In any case, she was a far cry from a nameless dame.

"Yeah, that's Ruthie," Coolican said. "Taken when she was in her early twenties. I remember the day when she gave me the photo. I was walking downtown in Guerneville and ran into her coming out of the pharmacy. It was a few years after high school. I think I was done with college. Who knows when I'd last seen her? So, I'm standing beside her, chatting, and I notice my breath is fucked up—I can't draw a deep breath. Can't get to the bottom of it. I s'pose that's what they mean by the phrase, 'She took my breath away.' Anyway, she reaches into this envelope and pulls out a folder of photos and hands me one. She said she was going to start doing some acting and needed head shots. I barely looked at the photo, but I took it. I figured she was trying to break my heart."

Coolican nodded his head and bit his lower lip, presumably to keep from crying.

I walked away from the photo and a fat tabby came over to check me out.

"That's Maverick," Coolican said. The cat sniffed around at my feet. A moment later, done with me, he went back to his carpeted cat shelf, under a hanging coleus.

Coolican pointed toward the red futon and said, "That's where you'll sleep." Then he heated some water and brewed a pot of chamomile tea. He asked if I minded if he lit some sage before we went to bed. I was new to this ritual of lighting sage, but whatever it took.

As we sipped tea, I asked Coolican about the paintings and he told me that he made them during college.

"They're very good," I said.

"You know art, Augie?" he asked, regarding me with amusement.

"Not really. I go to museums. I know what I like."

The Indian nodded toward the paintings. "They're derivative."

"Everything is derivative."

Coolican smiled. "Yes, some things derive from tradition; others, like these, are facile copies."

"You're pretty hard on yourself, Deputy."

"Aren't you the same?"

"No, I treat myself with kid gloves. That's the secret to my success."

Coolican smirked. "Maybe I'll come study with you in Minnesota."

"Trouble is, I don't have any success."

"You're kind of modest for a white man, Brother Bear."

I looked around the large room to see if I could spot any painting materials, but didn't see any. "You still paint?"

"Not since college. I didn't see a whole lot of future in an Indian painting Franz Klines."

"But you still like to look at them."

"If I could find something better, I'd stick it up there."

I watched Coolican furrow his brows. "May I ask you how old you are?"

"I'm thirty-five," he said, "if that's any kind of measurement."

He was the oldest thirty-five I'd ever seen. Maybe it was the crooked trail that grief left on his features. Maybe the deep pockmarks. Clearly there were things that had seasoned him in ways I couldn't imagine.

"Personally," I said, "I've discovered that angst is overrated. From my ancient perch of fifty-three, I can tell you that life gets easier."

"For some," he said.

"For some," I echoed, sadly.

The smell of sage,
a thin trail of grief
unites us.

A Stinking Macramé

In the morning Coolican built a nice fire and we shared a pot of coffee. The deputy wore a pair of red, waffled long johns and I, feeling a little crusty, sat in the clothes I'd traveled in the day before.

At first we said very little to each other. Coolican jabbed at the fire with a poker. He took small sips from his mug of coffee and, facing the flames directly, apologized for getting emotional in the car and again at the Last Judgment Campground.

"You don't have to apologize to me," I said.

"No, it's pathetic, man. I'm an Indian. I'm not some fucking crybaby Mormon politician."

"Hey, emotion has become one of my best friends," I said.

"With friends like that, a man can drown on dry land."

"I'm all about treading water."

"I don't know how to swim, which is why I like living along a river that floods. Keeps me on my toes."

Coolican excused himself to dress for work, but he had more to say and kept walking in and out of the main room. It was strange to watch an officer of the law assume his official look at the same time as he bared his soul. "I thought I was prepared for it," he said in a soft voice. "But when I realized there was no bringing her back, man—it blew me away."

"You can't prepare for that."

"They shot her in the head like she was an animal, a varmint. The bastards."

I wondered if it meant anything that Coolican thought of Ruthie's killer(s) in plural.

"And fuck me," he said, swatting a pile of unopened mail from a side table. "If I'd been a better friend to her, her life might have been different. She might still be here."

"You can't second-guess yourself about stuff like that," I said. "You can't beat yourself up."

"Bullshit," Coolican said. "I can and I will."

He walked over to the fire and spat into it a couple of times. Just when I thought he'd calmed himself down, he dashed across the room and scattered a pile of books from a plant stand. Cowering against the wall, I noticed Michel Foucault's *This Is Not a Pipe* bounce open as if it wanted to be read.

"Sorry, sorry," Coolican said.

A moment later, the deputy stood in front of the fire in full uniform, his brown eyes shooting huge out of his pocked visage. "There are times when my life seems like nothing but an assemblage of weak moments. A stinking macramé hanging on the wall, woven from my vacillations, my acts of cowardice, my hiding in the dark. Do you have any idea how much has been invested in me? Do you know how little I've delivered? A smart boy Indian without a tribe. Too smart for his own good. What kind of fool Indian studies literary theory at Berkeley? Who does he think he is? What's he prove buying into that high-minded irrelevance? What more does he know about being a human being?"

When he finished his rant, Coolican added a log to the fire and sat down in the chair beside me. Through the room's large window, I could see the fog lifting up the tops of the redwoods. The deputy kept his eyes closed as if he were meditating.

"Augie," he said.

"Yes." It was odd the way he said my name, as if we'd known each other for years, not just since the night before.

"I want to ask you a favor. I don't ask many people favors."

"So I should be honored?"

"Or you could be an asshole about it."

"Shoot," I said.

"I want to spare myself getting caught up in who killed Ruthie. . . ."

"I think that's a good idea."

"Good, because I want you to fill in for me. The sheriff's department is going to do its thing, but somebody's got to be looking at it another way. I'd have asked Poesy, but he's distracted. He says you're a decent detective."

I started to protest, telling Coolican that I'd only be in California a couple of weeks and didn't know my way around.

"Hush," he said, "you're blessed with dumb luck. Any fool can see that."

Coolican let out a contented sigh.

By the time he stood up and put on his cap, he looked as if the demons had left him. I feared that I'd be the one who absorbed them.

Drifters and Dirty Underwear

From Coolican's cabin, I walked fifteen minutes or so into downtown Guerneville. As I crossed the bridge, the river looked swollen. It had rained during the night and, from what I understood, for much of the last month. I found a restaurant on Main Street where I got a bowl of steel-cut oatmeal and drank some more coffee. I picked up a copy of the *Chronicle*, glad to see that you could get the city paper in this outpost. I scanned the paper, hoping to find an item on the Russian River murder, but it was too soon for that.

At ten, I wandered up the street to Ginsberg's Galley and found Sabbatini inside the barely lit tavern. It was cave-like, and so dark that I couldn't see much of anything.

"There he is," Bobby shouted from behind the bar. "How'd you sleep, man?"

"Better than expected."

"See. And how's Coolican?"

"He'll live."

"You're just the right tonic for him."

"I wouldn't go that far." I pulled up a stool across from Sabbatini at the long bar.

"How about a Bloody Mary?"

"Little early for that, isn't it?"

Sabbatini shook his head. "What's with this newfound sobriety of yours, Augie?"

"Just trying to keep my nose clean, but I s'pose a single bloody won't hurt me."

In response to the breakup of my marriage, I'd become a prodigious pothead. Weaning myself from the herb had been difficult. I could see that my resolve would be tested, here in Weed Central.

Now I watched Sabbatini mix a couple of bloodies with a grand flourish. We clinked glasses and Sabbatini proposed a toast to Jesse Coolican. I found myself gulping at my drink, enjoying its spicy kick. I also liked the aura of darkness as the spirit of unreality became pervasive. Nothing like sitting in your dirty underwear on a dark morning in a rumpled river town. Add the bloody and the shadow of a nearby murder, and there was hardly any need for night.

Sabbatini looked across at me. "I don't know if you've been around him long enough yet to realize what an amazing man Jesse Coolican is. He's really quite brilliant. He tries to make like he's a regular guy, but he's not. The Monte Rio Rancheria, an unincorporated band of Indians, have tried for years to recruit him to be their chief, but he won't have any of it. More recently, a Nevada gaming company that runs casinos tried to get Coolie to support a possible gaming facility in the town of Monte Rio. The Rancheria has sovereign rights to 2,500 acres right outside town, and the outfit offered Coolie some large sums to lobby for them. He wouldn't have any part of it. The man has some genuine dignity."

"To Coolie," I said, and we clinked glasses again.

"The guy also has a feel for poetry that's very special."

"That's what matters most," I said, jesting.

"You laugh," Sabbatini said, "but to hear Coolican recite Robinson Jeffers' 'In the Hill at New Grange,' with all of Jeffers' severity and crisp diction, is one of life's great pleasures."

"You sound like you're doing a Mastercard commercial, Bobby."

"There's nothing commercial about it. But I'm worried about Coolican," Sabbatini continued. "I don't think he's been so successful wrestling with his mental Satan. And the way he's taking the murder. He really loved that girl. Everything that I've heard about her is that she was a real loser. Smart, good-looking, and fatally hooked on crack."

"But that's not what killed her," I said.

Sabbatini shrugged. "Not directly."

"You never met her?"

"Oh, I met her. One time I ran into her in downtown Guerneville. She was pretty whacked out. She tried to sell me her body."

"Hmm. Coolican asked me to do some poking around about the murder, but I told him I was only visiting."

"You're not visiting anymore, Augie. The man needs you. The sheriff's department detectives are going to spend a lot of time linking this to the two Christian kids killed in their sleeping bags a few years back. That one's still eating them. Maybe the link pans out, but maybe not. People disappear easily out here. There are plenty of drifters around. It's easy to blame it all on a phantom drifter."

I threw up my arms in protest. "This kind of stuff's not my forte, Bobby. I don't even know the area. Nobody's going to talk to me."

"That's where you're wrong, my friend. Everybody knows Augie Boyer."

"How's that?"

"Everybody's heard about your heroics in Minnesota. You're Paul Bunyan with a paunch come to Rivertown."

"That's a crock of shit."

"You know that and I know that, Augie, but the rest of the folks out here in the Occident are willing to give you carte blanche. It's a very valuable currency. Don't underestimate what you can do with it. And don't forget, if Coolican has asked you for his help and you withhold it, you're not only insulting a man, you're insulting a nation."

The Galley Illuminated

With that, Sabbatini burst into a laugh and came out from behind the bar. He flicked some light switches, and the cavernous pub came alive. I could see that Bobby had sunk a lot of dough into the joint. The middle of the room was wide open. To the left were several cozy booths. On the right was the bar at which I'd been sitting, a monstrous slab hewed from a giant redwood. An impressive inventory of bottles glowed majestically in the mirrored spotlights. A photo of a bearded Allen Ginsberg had a place of honor behind the bar. The visage of the poet, all eyes and beard, leapt like a powerful ancestor out of its knotted-rope frame.

The nautical theme was one of the pleasures of the place. Sabbatini led me on a silent tour of his church. He had us stand under a fishing net suspended from the high, pressed-tin ceiling. A couple of dozen abalone shells gave off their marbled enamel shine. Sabbatini had rounded up a collection of French sailors and pirates, boldly rendered on beer platters. They were roguish eighteenth-century creatures with great mustaches. Some had red pom-poms on their sailor caps.

Poster-sized photos of poets were everywhere I looked. As we strolled, I recognized a number of them enshrined in matching gilt frames. There was Ezra Pound and Marianne Moore and Robert Creeley. Gary Snyder looked especially puckish, while W. B. Yeats appeared like an effete priest in his wire-rimmed specs.

At the front of the room was a stage built to look like a captain's bridge, with an old wooden helm and a brass compass.

I patted Sabbatini on the back. "This is quite an enterprise, Bobby. I had no idea you were taking it to this level."

"Me neither. It just kept growing."

"You look like you're ready to go."

"Pretty much. I've got staff hired. Have done my publicity. A couple of newspaper features are coming out on the place next week. The karaoke machine is ready to fly. I dropped a bundle on a software designer with a background in book design. We've got 3,000 poems loaded in and fifteen different broadside templates. Get this, some of the poems are set up as responsive readings. We take recordings of the poet reading, delete every other line, and the bar crowd collectively fills in the missing lines, highlighted in the projection."

"The church of Sabbatini."

"I guess so."

"You got enough folks around to fill the congregation, Bobby?"

"Listen, I've been in West County a year and a half now, and I've really cultivated the population. I used to run a morning meeting on Wednesdays. People came in, brought coffee and sweet rolls, and recited poems. Now the demand has become so great, I'm doing it five days a week. The city of Guerneville lets me use the chapel of an empty mortuary up the street. People come from all over the county. I betcha I have more than two hundred folks memorizing poems."

"Father Poesy."

Sabbatini raised his hands in benediction. "Bless you, my child." Then he went back behind the bar and pulled out an ashtray, fished in his shirt pocket for a joint, and fired it up. When he offered it to me, I declined.

He took another hit, shook his head, and said, "You're not the Augie I know and love."

"Sorry to disappoint."

Sabbatini leaned across the bar, drawing leisurely on the joint. Master of his realm, he reminded me of Groucho Marx with a cigar. A moment later, he snuffed the fatty and flashed me a stoner's smile.

A New Wife

I watched the old police-detective-turned-poetry-priest mix himself another bloody and then take a long, slow sip. "So, we have a little change of plans on the home front," he said.

"I didn't know we had any plans."

"Well, it turns out that our wife's arriving early."

"Your wife?"

"Yeah, Blossom thought it'd be wise for us to hire a wife, what with the Galley opening next week and no day care for Milosz."

"You've hired a wife?"

"Yeah, an old friend of Blossom's."

I chuckled. "Where did she meet her, in prison?"

"That's right."

"You're kidding."

"No."

"Come on, you're going to entrust your child to an ex-con?"

"Blossom's an ex-con."

"That's different. She's Milosz's mother and she's been fully vetted."

"Oh, yeah," Sabbatini said between gulps of his bloody, "and I really enjoyed the vetting process."

"I bet you did. So now you're going to have two wives, huh, Bobby?"

"Yeah, but it's not like that. We're not doing the Mormon thing. Quince's just providing domestic support."

"Quince?" I asked.

"Yeah, like the fruit."

I stood up off my stool and began pacing. Sabbatini was making me nervous.

"Have you even met her?" I asked.

"Haven't met her yet."

"What was she in for?"

"Armed robbery."

"Come on, Bobby, have you gone soft? Has the Fuck Face fucked with your reason?"

Sabbatini went to the double sink and washed out his cocktail glass. "Oh, you know these young women, like Blossom, they fall in with the wrong crowd and next thing you know they're holding up a chain of dry cleaners in Duluth."

"Yes," I said, disgusted, "and some of them end up like the dead girl out at the Christian campground."

Sabbatini waved me off. "I've always believed in giving people second chances. It certainly worked out with Blossom."

I lifted my head off the bar. "It's a hell of a chance to take with your own child."

"Augie, when we project good energy, that's likely what we'll get in return. I see it every day. It's hard to appreciate in Minnesota, surrounded by all that stoic negation. Always a hanging cloud of suspicion. But here, we don't have to live our lives with our shoulders hunched in fear."

I listened to this new age drivel and considered the possibility that I'd lost my friend. What about Ruthie Rosenberg, the nameless dame, who actually had a name but no longer a life? Hadn't she gotten shot in the head, right in the middle of Shangri-La? Had she lost her feel-good exemption? Had she met up with an outsider like me who was still clouded in suspicion, who didn't subscribe to the West County good life?

Sabbatini had been living in Northern California for a year and a half, but he'd already been fully converted. He grinned at me as if to confirm my suspicions.

I swiveled on my stool. "And how exactly does the arrival of your new wife affect me?"

"Well, turns out she's coming today and she'll be sleeping on the rollaway."

"So, you're kicking me out of your house before I even get there, Bobby?"

"It's not like that, man," Sabbatini said, lighting up what was left of his fatty. "You can sleep on the floor or the ratty couch if you like. But I thought it might be best if you stayed with Jesse. He needs you now, man, he really needs you."

"And what do I need, Bobby?" I shouted. "I come across the country and you toss me out for the sake of some felon. What do I need?" I repeated, this time as a hiss.

Sabbatini grinned at me. "Now that's a key existential question, but I'm afraid you're the only one who can answer it."

"Fuck you, Bobby."

Sister Everlast

Before I could storm out of the Galley in minor tantrum mode, a tall man, wearing a leather halter with fake boobs, strolled in. The guy had an enormous pair of biceps to go with his boobs and wore a black stocking cap branded in large letters with the EVERLAST logo. It was a lot to take in. I focused on his stocking cap and found myself remembering the Gillette Friday Night Fights. I'd watched them every week with my father, a normally meek man who became animated as he downed a half-dozen cans of Schlitz. Toward the end of the evening, my father would have me up shadowboxing with him as the pugilists on the flickering screen boxed in their Everlast trunks.

When the guy spotted Sabbatini behind the bar, he hollered, "Did you get it, Sister Poesy?"

"Sister Everlast," Sabbatini said, "come meet my old buddy, Augie Boyer. I think he may be ripe for the order."

"Oh, Augie," the breasted man said, "Sister Poesy's told us so much about you. We'd love for you to become a member of our order."

I didn't know what the fuck Sabbatini and the busty muscle creature were talking about, but before I could resist, Sister Everlast put quite a hug on me.

She repeated her question to Sabbatini, "So have you got it, Sister Poesy?"

"Not yet."

"I told you we're going to boycott you until you get it."

Sabbatini rolled his eyes and said, "*Ça ne pisse pas loin.* "

"What are you saying, Sister?"

"That doesn't piss far."

I stood up from the stool, ready to get the hell out of Sabbatini's joint. My quotient for bizarre local color had exceeded my capacity to absorb it. But before I could slip out, Sister Everlast made a florid apology.

"Augie, forgive me for barging in here and interrupting. You look confused. You're from the Midwest, aren't you?"

I nodded meekly.

"You don't know about us, do you?"

I shook my head.

"He doesn't know about us, Sister Poesy."

"No," Sabbatini said, "but I figured it was only a matter of time."

"We're members of the Sisters of Perpetual Indulgence. I'm Sister Everlast, as you've heard, and this is Sister Poesy of the Rose. The order's been around for years. We do a lot of charity work."

I swallowed hard. "I see."

"Even though we like to dress in drag, we're a hell of a lot more transparent than the brethren up at the Bohemian Grove. You're hip to the Bohemian Grove, aren't you, Augie?"

I nodded, though my awareness of the elite men's club, made up of Republican captains of industry, politicians, academics, and defense contractors, was very limited.

"Don't get started on the Bohemians, Sister," Sabbatini said.

"Don't you think we should give a fuck when the leaders of the so-called free world are engaging in mock human sacrifices to sixty-foot wooden eagles?"

"Sounds like good wholesome fun to me," Sabbatini said, with a wink.

Sister Everlast wiggled her nose at Sabbatini. "Augie, you should see how lovely Sister Poesy looks in drag. Sister Tart of the Tattoos really does a fine job making him up."

Sabbatini shrugged.

"You've come a long way, Bobby," I said. Although I wanted to get out of there, I stood frozen on my spot as Sister Everlast hectored Sabbatini for not acquiring any songs by the Singing Nun for his karaoke machine.

"*Changer de refrain*, Sister Everlast."

"But Sister Poesy, you're denying satisfaction to an entire community," Sister Everlast bellowed. "Just get one song. We can be satisfied with Soeur Sourire's 'Dominique.'"

The well-muscled nun began to sing the catchy ditty, but stopped abruptly. "Remember, I have the power to keep the whole order from patronizing your establishment."

Sabbatini wasn't intimidated. He simply shrugged. "I'm not doing songs, Sister, I'm doing poems."

"But the Singing Nuns are poets at heart."

"We've got bigger fish to fry."

Sister Everlast nodded, suddenly solemn. "Yes, I heard they found Ruthie's body out at Last Judgment. How's Jesse doing?"

"Ask Augie. He spent the night at his place."

Both sisters turned toward me.

"I think he's taking it hard."

The muscled sister closed her eyes and nodded. She pulled off her stocking cap and, with a handkerchief, mopped at her shaved head. Circling the top of her forehead were the tattooed letters *P-E-N-E-T-R-A-T-I-O-N.*

"What a thing," she said, "to happen in our community."

CHAPTER SIX

Spud and Derek in the Rain

I WAS COLD and I was starving. I'd made the mistake of eating nothing more than a demure chicken Caesar salad for lunch. A cold rain had been falling all afternoon, and even to my freeze-dried Minnesota body and soul, the dampness seemed particularly penetrating. It was fucking rheumatism weather. Still, I'd wanted to see if there was any news on the Ruthie Rosenberg murder and hoped to have a look at the Last Judgment Campground during daylight. As my car was still back at his cabin in Cazadero, Sabbatini agreed, against his wishes, to take me out to the murder site.

"You're not going to find anything out there, Augie," he'd protested.

"You might be right, Sister Poesy," I said, winking at the former police detective, "but if you're selling me down the river and pawning me off on Coolican, then I'm going to poke around on his behalf. Tomorrow I'll have my rental car, but today I'm stuck with you."

The campground remained closed. A TV news crew was packing up their truck after shooting some atmosphere.

"Anything breaking?" I asked a sandy-haired man who looked like the television reporter.

"They're not talking."

Two sheriff's department cars were parked in the lot. Police tape now stretched in all directions.

Sabbatini introduced me to one of the deputies, a cheerful character named Spud who sported a huge red blotch of birthmark across the left side of his face. I tried not to stare, but couldn't get over how closely the birthmark resembled the shape of Idaho, hence the man's nickname. Spud couldn't have been much more than thirty.

"So this is Augie?" Spud said with a grin.

Sabbatini nodded. "The Augster."

Spud's eyes opened wide. "How's Rose? I'm a real of fan of hers."

Sooner or later everybody got around to asking about my famous daughter.

"She's fine," I said. "She's on some kind of an all-star tour with the Boss."

We stood in the rain with Spud and the other deputy, whom Spud introduced as Derek, a gangly fella with a thin black mustache, no older than his partner.

"I think Rose is hot," said Derek, bouncing boyishly on his toes.

"You don't tell a man that you think his daughter's hot," Spud said.

Derek apologized to me. I shrugged.

I noticed Spud wink at Sabbatini. "Hey, Poesy, I've been memorizing some Gary Snyder."

"Good man."

"But it's kind of hard for me to keep the lines straight."

"What are you smoking these days?" Sabbatini asked.

"Just a little Fuck Face."

"Maybe you should switch to Monte Rio Brio. Coolie tells me that's the best for the memory."

"I do have one down, Poesy," Spud said proudly.

"Yeah, give it to us, man."

The deputy blushed, and the map of Idaho seemed branded a little deeper into his face. "It's a short one. Called 'On Top.'"

"Excellent choice," Sabbatini said.

Spud stood up straight and took off his sheriff's cap.

ON TOP

BY GARY SNYDER

All this new stuff goes on top
turn it over   turn it over
wait   and water down.
From the dark bottom
turn it inside out
let it spread through, sift down,
even.
Watch it sprout.

A mind like compost.

"Fantastic," Sabbatini raved. "I've never thought of the mind the same way since learning that poem. Gives you a new respect."

Deputy Spud had a big grin on his face. Then he nodded over to his colleague, Derek. "He's jealous 'cause he doesn't have a poet."

Derek protested, "I'm not jealous."

"We can find him a poet," Sabbatini said. "What kind of stuff do you like to do, Derek?"

Derek shrugged. "I don't know. Hunt."

Sabbatini mused for a moment. "I'm thinking Richard Hugo. I don't know if he hunted, but I'm thinking he's the poet for you. I'll bring some by."

I stood a moment longer in the dripping rain, not believing that we were standing at a murder scene. Trying to get myself back on task,

I caught Spud's eye. "So, tell me, has the sheriff's department made any discoveries out here?"

"Nothing much," Spud answered, too quickly. I watched his birthmark stretch as he grimaced for effect and shook his head.

"Nothing, huh?"

"No."

I expected Sabbatini, the veteran homicide detective, to jump in, but apparently he'd abdicated, leaving the initiative to the small-time P.I. I glanced around the expanded crime scene. "How come there's so much more cordoned off than there was last night?"

Spud shrugged.

"All due respect," Sabbatini said, "these guys don't know anything. They're not detectives. The detectives have already come and gone."

I couldn't tell if Sabbatini was playing with the deputies or not, but I made a point of contradicting him. "I think these guys know a whole lot more than they're letting on. Okay, what happened here? Did your perp go in more than one direction? Or was the victim still alive out here?"

Spud shook his head, still trying to play poker.

"Are they thinking there might have been more than one killer?" I asked.

Derek picked up the pace with his toe bouncing.

"That's what it is, isn't it?"

"Too early to say for sure," Derek volunteered, "but they've isolated two distinct sets of footprints, one set in shoes, the other barefoot."

Spud glared at his colleague.

"So," I continued, "that would suggest that we're dealing with both a man and a woman, the assumption being that the barefoot tracks belong to the victim. . . ."

"We can't assume," Spud said.

I winked at Spud. "Unless we're dealing with a pair of killers, one barefoot, who brought the victim here already dead. Anything come back on the weapon?" I asked.

Both deputies shuffled their feet.

"Look, I'm staying with Deputy Coolican and I think it'll be best for everybody involved if we keep him out of this. But he's going to want to know some things as they develop. What did they find on the weapon?"

Stalling, Spud poked his birthmarked cheek with his tongue so the mark took on dimension. The map of Idaho suddenly had topographical scale. I watched it rise and fall. "We're not supposed to know this stuff," Spud said, finally.

"But you do."

"It was a .45 caliber rifle, the same kind used in the 2004 double murder."

"Is it the same weapon?" I asked.

"That we don't know," Spud said, nodding now, his marked cheek falling back into place.

"Anything else?"

Both deputies shook their heads.

Walking to Sabbatini's car, I turned back to the deputies. "Hey, Derek, I'll see if I can get you a signed photo of Rose."

Derek grinned. "Would you?"

"I'll take one, too," said Spud.

"I'll see what I can do."

As we drove away, Sabbatini said, "I think you've got those boys where you want them."

Cold rain in the redwoods—
the old detective perks up
like a fresh shoot.

CHAPTER SEVEN

The Wife and the Bloodhound

THE MOMENT I set eyes on Blossom and Sabbatini's new wife, I wanted her to be my wife. Once I saw her bent over the ancient O'Keefe and Merritt in the small kitchen, she captured my heart.

Of course, my hunger had grown gigantic by the time I witnessed Quince, the ex-con, murmuring with her lips, in breathy concentration, as she pulled an earthenware casserole from the oven. I stood in the kitchen doorway while she pivoted with the casserole, noticing me for the first time. Her nostrils flared and she grinned at me, the dimple on each cheek deepening, as if she'd been expecting me.

Sabbatini had walked in ahead of me and was now in the main room with Blossom and Milosz. The aroma from the stove had lured me into the kitchen. I stood flat-footed, most likely with my mouth open. But at least I hadn't come empty-handed. I held a large bouquet of red tulips, having forced Sabbatini to stop on the way back through Guerneville. I wanted to leave something for the house from which I'd already been expelled, a curious way of thumbing my nose at my hosts' hospitality.

Quince placed the casserole on a trivet. "You must be Augie. I've heard a lot about you."

"It's all true."

"I'm Quince," she said with a laugh.

"I've heard hardly nothing about you, except that you're taking my bed."

"Oh, no."

"Don't worry, it doesn't look like much of a bed."

Quince was facing me now, a tall, pretty woman in her early forties. Her eyes were a silvery green you could swim in, and her dark hair was cropped short. She wore a beguiling pair of conical earrings, each one with matching single dots that suggested dominoes, a pair of double ones. God, how I wanted to plant a little kiss on each of her ears. I bit my lower lip to keep myself in line. Quince had a sweet nose with a little bump on the bridge, and a pair of generous lips. And, of course, the dimples.

She wore blue teal corduroys and a yellow apron that featured a small pile of plum stones and William Carlos Williams's famous lines, "I have eaten the plums . . ."

"Those tulips are beautiful," Quince said. "Do you always arrive with flowers?"

I handed Quince the bouquet with a curtsy. "I didn't want to meet the new wife empty-handed."

"How thoughtful of you."

Quince opened and shut cabinets until she found a suitable vase. At the butcher block, she cut the stalks with a single whack of the chef's knife, gathered the tulips in her long fingers, and arranged them in the vase, with an uncanny sense of order, before going to the sink for water.

Next she crossed the room and briefly lifted the lid of the casserole. I sniffed the air theatrically. "Smells like creamed pearl onions glazed in bacon. And there's still a leg of lamb roasting in the oven. You don't want to dry it out, now."

Quince looked at me like I was clairvoyant.

"I have a good nose," I said, and walked up close to her. I sniffed again. "But I can't tell what perfume you're wearing."

"I'm not wearing any."

"Ah, au naturel."

"You could say."

"I did say."

Quince turned her head sideways and looked at me like I was a curiosity. "Are you always like this?"

"Like what?"

"So forward?"

I took a few steps back. "Forgive me."

"I'm only kidding."

"Don't kid a kidder."

Quince spread her lips in a wide smile. My attraction to her was so intense I had to find a way to change my focus. I repeated the words *armed robbery* in my head a dozen times and looked down at the ex-con's feet, half expecting them to be shrouded in prison slippers. But she was wearing a witty pair of checked high-top sneakers.

"Where have Blossom and Sabbatini gone?" I asked.

"They're giving us a chance to get acquainted," Quince said. She looked at me so directly I felt like hiding behind my forehead.

Who's the forward one now? I wondered. Again, I sniffed the air. "That leg of lamb smells like it's going from medium rare to medium in the next minute. If I were you, I'd quit flirting and get her out of there."

"Shut up," Quince said, just as Sabbatini chased Milosz into the kitchen.

"Have you already offended our new wife, Augie?" Sabbatini said, with a laugh.

"Grab him, Bobby," Quince said, motioning to the boy. She was standing at the stove. "I've got to take the lamb out."

Sabbatini grabbed Milosz's hand. "Watch out for old Augie," he said. "He might look ancient, but I think he has some game left."

Quince pulled out the lamb. Once more I sniffed the air. "Oh, I'm glad you weren't shy with the rosemary."

"What's with the nose over here, Bobby?"

"He's always had a well-developed stinker," Sabbatini said, as Milosz squirmed free and waddled out of the kitchen.

"Beware the bloodhound," said the glorious wife, sniffing the air.

One look, and the heart
points due north—
love at first sight.

A Woman Ready

At dinner, which waited until Milosz had been tucked away for the night, Blossom wanted to hear the news on the murder.

"They've got nothing yet," Sabbatini said. "They want to link it to the Jenner murders."

"It is linked," I said. "It's the same type of rifle, fired execution-style, as in the unsolved murders up the coast. It may be coincidence, but my bet is it's either the same shooter or a copycat."

"How's Coolie?" Blossom asked.

"I talked to him this afternoon," Sabbatini said, between bites of lamb. He winked at Quince. "Looks like we've got ourselves a great wife, Blossom."

Quince shrugged in an odd way, as if to say, "Baby, you don't know what you've got."

"But Coolie," Sabbatini continued, "he sounded distant. I didn't expect him to be back from work yet. Was just going to leave a message, tell him to come up for dinner. But he took off early. Said he'd lit some sage and had been reading Thich Nhat Hanh. We got to yakking about mindfulness. Coolie was nicely tuned on the

Rio Brio. Anyway, he's coming over for dessert. And to pick you up, Augie."

I didn't want to be picked up. I wanted to spend the rest of my life with the new wife. I smiled across the table at her and in return she gave me a cool, don't-get-too-interested-in-me-buddy-boy smile. I resisted the desire to pepper her with questions and simply asked where she'd arrived from.

"Well, I've spent the last five years living in Reno." She glanced meaningfully at Blossom and Sabbatini. Was she expecting them to cover for whatever fiction she concocted? I wondered if Reno was a euphemism for a brothel on the outskirts of town.

Sabbatini motioned to me with a fresh bite of lamb on the end of his fork. "Be forewarned, Augie, do not gamble with this woman."

"I made my living," Quince said, a bit sheepishly, "playing Texas Hold 'Em."

"You must be good," I said.

"Will you teach me how to play?" Blossom said, stabbing a slice of lamb from the platter. She nodded to Sabbatini. "I want to whip his ass."

"We're living in a new age, Augie," Sabbatini said. "Now the women want to do the vanquishing."

"It's about time," said Blossom.

I was ready to surrender. Let the woman with the dimples and the domino earrings conquer me.

Quince grinned. "That was the best part."

"What was the best part?" I asked.

"Beating up on the boys. Nothing as satisfying as taking money from young lads. They'd come to town, all studly, and see this woman with a few gray hairs sitting at the table. I could read them as easily as the funny pages."

So she could read me with her eyes closed. I crunched a couple of pearl onions as I prepared my next question. "How come you were willing to give up all that glory to come to the boondocks and work for these two?"

Quince turned to Blossom and said, "He's patronizing me, isn't he?"

With a nod, Blossom agreed. "He can't help himself. He's fallen head over heels for you, girl."

"Hey," I said, "you don't know me as well as you think, Blossom Dearie."

Sabbatini cracked up. "This reminds me of a poem by Robert Creeley."

"Everything reminds him of a Robert Creeley poem," Blossom said. "You'd think that Robert Creeley had already lived our lives."

"In a sense he has," Sabbatini said.

Blossom sneered at her husband. "What was I saying before he went Creeley on us?"

Quince winked at me. "Something about Augie falling head over heels."

"*Attention*, Augie," Sabbatini said in a compelling French accent, "*au bout du fossé, la culbute.*"

"Translation please," I said.

"Christ, he drives me crazy with his bullshit," Blossom whined. "If it's not the poems, it's the damn French. He sits for hours with headphones on repeating French phrases. And half the crazies in this county think he's God."

Sabbatini nodded to me. "Danger is imminent, buddy. Or—in the beautiful imagery of the French—at the end of a ditch, a somersault."

Quince grinned at Sabbatini. "Are you trying to warn Augie about me, Bobby?"

"Not at all. I was just struck by the association of the phrases. You know, head over heels with *la culbute*, the somersault. It also brought to mind a charming David Ignatow poem about a bagel."

"One of Bobby's strategies," Blossom explained to Quince, "is to wear you down."

Sabbatini stood up and bowed humbly toward the table.

THE BAGEL

BY DAVID IGNATOW

I stopped to pick up the bagel
rolling away in the wind,
annoyed with myself
for having dropped it
as if it were a portent.
Faster and faster it rolled,
with me running after it
bent low, gritting my teeth,
and I found myself doubled over
and rolling down the street
head over heels, one complete somersault
after another like a bagel
and strangely happy with myself.

"Charming," Quince said.

Blossom shook her head in faux exasperation. I chewed slowly on a piece of lamb and then reminded Quince that I'd asked her why she'd left Reno for the glories of Cazadero.

Quince shook her head back and forth in a lovely gesture of liberation, her witty earrings doing the to and fro.

"First of all," she said, "Blossom asked me, and I owe Blossom. But that's another story. And the gig in Reno, it was getting a little old. You could say I was facing a crossroads." The beautiful ex-con left her lips partly puckered after saying the last word. I was forced to look away.

"The amazing thing," Blossom said, "is that Quince just called out of the blue and asked if I knew of a place out here where she could stay for a while. 'I got the place,' I told her. The whole thing was serendipity."

"You see, I either needed to grow the business," Quince said, "which would have entailed a move to Vegas, a place I have personal reasons for not wanting to return to, or I had to downsize."

I glanced around the cabin, "Well, this is downsizing, alright."

"Now he's patronizing all of us," Blossom said.

I grinned. "You people are sure sensitive."

"We are all sensitive, Augie," Sabbatini said. "That's the point. California does that to you. But sensitive as we may be, we still have our small ambitions."

"Come on now, Bobby," Blossom said, "don't go deep on us."

Sabbatini forged ahead. "And that's what excites me about the prospects of Ginsberg's Galley. It's just a humble place in Guerneville. . . ."

"It didn't look so humble to me," I chipped in. "It's spectacular. You guys sank a lot of dough into that joint."

Blossom shook her head.

"Don't start trouble, Augie," Sabbatini said. "We couldn't just have an ordinary dump. This tavern is going to be special. It'll be a place where people can bring their sensitivities, their broken ambitions, their burst hearts, where they can come and watch others dive into the sunken wrecks of their souls. . . ."

"Enough, Bobby," Blossom hollered. She shot Quince a see-what-I-mean look. "I'm afraid they're going to cart my husband away in a straitjacket."

"He was really a homicide detective?" the beautiful wife asked.

"One of the best," I responded. "What are you going to do? He found poetry and become an evangelist."

"I'm reminded of that old W. C. Williams poem," Sabbatini said, rolling right along.

Blossom shook her head. "No Williams tonight, Bobby."

"But you love Williams, honey."

"There's a time and a place."

I smiled at Quince and she smiled back. We were amused by our hosts. I remembered how much Blossom resisted Sabbatini and his poems in the days when he courted her. Finally, she gave in and began laying poems on him as quickly as he showered her with verse.

Briefly discouraged, Sabbatini got up and poked at the good, crackling fire he'd started before dinner. He added a furry log that sizzled as soon as the flames reached it.

"Once the Galley opens," Sabbatini said, with a knowing grin, "the poems will be flying."

Blossom shook her head. "That's just what the world needs, Bobby, flying poems."

I smiled over at Quince and realized that she'd been watching me, her mouth half-open like a woman ready to be made love to.

She quickly got hold of herself and closed her mouth. Then she winked at me and whispered: "*Bloodhound.*"

Roadkill and Porkpie

Before I could digest what had just transpired, there was a hearty rap on the door. Sabbatini opened it to Jesse Coolican, dressed in black, including a porkpie hat that made him look like a cross between the great tenor sax player Lester Young and a nineteenth-century Indian photographed by Edward Curtis. He walked into the cabin and doffed his hat but put it right back on again.

Blossom said: "I love that hat, Jesse. You look beautiful in black."

"Thank you, Blossom. I'm made for mourning. It's in the genes."

"Any news?" Blossom asked.

"Nope, I've turned my professional interest in the case over to Augie here."

"The great one, huh," Sabbatini said. "Good choice."

"Well, I figured you'd be good for nothing."

Sabbatini laughed briefly. "And what about your personal interest in the case?"

"I've buried that in a mound with my forgotten ancestors."

"Hey, meet Quince, an old friend of Blossom's. This is Deputy Jesse Coolican."

Coolican bent over and shook hands with the new wife.

"You're a deputy?" Quince asked, trying to mask her incredulity as soon as she heard her own voice. I enjoyed her discomfort.

"I am indeed, but off-duty at the moment."

"Guerneville's finest," said Sabbatini. "There's no cops in town."

Coolican nodded. "Welcome to Sonoma County, ma'am."

Sabbatini pulled a spare chair up to the table. "Come on over and join us, Coolie."

Blossom stood. "I've got a mincemeat pie cooling that I'm about ready to serve."

Coolican walked over to the fire and stood warming himself a moment. "Sounds good. Did you prepare it with genuine suet?" he asked.

"You bet," Blossom said, cheerfully, "made from fresh roadkill venison."

Coolican grinned. "Way to go, Blossom. Won't be long until you become a native."

Quince and I exchanged glances regarding the roadkill, as Blossom went back to the kitchen and Sabbatini excused himself to look in on Milosz.

Coolican gazed first at Quince and then at me. "I know you civilized people would rather we leave the dead animals for the vultures. But we savages think that's a waste. We can tell when it's fresh and when it's gone bad. Do you know how many people a full-grown deer will feed, ma'am?" Coolican asked, looking directly at Quince.

She shook her head and narrowed her eyes. It was the first time I saw her look mean.

"I bet you hail from one of our major metropolises, ma'am," Coolican said.

"Right," she said, "but I've learned how to disassociate from things I find unpleasant. People, too."

"I'm good at that, too," the deputy said. "Maybe we should get together sometime and disassociate."

Was Coolican actually coming on to Quince, I wondered, *or just jiving?*

In any case, Quince seemed to take the deputy seriously. She looked him up and down. Using her most breathy voice, she said, "I don't know if that'd be a good idea."

"Maybe not," Coolican said, winking at the beauty.

I'll admit I was confused by the exchange. Blossom, back from the kitchen, rushed in to fill the vacuum. "Quince's going to be our new wife," she said. "She'll be looking after Milosz and bringing a little order to the place as we open the tavern."

"That's what I understand," Coolican said. "So how did you women get to know each other?" he asked.

"We met in prison," Quince said, facing Coolican directly. "Taycheedah, right outside of Fond du Lac, Wisconsin."

"Bunch of Indians in there?" Coolican asked.

"Well, it's close to the Rez."

"So, you were working there?" the deputy asked. "Doing a little social work, teaching a writing class?"

"I was a prisoner," the new wife said.

"What do you know? Did you get caught up in a little white-collar crime?"

"I'm not sure what color the crime was. But I was holding an automatic rifle in a Milwaukee credit union when everything went down."

I pictured the famous shot of Patty Hearst holding the assault weapon in the old Hibernia Bank in San Francisco.

Coolican nodded his head like a therapist. "I see, but you didn't shoot it."

"I didn't get a chance."

"So you served your time," Coolican said.

"Damn right. Seven and a half years."

"Well, good for you."

"I don't know how good it was for me."

"You met Blossom, though."

"Baby Blossom," Quince said with affection.

Sabbatini passed through the room and then went out back to bring in more wood. He shook me off when I offered to help. For a moment, I was willing to cede the new wife to Coolican. I'd seen the streak of mean in her. I couldn't tell if she was flirting with the deputy, nor could I really feature myself with a woman who seemed so cavalier about her crime.

Pretty soon Sabbatini got the fire roaring again and Blossom walked in and out of the kitchen with a pot of coffee and plates of pie. "I just cut a sliver for you," she said to Quince, as we gathered back at the table, "so you could try it. But there's plenty more."

Quince eyed the little slice of mincemeat. "Roadkill pie," she said, and bent her fork through the flaky crust and the black meat of the pie.

"You only live once, Quince," Blossom said.

"Speaking of which," Coolican said, "I once knew a woman who prepared a honey-quince pie."

Quince glared at Coolican as she put the fork in her mouth. "Hey, that's good, Blossom, a hell of a lot better than that shit they fed us at Taycheedah."

The pie *was* good. I did my best to forget about the roadkill.

In a celebratory mood now, Sabbatini rolled up a huge fatty.

"What do you got going there, Poesy?" Coolican asked, with a hint of disdain. "Some more of the Fuck Face?"

"Hey, it's a helluva lot better than your Monte Rio Brio."

Coolican shrugged.

When the fatty came around to me and I passed, Coolican let out a squawk. "Come on, Brother Bear, be a man. You ate the roadkill, now smoke the Fuck Face."

I took the fatty between my fingers. It felt as comforting and familiar as cuddling with my ex-wife in bed. I sucked down an Olympian toke and passed the joint to Quince, whose head was rocking back and forth to an imaginary beat, the domino earrings bobbing like a pair of buoys in the sea. She smoked like a natural and I wanted her again, more than ever.

"I was about to recite a little William Carlos Williams before you came, Coolie," Sabbatini said.

Coolican nodded. "The good doctor, what do you know? Myself, I was reading some Yeats this evening before dinner."

"Are you people for real?" Quince asked.

"That is open to debate," Coolican said. He nodded to himself a few times and then became distracted. I looked into his pockmarked face, shadowed by the short brim of his hat. I thought of the phrase "old soul" but, in Coolican's case, I figured that *ancient* was closer to the truth. The man looked a hundred years old.

Sabbatini stood and gave the deputy a nice pat on the shoulder. "Why don't you give us one, Coolie?"

"Don't mind if I do. Here's a little Yeatser called 'Spilt Milk,'" he said, without expression.

> *We that have done and thought,*
> *That have thought and done,*
> *Must ramble and thin out,*
> *Like milk spilt on a stone.*

"Interesting choice, Coolie," Sabbatini said. "That's from *The Winding Stair*, isn't it?"

Coolican nodded.

"Published in 1931. Yeats was sixty-six."

"Sensing his mortality," Coolican said. "It's my favorite subject."

I glanced across at Quince who, wide-eyed now, was taking everything in.

"You didn't know what you were getting yourself into, did you?"

She smiled at me and I could see her pretty row of teeth. Then her toes touched mine under the table. I sensed the others watching us and tried to think of something to break the spell.

"Maybe it's time to initiate Quince," I said.

The new wife glared at me while the others regarded me quizzically.

"With a poet of her own."

"I don't do poetry," Quince said.

The rest of us laughed broadly.

Sabbatini said, "We'll leave that to Blossom."

Blossom nodded. "I've been thinking Kay Ryan."

"An inspired choice," Sabbatini said, relighting the fatty and passing it to me. "Our former poet laureate. Winner of the Pulitzer Prize. Recipient of a MacArthur Foundation genius grant." He winked at Quince. "She hails from Northern California, as well."

As I sat there sucking on the fat roach, I took in the scene at Sabbatini's: The priestly Bobby stood at the fire in his Sufi-wear, with his arm around Porkpie Coolican, who chattered about W. B. Yeats, while Blossom sang the praises of Kay Ryan, gesticulating with her tattooed hands while making her points. For her part, Quince looked a little bit like a bride with buyer's remorse.

As for myself, I kept sucking on the roach of Fuck Face, since nobody else seemed interested. Nicely ripped, I told myself it wouldn't be long before Quince was reciting poems and the two of us were in bed together. The only question was which would happen first.

Finally, Blossom stood up and commanded everyone's attention. "Here's the proof of the pudding," she said, nodding toward Quince.

SAY UNCLE

BY KAY RYAN

Every day
you say,
Just one
more try.
Then another
irrecoverable
day slips by.
You will
say ankle,

you will
say knuckle;
why won't
you why
won't you
say uncle?

It was a fine performance, and after everybody cheered, Quince relented. "Alright," she said, "set me up with some Kay Ryan."

CHAPTER EIGHT

Eggs, Bacon, Grief

I SLEPT FOR ten hours on Coolican's lumpy futon, not even waking to pee. Although I had a slight kink in my neck, I felt remarkably fresh, and greeted myself in the bathroom mirror with a hero's welcome: "Well done, old boy."

Coolican had already left for work. There was a three-word note—*eggs, bacon, grief*—on the kitchen table. It sounded to me like either the beginning of a poem or a suicide note. When I opened the fridge, there was nothing in it but a dozen jumbo browns and a slab of bacon. Grief, though hard to see, I supposed, was everywhere.

I had no interest in making breakfast, but found coffee and dripped a robust carafe of French roast. The sun was out. I opened the dining room window and perched on the sill, feeling like a cat sunning himself. As if my thought drew him, Coolican's cat came over and sniffed at my socks. After a second cup of coffee, I walked by the shrine and had another look at Ruthie Rosenberg. She was lovely, large-eyed, buoyant. Then I thought of her with her face blown off.

After a while, I burnt a little sage in one of Coolican's pots because it was there for the burning. Bemused in the pungent swirl, I turned over the book of matches and discovered a number scrawled with the name *Yevgeny*. I dialed it a bit absently and a man with a Russian accent answered: "Good afternoon. River Rose." When I didn't answer, the voice grew angry. "Hello?! Hello?!"

The night before, I'd followed Coolican back to Guerneville in my rental car, and now revved on coffee and sage, I was raring to drive down to Jenner, where the river met the sea. From what I understood, the River Rose sat high above the ocean. I wanted to meet Yevgeny. Maybe I could eat at the bar and get him to recite a little Yevtushenko.

Wild Mushroom Soup

The young woman behind the bar was a local. A lass with flaxen cornrows. I took a stool at the bar, facing an elegant shelf of premium gins and vodkas. A man like me, who doesn't even go in for that kind of stuff, could still become intoxicated by the display. I gave the stool a swivel and caught a glimpse of the ocean. The Russian wasn't anywhere to be seen, but I sensed he was close.

I asked for a lunch menu. Johnny Cash was singing, "Give My Love to Rose." A few stools down, an aging dandy sat with a woman he'd lost interest in. He kept looking over his shoulder as if somebody more to his liking might walk in. I could smell the man's cologne from halfway down the bar. He tapped his arthritic fingers on the bar and wore fat rings that had become knots in his gnarled digits. An ancient athlete. The woman ate oysters greedily while the gent tapped his fingers and remained on the lookout.

I gazed past them toward the deck, which faced across the river to the sea. It was too cold to dine out there. The barkeep handed me the menu and filled a water glass.

"What's good today?"

She took my question seriously, biting her lower lip and getting momentarily dreamy. "The wild mushroom soup," she said.

I could see she meant it. "It's really good?"

"Oh, man. I mean, I know you're not supposed to apply the term *terroir* to anything beside grapes, but, really, if you can't talk about the earth when it comes to wild mushrooms, especially these wild mushrooms, when can you?"

I smiled across at her. "I see your point. Where do the mushrooms come from?"

She grinned at me like I was silly. "Someone forages for them."

I wanted to keep the silliness going. "Do you have a staff forager?"

"That's me!" came a booming voice with a Russian accent.

I swiveled and took my first gander at Yevgeny. Tall and muscular, the Russian had a shaved head, dull blue eyes, and a pair of thin eyebrows that looked as if they were regularly plucked.

"Where did you learn about mushrooms?" I asked, once the big man crossed to the working side of the bar.

"He knows a lot," the cornrowed barkeep said, before migrating to the restaurant side of the establishment.

"My family always gather mushrooms."

"In Russia?"

"Of course. Outside of Voronezh. This is near Ukraine." The Russian polished off his sentences with a quick sneer. He looked me over for two seconds and I felt like I'd been fully frisked. Maybe I was missing something, but I couldn't pick up the charm Bobby was alluding to when he had described the Russian.

I persisted. "So what's different about foraging in California?"

The bartender looked at me as if I were a pest, but he didn't answer. I watched him wash some glasses and then towel down the area.

Finally, the Russian looked up at me. "So, you want to try the mushroom soup?"

"Maybe I'll have a Bloody Mary first." Sabbatini had nurtured my taste yesterday, and I was curious to see who mixed a better one, the professional or the divine one.

"A bloody," Yevgeny said, and went about the business of mixing it with such nonchalance that I wanted to give him the prize before even tasting the product. "The real difference with mushrooms," he said, "is safer here, easier to tell what will kill you." The Russian put down my drink on a cocktail napkin and gazed at me for a long moment. "Do you know mushrooms?"

"No."

"You have to be a dummy here to pick the poisonous. The Death Cap or the Death Angel."

"Those are the names of the mushrooms?"

The plucked-brow forager sneered at me. "This is the popular name. You want the Latin name? I give it to you. The Death Cap, they call it *Amanita phalloides.* The Death Angel, they also call this one the Destroying Angel—isn't that a nice name? This mushroom is called, technically, *Amanita orceata.*"

"You're a genuine scholar," I said, sipping my drink.

"Yes," he said, "I'm an expert on things nobody else wants to know. Back in 1992, in the region of Voronezh, forty-four people died from bad mushrooms. Hundreds of people sick. Worse case in all of Russia. I have no sympathy for these people because they are morons."

"Hard to stop people from following their appetites."

"Better to follow your dick."

"I've got into some trouble that way."

"But you are not dead," the Russian said. "Yet."

"So you don't think the soup will kill me?"

The bartender shrugged. "Live dangerously, my friend."

I stuck out my hand. "Augie Boyer."

He shook my hand and repeated my name, running it together into one word. It sounded to me like the name of a root vegetable stew.

"I know that name," he said.

"I'm a friend of Bobby Sabbatini's."

"Ah, *Augieboyer,*" he repeated, with delight. "You here with a visit for Bobby?"

"Right. For the opening of Ginsberg's Galley."

"It's wonderful. Bobby said he put some Yevtushenko in the karaoke machine."

"Yes, he told me you're a great one for Yevtushenko."

For the first time, a flash of pride spread across the Russian's face. "Yes, they call me Yevtushenko. I love his long poems."

The way the Russian pronounced *long* sounded to me like *lung*, and I wondered at first if Yevtushenko had written a series of poems about breathing.

"All I do," he continued, "is repeat the poem over and over to myself till I learn it. I get so proud, you'd think I wrote it." The Russian bowed his head slightly as a boyish smile leapt into his powerful face. "Let me get you a bowl of the soup. It's on me, Augieboyer."

So now the Russian was turning on the charm. He laid a woven place mat and silverware rolled in a linen napkin in front of me and went off to the kitchen. On his return, he held up a finger to indicate that my meal would soon arrive and then freshened the drinks of the old linebacker and his escort. Just as I took a stroll out to the deck, Muddy Waters broke out with "Baby, Please Don't Go." I stood a moment in the open breeze, noticing a couple of dozen seals sunning themselves on the far side of the river.

A few moments later, a slim Latino in a chef's hat bounced through the kitchen door with my soup and a few slices of sourdough.

I sipped the dark, wild broth slowly, trying to imagine how quickly the twist of poison would arrive, if it were coming. I wasn't thinking of myself but some poor, unsuspecting soul who, after just a couple of spoonfuls of such savory refreshment, began to sense the first twists of the knot. Did it happen this quickly? I wondered how often mushrooms had been used as a lethal weapon, but decided to suspend the thought. Yevtushenko had returned to my spot at the bar and was hovering over me.

"So, what do you think about it?" he asked.

"It's very good; you can pick up the wildness." The barkeep's word *terroir* echoed in my head. "The flavor tastes like it has really been earned. It's very rich."

The Russian laughed. "This is the only wealth the peasants ever had, but they did not have to earn it; it was given to them by the forest."

"They had to forage for those mushrooms," I said. "They had to get down on their knees."

The Russian shrugged. "A man farts," he said, "before he shits."

I pondered the phrase a moment, wondering if Yevtushenko had just laid a Russian proverb on me that had lost a little in translation. Sabbatini probably had a version of it in French. The Russian stood nearby as I took slow, savory spoonfuls of the rich soup. He leaned against the bar's double sink, lost for a moment in some brooding reverie. I reminded myself that his on-again, off-again girlfriend had been missing for five days and just yesterday had turned up dead. What was he doing back at work? I looked up and caught the Russian's eye. "By the way, I was very sorry to hear about your loss."

"What did you say?"

"Your loss, I was sorry to hear. Sabbatini told me about the young woman."

Yevtushenko's face turned grim. I tried to read it, but it was like reading a line of Cyrillic characters.

With furrows now running across his forehead, Yevtushenko resembled a stolid figure cast in bronze. Then his eyes narrowed. "A very sad business, what happened to her. Did Bobby send you out here?"

"No, I was just out driving. Sabbatini mentioned I could get a good lunch here." I forced a smile. "He was right."

"I've already talked to the sheriff's department for three hours. I try my best to cooperate." Yevtushenko sighed. "You can't believe the questions they ask me. I don't even think they suspect me, but they ask these questions. Like a dirty game, this is. You know what they ask me, Augieboyer? They ask, 'When did you last fuck her?' They don't ask, 'When did you last hold her in your arms? When did you last kiss her good-bye?'"

"They're not poets," I said.

"You got it right." He shook his head. "'When did you last fuck her?'"

The Russian looked at me for me for a reaction and I shook my head, dutifully, as if in sympathy with his disgust. Of course, I, too, was wondering when he last fucked her, but thought it better not to inquire.

Yevtushenko gazed at me, suspicious again. "Bobby sent you out here."

"No, I already told you he didn't." I stood up from my stool and fished a twenty out of my wallet.

"You're not going to finish your soup?"

I shook my head.

The Russian shrugged. "Well, I don't take your money."

"Thank you."

"You see, Augieboyer, you a Russian in this country, they always suspect you."

I moved toward the door. "I thought you said you didn't think they suspected you."

"No, in general." Yevtushenko's voice got louder. "A Russian in this country, they always suspecting. It doesn't matter how long I be here. They see Russian, they see mafia. I got no dirty business. I work. I live cheap, a tiny place near the ocean. Sonoma County sheriff, they lazy. They always look for easy target. If they were picking wild mushrooms, they all be dead. They ask me if I have any idea who kill her. I tell them, follow money. Look who bring money in Sonoma County. Marijuana syndicate. Nevada gaming. They say, 'What's that got to do with a crackhead whore?' That's how they talk about the dead."

Yevtushenko's expression changed, almost on a dime, from furious to obsequious, as the ancient athlete signaled for a fresh drink.

I waited for Yevtushenko to fill the order and then walked back toward the bar and asked, "What was Ruthie's relationship with the outside money?"

Yevtushenko bent over the bar and, in a much quieter voice, said, "Ruthie was not anymore Ruthie. The crack make her crazy. She work when she can out of a massage joint in Monte Rio. She meet a lot of men. Locals. Tourists. Guys who come here to do business. She take anybody's money. I remember she could be so lovely."

"Did she live with you till the end?"

"She come, she go." The bartender pushed back from the bar. He bent over the double sink and washed glasses.

I dropped a five-dollar bill on the bar. "You don't mind if I leave a tip?"

"Thank you."

"Thanks for the soup."

"This is my pleasure, Augieboyer." The Russian shook his head back and forth and then cleared his throat a couple of times like a man having a hard time swallowing his grief. "Next time you finish your soup," he said. "Please, you tell Poesy, I be there at opening night."

CHAPTER NINE

Priorities

SABBATINI WAS MOPPING the floor of Ginsberg's Galley when I dropped by. In ten days the joint opened.

Bobby hailed me with a burst of enthusiasm. I guessed Fuck face. "How ya doing, Augster?"

I put up a hand in greeting, but stopped just inside the entry to try and guess the identity of the poet intoning through the sound system. The poet's gasping breaths and reference to Gloucester, Massachusetts, gave him away as Charles Olson. "You always mop the floor to Olson?" I asked, slipping out of my shoes in deference to the freshly washed floor.

"Nah, Creeley's a better mopping poet. The short lines do a better job of matching my strokes. But sometimes you just have to go against the grain. Sleep okay last night?"

"Like a babe. Coolican was gone when I woke up. Then I drove out to Jenner and met Yevtushenko."

Sabbatini leaned his mop against the wall and regarded me with interest. Then the karaoke voice switched from the gruff Charles Olson to a demure female musing about a secret. Sabbatini watched me to see if I could identify the poet. When I shrugged, he switched to a mild British accent that perfectly mimicked the poet: "Denise Levertov. She's a trifle on the earnest side, isn't she?" He hit a remote device and the voice went dead. "So, did Yevtushenko lay any verse on you?"

"No, we talked wild mushrooms."

"Man's an expert."

"So I understand. They doing toxicology on Ruthie's body?"

"I suppose they will to see what drugs she had in her system. You ask me, that's kind of beside the point. Poor woman had two bullets in her head."

"Who knows, maybe the bullets got there later."

Sabbatini took a few giant strides across the room in his stocking feet. With his hand on his brow like a brainy vaudeville clown, I could see that he was about to mock my instincts as a detective. "So the reason the Rooskie poisoned the victim with wild mushrooms before shooting her in the head is . . . ?"

"He's a sadist," I said, thinking not so much about the Russian but of some fictive criminal mind.

"So if he poisons her to get his jollies, why does he bother to shoot her?"

"To link her killing to the unsolved double murder in Jenner."

"Or maybe he's not a sadist at all and shoots the poor lass to put her out of her misery. So, you like Yevtushenko for this thing, Augie?"

"No, I'm not saying that. I actually found him quite sympathetic. I'd just feel better if they ran toxicology on her. At first, the man seemed rather defensive. Once I introduced myself, he suspected you of sending me out to gather dirt about him."

"You think he's going to boycott the opening?" Sabbatini asked, with genuine concern.

"No, he made a point of saying he'd be here. That's unless he gets arrested in the meantime."

"Good, because I put a lot of Yevtushenko on the karaoke machine and I'd hate for it to go to waste."

"Well, I'm glad to see you have your priorities straight."

Marriage

Sabbatini booted the sound system back on, and after a charming reading by the patron saint, Ginsberg, of his poem, "A Supermarket in California," it kicked over to an interminable poem by Marianne Moore called "Marriage," which got me thinking about my ex-wife Nina. Although I'd done my best to consign her to the junkyard of memory, I still missed her. I muttered a couple of lines with the poet under the high volume of her post-Victorian cadence:

Psychology which explains everything
explains nothing,
and we are still in doubt.

A fitting sentiment for my ex-wife, the therapist, the anger specialist. And how did Marianne Moore, a woman who never married, know so much about the institution? For an instant, I was sick of all specialists and poets, but before I could turn genuinely sour, Quince, the temporary wife of Cazadero, strolled into Ginsberg's Galley, and I silently renewed my vow to make her mine. What synchronicity.

When Quince smiled at me and lowered her eyes, it was all I could do to keep myself from dropping to a knee. All this with Marianne Moore intoning delightfully in her high, nasal glory:

What can we do with them—
these savages. . . .

Quince went over and greeted Sabbatini. I heard her say something about Blossom taking Milosz to the doctor in Sebastopol for a checkup.

"So you're footloose and fancy free," Sabbatini said.

Quince grinned. "Yeah, and right in the heart of Guerneville." She walked over toward me and punched my arm like we were old pals. "Hey, Augie, you want to take me for a ride?"

It sounded like a joke question, too good to be true. I tried to play it cool. "Yeah, sure. Where?"

"You guys should go wine tasting out West Side Road," Sabbatini offered. "They make some great pinots."

"I like wine," Quince said, "but I'm hardly a connoisseur."

"Me neither," I said.

My heart sank when Quince turned to Sabbatini and asked him if he wanted to join us.

Sabbatini shook his head. "Nah, you kids go. I've got a little more tidying up to do."

Meanwhile, Marianne Moore was winding down her matrimonial epic:

Liberty and union
now and forever

Quince, apparently, had had her fill of the poet. She turned to Sabbatini and asked, "What is that hag hollering about?"

"Marriage, wouldn't you know?"

I led my future wife out through the swinging doors of Ginsberg's Galley as Sabbatini smiled beneficently upon us.

Fuck First, Talk Later

We picked up a couple of burgers down the street after deciding that we shouldn't taste wine on empty stomachs. I hadn't had enough of the wild mushroom soup to constitute a meal, and wanted my only hunger to be for Quince. She walked beside me back to the car, smiling joyously, as she swung the white sack with the burgers back and forth in her right hand.

Once we got onto West Side Road, Quince handed me a burger and took the other out for herself. It felt a bit like a high school date, leaving Mel's Drive-In on Geary, with the goods and the girl. Instead of cheap milkshakes, we'd wash it down with good wine.

I wasn't ready for my burger, but enjoyed watching Quince take quaint bites. I figured I'd wait for her to nearly finish hers before I inhaled mine.

"You're cute, Augie," she said between nibbles.

"Me?"

"Yes, you. I like to watch you when you're thinking. You get little furrows on your forehead. You go all serious and everything. What are you thinking about?"

I smiled at Quince.

"Uh-oh, now you're thinking before you answer."

"I was thinking about you," I confessed.

"Oh, and I figured you were trying to come up with who killed that girl, Ruthie."

Quince pulled out a pouch of fries and offered them to me. I demurred, difficult as it was. "Blossom said you'd be out nosing around on the case."

"Yeah, but I'm at a bit of a disadvantage, not knowing anybody out here beside Coolican, who's all messed up by the murder, and Bobby, who, despite being a helluva homicide detective at one time, is useless now."

Quince nibbled a fry. "Blossom said this Ruthie was all fucked up."

"Did Blossom ever meet her?"

"I don't think so, but that was the word on the street. She was a wild girl with an attitude. The type with a chip on her shoulder. I know the type."

"Hand me that burger," I said. "You sound like you've taken a special interest in her."

Quince shrugged. "I don't know. I was a wild girl, but I never really had a chip on my shoulder. I just had a thing for danger. That was my drug and I guess that's what got me into trouble. Blossom and I got to talking about some girls we knew in prison. Lots of 'em in there had a death wish. They were the black sheep and got themselves in trouble hanging with the wrong guys."

"That's what happened to Blossom, from what I heard."

"Yeah," Quince said, a bit absently.

I munched away at my burger.

Quince shot me a sideways glance. "I was a party girl. I always liked boys. And I liked sex." Quince winked at me. "Still do. But back in high school, even before, my attitude was fuck first, talk later."

I didn't particularly want to think about Quince as a teenage fucking machine.

"Have I shocked you?"

"Not particularly," I lied.

"I've never been a puritan, Augie."

"I can see that."

"I'm not the type of person who feels a lot of shame for what I've done."

"Lucky you."

"How about you? What were you like during high school? I see you as the loner type."

I didn't respond to that, but looked out over the vineyards, which now stretched in front of us on each side of the road.

"So, does Blossom have a theory about Ruthie's killing?" I asked.

"Not really."

"Maybe she just ended up partying with the wrong guy," I suggested.

Quince held a fry aloft in the air. "He was definitely the wrong guy. Maybe she didn't even know him."

"Or maybe she knew him really well."

"You don't think it was random?" Quince asked.

I shrugged. "I don't want to speculate about the murder anymore."

"I was just asking," Quince said with a pout.

"I know; you're the inquisitive type."

"I'm not any type," she said, sticking out her tongue at me.

"Oh, I see. But the woman who got murdered, whom neither you or Blossom met, is a type. And, even though you just met me last night, you're pretty sure that I'm the loner type."

Quince flipped me off, and just in case I missed the sign language, said, "Fuck you royal."

Interesting phrase. I kept my eye on the road which had narrowed. Things had gotten off to a difficult start. Could our marriage be on the rocks before it commenced? I dropped the stub of my burger in the bag. Quince, who'd finished eating, was biting the nails on her right hand.

"Sorry," she said.

"Hey, I shouldn't have egged you on."

"Well, I guess I am a little on the inquisitive side. Seems like I've come a long way since the fuck-first, talk-later days."

"I suppose so," I said, forced to shift the hamburger sack onto my lap.

In the vineyards,
their first spat,
guess who has a hard-on.

What Do You Need?

We took a dirt road to the first winery we hit, Porter Creek. The small tasting room was at one end of a farmhouse.

Quince shook her head. "This is it? This dink-ass thing is a winery?"

I thought the place looked charming. "All they need is grapes and a little know-how."

"Grapes and a little know-how," Quince echoed, as we got out of the car. Then she looked me up and down. "And what do you need, Augie Boyer?"

The question choked me. Literally. It may not have lasted much more than a minute, but it seemed like it took quite an era of coughing and digging phlegm from my throat to recover. Quince ran around the side of the car and slapped my back and told me to lift up my arms, which I dutifully did. Meanwhile, the chartreuse Neon with the key still in the ignition and the door open was ding-ding-ding-dinging, as if to underscore the danger of my condition.

When I finally pulled myself together and yanked the key from the ignition, a glorious calm ensued. I breathed deeply three or four times, noticed the sun high in the sky, and heard birds singing in the trees, as if for the first time.

Quince placed a soft hand on my cheek. "You okay?"

"I think so."

Then she shot me a wry smile and harkened back to the trigger of my choking episode. "We're a little sensitive about what we need, aren't we?"

"A wee bit."

"Well, get back to me on that, will ya?"

I nodded and escorted Quince toward the door of the winery. She had a spot of mustard on her upper lip. A souvenir from her burger. Quite fetching. I had no plans to mention it.

Kidnapped

We sipped pinot noir at both Porter Creek and Davis Bynam and liked the Syrah so much at Belvedere Vineyards that we bought a bottle and a pair of wineglasses.

It was lovely on the patio. On that cool spring day, we were the only folks out there. We chose a table in the sun and sat side by side so that we could both look over the vineyards. I got out my Swiss Army knife and yanked the cork with a flourish.

After I filled her glass, I asked Quince to describe the color. The lovely ex-con swirled the wine around and watched it thin a bit as it slid back down the sides of the glass. Clearly, she was taking my question seriously.

"It's a very deep purple," she said, "the purple of a velvet coat worn by a nineteenth-century Russian woman of means."

I was delighted with the response and tried to nudge it a bit further. "You mean, the very deep purple of a velvet coat worn by a nineteenth-century Russian woman of means and ample bosom."

Quince nodded. "Exactly. Now, tell me what you taste."

"You realize you're asking a lot."

Quince rested her right hand on my thigh. "I think you're the man for the job."

I swirled the wine in my glass and a little spilled over the side.

"Oops," Quince chirped, clapping her hands. She returned a hand to my thigh as I tasted the wine and tried to remember some of the tasting notes the server suggested.

"I get a hint of cassis."

Quince sipped from her glass. "Yes."

"But, also, a bit of the barnyard."

"Don't you know it," my tasting partner said with a smile.

"I get burnt butter."

"Bacon fat."

"Cherry."

"Plum."

"Licorice."

"Rubber."

I took a deep sip from my glass and said, "Roasted oak."

Quince shook her head. "Seaweed," she said, and slid her hand up to my crotch.

I did my best to carry on. "But what about the aroma?"

Quince dipped her sweet nose, with the little bump on the bridge, into the bell of her glass. "Cedar closet."

I waited for a further articulation as she squeezed my thickening prick. "That's it? That's all you've got?"

Quince glared at me and took a couple of deep snorts of her glass. "Cigar box," she said. "Leather. Anise. Eucalyptus." Then she climbed on my lap and shifted around so that she was facing me.

I put down my glass and looked into Quince's moon face and watched it soften. It was the first time I'd seen her so close. I looked into the crystal green of her eyes. Her earrings, thin, silvered crescent moons, seemed to tinkle. I wanted to twist a finger into the dimple on her right cheek. "I didn't think this would happen quite so quickly."

"What's happened?" she asked, her face turning into a comic puzzle of tics and winks.

"You're goofy," I said.

"If you only knew."

"So, what time do you need to return to your wifely duties?"

Quince blew me a kiss from a foot away. "I have the night off."

I went hard again. "Wow, for just starting the job yesterday, I'd say you've got yourself a pretty good deal."

"Yeah, well, for what they're paying me, I can pretty much set the terms. I told Blossom that I was going to kidnap you today." Quince planted a sweet tattoo of a kiss on the corner of my lips. I responded in kind, managing to dissolve the spot of dried mustard she'd been wearing.

"How did you know you'd find me?" I asked.

"I knew."

"And what are you planning to do with me?"

Quince grabbed hold of my prick again. "We'll see."

Another couple, Aussies from the sound of their chatter, wandered out to the patio, and my sweet abductor waved to them before slipping off my lap. The couple made a quick exit from the patio.

For the next half hour, Quince and I quietly admired each other, slowly downing the bottle of Syrah.

Target

The spell was broken by the ring of my cell phone. It was Bobby Sabbatini, breathless.

"Where . . . where are you guys, Augie?"

"I don't know, a winery out on West Side Road. What's going on?"

"Somebody just took a shot at Jesse Coolican with a crossbow, outside Hemp and Chocolate in Guerneville."

"You're kidding. Is he okay?"

"Yeah, the arrow just grazed the side of his head."

Quince tugged at my arm. "What happened?"

Sabbatini kept talking. "Now there's all sorts of law enforcement out here, Augie. They've cleared everybody off Main Street. He was coming out of the shop after buying a couple of packs of smoking papers. They've surrounded the building across the street. They think the shooter's in there. Imagine, shooting an Indian in this day and age with a bow and arrow. Of all the people to be a target."

I whispered what I'd heard to Quince.

"They brought Coolican to the hospital in Sebastopol. He should be okay. The wound was superficial."

"We'll come right back," I said.

"No need for that. But I got something I'd like you to do," Sabbatini said. "It's not a good idea for Coolie to stay in his place tonight. Everybody knows where he lives. So he'll stay with us, to be safe. We'll have a big slumber party. See if you can find a sporting goods store or something where you can get a couple of decent air mattresses. I gotta go."

CHAPTER TEN

Silk

We picked up the air mattresses and then parked in Healdsburg's luxe town square. Boutiques and small restaurants, kitchen shops, a dozen wineries with honey-toned bars.

"We got time for a walk around the square?" Quince asked.

I nodded and took her arm, feeling more chivalrous than I had in years. She kissed me on the neck as we walked slowly past a string of storefronts. "I like to see how the other half live," she said.

"Which half would that be?"

"The rich and the carefree."

Quince stopped in front of a boutique called Silk and led me in. The place made me dizzy with the smell of incense. Before I knew it, my lovely companion had wrapped a long paisley scarf around me.

She stood back and looked at it on me. "God, it's gorgeous. And beautiful on you, Augie."

I had to admit, the rose-colored fabric felt pretty luxurious.

"Come, look at yourself," Quince commanded.

Obedient as ever, I marched over to the full-length mirror.

"Look," she said, "it brings out the color in your cheeks."

"I didn't know I had any color in my cheeks."

"That's the point. You need something to accentuate the little color you have."

I studied myself with the long, flowing scarf draped around me. I wasn't exactly pallid. "Don't you think it makes me look a little like a dandy?"

"It might make a normal guy look like a dandy, but not you."

"What's that supposed to mean?"

"You're the salt of the earth, Augie. You look like a comfortably rumpled hat."

"A comfortably rumpled hat?"

"You know, like somebody who doesn't spend a whole lot of time thinking about your appearance."

"If you only knew, honey."

"Okay," Quince shrugged, "so you've successfully calculated the look of a guy who's entirely indifferent to his appearance. Look, all I'm saying is that you put something like this scarf on, and it's a surprise. It's counterintuitive."

"I think it makes me look like a dandy."

"No, like a man who knows who he is, who's so sure of himself he could wear a pink shirt, a gent not afraid of his feminine side."

Quince stepped up to me and kissed my nose. "You look so good." She caressed the fabric of the scarf and then investigated its various labels. "It's a silk and wool blend. Made in Italy. I mean, think about those Italian guys, the most macho men in the world. You know why that is?"

"Higher testosterone levels?"

"No. It's because they're not afraid of beauty."

I took a little bite—halfway to a hickey—out of Quince's long neck. "I'm not afraid of beauty either," I said.

Quince checked another label on the scarf. "It's only ninety dollars on sale."

I slipped the scarf off. "Ninety dollars. That's a small fortune."

"Not if you think of what it is."

I draped the scarf back on its rack just as the store clerk approached. His eyes were made up with blue eyeliner and he had a scarf of another flavor wrapped around his waist. Here was a guy who'd embraced his feminine side.

"How can I be of assistance?" he asked, and then preened a bit with a hand on his waist.

"We are just looking," Quince said, annunciating her words so icily that even I got a chill.

I followed after Quince as she flipped through a rack of women's jackets. "Did that guy rub you the wrong way or something?"

"I don't care for that kind of obsequiousness," she said.

I was tempted to ask her what kind of obsequiousness she did like, but figured she'd bite my head off. I took a final whiff of incense and told Quince that I'd wait for her outside.

A few moments later, we wandered into Healdsburg's Hand Fan Museum. Quince seemed captivated by a collection of eighteenth-century Chinese fans. Art snob that I am, I trailed behind her, looking on indifferently. Nothing wrong with the decorative arts, I thought. They deserve their own places, and here was one of them. Personally, I preferred the hand fans I used to see as a kid in black churches, when I went with my uncle Ted to hear the *Messiah.* Large cardboard paddles stapled to a stick, blank on one side, with the name of the funeral home that sponsored them on the other. I loved watching the stout, beautifully primped ladies working their fans so close to their painted faces, their wrists jangling jewelry in a steady beat. Would the Hand Fan Museum be interested in mounting an exhibit of vintage funeral fans?

As I was ruminating thus, Quince turned to me with a devilish grin and said, "Look what I found, Augie."

I expected her to point to a lascivious detail she'd discovered in the corner of a particular fan, but instead, she bowed and demonstrated a magic trick of sorts, pulling a stream of fabric from the left sleeve of her jacket. It kept coming and coming until I realized in horror that it was the Italian scarf we'd been playing with in the shop up the street.

"You stole that?" I whispered.

"I liberated it," Quince said in full voice. "It looked so good on you, I think it belonged to you."

"That's some rationale," I said, and, furious, walked out of the Hand Fan Museum.

A moment later, Quince joined me on the sidewalk. "Oh, he's angry," she said, pushing her lips out in a fake pout.

I didn't speak for a moment, but finally told Quince that I wanted her to take the scarf back.

"Oh, I'd never do that."

"Why?"

"Because that's when you get caught."

"Alright, then I'll do it." I unknotted the scarf, which Quince was wearing, and yanked it from her.

As I stormed up the street toward the shop, Quince hurried after me, shouting, "Don't do it, Augie; it's a mistake."

The only mistake, I thought, was losing my head over this crazy thief of a woman.

What a Bargain

Back at the shop, I decided to hang the scarf on its rack rather than explaining the "accidental theft" to the flamboyant clerk. I'd stuffed the scarf up the left sleeve of my bomber and imagined pulling it out, inch by inch, like a stealthy wizard.

"You're back again," the clerk said, and smiled at me coyly, as if I'd come back for him. But then he surprised me. "Where's your partner in crime?" he asked.

The phrase momentarily stunned me, but I decided it was less intentional than coincidental.

"She's just moseying up the street," I said.

"And how come you're not moseying after her?" he asked, with his hand on his hip. "Something grab your interest in here?"

I turned to the scarf rack without answering and could see the clerk, oh so pleased with himself, cross behind the counter.

As I crouched to avoid detection, before beginning my operation, I heard the clerk engaged in an amused phone chat. Little did I know that the trap had been set and I was about to step into it. Although I'd spent years detecting the crimes and misdemeanors of others, I was clearly not immune from detection.

I began tugging the pricey scarf from my sleeve, all the while coaching myself to breathe. It seemed a blessing when the shop's front door opened with the tinkle of a bell. A little distraction for the clerk. I hoped for a party of five women, smelling of money. I held my breath and listened for voices but heard only single footsteps, not even a greeting from the clerk. When I glanced toward the sound of the steps, a Healdsburg cop sneered at me.

"Stand up," he said.

I did, with a shrug, and offered the only words I could think of: "It's not how it looks."

"No, it never is."

The clerk came over and stood beside the cop. I looked into the cop's face, hoping that he, like the clerk, was wearing eyeliner and I could wake myself from this nonsensical dream. No such luck.

"I think he was trying to steal another one," the clerk said.

"I wasn't stealing anything," I said.

"Then what's that?" the cop asked, pointing to my left side.

I glanced at the long length of twisted silk scarf hanging from my sleeve, and in my current nightmare it spilled from me like the rose-colored entrails of a good-sized salmon.

"I was putting this back."

"Sure."

"I got outside and realized I'd mistakenly kept this on."

"Why not just explain that to Georgie here?" the cop asked, "instead of slinking around?"

I didn't have a decent answer, so I said nothing.

"Let me see your identification."

I pulled out my Minnesota driver's license and handed it to the cop. As he squinted at it, I yanked the rest of the scarf from my sleeve and draped the damn thing on the rack.

"Minnesota," the cop said, "what the hell are you doing here?"

"I'm on vacation."

"Is this the kind of thing you do on vacation?"

"Ask him where his accomplice is," the clerk piped in.

"I have no accomplice," I said, pissed now, "because I've committed no crime."

As the cop handed me back my driver's license, I pulled out my P.I. license and flashed it at him.

"Let me see that."

Meanwhile, the asshole clerk pulled the paisley scarf off the rack and shook his head. "He's messed this thing all up," exclaimed Boy George.

"A Minnesota dick, stealing scarves," the cop said.

"I wasn't stealing anything."

"How can I sell this thing?" George lamented.

"How about I just buy the damn thing from you," I said in a flash of lucidity, "and we call everything even?"

"That's one solution," said the cop, who looked like he was getting bored with this business.

The clerk flashed me a satisfied grin.

I pulled the scarf off the rack and flipped the tag to see the price. "Ninety bucks. It's overpriced, especially in this economy."

"For you," the cop said, "it's a bargain."

Swooning Again

I barely spoke to Quince during our drive back to Cazadero.

Finally, she dropped a hand on my knee. "I'm sorry. It was just a lark."

"A lark?"

"Don't pout, Augie. It doesn't become you. I wanted to see what you'd do if I threw you a hot potato."

"Well, I dropped it."

"I told you not to go back into the store," Quince said in soothing tones.

I wasn't soothed.

"The scarf," she said, "it really looks good on you."

I couldn't believe I was still wearing the damn thing.

"You realize that if you had tossed a hot potato to me, I'd have responded a little differently."

"Well, fuck you royal," I said with a certain relish.

"Alright, Augie!"

"Don't patronize me, sweetheart."

Quince puckered her lips and blew me a sweet kiss. I stared ahead at the road.

"I think this all bodes well for us," she said.

"Nothing bodes well for us." I wasn't going to yield.

She smiled at me in a way that surprised me. As if she were vulnerable.

"I love the way we temper each other," she said. "You're so good, and I only play at being bad."

"Maybe I'm not so good," I said, "and maybe you're not playing."

Quince let out a delighted whoop. "That would make us both bad. Imagine the trouble we could get into together."

"A regular Bonnie and Clyde."

"I'll be anybody you want," Quince said, her eyes widening in either sincerity or fraud. "I'll be anybody, if you'll be my man."

And that was it. I was swooning again.

Quince kissed me on the ear and whispered, "You do look beautiful in that scarf."

Two Russians and a Whore

I kept my eyes on the road as it curved with the river. We drove in silence for a few minutes and then Quince dropped her bombshell.

"I have a confession to make, Augie."

"You stole something else?!"

"No," she said. "Pull over when you can."

Once I found a turnout, I assumed a posture of indifference.

Quince gazed at me and I did my best to shoot her the cold eyes of a fish. She asked me to turn on the ignition so she could buzz down her window.

"Okay, here's the deal," she said. "Bobby won't like my telling you, but I don't give a damn. You're more important to me than any of the rest of this."

Why did I feel like I was being conned again?

"The whole thing about me being a hired wife is a ruse that Blossom and I cooked up."

"Why?" I asked, my mouth open wide, no longer indifferent.

"I don't make my living anymore playing poker. I used to, but now I work for a company called Red Carpet Casinos. It's run by two Russians who develop casinos in five western states."

"So, why the ruse?"

"Here's the deal. Boris and Dmitri, the Russian partners, came out here scouting for new locations and they fell in love with the Russian River area. Apparently, Russians had a colony out here in the early nineteenth century and these guys loved the idea of a Russian-owned casino on the river."

"Yeah, so what's that got to do with you becoming a phony wife?" I grumbled.

"I'm getting to that." Quince cradled her chin between her thumb and first finger as she considered how to spin her story. "After doing a little reconnaissance, Boris and Dmitri determined that the two most important folks to have on their side, for rounding up local support, were Jesse Coolican and Bobby Sabbatini. Jesse, because they need an Indian tribe to front the deal, and Sabbatini because he seems to be the most popular and trusted guy around. Coolican wouldn't play ball with them."

"Good for him," I said.

"Yeah, well, Bobby took the money."

"No," I said, shaking my head, "I don't believe it."

"Believe it."

"So, that's where he got the dough he dumped into Ginsberg's Galley?"

Quince shrugged.

"So what's your role?"

"I'm in public relations. I go into communities and try to strengthen support for the casino projects. They wanted me out here for the opening of Bobby's tavern. And when I realized that Blossom was in the area—I got a Christmas card from her—I decided it might be better for everyone if I worked, you know, undercover."

I thought of the last Christmas card from the Sabbatinis—Bobby, Blossom, and Milosz standing in front of the Cazadero cabin. It still adorned my St. Paul refrigerator.

"So your job is to get Coolican on board?"

"It would be a big plus."

"And how do you do that, you sleep with him?"

Quince gave me a long, hard look and then turned away. "It doesn't always turn out that way."

"Just some of the time, huh? Well, Coolie seems ripe for the plucking now, with his old girlfriend dead and people shooting arrows at him. Anyway, I think he took a shine to you. What I don't understand is why you wasted your affection on me. There's nothing I can do for you. I don't even live out here."

"Fuck you, Augie," she said. "I fell for you, just like a fool."

"Acting isn't your forte, darling," I said, channeling five cents' worth of Bogart.

"Like I really needed to fall for some paunchy, middle-aged P.I. from Minnesota."

Quince had actual tears running down her face, which she patted with the sleeve of her coat. I reminded myself that the woman was an ex-con, a thief, and, for all practical purposes, a whore.

"I'm quitting my job. I am. I don't have to work like that. I don't. It's bad for my self-esteem. That's what my shrink says. And you don't even care," she cried.

I pulled back onto the road and hit the gas hard. I focused on getting back to base camp as quickly as possible, though the curves were a bit of a challenge. I imagined dropping off the counterfeit wife and finding myself a motel room for the night. The room didn't have to be fancy, though I pictured a microwave and a couple of packs of popcorn. I'd put on some mindless show on the TV, maybe the kind of thing I never watched, like mud wrestling, and just gorge myself. That would put some distance between me and the whole pack of liars.

Meanwhile, Quince faced out the side window, sniffling. "I never learn," she said, sotto voce.

"Maybe you're studying the wrong material," I suggested.

"I'm not talking to you," she hissed.

CHAPTER ELEVEN

Mermaid

DEPUTY COOLICAN MET us at the door. He must have heard the car drive up. His head was mostly covered in a bandanna, but he had a big grin on his face. "We were worried about you guys," he said, winking at Quince. "Hey, nice scarf, Augie; you're getting stylish in your old age."

Coolican had picked up that things weren't so swell between the wife and me. He stepped out of the doorway so Quince could get into the cabin. Then he threw an arm around my shoulder and walked me around the side of the cabin, past the fifty yards of stacked firewood, to the freestyle backyard.

"What did you do to her, man?"

"You've got the question backward," I said, gnashing my teeth.

"Oh, so she's the evil one," he said.

"What are you so happy about, man? You've got people firing arrows at you."

"Hey, I'm alive. That may not mean a whole lot to you, Augie, but I'm kind of stoked about it. I didn't realize I cared."

"Kind of a sea change." I took a look at Coolican's head in the moonlight. A bit of bandage was visible under the folded kerchief.

"You okay?"

"Yeah, I was barely grazed. I don't really need to wear this thing. But, between you and me, I've always wanted to wear a headband."

"So, what do we have here, a new Indian war?"

"Nah, I got no trouble with Indians. I keep to myself. Anyway, an Indian would have got me in the middle of the forehead. Whoever shot at me was a helluva marksman. He just wanted to scare me."

"Yeah, and what does Sabbatini think?"

Coolican shrugged.

It was turning from dusk to night. I noticed a clothesline stretched between two redwoods and I could make out a couple of pairs of Sabbatini's Sufi pants, flapping in the breeze beside a half dozen of Milosz's cotton diapers and one of Blossom's black bras. A wild thought flashed through my craw, something about tying Quince by the silk scarf to the clothesline. I gave an involuntary shudder.

"You okay there, Augie?" Coolican asked.

"Yeah, I just had a chill. Look, I'm going to check into a motel tonight." I remembered the air mattresses in the backseat and started toward the car.

"What are you doing?" Coolican asked. "Aren't you even going to say hello to the mister and missus?"

"I've gotta get something from the car."

Coolican followed after me. "You want to tell me what went on with you and the wife?"

"Later."

Back in the cabin, Blossom and Sabbatini were sitting by the fireplace, but neither baby Milosz nor Quince were to be seen.

Sabbatini stood, regarding Coolican and me, before poking at the fire. "What have you guys been doing out there, having a little powwow?"

"Watch it, Bobby," Coolican said, grinning. "It's a slippery slope from talking powwows to out-and-out racism."

"That arrow put a spark of life into you, Coolie," Sabbatini said.

I dropped the bundled air mattresses on a chair.

"What did you do to Quince, Augie?" Blossom snapped. "She's more unhappy than I've seen her since we were in prison."

"You haven't seen her since you were in prison," Sabbatini offered.

"What did you do?" Blossom persisted.

"Why don't you ask your wife?"

"I did."

"She's not talking, huh?"

"I'm talking," Quince said, walking in from one of the back rooms. She had Milosz bundled in her arms. "I'll talk all you want. I'm not afraid to spill the beans. I'll tell you what it really was: I started to fall for the guy and it freaked him out."

"That's not quite it," I said. "*What freaked me out*, if you want to stick with that vernacular—"

"Oh, please, show us how you can go slumming with the vernacular, Augie." Quince secured Milosz with her left arm as she placed her right hand defiantly on her waist.

"What bothered me," I started, but then realized that everybody was staring at me. I took a breath and mentioned the smallest infraction. "I was bothered by your wife's shoplifting, and the fact that she left it for me to clean up after her."

"Tattletale," said Quince.

Coolican roared with laughter. "But it's a really nice scarf, Augie."

"You know what the French say," Sabbatini teased.

"Fuck the French," said Blossom.

"*Qui vole un oeuf vole un boeuf.*"

"And what does that mean?" Quince asked

"He who steals an egg will steal an ox," Coolican said, grinning.

"There are no oxen around here," Blossom said.

"There's just Augie," Quince said, sticking out her tongue at me again.

I shrugged and said to no one in particular, "I'm going to check into a motel in Guerneville."

Sabbatini shook his head. "Aw, man, we were looking forward to a slumber party."

Blossom said, "If you're going, why don't you take her with you, Augie?"

"I'm not going with him," Quince hollered. "He humiliated me."

I fired back: "There's a classic bit of projection."

"And now he comes with the psychobabble," the phony wife said.

Still grinning, Coolican said, "This is getting good."

Sabbatini, down on his knees trying to revive the fire, said, "All we need is a poem."

"Maybe you're right, Bobby," Blossom said. She smiled benevolently at Quince and then at me. "You're having your first quarrel."

"And last," Quince said, bouncing Milosz on her hip.

"How about a little Yeats?" Sabbatini asked.

"*Pourquoi pas?*" Blossom said, shrugging cutely.

I figured that she was trying some reverse psychology on Sabbatini—trying to get him to lay off the poesy—but it didn't work.

Once the fireplace was roaring away again, he stood up and cleared his voice like a public speaker expecting the attention of everybody in the room. "Coolie's recital last night got me thinking again about that old bird. Here are six lines that might be apt, from 'A Man Young and Old.'"

THE MERMAID

BY WILLIAM BUTLER YEATS

A mermaid found a swimming lad,
Picked him for her own,
Pressed her body to his body,
Laughed; and plunging down
Forgot in cruel happiness
That even lovers drown.

Blossom shook her head and spoke to her husband as if he were a fourth grader. "Thank you, Bobby, that was very helpful."

"You people are crazy," Quince said.

Coolican's grin grew wider. "Now she's catching on."

"I'm off," I said.

Milosz gurgled in Quince's lap.

"I guess the boy doesn't mind you leaving," Sabbatini joked.

I made my way toward the door.

"Wait," Quince said, and handed Milosz off to his mother.

A triumphant Coolican bellowed, "Looks like I get the rollaway."

Broken Glass

I turned back to glare at Coolican, but suddenly his grin disappeared and he held up his hands in a gesture to quiet us. The deputy's pocked face became strangely angelic. His mouth opened in wonder as he listened to something I couldn't yet hear. I heard frogs from the stream just west of the property and the shallow breathing of a generator, which I assumed came from one of the off-the-grid pot farms nearby. Then the wheels of a car getting closer, the hearty purr of a large motor. The car came to a stop. Then it backed up as if it were turning around. Coolican gestured for all of us to get down. Sabbatini helped Blossom and Milosz to a place under the oak dining table, and I led Quince to a spot by them.

"Get down," Coolican hissed at Sabbatini and me, both still in a crouch. The large Indian, with his gun drawn, had flattened himself against the wall adjacent to the door.

Sabbatini motioned me to get down with baby Milosz and the women, which I did without bothering to consider the implications, as he dashed in a crouch to the cover of a cabinet across the room.

"Bobby," Blossom called. It was the first time I'd ever seen anything approaching terror in her eyes.

Quince caught my eye and whispered, "I'm sorry, Augie. Really."

Sabbatini pulled his revolver from a drawer of the living room cabinet and clicked off the safety.

I'd never carried a gun, which I'd always considered a curious badge of courage, given my line of work. Now I felt a bit emasculated, crouching under the table with the women and child. I guess the alternative was to make a fool of myself.

The vehicle stopped, but the engine was still purring. I listened for a door opening. Footsteps. I wondered why Coolican sensed that this was more than a benign visitor. *Maybe,* I mused, *that's what comes with being attacked.* The frogs and distant generator receded into a mesh of white noise. I could hear Coolican breathing. I watched him concentrating with his ears. He winked at me, which I found even more surprising than his patience.

Bobby Sabbatini appeared to be losing his. He stood to the side of the cabin's front window and inched closer to it.

Coolican called, "Get back, Bobby."

"Bobby," Blossom cried out, "be careful."

As soon as Sabbatini pulled back a corner of the curtain, I heard the shimmying approach of the vehicle and then a quick stop. Coolican motioned for us to stay down. I heard the squeaky hinge of a door, followed by an eerie *swoosh,* and, faster than seemed possible, the gaudy shock of shattering glass.

Pandemonium ensued. Blossom issued a squealing scream. Milosz wailed in perfect sympathy with his mother. The vehicle door slammed. Sabbatini's shoes crunched over broken glass. He and Coolican hurled themselves out the cabin door as the vehicle blasted off down the road.

Only Quince was quiet. She took my hand and placed it over her heart, which I could feel ticking like a little bomb about to go off. I held her close for a moment. Then I crawled out from under the table.

A gold-tipped arrow sat amid the piles of glass. A tight scroll of paper, fastened by rubber bands to the arrow, had begun to unfurl.

Without touching it, I peeked at what I could see of a message, handwritten in fat Cyrillic characters.

Sabbatini rushed back into the cabin. “Everybody okay in here?” Without waiting for an answer, he hustled to the phone on the wall. It was an old turquoise rotary job. “Custard,” he said breathlessly into the phone, “it’s Poesy. Somebody just took a shot at us up here. Thought you could maybe catch his license as he barrels down the hill.”

Once he hung up, Sabbatini helped Blossom and the still whimpering Milosz out from under the table. I extended a hand to Quince. She stood awkwardly and surveyed the damage. Then she whispered, “I’m a little embarrassed. I peed myself.”

Somehow, I found her admission endearing.

As Quince hurried off to the bathroom, I went outside, hoping to find Coolican. He was a little bit down the road, crouched with a flashlight from his cruiser, studying the tire tracks.

“Can you identify them?”

Coolican glanced up at me. “My guess is a Jeep Cherokee.”

I nodded toward the cabin. “Looks like your friend sent you a little written message along with the arrow.”

“What did it say?”

“I left it for you, Coolie. My Russian is a little rusty.”

“It’s in Russian?”

“I believe so. Tell me something—what tipped you off that evil was approaching? The most I heard was an engine in the distance.”

“That’s my ISD—my Injun Sense of Danger.”

“You got an idea who’s behind the entertainment?”

Coolican shook his head. “I’ve got nothing.”

“You going to let the sheriff’s department know about this?”

“I am the sheriff’s department. Soon as the powers that be find out about this, they’ll want me to leave the area for my own protection.”

“Maybe you should.”

Coolican looked at me a little sadly and shook his head.

Marked Man

By the time we got inside, Blossom had hung a heavy wool blanket over the window and was beginning to sweep up the broken glass.

She leaned on the broom for a moment and greeted us. "Welcome to Appalachia."

Sabbatini had a pair of work gloves on and was sitting at the kitchen table, having flattened out the scrolled message.

I looked around the room for Quince with a longing that surprised me. And as if my longing beckoned her, she strolled into the main room, dressed now in a pair of tight turquoise pedal pushers. I had to concentrate to keep my eyes off her. She walked toward Blossom and said, "I think Milosz will sleep now." It was nice to think of Quince performing one of her wifely duties for the house, even if she was a phony wife.

We all jumped a bit when the phone in the kitchen rang. Sabbatini ran off to answer it. I stood with my arms around both Quince and Blossom.

"That was Custard calling back about the vehicle. Damn thing went by too fast for him to catch the license. He said it looked like a Ford F-150 pickup. Know who it might be?"

Coolican shook his head. He muttered, "No way that was an F-150. Didn't sound like it and the tracks don't match it."

Sabbatini went back to the dining room table and the letter that had been so rudely delivered. I walked up beside him. Coolican came over and shined his flashlight on the page. There were three lines printed in large, wobbly letters.

Sabbatini looked up at the deputy. "The light's nice, Jesse, but it doesn't change it into English."

"It's Russian alright," Coolican said.

"Think it's Yevgeny sending you a little message?" Sabbatini asked.

"That's too obvious."

"Somebody trying to set up the wild mushroom man?" I asked.

Coolican shrugged. He was still bent over the lines of Russian. He began to sound out the words in a credible Russian accent.

Sabbatini shook his head. "Don't tell me you studied Russian at Stanford."

"Cal," Coolican corrected. "I had four years of it."

"Don't bullshit us."

The Indian was quiet for a moment. "It's Yevtushenko."

"The bartender?" Sabbatini asked.

"No, the poet. I think they're lines from 'Babi Yar.' But I'll tell you this, the letters were written by someone who's never written Russian before."

"Can you translate them?" I asked.

"Roughly. 'Blood spills in rivers on the ground' . . . maybe 'on the floors.'" He paused. "I don't know this word. 'The bosses of taverns holler freely. And stink . . . stink like vodka and onions, half and half.'"

"What the hell is that supposed to mean?" Sabbatini asked.

"Somebody's trying to frame Yevgeny," I offered.

"Or target me," Sabbatini said. "A slightly looser translation would have the boss of a poetry karaoke bar reciting freely. Could be a little intimidation from the Christian fanatics. Rivers of blood spilling on the floor."

"Why in Russian?" I asked.

"Just to fuck with our heads," Coolican responded.

Sabbatini nodded. "I think someone ought to have a little conversation with the minister down at River of Blood."

Coolican turned off his flashlight and stood to his full height. "And I guess it's time for me to have another conversation with Vlady. See if he can shed some light on all this."

"Who's Vlady?" I asked.

"Vlady Babiansky," Coolican said. "That's the bartender's real name."

The Indian turned toward Blossom. "Hey, I'm really sorry to bring this on you people. I think it's best if I leave."

"No way, Coolie," Sabbatini said. "We're all in this together. Anyway, how do you know it was you they were shooting at? They could have been after me. It's my house."

"Nope," Coolican said, "I think I'm the marked man." He picked up the arrow. "I'm going to take this to go with the other one. Pretty soon I'll have quite a collection."

Sabbatini flashed anger. "Who the hell's doing this?"

Blossom, still looking a little tense, turned to her husband. "It sure as hell's not Robin Hood."

I wondered whether Blossom wanted Coolican to leave. It would be only natural. Maternal instincts. But Blossom was such a defiant woman and so loyal that I guessed she stood right with Sabbatini.

Sabbatini said, "Nice knickers, Quince. You look like you're ready to party."

"May as well."

"I can roll us a nice smoke of Fuck Face," Sabbatini offered.

"You people are really a bunch of potheads, aren't you?" Quince said.

Sabbatini pulled his stash out of a coffee tin. "Absolutely. This will settle us down."

Coolican looked around at each of us. "I'm off."

"You're not going anywhere, Coolie," Sabbatini said. "You can't do anything tonight but worry, so you might as well relax."

"Somebody ought to stay straight around here," Blossom said.

"Yes," Sabbatini agreed, "we need a sober witness."

"That would be me," I offered.

"It boggles the mind," Blossom said. "Augie Boyer has gone straight."

Charades

It was a slumber party at which very little slumbering occurred. At first we played charades. Sabbatini and Coolican were declared the winners after the deputy got Sabbatini to quickly guess Gaston Bachelard's *The Psychoanalysis of Fire* in the book title category.

Gloating, Coolican said, "I was thinking about going with Bachelard's other big title, *The Poetics of Space,* but I got to wondering how many abstractions a guy ripped on Fuck Face can communicate to somebody in a similar condition."

"We'll never know," Sabbatini lamented.

Then we played cards for hours. Hearts, mostly. Quince created a bit of a scandal when she proposed playing strip poker.

"You're not in prison anymore," Blossom said.

"I know, but the weed makes me amorous."

"Then take Augie into the spare bedroom. See where you can get to on the rollaway."

Quince grinned. "No, Augie's too good for me. He's pure."

"Yeah, as the driven snow," Blossom added, with a guffaw.

Pretty soon all four of them, humming on Fuck Face, were laughing their asses off.

CHAPTER TWELVE

The Root Is One

I WAS THE only one to wake to the knocking at the door. I stumbled toward it, but before I could get there, Custard, the anti-Semitic pot rancher, walked in. It was hard for me to believe that after our little siege, we'd left the cabin door unlocked. Custer looked around at the chaos—empty glasses and wine bottles, books of poetry scattered everywhere, the remains of late-night nachos crusted to plates—and shook his head. Quince was snoring sweetly, wrapped in an army surplus blanket, but Coolican, on his back on a half-inflated air mattress, rumbled like distant thunder. He wore his hat over his face like an old cowboy. Why none of the three of us took advantage of the spare bedroom, I'll never know. The sofa remained empty after Blossom mentioned the family of mice that kept house inside it. As far as I knew, Blossom and Sabbatini were in their bedroom.

"Hey," Custard said, "if you guys were having an orgy, how come you didn't invite me up?"

I assured Custard that nothing very exciting went on in the cabin after the window had been smashed by the night arrow.

"What were you guys doing, reciting poetry in the raw?"

"Pretty much."

"Who's that?" Custard asked, noticing Quince's head poking out from the blanket.

I put a finger over my lips to shush him.

"Poesy's one crazy shit," Custard said, in a whisper now. He motioned toward the thundering Indian. "And how about Coolican, bet he was chanting some Indian poetry, huh."

"Matter of fact," the deputy said, lifting the hat from his face and surprising us both, "I've been working on W. B. Yeats." Coolican sat up and looked directly at Custer. "He's Irish, Mr. Cust. I believe that's your tribe, isn't it?"

Custard nodded. "Partly," he said, "partly." He turned aside as Coolican threw off his blanket and stood up, naked except for his boxers and the plaid bandanna. It had curled up a bit to reveal more of the medical swathing around his forehead. Custard went over to the window that had been shot out and rubbed his hand over the coarse blanket covering it.

He sighed, as if the strange attack, for which he hadn't been present, had already wearied him. "I heard some prankster took a potshot at you in town."

"You think he was a prankster, Mr. Cust?"

"Well, I'm told it's kind of hard to miss with those crossbows."

"Oh, I don't know about that."

Custard touched the window blanket once more. "Any thoughts on who's been playing with you?"

"Yeah, I have a few thoughts," Coolican said.

"Who?" Custard asked.

"At this point, I'd rather keep my thoughts to myself."

Coolican was still standing there in his briefs, a mighty figure with shorter legs than I had realized, but with a long trunk and powerful arms. He'd clearly done his share of bodybuilding. It surprised me that in the age of the tattoo, Coolican didn't have a single one. Finally, he pulled on a ribbed T-shirt.

He turned toward Custard. "Hey, Poesy said you got a good look at the vehicle as it went by."

"Yeah, it was an F-150 pickup," Custard said.

"You sure about that?" Coolican asked.

"Hey, I know an F-150 when I see one."

With that, Custard shuffled around a little bit and asked if he could be of any help with anything.

"Ask the mister and missus about that," Coolican said. "I'm about to get my britches on and get the hell out of here."

"I won't bother them," said Custer. "Tell them I've been by." He nodded to me and, facing Coolican, said, "Yeats, huh?"

"Yes. William Butler Yeats, 1865–1939."

"You giving history lessons, Deputy?"

"No, I don't teach, Mr. Cust. But I did wake up this morning with a line from Yeats in my head: 'Though leaves are many, the root is one.'"

"And what exactly does that mean?"

"I can't really say. I'm not much for interpretation, Mr. Cust."

Protected Entity

Right after Custard left, Quince sat up and said, "I don't like that man."

"How long have you been awake?"

"A while."

Jesse Coolican, dressed now and pulling on his boots, winked at Quince. "I don't like him either. He's a racist, among other things. And I'd like to bust his ass for growing about a thousand times more herb than he's licensed to."

"Why don't you?" Quince asked.

"He's one of the protected entities."

"How's that work?" I asked.

"In his case, a couple of reasons. Sheriff's running for reelection and he's pledged no busts of folks with a license to grow. 'Course nobody's licensed to grow anywhere as much as he does."

"What's the other reason?" I asked.

"Well," Coolican said, as he walked around the room picking up books of poems and dirty glasses, "his wife happens to be the county supervisor in this district, a pretty powerful woman. She also happens to be one of the flakiest born-agains around here, a fact she keeps from the voters."

I joined Coolican in the general cleanup as Quince, wrapped in a blanket, hurried off to the bathroom.

"You know where Mrs. Cust goes to church?" Coolican asked.

"Yeah, River of Blood."

"Bingo. I bet she's a deacon down there."

When Quince returned, dressed in the tight pedal pushers of the night before, Coolican nodded to both of us and turned to the door.

"Where you going?" I asked.

"I don't know."

"I want to go with you."

Coolican shrugged. "Suit yourself."

Quince gave me a long, anxious look.

"I'll call you later," I said, "and let you know what's up."

She walked to the door and bent toward me as if she expected me to kiss her. Too many things were swimming around my head at once, but I managed to give her a peck on the forehead.

"Why don't you take your scarf?" Quince said, handing a tail of it to me.

It seemed a daft idea, but was clearly the path of least resistance. Quince smiled in the doorway as I wrapped it around my neck.

"Nice," Coolican said.

I could see a glow emanating from Quince as she waved good-bye to us.

Not the Only Game in Town

It was nearly noon before we got to the coast. There were a few detours along the way. Coolican wasn't talking. He answered the couple of questions I asked with monosyllabic grunts, so I stopped asking. As he hadn't said no to me coming along, I figured he'd talk to me when he was ready.

After the pretty road from Cazadero, the deputy turned east on 116 and, twenty minutes later, pulled into Guerneville. The sheriff's department shares small digs with the highway patrol, in a little strip next to a Chinese restaurant that specializes in whole fish. Coolican asked me to come in with him. He nodded to a patrolman and then introduced me to a clerk named Betty. Late thirties. Lovely. Beautiful brown eyes. She seemed excited to meet me. Told me she was a great fan of my daughter. They all are.

Betty laid her hand on Coolican's shoulder the way I wanted to the night I met him. "Heard about the attack over at Hemp and Chocolate. You okay, Jesse?"

"Yeah, fine. Barely nicked. Look," he said, "I'm in the middle of something. I'll check back in this afternoon."

"You be careful."

Betty asked how long I'd be staying in West County.

"Another ten days."

She winked. "Oh, good, maybe we'll get a chance to see more of you. Don't be a stranger."

"What was that about?" I asked Coolie, back at the car.

"I wanted you to know that Quince isn't the only game in town."

"Obliged."

"Hey, Betty seemed sweet on you from the start. I've never thought of her as hard to look at. Women around here get lonely after a long, rainy winter."

I glanced at Coolican. "So what's your take on Quince?"

The deputy chuckled. "You want me to tell you what you want to hear, or what I think?"

"The latter," I said.

"Oh, brave man." Coolican studied me for a long moment. "I don't trust her."

"Why's that?"

"Can't exactly tell you. Probably doesn't mean anything. Maybe I'm just jealous, Augie. She's quite a fox."

"She is that."

"I mean, where did she come from?" Coolican asked.

"Reno is what she claims."

"And why did she show up now?"

I shrugged, playing dumb.

Coolican shook his head.

"You know something you're not telling me, Jesse?"

Coolican revved the engine. "Not half as much as you're keeping from me."

Lyrical Homicide

Next we drove to the deputy's house, where he dropped off the sheriff's department car and backed a dented tan Corolla out of his garage.

"We'll be a little less conspicuous in this," he said.

At first I figured we were headed out to see Yevgeny, or Vladimir Babiansky, at the River Rose, but after driving through Monte Rio and Duncans Mills, Coolican drove past Jenner and the restaurant. He wove through the winding roads north of the hamlet, seeming to take fresh pleasure in each turn. A few miles up the coast he pulled off at a scenic turnout.

It was one of those views that could break the heart of a guy who grew up by the ocean and spent more than a generation away from it. Although the beach was not fully visible from the road, heroic rock formations rose from the sea. A lush green hillside, east of the road, featured munching cows, indifferent to both the cars and the scenic majesty.

"Mind a little hike?" Coolican asked.

"I guess not."

Coolican took a long look at me. "I think you can manage it."

I had an idea where Coolican was taking me, but decided to keep quiet. I felt almost boyish hustling behind the sheriff down a steep, twisting path. The beach was a Sargasso Sea of driftwood. The Russian River spilling into Jenner, just to the south, provided the timber.

Once we reached the sand, Coolican led me up the beach to a little cove. He pointed toward an expanse of small pebbles. "That's where they found the bodies. The two of them were in their sleeping bags, snug as bugs. Just happened to each have a pair of bullets put through their heads, fired at point-blank range. These kids, they had wedding plans. And some nut comes along, and for no discernable reason, erases their lives."

I wondered out loud whether Coolican saw a connection between these murders and Ruthie's.

The deputy shook his head. "It's only a phony connection at best. Somebody wanting us to waste time linking the murders. No, I just like to come down here from time to time. I'm not really sure why. To punish myself, I suppose. Even though I'm not with homicide, I've spent a lot of time thinking about this case. It breaks your heart." Coolican looked out toward the ocean. "Most people come out here and all they see is the beauty. And, goddamn, it is beautiful. But there's also the dark history. There's blood in the sand, and it's going to take a helluva lot more tides, coming in and going out, to wash it away. More than I'll see in my lifetime."

We were quiet a moment, just listening to the waves and the squawking of the seabirds. Then I dropped a hand on Coolican's shoulder.

"You're starting to talk like a poet, Jesse."

"Yeah, that's what comes from reading too much of that damn Yeats."

I smiled at the soulful sheriff. "I've got a confession to make."

Coolican gave a hearty laugh. "This will be good."

"Not only has Sabbatini had me memorizing poems for years, I've started to write them."

"Oh, God," the sheriff cried in faux despair, "what next?"

"I don't mean real poems."

"That's what they all say."

"No, they're just little haiku-like creatures."

"I know what you're talking about," Coolican said, kicking at the sand in front of him.

"Have you been writing them, too?"

"No comment."

"You too, Coolie?"

"Yeah, well, mine aren't haiku, per se. I just think of them as poetic burps."

"Funny, I think of mine as little farts."

"Little stinkers, huh, Brother Bear?"

"Yeah, we should shower Sabbatini with a wave of poetic product."

"Are you kidding, man?" Coolican said, looking toward the sky, as if it held some explanation for my lunacy. "We'd drip our wee offerings on the man, and Poesy would bury us in whatever epic crap he's been knocking out on the sly. We're better off staying in the closet."

I turned toward Coolican. "Here's a new one for you."

"How new?" the sheriff asked.

"The last minute or so."

"Let me have it."

I nodded.

On the bloodied beach
the two detectives
wish they were poets.

Coolican smiled his approval. "Give me a second here," he said, and turned his back. He pulled a small Moleskine notebook with a mechanical pencil out of one of his pants pockets. I watched him jot lines, scratch out a couple, write some more. After a few minutes he spun back toward me.

"This is called 'Lyrical Homicide,'" he said, and then read the poem.

The evidence slips like sand
through his hands.
The air is clear.
No suspect, no witness.
Once the ghosts stop
singing their damn songs,
he'll call it a day.

Cuckolds Anonymous

I followed Coolican up the beach and took a seat beside him on an enormous log.

"Okay," Coolican said, "what do you want to know?"

The question surprised me.

The deputy untied the handkerchief from his forehead and unwound the bandage. There was a long red scratch across his temple. A day after the fact, it looked like it was already on its way to disappearing.

"I know you have a lot of questions about what's been going on around here, so let's have 'em."

"How many do I get?"

"How many do you need?"

I shrugged. "Alright, tell me what I don't know about Ruthie."

"That's not a question," Coolican informed me.

"Okay, how come you and Ruthie broke up?"

Coolican turned away, cleared his throat, and spat into the distance.

"It was a long time ago, man," Coolican said.

"So why'd you break up?"

"She became too much trouble for me."

"What kind of trouble?"

"You name it."

"You're not telling me anything, Jesse."

"She was using all the time."

"What?"

"Marijuana, coke, finally, crack."

"What else?"

Coolican took a deep breath and his nostrils flared. "That should have been enough."

"But it wasn't."

"As an officer of the law. . . ."

"What kind of people did she hang around with?"

"That was a big problem. They were mostly small-time stoners. River rats. People not worth worrying about as long as they stayed away from my place. That was the rule—she couldn't have anybody over at my place without me being there."

"Did she play by the rule?"

"Mostly."

"But not always. So, you walked in on her one time while she was smoking crack with some deadbeats."

"No, I walked in on her after she'd already gotten high, and there was just one guy, a guitar player named Rabbit, whose dick she happened to be sucking."

Coolican looked directly at me as he reported this. I did my damnedest not to look away, but it was hard when I saw Coolican beginning to tear up.

"And that was the end of that?" I asked.

"Not quite."

Rather than pressing on, I decided a little commiserating chatter might be in order. "Hey, Jesse, did Sabbatini tell you about my ex-wife?"

Coolican looked toward the waves without responding.

"Okay, she's a therapist, an anger specialist, who writes books. You may have heard of one of them—*I'm Going to Kick Your Ass: Anger and the American Dream.* It did really well. So, things were going along quite merrily, or merrily enough, when I found out my wife was having an affair with another therapist. The kicker was she got herself knocked up at age forty-five."

Coolican shrugged. "So, what do you want to do, form a support group? Cuckolds Anonymous?"

"Sure," I said, "that's good. The California chapter can be called CA of CA. We could call it kaka." I forced a laugh, but Coolican wasn't having any of it.

"She have the baby?" he asked.

"Yeah."

"And you divorced her."

I nodded. "But the baby didn't have anything to do with it." We sat in silence for a moment and I found myself wondering about Nina and the baby, whom she was raising by herself.

"Well, Ruthie didn't get pregnant," Coolican said. "She got murdered." Coolican stood up and spat toward the ocean.

"So, what's your current theory?" I asked.

"Don't have one."

"I think you do."

Coolican went mum. I watched him gather more spit and shoot it toward the ocean.

I pressed on. "Yevtushenko said that she was working out of some massage studio in Monte Rio, providing full-service massages."

"I don't doubt it." Coolican started walking up the beach. "I knew she was hanging out at McCluhan's."

I hopped off the log and followed Coolican up the beach. "He said she might have got mixed up with somebody from outside the area."

"Could have. We closed down McCluhan's for a while a few years ago. They were whoring right out of the place. Now they keep it clean in the shop, far as I know. Straight massage. But I'm sure they still send out girls to the resorts. There's no way of policing that. They probably make calls out to the Bohemian Grove, during the season, when all those gaudy Republicans gather to urinate on the redwoods. For all I know, Ruthie sucked Dick Cheney's cock for the price of a few pipefuls." Coolican turned toward the ocean and spat once more. "That's not the way you want to think of the dead."

I thought it best to change the subject. "So what do you think the deal is with Yevtushenko?"

Coolican shrugged and then scratched the side of his head where the arrow had grazed it. "I don't know. Sounds like his experience with Ruthie was similar to mine. You know, when she wasn't fucked up, she had a soulful beauty that teased you into believing in a future with her. But that became less and less of the time. That damn woman broke some hearts, not just mine."

The deputy reached into his wallet and handed me a photo of a dark-haired, olive-skinned young woman wearing a blue-striped sweater. It was the same woman I'd seen before, but a different photo. She looked French.

"That was maybe ten years ago," Coolican said. He took the photo and slipped it back into his wallet.

"She was very lovely," I said.

I was afraid the deputy would start weeping. He sped up the beach and I left him some space. When I finally caught up, I shifted back to the Russian. "Who do you think's setting up Yevtushenko?"

Coolican, glazed in grief, looked at me blank-faced.

"Shouldn't we go over and have a talk with him?" I asked. "We could have a little wild mushroom soup for lunch."

"He's not going to be there," Coolican said, speeding up again.

"He was there last time I was out there."

Coolican shook his head. "Circumstances have changed a little since then. My Injun instinct tells me the Russian knows there's somebody out here taking target practice and that he and I may be the prime targets."

"Why?" I asked.

Coolican shrugged. "How should I know? Jealousy? Maybe some other dumb fool fell for Ruthie. Some joker with a crossbow."

"I don't get it," I said.

Coolican looked back at the ocean and laughed. "Of course you don't get it. Welcome to West County."

CHAPTER THIRTEEN

Manzanita

JESSE COOLICAN WAS so certain that Yevtushenko wouldn't be inside the River Rose that he stayed in his car. The cornrowed young woman who'd been behind the bar the day before was holding down the fort again.

"Hey," she said, "bet you came back for some more wild mushroom soup?"

"Matter of fact."

"We're out. Sorry."

"How could that be?"

The barkeep wrinkled her nose. She was cuter than I had realized the first time.

"Yeah," she said, "I was surprised, too. We had plenty of soup when we were done last night."

"You're saying a good-sized tureen of mushroom soup disappeared overnight?"

"I didn't say *tureen.* That's not a word I'd use."

"Weren't you the one talking *terroir* yesterday?"

The cute barkeep stuck out the tip of her tongue at me.

I took a stool. Van Morrison's "Crazy Love" was playing. "Is your Russian forager around?"

"He left right after you split yesterday."

"Is that right?"

She glanced down the quiet bar before confiding that Yevtushenko hadn't even called in today.

"Sounds like he made off with the mushroom soup."

She laughed. "Now all he's got do is take it home and add poison."

Her offhand comment nearly made me choke. "You've got quite an imagination."

"Yeah," she sneered, "so, you still want lunch?"

"I haven't decided. I think you may have taken my appetite away."

"Sorry about that. You want something to drink while you think about it? How about a Bloody Rose? That's our signature drink. We splash the bloody mix with pomegranate juice."

Once she made the drink, she gave the bar a quick wipe and stood directly across from me. She smelled faintly of a good French-milled lavender soap.

The day before, I hadn't noticed henna markings on her arms: a bevy of insects—red ants, ladybugs, spiders, running through a labyrinth. She watched me studying them.

"I like the bugs," I said. "Did you have them yesterday?"

She shook her head and flashed me a coy smile. "You're very observant. My roommate's a henna artist, and I just kinda had this vision last night."

"Were you high?" I asked.

"You don't want to know. Hey, I like your scarf," she said, nodding to the silk job that had caused all the trouble. "You didn't have that when you were in here yesterday."

"Nope. So, what's your name?"

"Manzy."

"Manzy?"

"Yeah, it's short for Manzanita. Don't laugh; the 'rents were thinking of naming me Madrone. Then everybody'd call me Drone."

"My name's Augie."

"I know who you are. You're Minnesota Rose's father."

"My claim to fame."

"We have a lot of her songs on the system here."

"Do you?"

"Yeah, you know—'River Rose,' 'Minnesota Rose.' Sometimes, when the crowd's right, we crank up Guns N' Roses."

That sounded to me like a night to miss. I sipped my drink. A little too sweet for my taste.

"So how do you know who I am?"

"Vlady told me as he was leaving."

"Did he know about my daughter?"

"'Course. Everybody knows about your daughter. Even one of the guys who came by looking for Vlady asked for you. But he didn't know your name. He just said, 'How about Minnesota Rose's father, is he staying with Sabbatini?'"

"And who are these guys?"

Manzy looked at me sideways. "You know, I get so few tips on weekdays."

I pulled a ten-dollar bill out of my wallet.

Manzy regarded the tenner. "That's hardly worth getting out of bed for."

"You're already out of bed." I took the ten back and put down a twenty. "What are you, a baby extortionist?"

Manzy looked again to each side of the empty bar. "One of the guys who came in looking for Vlady was also Russian. I'd never seen him before. Short. Kind of a mealy face."

"What's a mealy face?" I asked, and sipped at my drink.

"You know, a guy who's spent his life eating white bread and his face kind of turns into Wonder Bread."

"No Russian rye for him, huh?" I figured Manzy was having a bit of fun with me now that she'd pocketed my twenty. "What else can you tell me about him?"

"He wore gold rings on each of his pinkies, and no other rings. I always check out a man's hands; you can find out a lot about them. Like you, Augie," she said, looking me straight in the eye, "you should probably clip your fingernails."

I took a quick glance at my nails and discovered that she was right. I was tempted to ask her if my unclipped nails signified anything aside from my personal hygiene going derelict.

"This Russian guy with the pinkie rings," she went on, "was very fastidious. I'm sure he goes for regular manicures. He wore a nice clear polish that made his half-moons shine."

At this point Coolican strolled into the bar. He had the bandanna tied back around his forehead.

Manzy looked up and said, "Hey, Jesse."

He nodded. "Manzy. No Vlady?"

Manzy shook her head.

"Yeah," I said, turning toward Coolican, "Manzy's been telling me about this Russian guy who came looking for Vlady. About his manicure."

Coolican rolled his eyes and then surprised me by asking the barkeep about Yevtushenko's nails.

"He cuts them himself," she said, casually, "but he tends to keep them long. Sometimes he doesn't clean the dirt out of them after he's been foraging. Care for something to drink, Jesse?"

"Yeah, give me a tonic water and a twist of lime."

Some anonymous bluegrass twanger was twanging with a brittle fiddle in the background.

"So, Manzy, did the well-manicured Russian give you a way of getting in touch with him?" I asked.

Without answering, she reached under the counter and pulled up a business card. The printed side was scratched out—it looked like some kind of plumbing service. On the back was scrawled a number without a name. I jotted the number down in my head, wondering if the 770 area code was somewhere in Nevada. I handed the card back to Manzy. "Did the Russian guy give you his name?"

"Yeah," she said, "Fred."

"Fred," I echoed. "That doesn't sound very Russian. How about Fred's buddy? Was he Russian, too?"

"No, he was a local."

Coolican looked up at the barkeep. "You know him, Manzy?"

"No, but I've seen him around."

"What can you tell us about him?" I asked.

Manzanita gave me a blank stare and I realized I'd already got my twenty bucks' worth.

Coolican had the same idea. He tapped me on the shoulder. "How much are you into her for, Augie?"

"Twenty bucks."

"Twenty bucks," he repeated. "How much did the Russian give you, Manzy? How much did Fred lay on you?"

The barkeep looked like she was going to cry. "He didn't give me anything, Jesse. He just scared the hell out of me."

"Did he threaten you?"

"Not exactly."

"But he scared you."

Manzy nodded. "He said he was an old friend of Vlady's and he had something for him. He asked for Vlady's cell number, and when I said I didn't have it, he said, 'Then find it, honey. You don't expect me to believe that the management doesn't have its employees' phone numbers, do you?'"

"And he said all this with a thick Russian accent?" I asked.

"No, no," she said, her eyes open wide, "he hardly had any accent. I mean, it was more like an English accent, you know."

Coolican chuckled. "So, did you find him Vlady's number?"

"Well, I crossed over to the restaurant to make like I was getting it, even though I have it in my cell phone. And when I came back to the bar, they were both gone."

"Just like that," I said. "You didn't tell us about the local guy."

Manzanita repeated her blank stare.

Coolican poured down the rest of his tonic and nibbled on an ice cube for a minute. "Augie's not going to give you any more money, kiddo. I won't let him. In fact, you might find yourself in some deep shit for withholding information in a criminal case."

Manzy refilled Coolican's glass with ice and tonic. You could tell that she was wondering what to say next. She looked at Coolican. "Is the Russian a criminal?"

The deputy shrugged.

"What can you tell us about the local guy?" I asked.

"Where do you know him from?" Coolican followed.

"I don't know him," she answered, a little angrily.

"Where have you seen him?" Coolie asked.

Manzanita took a deep breath. "I've seen him around Guerneville. I think he was one of the guys making trouble at the pancake breakfast last fall."

Coolican sipped his tonic. "Sisters of Perpetual Indulgence?"

"Yeah," Manzanita said, "I think he was one of those creeps chanting."

Coolican gave me a sideways glance. "Are you hip to the Sisters, Brother Bear?"

"Your local order of cross-dressing charity workers?"

"Right. Once in a while the rednecks get a little threatened and there's a small rash of homophobia."

"But the sisters aren't all gays, guys, and lesbians," Manzanita said, perking up. "More and more of the initiates are straight. In fact, I'm thinking of joining the order."

Coolican flashed her a thumb's up. "Good for you, Manzy."

"Yeah, I've already picked my name: Sister Savory Morsel."

"Very tasty," I said, "but back to the guy. What else can you tell us about him?"

"I don't know."

Coolican loosened his headband and waved it at the barmaid.

Sister Savory nodded. She filled a glass with ice, Bloody Mary mix, a few gulps of vodka, a shake of Worchester, and a couple of grinds of pepper. "The times I've seen him, he's been wearing a string tie," she said, and spun a swizzle stick through the drink before lifting it to her lips. No sweet pomegranate swill for Manzy.

"Nice, shiny knob of agate over the clasp?" Coolican asked.

Manzanita nodded with her head down and sipped her drink.

Coolican pulled out his wallet and dropped a ten-dollar bill on the bar. "Thanks for that, Manzy."

Tug the string tie
of the man wearing it—
a suspect is born.

About the Filly

As soon as we got back to the car, Coolican said, "Sounds like Mr. Cust is doing a little business with the casino Russians."

"Yeah, I picked up on that. Tell me about the casino business, Jesse."

Coolican started the car and headed back down Highway 1. "How much has your girlfriend told you?"

"I'm sure I was the last to find out."

Coolican shot me a big grin. "You've really got the cuckold's complex going, Bear. I didn't buy the wife bit from the start and asked Poesy about it. He thought it'd be best if you got it from the horse's mouth, since you and the filly were already engaged, so to speak."

"That was very thoughtful of Bobby," I said, pissed all over again. "He told me you resisted the casino's offers."

"Right, I didn't want their stinking dough." Coolican grinned at me. "But I haven't gotten any offers from the lovely Quince yet."

"Sounds like it's all fair game, Jesse."

"No worries, Bear, I'll leave the Quince pie for you."

"This whole scene stinks, if you ask me. And Sabbatini didn't bother to tell me that he *did* take the money."

"Yeah," the deputy said, nodding, "I guess he figured it was money going directly to the poetry church. You disappointed in him?"

"I don't give a fuck anymore."

"Now you're talking," Coolican said. "And about the filly, I think you should be flattered that she's got the hots for you. It's not like you represent any strategic value in West County."

"She tells me that getting you on board is her next assignment."

"She told you that? I promise you, Bear, I won't be jumping her bones."

Coolican rearranged his headband before turning onto Highway 116 and heading back toward Guerneville.

"She said she was going to retire from the gig."

"That's what they all say."

"So how many of the Russians did you meet, Coolie?"

"Just Dmitri."

"Not to be confused with Fred of the pinkie rings and the nice manicure."

"Yeah, that's him. Though I have to confess I didn't check out his manicure. He seemed like a decent enough guy. Just going about his business, trying to buy support for his pet project—the return of the Russians. The way he talked about it, you'd think these guys were a bunch of ancient Jews returning to Jerusalem."

"So what about Custard and the Russians?"

"That's a new one on me. Custard's always had a nose for money. I figure he's trying to milk the Russians for swinging the county supervisor's support their way. But that doesn't really give me a clue as to who's shooting arrows at me. I'm going to go have a little chat with Mr. Cust. I don't think we should both go. He'll feel ganged up on."

"How about you drop me off in Monte Rio? I want to have a look around."

"That major metropolis?" Coolican glanced at his watch. "Okay," he said, driving through Duncans Mills, "it's a quarter to one. You might have to hang for a while. I'll pick you up at the café at 3:00."

CHAPTER FOURTEEN

Introducing Mr. Newborn

I PICKED UP a coffee and strolled under the neon sign that looked like it dated from the 1930s: MONTE RIO AWAITS YOUR RETURN. The marquee of the old movie theater spelled out the words BLOOD SIMPLE. Apparently they were having a Coen brothers festival. I waded through the three-tent village of hippie craftspeople, looking at the roach clips. McCluhan's, the fabled massage parlor, was housed in an old stucco building painted smoky blue. The awning displayed the shop's motto: THE MASSAGE IS THE MESSAGE.

Who knew what I'd find inside, but I wanted to see the place. Would anyone talk to me about Ruthie Rosenberg? I wasn't holding my breath, but I imagined it was warm inside McCluhan's. My body had been chilled since I got to Sonoma County. Early March in West County, rather than being a reprieve from the Minnesota winter, was a new adventure in chilblains. The idea of a massage, a pair of warm hands on my back, had some appeal. What I really wanted, of course, was a night in a room with Quince.

I opened the door to McCluhan's. The waiting room had a pair of kneeling chairs and a chaise, constructed in an S-shape of corrugated cardboard. A redwood burl served as a coffee table. It was covered with volumes of poetry. I noticed books by Frank O'Hara, Jane Hirshfield, Hayden Carruth, and Andrei Codrescu. Sabbatini had been here.

Across the room, a bubbling aquarium showed no sign of a live fish. Above it on the wall was a framed bit of needlepoint that spelled out an alternative motto: THE MASSEUSE IS THE MEDIUM.

It was indeed warm inside. A large, dark-haired woman name-tagged RANDY came through a door from the business part of the establishment. "Can I help you?"

"I hope so," I said at the counter.

Randy perched, a little wobbly, on a tall stool that didn't look good for anybody's back. She had a paperback ready to go that didn't appear to be poetry. I squinted to catch the title: *Your Risk, Your Gain.* She flashed me a curt smile.

I nodded toward her book. "Are you looking to take a risk?"

Randy rolled her eyes. "Not without a significant gain pretty much assured."

"Then that wouldn't be much of a risk."

"I guess not," she said, with a calculated weariness that made it clear she wasn't interested in bantering.

Randy wore a vintage velvet dress with a couple dozen teenie black buttons. It caught my attention because Randy hadn't bothered to fasten the top dozen buttons, opting to feature her pretty black camisole and the heaving swell of her breasts.

"I don't have an appointment but wondered if you have any openings this afternoon. I'm in need of a massage."

For a large woman, Randy was delicately featured, with a short, upturned nose and lips that formed an elegant *O.* She flipped through a clipboard pad on the counter.

"Jamie's got a half hour at two."

Behind me the door opened and a tall, bearded man with a ponytail walked in. Despite his muddy jeans and rawhide jacket, he shivered as the door closed behind him.

"Cold out there, Randy," he said, slipping into a kneeling chair.

I nodded to Randy. "Two o'clock's good."

"You understand, we don't do full-body massages in the shop."

I nodded.

"They don't do half of what they used to do," the guy said from the kneeling chair. I noticed he'd picked up the O'Hara book, *Meditations in an Emergency*, and was mumbling lines of it.

"Name?" Randy asked.

I hesitated. "Phineas Newborn," I blurted, assuming the moniker of the great Memphis pianist, long gone. An esoteric persona.

Randy winked at me. "You don't say."

I repeated the name to myself, wondering what its choice said about me.

Old Ezra and the Lymphs

"Mr. Newborn, Mr. Newborn, Mr. Newborn." I was leaning against the wall and must have snoozed off. Randy said, "First door on the right," but I'd forgotten where I was going. Once she buzzed me through, I heard a familiar voice looping toward me. "Come right in, Mr. Newborn."

Sister Everlast turned out to be a masseuse. Here, he was clearly a man, in tight muscle shirt sans breasts. For flash, he wore a pair of red boxing shorts, branded EVERLAST. Standing there barefoot, he looked like a martial arts master.

"Look who's already seeking anonymity in West County."

"Sister Everlast."

"The one and only." My flamboyant masseuse curtsied. "So, Mr. Phineas Newborn is looking for a massage. Very interesting. Tell me, what's it been like to live your entire life as a Newborn?"

"Where do I begin? And you go by Jamie?"

"Correct. Jamie Holmes, the given name. Alright. Now, do we have particular things bothering us, Mr. Newborn? Or are we just looking for our basic rebirth?"

"Nothing out of the ordinary. A bit of a kink in the left shoulder, some tightness at the back of the neck. I've been freezing since I've gotten to California. Try to explain leaving a Minnesota winter and freezing in California."

"I'll leave the explanations to you, Mr. Newborn."

"Augie," I suggested.

"No, no, you've come here as Mr. Newborn and you should leave as Mr. Newborn. If there's anybody who knows that formality has its value, it's me. For instance, there are certain things I could tell Mr. Newborn that I wouldn't think of mentioning to Augie Boyer. Why don't you get down to your shorts and climb up on the table? I'll be right back."

I did as I was told, wondering what I was letting myself in for. Down to my jockeys, I sat on the massage table, with the familiar passivity of a patient waiting, half naked, for his doctor.

Sister Everlast returned with a shopping bag and a CD, which he slipped into a boombox across the room. I was a bit horrified to hear the Singing Nun's hit song "Dominic" blast into the room.

"Can you deny her charm, Mr. Newborn?"

"Not at all, Jamie, but could we please have it quiet during the massage?"

The masseuse shook his head. "You breeders are all the same," he muttered. "One moment, please."

After he clicked off the CD, Jamie turned his back and pulled something from the shopping bag that he slipped over his face. When he turned back, I let out a small shriek. His face was covered in a mask that bore an uncanny likeness to Ezra Pound in his dotage. The remarkable mask had been crafted of papier-mâché or the like. Little tufts of white hair grew from the chin. Terraces of bushy, bone-colored Brillo, somehow stitched to the top, gave the wig volume and suggested the pompadour the old man wore in his youth. Pound's expression was resigned. His cheeks were puckered with age like an old peach going to rot.

Sister Everlast stretched out his arms and proclaimed, in an aged voice full of tremolo:

And the days are not full enough
And the nights are not full enough
And life slips by like a field mouse
Not shaking the grass.

The masseuse pirouetted, his arms high in the air. "That was Pound's epigraph to Lustra." It was very odd to see the ancient face attached to the toned body in boxing trunks.

"It's a striking likeness," I offered.

"Have you heard about the masks?"

I shook my head.

"Well, Poesy's commissioned a trio of master mask makers in Graton to create fifty poets. It's exceptional work. I'm thinking of buying a couple more. And believe me, Mr. Newborn, they ain't cheap."

In hopes of overcoming my queasiness, I looked directly at the face of the aged poet. "Might I ask why you're wearing the mask now?"

"You might ask, Mr. Newborn, but an answer may not be forthcoming."

Suddenly I was pissed. "How come you're playing games with me, Jamie?"

"Oooh, what an aggressive question. Do you suspect me of some sort of duplicity beyond my normal cross-dressing, mask-wearing behavior, Mr. Newborn? Or are we witnessing a blush of homophobia?"

I thought of rising from the table and getting the hell out of McCluhan's, but reminded myself of my purpose.

"Time's a-wasting, Mr. Newborn," my masseuse said. He ordered me onto my back and stood just north of my head. I felt a bit of vertigo. What was I doing on my back? Wasn't he going to massage my back?

The masked Pound sensed my question. "I'm going to get under you with my hands, Mr. Newborn."

I looked a little skeptically into the aged face. After barely touching my lower back, the disembodied voice said, "You don't sweat easily, do you?"

"No."

"You retain a lot of water."

I nodded, feeling like I was confessing something very deep about myself that I wasn't sure I knew.

"We'll work the lymphs and see if we can drain a little. You should be taking a steam bath every day, or bathing in a hot tub with Epsom salts. Anything to draw the water out."

I didn't really know what he was talking about, but as he worked the flab and muscles at the base of my spine, my nose began to run. Then tears ran involuntarily down my face. After a good twenty minutes of this, I became sopping wet. The masseuse shifted to my upper back and shoulders. I opened my eyes very slowly. Old Ezra shook his head dismissively. "My, my, Mr. Newborn, you've got some genuine blockages here. No way we can say that your emotional life is squeaky clean."

The masseuse peeled off his mask and dabbed at the sweat on his face with a towel. He repeated his recommendation about the steam and Epsom salts.

Drained, I sat up, and then climbed off the massage table. As I dressed, I focused on my original purpose. "Jamie, did you know Ruthie Rosenberg very well?"

Jamie didn't answer at first. He boosted himself onto the massage table and crossed his legs. "Of course, I knew Ruthie. How well is debatable. After a while, I'm not sure that anybody really knew her. Or that anybody really knows anybody, for that matter.

"Ruthie and I worked together at times and she also took a genuine interest in the Sisters. I think it's fair to say that she had sister-envy. She could see the fun we were having. I told her she'd be welcomed in the order, that it was open to straights. She'd come to our monthly bingo games in Guerneville once in a while. But she couldn't get it together to join us. You didn't come here for a massage, did you, Mr. Newborn?"

"Why do you think she couldn't get it together to join the Sisters?"

"The drugs, of course. And she had a little problem with her identity, which didn't exactly make her unique. Ask me why people don't accept that they have multiple identities. Ask me about repression. Ask me what I see in people's backs. I try to embrace all my identities. How about you, Mr. Newborn? Are you free to embrace all your identities?"

"*Embrace?* That's not the word I'd use. But back to Ruthie. What else can you tell me?"

"You had to be jealous of the way men fell for her."

"Were you jealous of her, Jamie?"

My masseuse gave me a sideways look. "I was using the word loosely."

"As in 'loose woman'?"

"I don't know what you're getting at, Mr. Newborn. My motto's 'Live and let live.'"

"It's obviously not everybody's motto around here," I said.

"No," Jamie said, solemnly.

"Go back to what you were telling me about Ruthie's ability to attract men."

"I've known people with that talent. Both men and women. Ruthie could get them to fall, and stay fallen, even when it was clear she couldn't respond."

"What about Deputy Coolican?"

"He had it bad. He'd come here looking for her. He'd be off-duty. Ruthie wasn't always here when she was supposed to be. It's a wonder they kept her on. I'd see the deputy, anxious in the waiting room. He didn't want to be seen here. People talk about this place like it's a whorehouse, but some of us are legit masseuses."

"Who else had a thing for Ruthie?"

Before Jamie could answer, the intercom buzzed that his next appointment had arrived.

"Can you tell me anybody else who was under her spell?"

Jamie vaulted off the massage table, squeezed sanitizer onto his hands, and then rubbed them together. "We should probably settle up. I don't want to keep my client waiting any longer."

"How much do I owe you?"

"Fifty dollars."

I was afraid to look inside my wallet. It had been thinning out in such a hurry. I plucked out four twenties and fanned them across the massage table.

Sister Everlast looked down at the money and hesitated a minute before picking it up. "Two other guys come to mind. One lives out by Sister Poesy. He's got a pretty big pot operation."

"Cust?"

Jamie nodded. "Yeah, and I think there was a guy from out of town, a Russian. Of course, she always snagged a few from the Bohemian Grove when they had their annual pissing contest. I don't know if a girl can go any lower than selling her body to those arrogant Republican pricks."

"Can you tell me anything more about the Russian you mentioned?"

Jamie shook his head. "That's all I got." He put his hand on my back and led me toward the door. "Steam, Mr. Newborn, don't forget to take the steam," he said, as he opened the door and ushered me out.

Face of an ancient poet—
the multigendered masseuse
opens my pores.

Phone Sex

My head was swimming by the time I got out to the street. Coolican wasn't anywhere to be seen. I crossed over to the café, got myself an Americano, and walked through the outdoor pottery market, keeping my eyes open for the deputy. By four, an hour past our agreed time, I realized that I was stranded in Monte Rio with a cell phone that had no service. I begged a phone call from the proprietor of the café, who wanted a dollar for the courtesy.

"It is a business, after all," he said.

I didn't argue, dropping four quarters on the counter.

Blossom answered and could hear the anxiety in my voice. "What kind of trouble have you got yourself into, Augie?"

"Who said I'm in trouble?"

"The truth is we're all in trouble."

"Don't go deep on me, Blossom. Is our prophet around?"

"He's down in Guerneville at the Galley. He's got a phone down there." She gave me the number. "Wait a minute. Quince wants to talk with you."

"Augie," the voice said, surprising me with its tenderness, "are you okay? I'm worried about you."

"Why?" I asked, intoxicated by her voice.

She made kissing sounds into the phone.

I couldn't believe the effect the woman had on me. I looked around to make sure the café guy wasn't watching me and then smooched back into the phone.

"Let's run away from here," Quince said.

"Where would we go?"

"Farther west."

"This is the western edge," I said.

"There's always Hawaii. Bali."

"What'll we do?"

"Don't be so practical, Augie."

"It's part of my nature."

"We can change that."

"I've got to go," I said, and smooched once more into the phone.

Next I dug a coiled dollar out of one of my pants pockets and smoothed it out on the counter. "I need to make another local call."

"Alright," the guy said, scooping up the dollar, "but no more phone sex."

Alas, I got Sabbatini's answering machine. His message was the first couple of lines of a William Carlos Williams poem, from a recording made when the poet was an old man:

I'm persistent as a pink locust.
Once admitted to the garden
you will not easily get rid of it.
Tear it from the ground,
if one hair-thin rootlet remain
it will come again.

I left a message for Sabbatini with the café's phone number and sat on a stool wondering if I should offer the café guy twenty dollars to drive me into Guerneville, or try to hitchhike over, seeing that it was just a few scant miles through the redwoods.

The phone's ring saved me. The coffee guy looked at me like he knew all my dark secrets. "You Augie?"

Hunch

Sabbatini drove over to get me half an hour later. In the interim he'd called around but could find no word on Coolican's whereabouts. He said he wasn't worried about Coolie, as if the burning of sage had earned the deputy some kind of cosmic immunity.

"He's probably off somewhere in the redwoods memorizing Yeats," said Sabbatini. I reminded him that the deputy had almost been killed by a flying arrow the day before and that his presence was likely responsible for the attack *à la maison.*

I wanted to wake the old detective in Sabbatini because I needed him. But the fucker had gone soft with weed and poetry, with living in Sufi-wear by the Russian River.

"Do me a favor, Bobby. Take me out to the River Rose."

"All the way to Jenner?"

"Take you twenty minutes."

"Yeah, twenty minutes out and twenty minutes back, and who knows how long waiting for you."

"You can just sit in the car with a fatty of Fuck Face."

"What kind of hunch are you playing, Augie?"

"You owe me, Bobby. You got me into all this bullshit."

Sabbatini was right. My desire to go back to the River Rose was nothing more than a hunch, a hunch that the Rose was the rendezvous point and a few of the players in this bad dream were about to show up.

CHAPTER FIFTEEN

Russian Glory

ON THE DRIVE back to Jenner, I asked Sabbatini to fill me in on the relationship between Coolican and Indian gaming.

"He's got no relationship, far as I know. They kept trying to throw money at him, but he wouldn't have any of it."

"So, he didn't take the money, but you did."

Sabbatini tapped a finger on his cheek. "Quince told you about that?"

I nodded.

Sabbatini cleared his throat. "It was a tactical move on my part."

"I'm not judging you, Bobby."

"Sure you are. But that's okay. So you've probably heard about the Russian principals of the company falling in love with the Russian River area."

"Yep. And who the fuck are these Russians?" I asked.

"They're named Dmitri and Boris. They came out here, got five cents' worth of feel for the locale, and realized that I was a pretty popular guy with the locals. I told them I wasn't interested in pimping a casino. They said they heard I was opening a poetry tavern, and Boris recited some Mayakovsky in Russian."

"That's what got you, a hunk of Mayakovsky?"

"Hell, no. For all I know, he was reciting some jive manifesto. Dmitri asked if I could use fifty grand for the tavern *tout de suite.* I said, of course I could use it, but I wasn't interested it endorsing their joint until the environmental impact studies were complete and the project was approved by the county. I'd endorse it, I said, after that. And they bought it, Augie. I'd call it a minor miracle for the sake of poetry. I got the dough and there's no way in hell that a fucking casino with an 180-room hotel is going to cut the environmental mustard anywhere along this river, especially not in Monte Rio."

"But they got their hearts set on Monte Rio?"

"The Russians are dreaming. It's hard to run a septic system for a mid-size restaurant in Monte Rio. And how do the people get out there? They'd have to build new roads, log out miles of redwoods. It ain't going to happen, Augie. The fucking Rooskies got blinded by some sort of bullshit chauvinism. The return of Russian glory to the California coast. I read some local history. There was no Russian glory out here. Bunch of Russians came down in the 1820s or something. Settled north of Jenner. Slaughtered all the seals and otters till the area was fished out. Couldn't figure out how to farm in the fog. The fuckers couldn't survive and left with their tails between their legs. That's the Russian glory these jokers want to return to."

The Russian River—
Russians coming,
Russians going.

Sea Ranch Tsunami

When we arrived at the River Rose, I asked the retired detective to pull around the side of the building as Coolican had. There were only a few cars in the parking lot. Sabbatini proposed dropping me off at the River Rose while he went down to the beach at Goat Rock to look for some driftwood. "I'm looking to create a little more ambience for the Galley."

I wasn't ready to go into the Rose. "Hang out a few minutes, Bobby, if you don't mind." I glanced at my watch as if I expected it to offer a clue. It only revealed that it was five to five.

I dozed off in the car beside Bobby, drifting into one shadowy, waking dream after another about Quince. I called up her lovely face, the hollow under her eyes where her soul seemed to reside. But then my reverie turned to a horror show—the lovely likeness of Quince dissolved and I was left with an image of charred skin hanging off Ruthie Rosenberg's left jaw. My body shuddered in the front seat and Sabbatini grabbed me.

"What's going on, Augie?"

I shook my head. "Funky dream."

Sabbatini regarded me suspiciously. "You okay, man?"

"Yeah, sure, sure."

I opened my eyes slowly, just in time to see Gordon Cust climb out of his candy-apple-green pickup and walk purposefully to the bar entrance.

Sabbatini pulled out a joint and lit it. When I declined a hit of it, he said, "You're not the man I used to know. Here, smoke this. It will give you courage."

"False courage."

"Who cares if it's true or false?"

For some reason, probably to release the images of both Quince and Ruthie Rosenberg, I took the joint. Once I started smoking, I couldn't stop.

"This is different weed, isn't it, Bobby?"

"No kidding. This isn't your run-of-the-mill Fuck Face. This is Sea Ranch Tsunami. Estate-grown Indica. I know a doc up at Sea Ranch that's really got his chemistry down. Hell of a guy. Man after my own heart—he's memorizing a lot of Milosz."

"Great. Isn't Sea Ranch a gated community or something?"

"Gateless and no longer exclusive. They've got their share of foreclosures. Cut back on the security. All the better for growing in peace."

The damn weed was so strong I felt fuzz growing on my face. As Sabbatini laughed, I swear I saw little green sparks flying out of his mouth.

"I'm buzzed out of my mind," I whispered to Sabbatini.

"Yeah, and you haven't seen anything yet. The Tsunami comes in waves."

The idea of being any more stoned was so terrible, I laughed in a rapid volley of cackles that sounded like gunshots.

"Augie's back," Sabbatini shouted.

My eyes seemed to grow larger. "I'm not sure I'm going to know how to conduct myself."

"Conduct yourself like you're a symphony," Sabbatini said, with a fire-of-green-sparks laugh. "Here's my advice. Concentrate on the beat. Give plenty of confidence to the violins, and don't forget to cue the French horns." Sabbatini demonstrated his technique, waving both hands, his face reflecting the rapturous sounds emanating from the small orchestra in the shadow of the windshield. I saw him cue the French horns and then realized that he was working on orchestral dynamics. First he brought a finger to his lips, and then he pushed downward with both hands. His closed-eyed smile made clear that the pianissimo he wanted had been achieved. "Come on, Augie, start conducting. What are you waiting for, a baton?"

I took a deep breath as a fresh wave of the Tsunami pushed and then tugged me with a fierce riptide. For balance, I braced myself on the door handle. After a half moment, I managed to open the door. "I guess I'm off."

"Do you know what you're doing?" Sabbatini asked.

"Hell, no. I'm playing it by ear without an instrument or a baton."

"That's alright. Keep it supple, Augie."

"Supple," I echoed, chewing on the word for a moment. "What exactly does that mean?"

Sabbatini flashed me a vaudevillian smile and reached into the backseat for a rubber-banded pile of fliers. "Here, take these in with you. Announcements for the opening of Ginsberg's Galley. They can be your raison d'être."

I nodded.

Sabbatini's head fluttered in a small Tsunami, and then he squinted at me. "Don't look Custard in the eye," he said. "It will freak him out. With guys like him, who are chickenshits by nature, it's best to stare at their balls. They don't realize why it's happening, but the little courage they have drains away."

"Are you serious?"

"Try it."

"Stare him in the balls?"

"That's the ticket."

"So you're telling me that Custard's benign?"

"I've never had any trouble with him. Just use your charm, Augie."

"My supple charm. How about Manzanita, the waitress?"

"Manzy?"

"Yeah. She linked Custard to the Russians. How should I play her?"

"Her, you can look in the eye, and she'll tell you which way to play it." Sabbatini winked at me and went back to his conducting.

As I walked toward the entrance of the River Rose, a fresh wave of Tsunami spun me around and I felt like I was frozen in somebody else's yoga pose. I held my ground a moment and then pulled a pair of horn-rimmed shades that didn't fit properly from my jacket pocket. "You're cool, man," I said out loud, not believing it, as I watched my own green sparks dissipate.

Rain or Hail

Manzanita looked up with surprise when she saw me walk in, but neither Custard nor the four or five others at the bar turned around. Custard sat in his Stetson at the end of the bar, with a leather bag propped on the stool beside him. He was either reserving a stool for a compadre or simply resting his bag there.

I decided to play it loud. "Hey, how are you, Manzy?" I called.

A trio of locals turned and checked me out with little interest. Custard grudgingly spun toward me in his stool, but he wasn't letting on that he recognized me. He looked past me, as if he expected someone else to come through the door.

The barkeep played it as I hoped—dumb. "Hey, how you doing?" she said. "You're Poesy's friend, aren't you?"

"Sure enough, I'm Augie."

Custard could no longer pretend he didn't recognize me. We'd actually had a short conversation early that morning at Sabbatini's, but that seemed like eons ago. Custard nodded my way, pulled a tin of tobacco from his back pocket, and positioned a couple of pinches inside his lips.

I flipped my shades and walked toward him with my hand outstretched. "Hey, is that you, Mr. Cust?"

"Augie," Custard said, "quite a night you guys had up at Sabbatini's."

I forced myself to look in the direction of Custard's balls. "Yeah, a little more excitement than I'm used to. I came for a little vacation in sunny California, you know, and suddenly find myself in the middle of a turf war between Tonto and the Lone Ranger."

Custard laughed, but I chided myself for saying too much. When you find yourself staring at another man's balls, less is more.

"So what are you doing out here?" Custard asked.

I handed him a flyer for the Galley's opening. "You're going to be there, aren't you, Mr. Cust? Didn't you say the other day that you've been working up an e. e. cummings poem? I know Sabbatini put some cummings on the machine."

"'Rain or Hail,'" Custard said. He stood up off his stool, shifted the tobacco around in his mouth, and began confidently reciting the poem:

rain or hail
sam done
the best he kin
till they digged his hole

:sam was a man

stout as a bridge
rugged as a bear
slickern a weasel
how be you

(sun or snow)

gone into what
like all them kings
you read about
and on him sings

a whippoorwill . . .

At that point, Custard paused with his mouth open. I had to look away; the sight of brown tobacco juice turned me a little queasy. I steadied myself through a fresh Tsunami. A woman sitting at the bar clapped, thinking Custard had finished his performance. He glared back at her and looked around at the rest of us, as if there were a prompter among us who was holding out on him.

"Goddamn it," he said. "I always get stuck after 'whippoorwill.'"

"The beauty of the poetry karaoke machine," I said, "is that you don't have to memorize the poems."

Custard looked at the flier. "Yeah, I'll be there."

I handed a flier to Manzy and asked her if there was a wall where I could post it.

"Sure," she said, shooting me a wry smile, "I'll take care of it."

"So, how about you, Mr. Cust, you come out this way much?"

Custard nodded grimly. "Once in a while."

I figured it was time to go with a gambit, a safe one at that.

"Where's your Russian bartender?" I asked, looking straight at Manzy. "I understand he's memorized a hunk of Yevtushenko."

Manzanita bit her lip before answering. "Yeah, he practices on me sometimes after the place has emptied out and we're tidying up."

I'd dropped the funky shades back over my eyes and watched Custard. He'd turned away from Manzy and pretended not to be listening, but I could see his ear growing into a fat cauliflower of curiosity.

The barkeep was enjoying the game and kept on talking. "He's got this long poem called 'Babi Yar' that's, like, really intense. At first I couldn't follow it at all, but pretty soon I found myself waiting for certain lines. One night, when Vlady said the line, 'I am older than the entire Jewish race myself,' I asked him if he was Jewish."

I watched Custard's cauliflower grow larger as he waited to hear Manzy's answer.

"He just laughed at me," she said. "Then when he could see that I was hurt, he said, 'No, the poet means it to be symbolic. You have to realize,' he said, 'everything is symbolic.'"

I could see Manzy had embarked on a wonderful performance for my benefit, and I began to wonder if I was missing any coded information.

Custard turned back our way and grumbled, "The only thing worse than poetry is talking about it."

"That's a bit of a surprise, coming from you," I said. "The way you recited the cummings, I thought you had a real feel for the stuff."

Custard only grunted and looked past me again. I wondered if Sabbatini was still sitting out in the car.

"You better not let Poesy know how you feel," I said.

"Or what?" Custard wanted to know, "he won't let me come into his poetry joint? I think he's got bigger fish to fry."

"Like what?" I asked.

"Like people shooting arrows at his cabin."

On the Floor

When Manzanita moved down to the other end of the bar to refill drinks for the locals, I headed toward Custard and asked if I could move his bag to sit on the stool beside him. I needed to get into his face.

He glumly shifted his bag to the floor. Nothing like a small territorial invasion. I applauded myself for keeping the Tsunami at bay, and flipped off my shades again. It probably wasn't a good idea to wink at Custard as he swirled a pale brown wash of ice water at the bottom of his glass.

"What are you drinking?" I asked.

"Maker's Mark."

"Can I buy you another? I owe you a drink for rescuing me in the Cazadero wilds."

Custard nodded and I dropped a twenty-dollar bill on the bar and signaled to Manzy to refill the man's glass and bring me a pint of Lagunitas IPA. I made a point of clinking glasses with Custard, who seemed a bit confused by my friendliness.

Once he'd poured down a gulp of whiskey, I went after him. "Sabbatini said you saw the vehicle go by last night."

"Yeah, it was an F-150 pickup, a few years old."

"Well, you know, we checked it out and there were some good fresh tire tracks standing up in the mud, but they were nothing like an F-150."

Custard inhaled through his nose and his face turned red. "Are you calling me a liar?"

"Not at all. I'm just thinking you were mistaken about what you saw in the dark."

Custard turned to face the other way. "So you think you're some kind of detective?" he grumbled.

"Nah, I'm pretty minor league."

"But you're poking around here," Custard said, swiveling to face me, "a place you know nothing about. You could get your Minnesota ass kicked if you're not careful."

"I'm actually from San Francisco, Mr. Cust."

"Yeah, and you've been gone a long time. Don't get yourself killed on vacation."

"I don't intend to. So, Mr. Cust, what seems to be threatening you? What are you afraid of?"

Custard flashed me a grin. "Are you for real?" he asked, slamming down the rest of his bourbon.

I took a cold gulp of Lagunitas. "Tell me how you're connected to these Russians. How's your marijuana empire involved?"

"Shut up, Augie," Custard said, in a controlled hiss.

"How much do you know about the recent crossbow attacks?"

"Fuck you."

Custard stood up from his stool and I did the same, doing a bit of a Tsunami shimmy once I got to my feet. With my footing more or less secure, I stared directly at Custard's balls, an act that didn't exactly make him wilt.

Behind the bar, Manzanita, eavesdropping, dropped a couple of glasses.

The crackling disaster made Custard laugh. "Need some help there, honey? Maybe your ugly tattoos, those fucking bugs climbing up your arms, are giving you trouble."

Manzy sneered at Custard and flipped him off.

"Fuck you, you little bitch," he said.

I took a step toward Custard and looked directly at his balls. "You're out of line, Mr. Cust."

"Yeah," said the woman sitting solo down the bar, "you bully."

Custard spat a stream of tobacco juice onto my right shoe. It had a vile odor reminiscent of something between singed hair and burnt cabbage. A small wave of Sea Ranch Tsunami washed over me. I forgot all about Custard's balls and threw a pretty good right hook at the creep's face. He caught my punch with his open left hand, as if I were a child. I heard him laugh and then saw his right fist form, and the shine of a brass ring on his middle finger. Next thing I knew I was on the floor.

Just once in my career as a P.I., I'd like to be the guy who nails someone else, but that doesn't appear to be my fate.

The paunchy detective,
finally the aggressor,
on the floor again.

CHAPTER SIXTEEN

A Little Character

As I CAME to, Manzanita was bent over me, holding a cluster of ice in a bar towel over my nose.

"I think he broke it," she said, though I couldn't tell if she was speaking to me or to someone else. Then I heard Sabbatini laugh.

"It will give his face a little character," my old buddy opined.

"Thanks a lot, Bobby," I said, though the words didn't come out clearly.

"Hey, look who's joined us," Sabbatini said.

I lifted my head.

"Don't try to get up yet," Manzy said.

"Where did Custard go?" Sabbatini asked.

"He ran out the back," said Manzanita.

"Coward."

I didn't seem to have any problem breathing in and out of my nose. The pain itself was surprisingly mild, a soft bruise to the bone.

It had been a surgical attack—one shot to the schnoz, with little collateral damage, save for a pulse of pain at the back of my head, which I must have tweaked on the ground. I reached behind and felt a good-size lump rising. I was most troubled by the fact that I had to pee and couldn't yet imagine how I'd get up and into the men's room. And yet, I felt mildly heroic that I'd survived the knockout without peeing my pants. I closed my eyes and licked my lips, catching a receding wave of Tsunami.

"*Le coup lui a fait voir trente-six chandelles.*"

"Are you talking to me?"

"I said the blow had you seeing stars, or as the French would say, thirty-six candles."

I closed my eyes and did see candles. I didn't try to count the number. "What did he hit me with?"

Sabbatini laughed again. He was enjoying the spectacle of me, KO'd on the floor of the River Rose. "Custard used to fight Golden Gloves."

I lifted my head. "Give me a hand here, Bobby."

Sabbatini crouched behind me. "We're going to take it slow, Augie. Sit up first."

Once he got me into a sitting position, I felt a little queasy. Bobby sensed this and asked Manzy to bring me a shot of whiskey.

"I got to pee," I whispered.

"Right," he said.

Manzy rushed over with a double shot of whiskey and handed it to Sabbatini. "It's on the house," she said, with a slight giggle.

"Jeez," I said, "I'm making out like a bandit."

Bobby made sure I could hold onto the tumbler before he let go of it. "Now pour that firewater straight down."

I did as commanded and my head jerked back as if I'd been clobbered again.

With a hand under each armpit, Sabbatini raised me to my feet, where I stood a moment, weak and bandy-legged.

The poetry priest took my arm and whispered a line from William Carlos Williams about the descent beckoning. I tried not to understand it.

"Let's go to the men's room and freshen you up," Sabbatini said.

He led me to the urinal. "I'd prefer not to hold your dick, Augie," he said.

"I think I can manage," I assured him.

I let it rip,
a flood of relief
that passed for pleasure.

I could see in the mirror that the area under my eyes and the bridge of my nose had already bruised blue-black.

"Hey, Rocky," Sabbatini said, "can you breathe okay?"

I nodded and washed my face gingerly.

Sabbatini took a close look at me. "Breathe in and out for me."

"Yes, doctor." I inhaled and exhaled deeply several times with only a small tingle of soreness.

"That thing's going to be crooked unless you have it reset. But such character."

I drew my ill-fitting horn-rimmed shades out of my shirt pocket—a wonder they were still intact—and slipped them on.

Sabbatini grinned. "That's a look I like."

Big Tipper

I was doubly surprised on my way back to the bar. The first surprise actually hit me as I washed my hands. One of my daughter's songs—"Littler Than I Thought"—cycled onto the River Rose's sound system. It struck me as bitter irony that this of all possible Rose songs shuffled on now. Sabbatini, walking with me back from the washroom, cracked up when he heard Rose's lyric at the chorus:

I fought and I fought—
turned out I was littler than I thought.

The second shock was to see Custard, his head down on a cocktail table near the bar. He stood and made a grand apology when he saw us.

"You want to file charges against this prick?" Sabbatini asked.

"Back off, Poesy," Custard said.

"You don't tell me what to do, you fucking redneck. You may have deviated this man's septum."

Custard looked confused. He turned toward me. "Like I said, I'm totally sorry. I kinda lost it there."

"You sure the fuck did," Sabbatini said. "This man needs to go to the hospital."

"Hey, I'll pay whatever it costs."

Sabbatini nodded. "Yeah, you will, and before I get him over to the clinic in Sebastopol, we're having a talk, Gordo."

Manzy came over to ask if we wanted drinks, but Sabbatini shook her off. "No, we're going for a little ride." To Custard he said, "You better leave Manzanita a gaudy tip for her trouble."

Custard reached into his buckskin wallet, pulled out a five, and dropped it on the table.

Sabbatini shook his head. "You can do better than that."

Custard protested, "All I've got is a hundred-dollar bill."

"Well?"

Manzanita, who was standing a bit back from the table, said that she'd be happy to change the hundred.

"You don't have to do that," Sabbatini said.

It was nice to see Sabbatini showing a little force. I was afraid his West County life had taken it from him. He and my assailant had a brief staring match, which Sabbatini won. His stare, I noted, was fixed directly on Custard's eyes.

Clearly a day of firsts. I'd never before seen a man in Sufi-wear stare down a strapping redneck. The old Golden Gloves champ picked up his five-dollar bill and extracted a C-note from his wallet, grumbling something under his breath as he tossed the bill onto the table.

A Higher Form of Being

Once outside, Sabbatini ordered Custard into the backseat of his Volvo. I was a bit amazed by the authority that the old police detective assumed and the way Custard minded it. I guess that's what comes from winning a staring match. I wouldn't know.

The Volvo smelled of Sea Ranch Tsunami. The sweet, smoky aroma brought on a fresh series of waves.

"Smells like you've been taking your medicine, Poesy," Custard said in his most pleasing voice.

"*Ca me met la puce a l'oreille. Il y a anguille sous roche.*"

"What was that?" Custard asked.

"I smell a rat."

"Hey, I've got some really righteous stuff to lay on you, Poesy."

Sabbatini didn't respond.

I flipped down the mirrored visor in the front passenger seat and had a look at my swelling nose. The blue-black of the bruise seemed to be marbling actively across a wide swath of my face.

"Where are we going, Poesy?" Custard asked.

Sabbatini didn't answer.

I could hear Custard rustling around inside his saddlebag in the backseat, but I didn't turn around to see what he was up to.

After we pulled out of the parking lot and headed north on Highway 1, Custard said, "No, I've really got something nice for you guys."

Sabbatini smiled at me. "Here's where the bribes begin."

As if on cue, Custard leaned over the backseat and handed us each fat baggies filled with premium, pinup-worthy buds. The stuff looked like it came straight from a centerfold shoot at *High Times.*

Sabbatini grabbed the bag offered to him, but I shook my head, and just as Custard was going to take back the second baggie, Sabbatini grabbed it.

"What would you say the street value of this is?" the old police detective asked.

"That there is some potent bud. We're not talking your run-of-the-mill Fuck Face."

"Then what are we talking here? What do you get for a baggie of bud this size?"

"Baggie like that," Custard said, pausing as if he needed to consider the price, "baggie like that, a fat ass of an ounce like that goes for $300, to friends."

"So that suggests that Augie and I are better than friends since you're giving us this shit." Sabbatini turned to me. "See, here's where a shyster like Custard is really shitting us. Nobody's getting $300 an ounce anymore. Too much of a surplus."

I groaned after the second of two hairpin turns and Sabbatini put a hand on my shoulder. "We're just about there, Augie."

"Where are we going?" Custard asked.

Sabbatini pulled into a turnout on the ocean side, parked, and turned the engine off. This was the same turnout that Coolican had taken this morning. It seemed as if the locals had an affinity for ghoulish tourist spots.

"You know what that beach is down there, Gordo?" Sabbatini asked.

"Nope."

I didn't bother to turn around but could see that the two were facing each other via the rearview mirror.

"You sure you don't know? That's Fish Head Beach where those two Christian kids were murdered in 2004. You know anything about those murders, Gordo?"

"Hell, no, why would I know anything about that?"

"So, you're telling me that you don't know about those murders."

"Just what I read in the papers, and various theories, you know, you heard people expousing in taverns."

"I hate to be the bearer of bad tidings, Gordo, but *expousing* ain't a word. You can go with *exposing* or *espousing*, but you've got to really make a choice between 'em." Sabbatini winked at me, clearly enjoying his little detour into the pedantic. "So what's your theory about who killed them, Gordo?"

"I don't have a theory. And quit calling me 'Gordo.'"

"Isn't that your name, Gordo?"

Custard winced audibly.

I'd started to become obsessive about my nose. I couldn't take my eyes off it in the mirror. I checked and rechecked my breathing, wondering if in fact I did have a deviated septum.

Sabbatini dropped a hand on my shoulder. "How's the schnozola doing?"

"I'm thinking it will live."

"I bet you'd like to smash Custard."

"Not especially."

"You're really lucky that Augie's a higher form of being, Gordo."

Love Underrated

Sabbatini turned around now and looked at Custard. "So you have no theory you're willing to *expouse* about the murders down there?"

"Probably was just some drifter," Custard said.

"Without a motive?"

"Hell, I don't know what his motive was. He didn't take any money from them."

"So are you saying that money is the only sensible motivation for committing a crime?"

"No, I'm not saying that."

I turned sideways so Custard could see my face. "I've always thought love was underrated as a motive," I said.

Custard narrowed his eyes, a nuance lost on Sabbatini, whose husky laugh at my line filled the car.

"That's so Augie." Sabbatini said. "He's such a romantic."

I supposed that was true, although I couldn't imagine myself far gone enough to kill for the sake of love.

"It takes one to know one," Custard said, with a sneer.

"What is that supposed to mean, Custard?" Sabbatini demanded. "What is that supposed to mean?"

Custard went mute and I did my best to disassociate.

Only the lovesick
detective sees love
as a possible motive.

Dark Deeds

A couple of moments later, Sabbatini changed his tune. He caught Custard's eyes in the rearview mirror. "Hey, Gordo, how many plants do you have growing?"

The pot rancher shrugged. Without turning, I could hear him trying to buzz down his window.

"Hey, how do I get this window open, Poesy? I got to spit."

Sabbatini unlocked the window, and just like that, Custard had the window down and was shooting long wads of tobacco loogie from the backseat.

"I'd guess you have a good two hundred plants or so, huh, Gordo?" Sabbatini continued. "You've really got great sun exposure out there. You should see this guy's operation, Augie. He's one of the biggest outdoor growers in the area. He's absolutely brazen, grows these big, motherfucking plants right out in the open. Nobody's gonna touch Custard's shit. Come harvest time, he's got these beatific two-pound shrubs, most ravishing bud you've ever seen in your life. How much you get a pound for that bud, Gordo? Around three Gs wholesale?"

"No, barely two. Like you said, prices are down. The indoor growers are the only ones making the big money."

"But you're not suffering, Custard, not by my calculations. So let's see, what's Custard's crop worth? That's, say, two hundred and fifty plants at two pounds, times two grand a pound." Sabbatini pulled a phone out of his pocket and punched in some numbers. "I've got a calculator on here. Damn, that's a cool million for one crop. How many crops you have in a year, Custard?"

"Believe me, it's not all profit. I've got plenty of expenses."

"How much do you pay in taxes, Gordo?"

"I pay taxes."

"How much you want to bet we pay more taxes than he does, Augie?"

"So what's your point here?" Custard shouted.

"Who said I have a point, anyway? Maybe I'm just making conversation. You see, Custard's part of the 1 percent. Instead of occupying Courthouse Square in Santa Rosa, we should be occupying the pot ranches of West County."

The pot rancher turned to the open window and spat out another wad of tobacco custard. I began to feel like a captive in the car and willed myself to open the car door and step outside.

"Where you going, Augie?"

"Just need a little air."

"Be careful out there."

I was surprised by the force of the wind. It had really come up since Coolican and I were there in the morning. Whitecaps checkered the belly of the ocean. I walked gingerly toward the cliff and looked down the hilly crags toward the beach. Hard not to picture the two young Christians dead in their sleeping bags. Killed the very same way as Ruthie Rosenberg.

CHAPTER SEVENTEEN

Detective Sabbatini Returns

I WENT BACK to the car, figuring that Sabbatini was probably waiting for me. No such luck, I realized, as soon as I settled back into the front seat. Custard and Sabbatini were still jousting.

"What the hell do you want from me, Poesy?" Custard asked. "I mean, I'm sorry I clocked your buddy."

Sabbatini ignored him and turned toward me. "How is it out there?"

"Big wind."

"Hey, Gordo, how many people do you have working for you?" Sabbatini asked.

"I don't know, maybe a dozen. It's seasonal work."

I turned to look at Custard. He'd taken off his Stetson and his thin, stringy hair looked as if it hadn't been washed in a while. I noticed for the first time that the skin over his chin and right cheek had small black flecks embedded in it. I guessed he'd once been sprayed with buckshot. His cheeks were both puffed with tobacco. I'd lied to

Sabbatini—I would have loved to clobber this creep. Sabbatini pulled a Swiss Army knife from his pocket and started poking between his teeth with the plastic toothpick. Custard yanked out his tobacco tin and took a few pinches. Jeez, if I'd had my clippers with me, I'd have given myself a manicure.

Before Sabbatini could ask his next question, I jumped in with one of my own. "Who was the Russian you were waiting for at the River Rose yesterday?"

Sabbatini winked at me.

Custard groaned. "Dmitri."

"Dmitri from the Reno casino outfit?" Sabbatini asked.

Custard nodded.

Sabbatini grinned. "What kind of business are you doing with him?"

Custard paused before answering. "He's . . . a good customer."

"What are you selling him," Sabbatini asked, "your ganja or your wife?"

"Fuck you, Poesy." Custard made a fist with his right hand.

"What are you going to do, clobber me, too, Gordo?"

"Hey," Custard said, with a snarl, "I hear you got a fat tub of shekels from the casino, Poesy. Now take me back to town. I don't know what you're giving me all this shit for."

"Sure, I'll take you back to town, Gordo. But one more question: How long did Ruthie work for you as a trimmer?"

I was surprised by the question, but Custard took it in stride.

"I don't know," he said, "a few years. On and off."

Sabbatini turned the key and let the Volvo idle for a minute. "And how about Yevgeny, how long's he been trimming for you?"

"I thought you said one question."

"It's one question with several parts. You should see this scene, Augie. Gordo's got a little cabin out on his property. I'm not talking about his house, but this small cabin where there's this big ol' oak table that practically fills the main room. So you got five or six people sitting around the table, smoking weed. There's usually a bottle of

Jack Daniel's going around, and these folks are just sitting there bullshitting. Meanwhile, they've got these small manicure scissors clip-clipping away through the buds with the mechanical fluency of hummingbirds."

"Maybe you should write a poem about them, Poesy," Custard grumbled.

"There's an idea."

I turned sideways so I could see Custard. He had his Stetson back on now and an inscrutable look fixed on his mug.

"A better idea," Sabbatini continued, "would be to have all those trimmers reciting poems as they trim."

Custard shrugged. "You think everyone should be reciting poetry."

"*Bien sur*! Imagine if you had all the trimmers in West County reciting poems. I'd start them out with Gary Snyder's 'Hay for the Horses.'" Sabbatini shifted into reverse, and then pulled the car back onto Highway 1, aiming south. He turned back to catch Custard's eye. "When did you start suspecting that Yevgeny and Ruthie might be stealing from you?"

"I'm not talking anymore."

Sabbatini nodded. "Fine, we'll just talk around you. Talk among ourselves, as it were." Bobby flashed me a big smile and continued rapping a blue streak. "The problem, Custard discovered, was that he couldn't be everywhere at once. If he was in the fields, he couldn't keep track of what was going on in the cabin, or vice versa. He thought he was paying his people well, but they were still stealing from him. He had some folks he trusted, but all of a sudden he couldn't trust anybody anymore.

"Hey, final part of the question, Gordo. Did Ruthie Rosenberg steal enough from you for you to want her dead? Take your time with your answer. I could even find you a pad of paper and a pencil, in case you'd like to write it down," Sabbatini said, sounding like the old police detective.

"Hey, Custard," I said, turning to face the man directly, "how long had you been sleeping with Ruthie by the time she died?"

I expected to get nailed again by the rancher, but he just puffed out his cheeks and looked grim.

"Wow," said Sabbatini, "that was a real blockbuster. Thing about Augie is he's a pretty good sleuth when he puts his mind to it. And you got to appreciate the foreshadowing, Gordo. I mean the way Augie laid that egg of a line about love being underrated as a motive."

"Hey, I had nothing to do with that girl's killing," Custard volunteered.

"No?" Sabbatini said, "you just slept with her."

"That didn't make me exactly unique." Custard buzzed down the window and spat again.

"Did you love her?" I asked.

"No," he said, but he squinted his eyes in a surprising way. "I tried to protect her."

"From whom?" I followed.

"I just tried to keep her safe."

"From whom and from what?" Sabbatini persisted.

Sabbatini eyed Custard in the rearview mirror while I looked at him directly, but the pot rancher had clammed up again.

Cazadero Castrato

"Well, think about your answer a little, Gordo. Meanwhile, how about we roll up a joint of your righteous bud? What do you call this shit? What do you call it, man? You can tell us that much."

Custard wasn't budging.

"Anyway," Sabbatini said, "I've got some slow-burning papers here. We'll take our time getting back."

Sabbatini pulled out one of the baggies of bud and juggled it in his hand for a moment. He tossed it to me with a pack of papers, and said, "Augie, will you do the honors?"

After I rolled up a decent fatty on the open tray of the glove compartment, I handed it to Sabbatini.

"Not bad for a teetotaler, Augie." Bobby fired up the doob and passed it to me. I wasn't having any. The waves of Tsunami were getting fainter and I didn't want to do anything to amplify them. I turned to my assailant and offered him the joint. He took it and spent a moment looking at it. Then he found his voice again.

"I'm not much of a smoker anymore," he said. "I've got so I prefer edibles."

"But weed's your business, Gordo. You've got to know your business; you've got to know it from the inside out. And to know it, you have to smoke it. It's like me and poetry." Sabbatini took both hands off the steering wheel and held them aloft for a moment. "Do I know my business, brothers, or do I know my business?"

Custard zipped down his window and spat a couple wads of tobacco. Then he drew on the fat joint, savoring it like a prize cigar. After taking a half-dozen hearty hits, he said, "You're right, Poesy, nothing wrong with the direct approach. All I'm saying is that with edibles, you're looking at the future." He passed the fatty back to Sabbatini.

The old detective nodded. "Could be, could be."

Custard reached into the pocket of his jean jacket and pulled out a handful of chocolate bars wrapped in bright lavender foil. "I just picked up some chocolate cannabis bars from one of my associates. They're supposed to be a killer high."

He offered both Sabbatini and me one, which we declined. Bobby kept puffing on the joint.

"Cazadero Castrato," Custard blurted out.

"What's that?" Sabbatini asked.

"That's the name of the shit you're currently smoking. This motherfucker's so strong, it could turn us into eunuchs."

"Not me," I said, "because I haven't had any."

"Watch out, Augie, even the contact high could bust your balls."

I buzzed down my window, hoping to escape the Castrato's effect.

Custard's Pussies

"So, how do you like it, Poesy?" Custard asked, sticking a chocolate bar into his mouth and chomping through it in a flash.

"Oh, it's a player," Sabbatini said, "no doubt, it's a player."

"Hold on, it's about to grab you by the balls." Custard peeled the foil of another chocolate bar.

"How many of those can you inhale at a time, Custard?" Sabbatini asked.

"I go three or four. But what I'd really like to do is open a line of edibles. With edibles, the sky's the limit." His mouth full of cannabis chocolate, Custard let out a high-pitched cackle that swelled into a bright falsetto. "Here's my fantasy; you guys want to hear my fantasy?"

"Do we have a choice?" Sabbatini asked.

"No, it's just this. I supply a beautiful lady in every town in West County with herb and kief. I'm talking Occidental, Valley Ford, Bodega, Bloomfield, Duncans Mills, Monte Rio, Rio Nido, Graton. From Sebastopol to Petaluma in the east, Bodega Bay to Sea Ranch in the west, and everywhere in between. And each of these ladies bakes herbed edibles. Blondies, brownies, bourbon balls, macaroons, Russian tea cakes, exotic fruit tarts, kief-crumbles, ginger bars, caramel popcorn balls, you know, real out-there yummies. I mean, these lasses are everywhere, like Swiss milkmaids."

"You putting them in uniforms, Gordo?" Sabbatini asked.

"Hey, that's a cool idea, Poesy." Custard packed another chocolate bar into his mouth as Sabbatini and I smiled at each other.

"And the best part," Custard continued, "is that as I do the rounds myself, I fuck each one of my milkmaids before leaving with her edibles."

"That's if the Castrato doesn't get you first," I offered.

"No way."

"You could call the line Custard's Pussies." Sabbatini said. "That's got a nice ring to it."

Black Bart

Custard began laughing hyena-like in the backseat, only pausing from time to time to shove another chocolate cannabis bar in his mouth.

He began pointing at things out the window and cracking up. "Did you see that?" he'd say.

"What?" I asked.

But by then, he'd be laughing at something else. Sabbatini nodded to me with a grin. From the front seat, we listened to Custard reading road signs and chuckling to himself.

Sabbatini drove past the River Rose where Custard's car was parked, and Custard grinned out the side window, muttering, "There goes the Rose."

A few minutes later, after Sabbatini turned east on 116, he pulled into the village of Duncans Mills and parked in front of a tavern called the Blue Heron.

"What are we doing here," Custard asked, cackling with pleasure, "stopping for a fried oyster sandwich at Cape Fear?" He nodded to the café across the highway.

"Nope," Sabbatini said.

"Aw, it's one of my favorite places when I've got the munchies."

"Brothers," our pilot said, "I thought it was time to pay homage to Black Bart."

The three of us climbed out of the car and into the sudden burst of late afternoon sunlight. We must have looked like three blinking hayseeds just evacuated from a movie theater.

"I've got to take a whiz," Custard announced before running off to the café next door to the Blue Heron. Sabbatini stretched his legs and then did a little shimmy in his Sufi pants.

"I think Custard's going to lead us to the murderer," Sabbatini said.

"You don't think it's him?"

"I'd be surprised. But if it is, he'll lead us there as well."

"I hope you're right. How's the Castrato?" I asked.

"I really couldn't tell you. I pulled a Bill Clinton."

"You didn't inhale?"

Sabbatini grinned and then led me over to a plaque commemorating the gentleman bandit, Black Bart. He gave me a brief history of the man who specialized in holding up Wells Fargo stagecoaches and sometimes left poems behind at the scene.

"Strange hero to honor with a plaque," I said.

"This was the Wild West. Everybody out here likes to think they have a bit of outlaw in them. Given the current status of Wells Fargo among the occupiers, Black Bart might end up with his dead old ass deified."

Custard tumbled out of the café with a take-out cup of coffee and joined us at the Black Bart plaque. "I'd have picked up some coffee for you guys, but I didn't know how you liked it."

Sabbatini grinned at me.

Custard pulled a small flask out of his back pocket and poured the rest of its contents into his cup. "Here's how I like mine—Scotch coffee." Then he read the poem off the plaque, purported to be Black Bart's last, left behind at the scene of his final stagecoach robbery.

I've labored long and hard for bread,
For honor, and for riches,
But on my corns too long I've tred,
You fine-haired sons of bitches.

Custard flashed Sabbatini an ingratiating smile. "We should do some Black Bart at the Galley."

What Rhymes with Crime

Once back in the car, Sabbatini had me roll another joint of Castrato. After lighting it, he passed it back to Custard.

The pot rancher sucked on the joint and passed a lavender-foiled bar to Sabbatini. "Try this, Poesy. They are so righteous."

Sabbatini chomped down on the cannabis bar and then had a big hit of the joint.

"Be careful, Bobby," I said. "I doubt that Blossom will appreciate the effects of the Castrato."

"You're right about that," Sabbatini said.

"My wife could care less," Custard said, grinning. "Could care less," Custard said, liking the sound of his echo.

"That must be one of the reasons Ruthie was so important to you," I suggested.

Custard shrugged and then unwrapped yet another cannabis bar and floated the thing in his mouth. "I should have divorced her twenty years ago," he said, thoughtfully, before bursting into a cackle that sprayed chocolate spittle through the air.

"How long have you been married?" I asked.

"Twenty-one years."

"That first year must have been pretty good," Sabbatini said.

"It was okay."

"Sounds like a sad gig," Sabbatini said, sucking on the joint. I watched him hold the smoke a moment in his mouth before letting it slowly tumble out. The force of habit.

I zipped down my window for air and then turned to face Custard, who was swaying back and forth to an imaginary song. "How did you meet Ruthie, anyway?" I asked.

"How did I meet her?" Custard said, before laughing at the question. "Yevtushenko introduced me."

"Had he broken up with her?"

"I don't know; he was just shopping her."

"So, he was her pimp?"

"Pimp, wimp, simp, primp," Custard said, laughing up the ladder into a true falsetto.

Sabbatini winked at Custard in the rearview mirror and sucked hard on the fatty. He may not have been inhaling before, but he sure as hell was inhaling now. I didn't like the way things were developing, or devolving, as the case may be. Sabbatini was driving on 116, back out toward the ocean, but was only going about forty miles an hour. A pickup had started tailgating us, and was hitting his horn in short bursts to get Sabbatini to speed up or pull over.

Sabbatini nodded his head backward. "It's clear that this guy is having trouble with the natural rhythm of things."

"All Meat," I said, remembering my first conversation with Custard, "All American." That was a mistake. It fed right into what was left of Custard's brain.

"All Meat," he chanted, "All American. All Meat, All American. Paul Revere Frankfurters, All Meat, All American."

I turned back to face Custard. He was still chanting and I wanted to shut him up. "Yeah, that's how you described yourself when we first met in Cazadero."

Custard slid down the backseat until he was practically supine, murmuring, "Cazadero, marrow, faro, sparrow, tarot."

"Where are we going, Poesy?" I asked.

"I don't know."

"Maybe we should have a plan."

"Don't get all hung up on the destination, brother. I can tell you, that's not the way home."

"Castrato, motto, jotto, risotto, ricotta." Custard flung the words out with big round vowels.

The pickup finally passed us, flipping off Sabbatini on the way by.

"Did you see that guy?" Sabbatini asked. "He's riddled with anger."

"Anger, bang her, hang her," Custard shouted, a desperate hitch in his voice.

"What rhymes with crime?" I asked.

Custard snorted and said, "Time."

I doubted that I could get more from Custard at this point, but I figured I'd keep trying.

"Hey, Custard, did Yevtushenko have other girls he 'shopped'?"

"Shop, drop, top, fop," he cackled.

"Did he have other girls?"

"Girls, curls, swirls," he said, going fetal in the backseat. I watched him mumble something unintelligible before closing his eyes. A nasty foam of chocolate and leftover tobacco swill began forming at the corner of his lips.

It wasn't long before Sabbatini hit Highway 1 and headed north again toward Jenner. When we pulled into the River Rose, I noticed a chartreuse Neon, just like my rental car, pulling out.

"Wasn't that Quince driving?" Sabbatini asked. "And Coolican sitting shotgun?"

I nodded, sadly.

Once he'd parked, Sabbatini smiled at me and said, "I'm really high, Augie."

"You were honking on the hooter pretty good."

"And that chocolate bar was wicked. Edibles aren't s'posed to hit so quickly. But I haven't eaten anything all day."

Sabbatini slid down in his seat, reciting from Ferlinghetti's "Coney Island of the Mind." I could see that Bobby was in outer space. Shrunken in his seat, he danced each line with his head like an old puppeteer.

The poet's eye obscenely seeing
sees the surface of the round world
with its drunk rooftops
and its wooden oiseaux on the clotheslines
and its clay males and females
with hot legs and rosebud breasts
in rollaway beds
and its trees full of mysteries
and its Sunday parks and speechless statues
and its America. . . .

After he hit *America,* Sabbatini went back and repeated the word *oiseaux* until he was scatting it. You could almost see birds flying. I stayed in the car until he drifted off to a whistling sleep, his head against the grips of the Volvo's steering wheel. I didn't notice any foam spilling out of his lips.

I left the sleepers to their slumber, and for the third time that day walked toward the entrance of the River Rose. Fucking Groundhog Day. The parking lot was fuller than during my previous visits. The happy-hour revelers had begun to show. On the way, I took out my handkerchief, mottled with dried blood, and gingerly touched the bridge of my broken nose. There seemed to be no fresh seepage, but, surely, I looked like a monstrous gargoyle.

CHAPTER EIGHTEEN

Je Ne Sais Quoi

I HOPED THAT Manzanita was still bartending. Flush with tip money, she'd provide some useful information. But Yevtushenko was back behind the bar. Lazarus of the mushrooms. He saw me walk in and gave a wary sigh. The barstools were taken by patrons who seemed to know each other. I noticed a little daylight between two women in their late thirties and sidled in.

"He's supposed to be hung like a horse," the curly-haired one said, with a throaty laugh.

The other woman, fair and freckled, guffawed before saying, "No lie."

Disfigured and heartsick as I was, I couldn't resist joining the conversation. "How'd you know? I just got here."

This brought a pat on the back from the curly-haired one, who introduced herself as Patty. Her freckled friend scooted her stool back to give me more room to stand and held out her hand to me. "Sky," she said, "as pure as the vodka but without the extra *y*."

I shook her hand. "Who needs the extra *y*? Anyway, in the natural order of things, the sky above us existed before the vodka."

I introduced myself and then caught a glimpse of my face in the mirror behind the bar. The skin on either side of my nose was puffed and bruised. In reflection, I looked like a cubist creature leaping out of a medical reference book.

"Augieboyer," Yevtushenko said, standing in front of me now. He extended his hand. I wondered if what Custard had said was true, and I was actually shaking hands with a pimp.

"I hear you have an accident with Custard," he said, "but I didn't know it was such a crash."

I excused myself to the women who'd befriended me, and asked Yevtushenko if I could talk with him.

"That's what you doing," he said.

I tilted my head toward the end of the bar, but Yevtushenko reminded me that he had a full bar to tend and that there was no place for the kind of conversation I wanted to have.

"What you drinking, Augieboyer?"

I rarely drink hard liquor, but wanted something to dull the throbs emanating from my nose and the back of my head. "Johnny Walker Black on a single cube of ice, with a couple of Advil."

"Excedrin," he said.

"And bring two more beers for these ladies," I said.

A moment later, Yevtushenko returned with the beers and left my drink, with *four* Excedrin, on a cocktail napkin in front of me. "I be back," he said.

I took my medicine and watched Yevtushenko gracefully manage his tasks up and down the bar.

"Who hit you?" the freckled Sky asked.

"Some jackass," I hissed, warming up to my scotch.

"Have you seen a doctor?" Patty asked.

"Not yet. He really rearranged my face, didn't he?"

"You look okay." Sky said, taking a frosty sip of her beer. A bit of the head stuck to her upper lip. She reached out with her tongue and licked it off. "So, you're like a man returned from battle." She kissed the tips of her fingers and then touched them to my chest.

"What was that?" I asked.

"A Purple Heart."

"You must be one of those women who like men who need nursing," I said, pouring down the rest of my scotch in a gulp.

"She's one of those women who like men," Patty said.

"I'm actually quite choosy," Sky said, and raised her neck in a mock haughty expression.

Although they were a bit older than Ruthie Rosenberg, I figured Patty and Sky probably knew her.

"Don't worry about your bruises," Sky said. "They'll heal."

"My friend says that the reshaping of my face gives me character."

Sky smiled at me. "You already had character."

"Yeah," agreed Patty.

"Thank you. But how can you tell?"

"You have a presence," Patty said.

"A certain *je ne sais quoi*," said Sky. She grinned to her friend and said, "I mean, check out that scarf. It's beautiful. But it takes a formidable man to wear a scarf like that."

I nodded my thanks. I was such a wreck I hoped I didn't begin crying because a pair of strangers were being kind to me. I glanced again in the mirror and was surprised to see that, despite all I'd been through, the scarf still looked dashing and seemed to have escaped the bloodbath.

"So what do you girls do?" I asked.

"She's a hairstylist in Guerneville," Sky said, pointing to her friend, Patty, "and I'm a holistic nutrition specialist there. You might try some arnica on that bruising, and then steep a couple of dry teaspoons of St. John's wort in vegetable oil and rub it over the affected area."

"She is so full of herself," Patty said.

"You guys are really good friends, aren't you?"

They both nodded.

"Did either of you know a woman named Ruthie Rosenberg?"

Patty looked away, but Sky met my glance. The corner of her upper lip quivered. "Ruthie was a friend of mine."

"I'm sorry."

"She'd come into the pharmacy sometimes. I liked talking to her, you know, when she was okay."

"What do you mean, okay?"

"When she wasn't, you know, cracked out. Did you know her?"

I shook my head.

"I liked her worldview. She believed a lot in good energy and bad energy."

"Well, she certainly ran into the latter."

"Yeah, I'm sick about what happened to her."

"Any idea of who might have done this?"

"You a cop?" Sky asked.

"No, a private investigator."

Both women regarded me with fresh attention. Sky leaned closer to me and whispered, "She slept with, you know, a lot of guys. The drugs, I think they took away her sense of danger."

"Maybe her common sense," I suggested, "but does anyone in particular come to mind?"

Sky raised an eyebrow.

Yevtushenko was suddenly standing in front of me with a fresh drink. "Augieboyer, what you want to say? You want to know about Custard?"

"Sure."

He gave a hard, get-lost look to each of the women and they hopped off their stools and moved to an empty cocktail table across the room. Along her way, Sky waved and said, "Good luck, Augieboyer."

Provocateur

"Custard, he's a little man," he said. "Not physical little, maybe, but mental. You are not man of violence. He knows this."

"I tried to throw a punch."

"But you no good at that. You good for things more important."

"I don't know what I'm good for."

The Russian gave me a cheering smile. "Ah, Augieboyer, you good for plenty."

I couldn't figure out Yevtushenko. Was he really a pimp? A small-time gangster? The trouble was, I'd been having difficulty reading just about everybody I met. I'd already been fooled by Coolican and Quince, Sabbatini and Blossom. Why take Custard at his word? What proof did I have that Sister Everlast was speaking the gospel? My only play was to try and smoke out Yevtushenko.

"Custard said something very disturbing."

"What he say?"

"He said he used to fuck Ruthie."

I watched Yevtushenko's face turn red. He looked like he wanted to spit, but pulled his lips together into a tight pucker. "He say that?"

I nodded, and then reached down for everything I had left. "He also said you introduced her to him, that you were her pimp."

Yevtushenko's lips turned to a snarl and he backed away from the bar with two empty pint glasses in his hand. I figured I was in for another bruising, but, with tears streaming down his face, the bartender slammed the glasses into the stainless steel sink. The echoing explosion forced everybody in the bar to look up at once. I sat there dumbly, waiting to see what would happen next.

As it turned out, Yevtushenko raised his arms in the air in silent apology, and then, in contrast to his rash act, he gathered a couple of bar towels and soberly cleaned up the broken glass. People settled back into their conversations, and I noticed both Patty and Sky watching me with looks of concern on their faces. They must have realized that I was the provocateur.

I studied my cubist visage in the mirror and poured down the rest of the scotch. Yevtushenko hissed a half-dozen words my way: "What Custard say is filthy lie." I was in no position to argue with him and would have been a fool to try.

The bartender hovered nearby for a minute, no doubt expecting a response. I had none. I stood up from the stool and noted a weariness in my legs. It was as if I'd taken a beating over ten rounds rather than getting KO'd by a single punch.

"How much do I owe you?"

"You owe me nothing, Augieboyer. You and me, we have the same enemy."

I nodded and peeked in my wallet. Time to hit the cash machine. I pulled a five-dollar bill out and laid it on the counter.

As I walked toward the door, Sky came over and handed me a folded piece of paper. "If you find you need something," she said, "call me."

I smiled gratefully. "What could I possibly need?" I said, feeling like a man who needed everything.

She kissed me on the cheek. "Something may occur to you in the night."

Malodorous

In my absence, Sabbatini's Volvo had turned into a disaster area. Custard had vomited all over himself in the backseat and turned a shade of yellow that wasn't particularly becoming. The stench was overpowering. I did my best to block it out as I tried to rouse Sabbatini, who was moaning in the driver's seat. He'd curled into a fetal coil under the steering wheel. I knew in a flash that both men had been poisoned.

I ran back into the River Rose and grabbed Sky. "I need you now."

She hurried out of the tavern with me. "Where's the closest hospital?" I asked her.

"Palm Drive. Sebastopol."

"How many miles?"

"It's less than twenty-five miles."

"I've got a couple guys here that look like they've been poisoned."

"With what?"

"I'm not sure. They were both smoking some powerful weed and also partaking of edibles."

Sky took in the disaster scene without noting the smell, which might seem like a normal response, but it struck me as heroic, given the power of the stench.

"How long for an ambulance to get here?" I asked.

"You're better off driving them in yourself. It could take a good half hour on that winding road. I'll come with you."

Once we uncoiled the moaning Sabbatini, Sky exclaimed: "That's Poesy."

"Yes."

She helped me extricate him from the driver's seat and load him in the back beside Custard.

I noticed Patty hovering near the entrance of the Rose and grabbed Sky's hands. "Go over and talk to her. Tell her we've got this under control."

There was no time to clean out the vomit, so we drove with all the windows open.

"Who's the other guy?" Sky asked.

"His name is Cust. He lives out near Poesy in Cazadero. It was his dope and his edibles, so I don't know why he ingested the stuff."

"Somebody spiked it without his knowing."

"He ate a lot more of the cannabis chocolates than Poesy," I said, "but at least he vomited."

Sky turned around to look at the two men. She reached over and took Custard's pulse. "He seems okay," she reported. "He's in a pretty deep sleep." Sabbatini was still moaning.

"Poesy's in bad shape," I said. "Any way to get him to vomit?"

Sky turned and looked at me. "You think that's what he needs?"

"Hey, you're the doctor."

"Hardly. And I've never seen anything like this before. Slow down a little," she said. "Don't kill me now."

I slowed down per Sky's request and she climbed halfway into the backseat, forcing two fingers down Sabbatini's throat. Barely conscious, he still fought her. Finally, she hit pay dirt and with an awful retching scream, he heaved. Sky managed to dive back just before the eruption. A fresh wave of pungent odor blanketed the interior of the car.

Sky settled back in the front seat and wiped her fingers on her red corduroy pants. “This is a helluva first date,” she said.

“It’s going to be hard to top.” I thought of my recent first date with Quince, which nearly got me arrested.

Sky smiled at me, closing her eyes with feeling. I realized that I represented more than a bizarre amusement to her. As fond as I was of Sky, my feelings didn’t go that way.

We drove a while in silence and then Sky asked why I hadn’t got sick like the others.

“I didn’t smoke or eat any of it.” I told her about having already had enough for one day, what with a deep massage, a punch in the nose, and some thundering waves of Sea Ranch Tsunami.

“For you, Augieboyer,” she said in a spot-on rip of Yevtushenko’s accent, “this is the day that keeps on giving.”

I shook my head and bombed right through the “Monte Rio Awaits Your Return” sign.

“Your phone work out here?” I asked.

“Should.”

I pulled Sabbatini’s number from my wallet and punched it in. When Blossom answered, I told her that I was driving a couple of guys who’d been poisoned to Palm Drive Hospital in Sebastopol. I told her that she should call ahead to the hospital to let them know we were coming.

“Where’s Bobby?” she shouted.

“He’s one of them, but he’ll be fine,” I said, no doubt betraying my lack of conviction. “Meet us there.”

“Bobby’s one of them,” Blossom screamed. “How am I supposed to get there? How am I supposed to get there? Bobby took the car!”

“Call your neighbor, Custard’s wife.”

“That Christian bitch!”

"Her husband's the other guy."

Blossom kept screaming into the phone and I handed it to Sky. I wasn't skilled enough as a multitasker to entertain Blossom and speed along the curving road through the redwoods. Sky did her best to calm the agitated wife. It was a hopeless chore. At one point I heard Blossom holler, "Who the hell are you?"

As I slowed down coming into Guerneville, Sky turned back and checked on our ailing passengers. With a handkerchief wrapped around her right hand, she took pulses and lifted eyelids.

"What's the deal?" I asked.

"They don't seem to be getting any worse," she said, sitting back in the front. "Pull up here," she said, pointing to a spot at the curb. "I won't be a minute."

I did as told, and before I could ask why, Sky was out of the car and darting into the new age pharmacy where she must have worked. It was only a few doors up from Ginsberg's Galley. I turned to look at Sabbatini, the heap of him, breathing amid his vomit in the backseat. Poor man. I kept my eyes from Custard. He was still breathing.

Good to her word, Sky returned in a flash, climbing into the front seat beside me. She opened her small purse, pulled out a package of blue sanitary face masks, and ripped it open, handing me a mask. "Here, put this on. I didn't think I could take the smell all the way to Sebastopol."

Once we both had our masks on, I winked at Sky and she winked back. I glimpsed a reflection of myself in the rearview mirror. The mask clearly improved my looks, covering my broken nose and vast patches of bruised and discolored skin. The horrid smell was hardly eliminated, but it seemed to back up a bit, coming closer to the memory of a malodorous event rather than the event itself.

Murder, the Theme Song

The curves in the road picked up once we got out of Guerneville. Sky kept her humor amid this grim scene, suggesting I slow down a titch.

"Imagine the crash scene," she said. "Two barfed-out guys coming to their senses in the backseat, and you and me, looking like a pair of masked bandits, dead in the front."

I backed off the pedal a bit. Pushing through the redwoods toward Forestville, I asked Sky how she knew Sabbatini.

"Oh, I don't really know him; I just know who he is. Everybody knows Poesy. I see him sometimes going into his tavern, you know, getting it ready for the opening. One day he came into the pharmacy. He told us about his morning meetings, and then handed out poetry books and suggested we pass them among ourselves until we found a poem that moved us. "

"Did you find one?" I asked.

"Yes, a Robert Creeley poem."

"Poesy's favorite. Which one?"

Sky shot me a sly smile. "I'm saving it for the opening."

If there is an opening, I thought, and glanced back in the mirror at what I could see of Sabbatini's breathing heap.

Sky took hold of my right hand and I let her hold it a minute before slipping free and grabbing the steering wheel.

"So, how did you know Ruthie?" I asked.

"She came into the pharmacy a lot and we got to talking. She was into holistic medicine. It became a real interest for her."

"Could you tell whether she was using?"

Sky took a moment before answering. I glanced over at her. Her eyes seemed to grow larger, but that perception may have been shaped by her face mask, which left only her eyes visible.

"Yeah, I could tell when she was using. I mean, it was so obvious anybody could tell. She'd come in and want to talk about diets. She was heavy into colonics. Had that addict's thing of wanting to do things all the way. She'd kill herself with the cure if she had to."

"Yeah," I said, "like one of those anorexics who go to Weight Watchers to stop themselves from overeating."

"Totally. Ruthie was going to kill herself one way or another."

"But somebody beat her to the punch."

"I can't believe it." Sky's forehead furrowed above her mask. "I mean, you sensed tragedy all around her, like that was her theme song or something. But murder? I mean, your heart went out to Ruthie. She had this earnestness about her."

"Was it real or a con?"

Sky shrugged. "She had nothing to gain from me. I had a little knowledge of questionable value to her. She never asked me for money or anything like that."

"Did she talk about the men she was seeing?"

"Her life was a mess with men. Once they fell for her, she felt responsible for saving them."

"Saving them from herself?"

"Right. Logic wasn't her strong suit."

"Did she talk to you about any of them?"

"Not to me. I only knew about two men, but they were common knowledge. Guerneville's a small town and Ruthie was one of its most flamboyant citizens."

"Who were the two men?"

"Jesse Coolican, the Indian deputy, and your friend the bartender, whom she lived with off and on."

"Wasn't she done with Coolican?" I asked.

"That was the trouble. She was never done with anybody, I mean, if they weren't done with her."

"And you don't think either of these guys was done with her?"

"Not from what I heard."

"What do you know about Yevtushenko, the bartender, being her pimp?"

Sky dropped her hands over her mouth. "That's the first time I've heard that."

"That seem plausible?"

"I really thought the Russian loved her."

"You don't think those possibilities are mutually exclusive?" I asked.

"I'm not that advanced a student of human nature."

"That would be abnormal psychology."

He's Alive

As we drove into the outskirts of Sebastopol, I heard somebody rousing in the backseat. Then came Bobby Sabbatini's familiar voice: "What the fuck?!"

Both Sky and I turned around to see Sabbatini wiping crud off his face with his shirt sleeves. "Hey Bobby, you're alive."

He gave off a small, frightened scream, probably at the sight of the two of us in face masks.

"Who the hell's that?" Sabbatini said, pointing at Sky.

"I'm glad you feel better," she said.

"I feel like shit."

"I'm Sky," she said, and took off her mask and smiled at him. "From the pharmacy."

"Oh, yeah."

"Sky's been very helpful."

Sabbatini got a sheepish look on his face. "Forgive me for the mess."

"Don't be silly," I said. "Custard's weed made you sick. It was laced with something."

"The Castrato?"

"It was either that or the edibles. I have the baggie of the Castrato up here. We'll get it analyzed."

"Is he dead?" Sabbatini nudged the inert body beside him and a soft groan issued from it. "I guess not."

Sky directed me through Sebastopol to Palm Drive Hospital. As soon as I pulled up, she ran in the emergency entrance and came out with a male nurse and an orderly, each wheeling gurneys. The nurse gasped at the sight of our backseat load.

At least it's not blood, I thought.

"What do we have here?" the nurse asked.

"They've been poisoned," I said.

They lifted the groaning Custard onto a gurney. His eyes opened for a moment but quickly closed. I walked alongside the gurney, remembering that Custard had pulled one cannabis bar after another out of his jean jacket pockets. I explained to the nurse that the patients' pockets might hold a key to what had poisoned them. The nurse shrugged as if to say, "Help yourself," but then I noticed that both of Custard's pockets were filled with barf. For a moment, I considered wrapping the silk scarf around my hand and diving into the wreck, but that seemed beyond the call of duty.

Sabbatini refused a gurney. He stood, a little shaky, beside Sky. Intent on walking, he wrapped an arm around my shoulder. I was glad to offer what little support he'd allow.

I conversed a moment with an ER doctor, explaining that Custard and Sabbatini had been poisoned and that Custard had eaten a whole lot more than Sabbatini. "Whatever it was, it knocked them out."

"How long ago was the substance ingested?" he asked.

"The last couple of hours."

"You had none yourself?"

"No."

I pulled out the baggie of weed. "This is what they smoked. Plus they had some chocolate cannabis bars. Cust, the guy on the gurney, had a half dozen of them. Sabbatini, the one who walked in, only had one, as far as I could tell. There may be more of those in the pockets of Cust's jean jacket." I didn't mention the barf.

The doctor nodded. "Did you happen to see how those bars were packaged? Were they homemade? Were they sealed?"

"They were wrapped in foil, but not sealed."

"Well, we will pump them out and hydrate them and go from there." The doc, an East Indian named Rajmahani, seemed to find the follies of us mortals amusing. He took a long look at me. "And what happened to you?"

I wondered what he meant until I remembered my nose. "I had a little accident."

"Let's have someone check that out," he said. "It looks like you should have it reset, though it's hard to tell because of the swelling."

CHAPTER NINETEEN

Waiting

BLOSSOM WAS IN the waiting room when I got out there. Sky, assuming the role of temporary wife, had Milosz in tow, and was lifting him to see the small tropical fish swimming around the aquarium.

As soon she saw me, Blossom hollered, "He going to be okay, Augie?"

"Yes," I said, without equivocation.

"What happened?"

I checked out the waiting room. There was a teenage boy, his face in his hands, beside his mother, or someone assuming the role. She whispered comforting words to him. Right across from them was a man in his seventies, with his arm in a homemade sling. He sat next to a woman his age reading a copy of *Prevention.*

I bent to Blossom and whispered, "It appears they ate or smoked something laced with poison."

"Fucking idiots," Blossom screamed. "Where did they get the shit?"

"Shhhh."

"Don't shhhh me, Augie."

"Custard had it, but he didn't mention where it came from. The doctor didn't seem worried about Bobby. "

"What the fuck does he know?"

The mother glared over at Blossom as I chuckled at Blossom's nasty disposition.

"And what the fuck happened to you?" she asked.

"Your neighbor, Mr. Cust, didn't like something I said. One punch and I'm flat on my back. Somebody should have told me that he'd been a Golden Gloves champ. I might have watched myself."

"You look like shit, Augie," Blossom said, with a hint of a smile.

"Thanks. It's been a hell of a holiday so far." I noticed Milosz's car seat on the floor beside Blossom's diaper bag. "So, did Mrs. Cust bring you over here?"

"Yeah, had to listen to her Jesus jive the whole way."

I waved at Sky and Milosz, who were getting along famously.

"Sky's cool," Blossom said.

"You know her?"

"From the Peoples' Pharm."

"She was a big help to me."

"Have you fallen in love with her, too, Augie?"

I shook my head and thought of Quince driving my rental car with Coolican sitting shotgun.

The trickster
made off with my heart
in the rented Neon.

Lover Boy

I excused myself, went over to the registration desk, and flashed my out-of-state medical card.

"Have a seat," the receptionist said.

Blossom paced back and forth, an obstinate scowl on her face.

"Come here," I said. "Sit down."

To my surprise, Blossom did as I instructed. "Is he really going to be okay, Augie?"

I took her hand. "I'm pretty sure he is."

Blossom looked up and smiled at me, and then her face turned to concern. "You sure that doesn't hurt, Augie?"

I squinched my broken nose like a bunny. "Only when I do that."

"Then don't do that," she said.

Milosz, on the ground again, ran over to his mom and grabbed her thumb.

"He wants you to see the fish," Sky said.

Both Blossom and I followed Milosz over to the fish tank, and after a moment of oohing and ahhing, Milosz ran off with Sky following after him.

Blossom and I stood together at the fish tank, watching the darting bursts of color. "Any word from the phony wife?" I asked.

"She went off to fetch Coolican in your rental. I got a call from him that his car had broken down."

"Do you really believe that?" I asked.

"What's not to believe?"

"I saw her behind the wheel of my Neon, hauling ass out of the River Rose with Coolican sitting shotgun. What do you think that was about?"

Blossom shrugged. "Maybe they found out who's been shooting arrows at Coolie."

"You don't think there's anything going on between them?"

Blossom shook her head. "No, Quince is soft on you."

I tried to ignore this piece of information, but couldn't keep from grinning.

"Look at you, loverboy."

We sat quietly a moment and then Blossom began tearing up. "He's not going to die, is he? Not now. He's so excited about the opening of the Galley."

I grabbed her hand. "What are you talking about? It's going to take a hell of a lot more than a poisoned cannabis bar to fell Bobby Sabbatini." I pulled a handkerchief out of my pocket, but the damn thing was all bloody.

In the years I'd known Blossom, I'd never seen her so vulnerable.

The old man with his arm in the sling got up and started pacing. "The fucking arm's broken," he said to nobody in particular. "I'm going to get rid of that animal. I am."

The woman he'd been sitting beside shook her head and said, "Language."

A moment later, Milosz waddled over to his mom, who boosted him onto her lap.

Sky smiled at us. "I'm going to take off. Patty's picking me up in the front lobby."

I stood to hug Sky and she held up a hand. "Sit."

"I can't thank you enough."

"It was an experience," she said.

Blossom joined in the chorus of thanks as Sky waved bye-bye to Milosz.

"See you guys at the opening," Sky said.

After she left, Blossom grinned at me. "I saw the way she was looking at you, Augie."

"What's with the women around here? Are they all love-starved?"

"Not me," Blossom said, bouncing Milosz on her knees. "I'm not starved in that department at all." Then she started tearing up again. I watched her eyes track a nurse who came to the waiting room door and called the man with the broken arm.

"The damn arm's broken," he mumbled, looking around at his wife.

Next the teenage boy was called in, and then they came for me. Each time the nurse appeared, Blossom asked for some news about Sabbatini's condition. The nurse had nothing. Blossom got back on her feet and paced across the waiting room, with Milosz in hand. "If he's going to be okay, what the hell is he doing in there so long?" Blossom shouted.

A bottled blonde with a nasty cough, who'd just signed in, shot daggers at Blossom.

Blossom stood with her hands on her hips and stared the poor woman down. "What the hell's the matter with you, bitch? You swallow some bleach?"

Unlikely Suspect

I was glad to be led to a little dark room, glad to have my blood pressure taken and to hear that it was normal, glad to be left with my thoughts as I waited for the doctor.

I must have slept for a while—the light in the room seemed different when the doctor came in. It was the same man I'd spoken to earlier—Dr. Rajmahani, a tall, slim gent who looked like he was always at the point of laughing. He examined my nose and asked about the pain, which I said was negligible.

"Negligible," he echoed, "this is a curious way of putting it. There's no need to be macho about this."

"Don't worry. I'm not the macho type."

Dr. Rajmahani wondered if I had any trouble breathing. I tested my breathing again and replied in the negative.

"Well, I'd like to look at it in a couple of days, when the swelling's down."

The conversation switched to Sabbatini. Dr. Rajmahani took a seat beside me. "He's going to be fine. Your friend has a very good mind. He was reciting poetry. We'll watch him for a while. Have him stay overnight in the hospital."

"You ought to talk with his wife; she's freaking out in the waiting room."

"Yes, just spoke to her. I'd like to have her take a sedative, but we need someone to look after the baby." The doctor winked at me. "She said you could be the lucky candidate."

"Of course," I said, "I can look after Milosz."

Dr. Rajmahani grinned. "It must be a good omen to name a baby after a poet. Maybe he'll speak in verse." The doctor chuckled. "Your friend told me about his poetry tavern."

I nodded. "So he'll be out tomorrow?"

"Unless we have some unexpected developments. A poetry karaoke bar." Dr. Rajmahani shook his head with pleasure.

I inquired about Custard.

Dr. Rajmahani bowed his head. "Mr. Cust isn't so lucky. I'm afraid we're looking at kidney failure. We'll flush him out and get him on dialysis. He may not make it."

"Oh, Christ," I said.

"I understand that Mr. Cust was the one who did the damage to your nose."

I nodded.

Dr. Rajmahani stood up and flashed me a cryptic smile. "I realize that these incidents are entirely unrelated, but because, how do they say, foul play is suspected, we're required to report this unfortunate incident to the sheriff's department."

I gave Dr. Rajmahani a sideways glance. "My broken nose or the poisoning?"

The doctor chuckled. "The poisoning, of course."

"You know, it wasn't me who provided Cust with the poisoned goods."

Dr. Rajmahani blinked a couple of times and shook his head. "Of course not, though it was you who brought the questionable substances to my attention."

"I wanted you to see what poisoned them."

The doctor shook his head. "Absolutely the correct action, but all the same . . ."

"It was Custard who offered the stuff to us," I said, wondering if I sounded like the not-so-wily suspect about to get nabbed.

"Of course, of course."

"And the man's not the type to plan a public suicide."

"No, no."

I was beginning to tire of the doctor. "Is Cust conscious?"

"I'm afraid not."

"Do you think he'll regain consciousness?"

Dr. Rajmahani's expression became too grim to hope for much.

"It's that bad?" I asked.

"I'm afraid so."

"Damn. Any idea what the poison was?" I asked.

He shook his head. "Too early yet, Mr. Boyer. Please come back and let us have a look at your nose in a couple of days."

"I will," I said, "unless they have me under lock and key."

The damaged suspect,
guilty since birth,
contemplates surrender.

Inventory

I was famished and exhausted by the time I got back to Cazadero with Blossom and Milosz. Blossom had taken two Ativans in the barfed-out car and passed out before we got home. I brought Milosz in first and dropped him, screaming, into his crib. Then I struggled to get Blossom out of the front seat of the Volvo and, like a whacked-out bridegroom with a broken nose, carried her over the threshold of the cabin and dropped her on her bed, pulling a white quilt, embroidered with a couple of lines of Hart Crane, over her. Milosz continued hollering in the crib, so I hoisted him out. We circled the kitchen, him in my arms, until I came up with a plan.

I sat Milosz in his high chair with a cupful of Teddy Grahams and some apple slices, and then warmed a bottle for him, squeezing out a little from the nipple onto the back of my hand to make sure the temperature was right. My ex-wife had taught me this method a quarter century ago. I became immediately nostalgic. For what? Thankfully, Milosz's squawking for his bottle cut my reverie short.

I strolled again with the boy in my arms, trying to burp him. But all he did was fart and I realized I had a diaper to change. Once I got Milosz cleaned and changed, he climbed off the changing table and brought me two board books with bright images of trucks. We settled into the rocker beside his crib and I made up stories about tow trucks, semitrailers, and cement mixers until we both fell asleep.

When I awoke a little after ten, with a knot of hunger in my tummy, I found Milosz nestled in my lap, dreaming of trucks. I lifted him gently into his crib for the night.

Three Calls

As I checked on Milosz like a dutiful guardian, the phone calls began.

First was Sabbatini from the hospital. "Get me out of here, Augie," he said. "I can't sleep in this place. They got me sharing a room with an old man who keeps screaming for his mother."

"Go Zen, Bobby." I explained that he'd be better off staying put for the night. "Chant a Creeley poem or two."

"Let me talk to Blossom."

"She's out for the count, man. She's two Ativan in. Let her rest. She had quite a shock. So, how you feeling, Bobby?"

"It's nothing to write home about."

"No, I wouldn't think so."

Then Sabbatini asked about Milosz and when I told him the routine I went through with his son, he started blubbering about how grateful he was to be alive. I decided not to tell him about Custard, though, for all I knew, he'd already ferreted out that information. Sabbatini signed off with a long poem about survival by Seamus Heaney. After he'd finished his recitation, he coughed into the phone and said, "Augie, you're snoring. Goodnight."

Next came Coolican.

"Where are you?" I called into the phone. "Where were you?"

He drawled, "Hello, Brother Bear, somebody's trying to kill me, so I'm holed up a while."

"Where?"

"Can't say."

"Why were you driving off with Quince in my rental car?"

"She was a big help to me."

"I bet she was. Where is she?"

Coolican didn't answer my question. "I wanted to tell you I was sorry about not fetching you in Monte Rio. Circumstances. I'm a victim of circumstances, as one of the Three Stooges used to say." Coolican sounded like one of the Stooges when he laughed and I realized that he was probably fuck-faced. I pictured a trail of sage swirling around him.

"I'm going to be okay, but you'd be smart to lay low for a little, Brother Bear."

Finally came a call from Yevtushenko that launched me into action. The Russian's voice sounded hoarse, but I had no trouble recognizing it.

"Is that you, Augieboyer?"

"*C'est moi,*" I said, channeling Sabbatini.

"You are in a very danger place, Augieboyer."

"What are you talking about?"

"I think I know who is the assassin."

I hadn't thought of Ruthie's murderer as an assassin, but what the hell. "Who's that?"

"I won't say on the phone. This very dangerous to tell."

"Sounds like it might be more dangerous not to tell, Yevgeny."

"You meet me, I tell."

"I'm out of gas," I said.

"You find station, twenty-four hour, right in Caz."

"Not that kind of gas. Energy."

"You need energy, Augieboyer, think about being dead."

"I'm not going anywhere tonight, Yevgeny."

"Only to the morgue?"

"If that's my fate . . ."

"Fuck you to your fate, Augieboyer."

"Any more days like today and I'd agree with you."

"I tell you this much. Is a woman, the killer. This I believe, Augieboyer."

"How do you know?"

"You meet me, I tell you more."

"Where?"

"Armstrong Redwoods."

"Where the hell is that?"

"You go through Guerneville, up Armstrong Woods Road. It twenty minutes from Caz. Then meet me at the Armstrong Tree."

"What the hell's the Armstrong Tree?"

"Giant redwood. Twelve hundred year old."

"How am I going to find this tree in the dark?"

"You bring flashlight. Follow signs. It's not any tree. It's giant tree."

"How long a walk is it?"

"Maybe a half mile from the park entrance."

"You expect me to drive out there and then walk a half mile in the dark into a redwood grove. What are we going to do, forage for mushrooms?"

"I not joke. People are dead."

"People?"

"You better come."

"How do I know you're not setting me up?"

"You? What to gain with you?"

"That seems to be the consensus."

"I promise I not ambush Augieboyer."

"Well, that's a comfort. How do I know you're not the killer?"

"If I the killer, why somebody shoot arrow with poem in Russian like it's me? Am I so stupid to do that? Why doesn't the sheriff's department lock me up? Why do they ask me to help?"

"Who asked you to help?"

"Coolican."

"Where's Coolican?"

"I don't know. I meet you at the Armstrong Tree at midnight. That give you time to pull up your pants, Augieboyer." The phone clicked.

CHAPTER TWENTY

Repent

THERE IS ABSOLUTELY no reason for a man to entertain such an invitation. Perhaps it was simple curiosity that got the better of me. After the day I'd had, I figured that giving up the ghost in the shadows of a twelve-hundred-year-old redwood might not be the end of the world.

Before I left, I brewed a pot of strong coffee and poured it down like it was medicine. I made a call to the hospital, trying to reach Dr. Rajmahani in the emergency room. He was off for the night. Back to the switchboard, I asked to be put through to Mr. Cust's room and was told it was too late to disturb patients. That left me with the hope that Custard had survived. Finally, I checked on both Milosz and his mother. Each was glazed with an aura of blissful sleep. How I envied them.

I dug around a utility closet and found a flashlight and some old rags. I'd hoped to clean out the car thoroughly and deodorize it somehow before anybody got in it again, especially me. But I had neither the time nor the patience for that, so I pulled the Volvo up as close as I could to the cabin, hooked up a garden hose, adjusted the nozzle to firehose mode, and blasted the backseat, sending clumps of vomit out the open doors into the driveway. After I buffed down the old leather seats with the rags, I took a long whiff through my broken nose. The car still stank, but no more, it seemed, than my fate.

Passing by First Christ River of Blood, I saw a tall woman, her head wrapped in a bandanna, standing beside the lit signboard. She was fiddling with the large letters. It seemed an odd time of night to be changing a sign. The last time I'd noticed it, it read: THE RIVERS OF AMERICA WILL RUN WITH BLOOD TO THEIR BANKS BEFORE WE SUBMIT. A real bleeder, as Blossom would say. The new sign offered an even simpler sentiment. Still in process, it read: REPENT, REPENT, REPE. I tried, to no avail, to get a clear look at the woman in the bandanna.

Once I hit 116, I focused on the task at hand—meeting a Russian bartender, mushroom forager, and possible pimp and murderer in the middle of a redwood forest at midnight. I wondered what he had to gain from me. Everybody I met knew more about what was going on than me. My elimination didn't seem worth the trouble. If Yevtushenko regarded me as an adversary, he clearly overestimated my prowess as a detective. If he saw me as an ally who could help him out of a difficult situation, he was really in trouble.

Lost in a labyrinth,
he forgets about will,
forgets about reason.

In the Redwoods

I walked slowly up the path toward the Colonel Armstrong Tree, which, according to the sign near the park entrance, was a half mile ahead. A deep fog shrouded the grove. Even though it was a dozen miles away, I smelled the ocean. It hung like an old buddy in the mist.

I aimed the flashlight's beam a couple of feet in front of me and followed the small circle of light up the path. Fortunately, the hike involved little elevation or rigor.

The hoot of an owl, which seemed to pitch its voice from alternate directions, accompanied me. The owl spooked me less than the realization that Ruthie Rosenberg's body had been found in a similar grove of redwoods.

Occasionally I aimed the flashlight's beam up the trunk of a behemoth and watched it fade into the mist. Closer to the ground, I saw the enormous hollows of fallen trees, some blackened by fires, others with stout branches arching across the path.

I smelled the savory campfire before I saw it. Soon, I flashed on a sign that pointed to the Colonel Armstrong loop and followed it toward a small, crackling fire built inside a giant burl. The beam of a flashlight scanned along the path until it found me.

"Augieboyer, you're right on time."

Yevtushenko sat cross-legged in front of the fire with his shoes off, warming his feet. In the firelight, I noticed a sleeping bag and a camp stove with a steaming saucepan, responsible for the savory redolence. One mystery solved—the runaway mushroom soup had been found.

Beside the stove was a canteen and a half-empty quart of Cutty Sark. I wondered if the Russian had been drinking for hours. In any case, this is where he planned to spend the night. I almost wished I'd brought a sleeping bag.

I nodded toward the fire. "Have you burned down that giant redwood?"

"No," he laughed. "Don't you see it, Augieboyer? It is right behind you."

I turned to look at the mighty tree and aimed my light at a plaque in front of it.

Yevtushenko aimed his light up the thick trunk. "You can't see it so much: the fog sits on its shoulder. They say it is 1,200 years."

"You sound like you don't believe it."

"It could be. Maybe it's older. Come sit here. Get warm. I step in a puddle. My shoes and socks got wet." He pulled a tin cup from his cook kit and said, "I give you some warm mushroom soup."

"No, thanks. I'm good."

"It's good," he said, licking his lips.

Yevtushenko looked like a hero from a 1930s film, his khakis rolled up and his bare feet dangling near the hot burl fire. Yes, a bald-headed Gary Cooper.

I walked toward the fire, crouched, and extended my hand. After we shook, I stood back from the fire.

"You not sit, Augieboyer?"

I held my place stupidly for a moment, trying to project five cents' worth of why-the-hell-did-you-drag-me-out-here defiance. But I really couldn't fake it. For better or worse, I'd already given myself to the experience. What the hell, it was beautiful in the dark, misted redwoods. I felt foolishly safe with these thousand-year-old brothers surrounding me. Anyway, I'd just lived a hundred years in a day, and if this was going to be the last night of my life, I decided that I might as well enjoy it.

With some effort, I folded myself into a high-kneed cross-legged posture to Yevtushenko's right. An owl hooted, again without revealing its location.

"You sure you not want some soup, Augieboyer?"

It smelled so damn good and I was still hungry. "Sure, give me a little cup."

The Russian took a swig from his bottle of Cutty Sark and then passed it to me.

I lifted the bottle and poured a couple of big gulps of scotch down my throat. Just like that, I was coated with a layer of well-being. Yevtushenko drank some more and passed the bottle back to me. I'd had enough and put it down. The Russian climbed onto his knees and dipped the tin cup into the saucepan. The steaming cup dripped wild mushroom broth down its side and Yevtushenko stanched the driplets with a wipe from one of his wet socks.

I took a long gulp of the rich soup and tried not to think about my impending death.

"So, why are we here?" I asked.

"I tell you, everything is bugged."

"Isn't meeting way the fuck out here a bit of overkill?"

Yevtushenko shrugged. "I don't know overkill. I just know somebody wants to kill me. Anyway, it's nice out here."

I could hardly disagree. I took another slug of the hearty potage and nudged a small conifer branch into the fire.

"What do you want from me?" I asked.

"Like I say, I'm in danger."

"Everybody around here seems to be in danger."

"You, too, Augieboyer," Yevtushenko said, and flashed his light on my face. "Your nose, it's become a bigger flower since this afternoon."

"Flower? So what's the reason for all the danger?"

"It start with casino money."

"Tell me about the casino."

"There is no casino; there be no casino. Everybody that lives here knows that, but still they take the money."

"How come there won't be a casino?"

"It fuck up the area," Yevtushenko shouted. "The traffic—it not work. The greens block it. The people not vote for it. The Indians not vote for it."

"What does Coolican think?"

"He hate it."

"Did he take the money?"

"Not Coolican. They want him to put together a bunch of Indians. Make a tribe. A tribe of Indians have rights to put casino almost anywhere. But Coolican not do it."

"You said you thought a woman was the killer."

"You know her. You have crush."

"Quince?!" I said, incredulous.

Yevtushenko nodded. He gulped from the bottle and then turned his head and spat.

"How do you figure?"

"Nobody suspect her. She pretend to work for Poesy and his wife, but she work for Dmitri and Boris. Those guys get what they want. They know lot of people try to fuck her, but she fuck them instead."

"Okay, but how does that make her a killer? And what does Ruthie Rosenberg have to do with the casino?"

"One question at a time, Mr. Detective. First, I tell you this—Coolican said they find two set of footprint at Christian campground."

"So?"

"They both woman feet. One wear shoes, one not. This is true. They sure they both women."

That was quite a scene to contemplate. A woman with a gun chasing a barefoot hostage through the redwoods. Pure horror show. I'd never seen one woman do another, but I'd lived a sheltered life.

The Russian stood up. He looked fetchingly disheveled from the drink, pitched forward, and then stumbled. "Ruthie," he said, "she not deserve that, murder like that." He called out into the mist, "You fucking bastard. You fucking bitch."

I shined my flashlight on Yevtushenko. "Hey," he said, stumbling again as he covered his eyes with his arms. I thought of the Old Testament God, shining his light on the shamed Noah. It had been some time since I'd equated myself with God. I switched the light off.

"So the only link to Quince is that she's got women's feet? Why would she want to kill Ruthie Rosenberg? She didn't even know her."

"You got denial, Augieboyer. That woman is the hired killer."

"Why would anybody hire somebody to kill Ruthie?"

"You lucky you get warning. You might be next."

"Why?"

"You know things. She know you stick your head around. Just like Coolican. Just like me. We all investigate. We all in danger."

"Tell me why any of this gang would want Ruthie killed."

"Dmitri, he want to fuck her, but she told him to fuck off."

"Who told you that?"

"Ruthie." Yevtushenko almost toppled as he reached for the bottle of Cutty Sark. He poured the rest of it down his throat. "I know those Russians, they ruthless."

I wanted to press the man about stereotyping Russians, since he'd raised the issue earlier, but there was another issue that I needed to get to the bottom of.

"Tell me something, Yevgeny, how come you disappeared from the Rose after I came by the first time?"

"Who told you that?"

I didn't answer.

With a bit of an effort, Yevtushenko sat back down by the fire. "I disappear because I have premonition."

"A premonition of what?"

"Somebody after me."

"Why you?"

"I know things." Yevtushenko spooned in a little more mushroom soup.

"Then why'd you come back?"

"To find out more things. I live dangerously, Augieboyer. I don't recommend for you." Yevtushenko belched a mushroom cloud. I tried not to breathe for a moment, but still absorbed a wave of wild mushroom smokiness. *Why had I eaten his damn soup?* The Russian picked up the flashlight and shined it on me. "Look at you, Augieboyer. You already beat up. You want to get killed. She kill you when you not expect. Maybe she take your shoes. Maybe somebody else get you. Or get me. By bullet, by arrow, maybe by poison."

I couldn't figure why Yevtushenko was trying to freak me out. He reminded me of a ten-year-old bully telling horror stories at camp. It was frighteningly effective.

Guilty as Charged

Suddenly a loudspeaker voice shook us from our reveries.

"PUT OUT THE FIRE IMMEDIATELY. STAY WHERE YOU ARE. DO NOT TRY TO RUN. WE WILL FIND YOU."

I could see fear leap into Yevtushenko's eyes. "Aw, shit," he said.

"That doesn't sound like Quince," I said.

The Russian didn't laugh at my joke. He stood up and grabbed the empty bottle of Cutty Sark and tossed it into the distance. It must have made a direct hit on a redwood trunk because we could hear its bright splintering. Yevtushenko looked like he wanted to run. I did my best to calm him down, explaining that it was only a park ranger. I'd read a sign at the entrance to the grove that prohibited overnight camping. Surely fires were not allowed.

The Russian and I started digging up turf to throw on the fire. A moment later a small park service jeep pulled up and aimed its headlights directly at us and the squalid scene. The Russian's old school sleeping bag and the cookstove with its pot of wild mushroom soup looked laughable. Then Yevtushenko's hands shot up in the air, reminding me of a bandit surprised by the sheriff in an old cowboy movie.

The park ranger chuckled out loud. "You can put your hands down," he said.

That was the moment I realized that, if the soup wasn't poisoned, I'd survive the night.

Ranger Rex, who with his little blond milk mustache looked to be about fourteen, had probably been off smoking Guerneville ganja.

"There's no camping overnight," he said, trying to sound official. "It's posted. And there are absolutely no fires in the park. You could have set the whole forest on fire. What were you thinking?" His light still shining on us, the baby ranger tried to shame us. "You guys look all messed up," he said, "but you don't look like you're homeless. How could you act so irresponsibly?"

Yevtushenko thickened his accent and said, "I don't so good read sign in English."

The ranger shook his head, and then stared at me.

"It was a lapse in judgment," I said.

After we were given citations, we walked back to our cars, parked just outside the grove. I asked Yevtushenko if he was sober enough to drive. I probably should have taken his keys, but I didn't want to be stuck with him. By now, any nobility I had was shot.

Before climbing into his old Skylark, Yevtushenko said, "Remember what I warn you."

CHAPTER TWENTY-ONE

What Happened to You?

IT WAS 3 AM by the time I drove off toward Cazadero. A few miles up the road, just past Monte Rio, I felt the hand of sleep slip over my face. The creeping paw forced me to park at the next pullout, where I granted myself a fifteen-minute nap. Five hours later, just after eight, I woke myself up, bouncing against the steering wheel and engaging the horn.

Half an hour later, I was surprised to find my homely chartreuse Neon parked in front of Sabbatini's cabin. It looked as if it had had a fresh visit to the car wash. I peeked inside to make sure it was mine. A shiny black Lincoln Town Car was parked beside it. The sight of the fancy, limo-style vehicle gave me a fright, as if it belonged to a messenger with grim tidings.

Quince was sitting at the dining table along with Blossom and a small man in a gray suit. I reminded myself of Yevtushenko's injunction. Was I about to face the killer? It was hard for me to take the idea seriously, but I still wasn't anxious to see her.

Blossom broke the ice in her inimitable way. "God, Augie, what happened to you? Did you sleep in the car, for crying out loud?"

"Matter of fact."

"And you really should have somebody look at your nose."

Quince had dropped her hands over her mouth at the first sighting of my rearranged face. She looked like she wanted to rush toward me. With what intention?

"Augie," she said, "I'd like you to meet my colleague . . . my former colleague, Dmitri." The man stood and extended his hand toward me. He was a gnomish fellow in his forties with a crooked smile reminiscent of Dick Cheney's, but with charm.

"It is my pleasure, Mr. Boyer," the man said, in a clipped English accent. "Dmitri Lermantov. I've heard many good things about you. You have some big fans around here, and from what I understand, you've only just arrived."

I was momentarily tongue-tied. "It's a strange place," I managed.

"Indeed," the Russian said, rolling his head around comically like a bobblehead doll, "we've noticed. Sit down, please." Dmitri motioned toward the empty chair.

Once seated, the clammy awkwardness of the scene kicked in. I wished for a deck of cards and for somebody to deal a hand. I'd be fine with losing whatever I had left in a game of penny-ante poker. Dmitri smiled at me and I smiled back.

"So, which one of you is no longer with the company?" I asked.

"That would be me," said Quince.

I tried not to look at her, though I'd noticed her short skirt and that she was wearing flip-flops. It looked as if her toes had been given a fresh coat of fuchsia polish. I shifted my attention to Blossom. She had her hands wrapped around a cup of coffee and looked groggy in her yellow chenille bathrobe.

"Augie," Quince said, "I'm sorry about borrowing your car without asking. I can explain."

I shrugged and kept my eyes trained on Blossom, who made a point of sniffling and blowing her nose into an old tissue pulled from the pocket of her robe.

Blossom looked up at me. "You really ought to have that thing reset."

"They need to wait for the swelling to go down."

A short silence fell across the table. I peeked at the Russian's hands. They were as Manzy had described them—impeccably manicured. The dandy wore gold rings on each of his pinkies.

"Mrs. Sabbatini," Dmitri said, clearing his throat for emphasis, "again, forgive me for the inopportune timing of my visit. My plane leaves earlier than I'd like from the city, and, as soon as I'd heard about Bobby taking ill, I wanted to pay my respects."

Blossom nodded, appearing thoroughly disinterested in Dmitri's patter.

"As I was starting to tell you earlier, we've come to the regrettable conclusion that building a casino on the Russian River isn't a viable option. Of course, this will have no implication regarding the funds advanced to your husband. This, we understand, is one of the many expenses of doing business."

Blossom made a queer, snickering sound and then stood up. She looked like she needed to sit down again, but managed to get as far as the old refrigerator, which she leaned against for balance.

The Russian stood. "Are you okay, Mrs. Sabbatini?"

With a wave of her hand, Blossom dismissed him. She looked directly at Quince and me. "I feel crummy. I don't know what they gave me at the hospital, but it didn't agree with me. I'm going back to bed. Will you guys do me a couple of favors? When Milosz wakes up, would one of you feed and change him?"

"Sure," the faux wife said.

"Thanks, Quince. And when Bobby calls and is ready to go, will one of you pick him up?"

I nodded. "I'd be happy to."

"Mrs. Sabbatini," the Russian said with a bow, "I hope you feel better soon. Please pass on my regards to Mr. Sabbatini."

"Thank you." Blossom nodded to Dmitri and gave that queer chuckle again as she stumbled toward the bedroom.

Irresistible

Once Blossom departed, Quince asked if she and Dmitri could explain some "developments" to me.

"Sure, what's up?" I regarded Quince with as much contempt as I could muster.

"Yes," Dmitri said, his fancy hands clasped behind his back, "let me explain the way things unfolded yesterday."

"By all means," I said, failing to repress a snicker.

"One of the locals we've worked with is a man you also know, Gordon Cust. It turned out to be a poor decision on our part to have anything to do with him. He's a very unscrupulous man."

I wondered if Dmitri was talking about a dead man.

"Well, I can't say Custard's one of my favorites," I said, pointing to my nose. "He left me with quite the souvenir."

"What a shame," Dmitri said.

Quince purred in sympathy.

"We think Mr. Cust may be responsible for the attacks on Deputy Coolican," the Russian said.

"Who's we?" I asked.

"Quince and I," the Russian said.

Quince stood up and began pacing. Against my will, I followed her steps with my eyes.

"When you went for your massage yesterday," Quince began, "Coolican drove over to Guerneville, and as he parked in front of the hardware store, an arrow shattered his passenger side window and penetrated his headrest."

I must have been holding my breath as Quince spoke because I exhaled, at this point, in stunned relief.

"When Coolican peeked through the shattered window, he saw Custard's green truck taking off west on 116. Coolican tried to chase after him but couldn't keep up in his old Corolla. That's when he called here looking for Bobby. It was just after you called. I told him you were probably having Bobby pick you up."

I slumped in my chair.

"Coolican was spooked and had driven out to a retreat he has north of Jenner and asked me to come for him because his Corolla was spurting oil."

"So you drove out there?"

Quince's pacing came to a stop. "Yes."

"And he wanted to stop at the River Rose."

"He thought Custard might be inside. His truck was parked outside, but Custard wasn't in there."

"He was driving with Sabbatini and me."

"That's what we heard. We tried to reach Bobby on his cell, but he must have had it turned off."

Dmitri's small head bobbed back and forth, trying to follow our conversation.

"What did you do after that?" I asked. "How come you didn't come back here last night?"

"I was freaked out," she said. "I went by the resort where Dmitri was staying in Rio Nido and rented a room. Then I took a sedative and checked out. Any more questions?"

I shook my head.

At this point, Milosz woke up and began wailing.

"I'll get him," Quince said.

"No, I will." I followed Quince into the baby's room and relented, watching her deftly handle the diapering chores, cooing at Milosz throughout the process. It was hard to feature her as a killer.

"You're good at that," I said.

Without looking up, Quince responded, "I have three younger sisters."

Dmitri was standing by the door, thumbing a text message, when we returned. He smiled at the baby in Quince's arms. "You look good with a baby, my dear."

Quince smiled and sniffed at Milosz's head. "I love the way he smells."

Dmitri gave me a half bow and said, "Very good to meet you, Mr. Boyer. I'm off."

I shook the Russian's hand. "One question before you leave."

"About Mr. Cust?"

"No, about your colleague here."

"My former colleague."

"I resigned, Augie."

"Right. Now, Mr. Lermantov, tell me why Vlady from the River Rose called me last night, terrified that Quince was out to get him."

"He said that?" Quince cried in alarm.

"Well, he was mistaken. He has Russian nerves," said Dmitri. "The only danger this woman presents is for men who fall in love with her."

"You sound as if you speak from experience."

"No comment."

I was getting tired hearing about the irresistibility of these women. First Ruthie and now Quince. It seemed as absurd a notion as love at first sight, a condition to which I'd recently fallen victim.

Quince handed Milosz off to me as Dmitri gave her a hug. "Don't be a stranger, my dear. We will expect a visit from you when you come through Reno."

I shook hands once more with the Russian and was glad to see him leave.

After we set up Milosz in the corner with a fleet of small trucks, Quince and I took a long look at each other. She leaned against the wall beside a framed broadside of a poem by Robert Hass. I read the poem's title—"The Problem with Describing Trees." I'd have no problem describing the way Quince looked. God, her legs were lovely in her short skirt, her eyes wistful, her lips cutely scrunched in an expression of contrition. The problem began if I tried to describe how I felt about her.

I bit my lower lip. Was she the killer? I figured not. It didn't add up. Even the world's best con artist could not fake the terror I saw in her eyes on the night of the flying arrow. Still, I didn't trust the woman. She smiled at me, barely parting her lips. Could I hold her responsible for the fact that I couldn't resist her?

What tempts him
is on the far side of a window
he's unwilling to close.

Showering with the Enemy

After I watched Quince heat a bottle and feed and burp the boy, with a clean diaper draped over her shoulder, she said, "You look like you really had a hard night. Why don't you take a shower, Augie? Then we can talk."

It was as if the woman had hypnotized me. Maybe she had. I'd like to think it was my weakened condition that left me vulnerable. That I'd been going for days with little sense of my bearings. "Take off your clothes," she said in calm, even tones.

I just stood there as she lifted Milosz into his high chair and wrapped a Velcro bib around his neck. My mouth fell open as Quince fed the boy stewed apples and graham crackers.

"Just get into the shower."

I hung my head. I stank. My clothes were smeared with blood and probably vomit.

"I don't even have a change of clothes here," I said. "Everything's at Coolican's."

"I'll lay out some of Bobby's clothes for you. They're loose enough that they should fit you."

Two minutes under the hot water, and I heard the bathroom door open. Next thing I knew, it was the door to the shower. Quince stood there naked. After the initial shock of flesh, it occurred to me that the woman might be hiding a knife. Was this my *Psycho* moment? I stood still in the steam, under the steady blast of hot water, trying to see more than I could see. Hard as it was to do, I forced myself to focus on Quince's eyes. Were the large, green, smiling orbs filled with treachery or simply amused by the absurdity of the moment? I couldn't decide. I took in the rest of her. The small, melon-shaped breasts with rosy nipples, thick and rounded as fresh berries. The slender flanks and smooth belly. The trimmed tawny brown of her bush. The long taper of her legs leading to the small feet, and the nails painted a pale fuchsia that nearly matched her nipples. The sight of her small feet gave me pause, as I remembered Yevtushenko's wild assertion.

"Is there any hot water left?" Quince asked.

"Where's Milosz?"

"In the playpen," she said, and reached for my cock.

I pushed her away, feeling my breath constrict.

"Can't I give you a little pleasure?" Quince asked.

"I don't trust you."

"What does that have to do with anything?"

"I'm not one of your clients," I said, noticing how the tufts of her bush had become matted under the shower.

"And I don't want anything from you," she said, "but you."

"That's quite a lot."

"Just share what you want," Quince said, smiling at me sweetly.

With that, I relaxed and Quince grabbed hold of me. Before I knew it she was working me into a lather. I suppose I could have protested. Absent all will, I might have cried, "Rape!" But then she bent over, and with no trouble at all, I slipped inside her from behind. We went at it for a good five minutes until she came, or pretended to, and I most definitely shot my wad, just as the water turned cold. Quince let out a little squeal and was gone.

Showering with the enemy is not all it's made out to be. As I toweled off, more confused than ever, I noticed a clean pile of clothes sitting on a wicker stool just inside the bathroom door. I panicked at first when I didn't see my dirty clothes. What had happened to my keys, my phone, my wallet? Had the last vestiges of my identity been pilfered? But then I saw the contents of my pockets in a small plastic bowl by the sink. It may have been a food bowl for a pet, but it reminded me of the little bowls they provide to clear your pockets at airline security. I wondered if what I had just experienced with Quince constituted a strip search. Had I already been through security, or was I still on my way?

Half dry, I stood naked in front of the mirror, trying to assess whether Quince had been through my wallet. Although nothing looked amiss, she'd clearly perused it. Not much to learn aside from the fact that I'm a peasant and a type O positive blood donor. Perhaps she uncovered a few scraps of paper with local phone numbers scrawled across them. Nothing she probably didn't already have. My phone had little to offer since my lousy service didn't pick up calls in West County.

It was time to dress. I regarded with suspicion the pile of Bobby Sabbatini's clothes that had been set out for me. Before slipping them on, I smelled the boxer shorts and T-shirt to make sure they were clean. A faint fragrance of lavender. Then I pulled on a pair of Sabbatini's drawstring Sufi pants, printed with a pattern of gestural markings in red and black, reminiscent of a handsome Robert Motherwell print. Next, I fastened fat buttons into the stretched-out buttonholes of a threadbare Guatemalan shirt, a refugee from the 1960s. This wasn't the type of shirt police detective Bobby Sabbatini wore, even in his leisure. Hard to imagine the man had once been legendary for his sartorial splendor. Now he did his shopping at hippie thrift shops. There were no socks, only a pair of rubber-soled huaraches that fit my feet surprisingly well. I had to admit the duds were comfortable. I regarded myself in the mirror. The bruised, cubist nose. The discoloring, a marbled blue and black around the eyes. The look of a stunned animal. I might have been a prisoner of war in a third world country, or a peasant holy man stoned by a gang of bandits.

When I walked out to the living room, Quince was all smiles. She'd traded her skirt for tight jeans patched at the knees and an embroidered peasant blouse. She'd kicked aside her flip-flops and was sitting on the old mohair sofa with a couple of issues of *Poetry* magazine in her lap. That suggested another level of enemy infiltration.

I greeted Milosz, who was happily sequestered with a handful of Matchbox cars in the playpen. He chuckled at the look of me.

"You look refreshed," Quince said. "Would you like me to make you some breakfast?"

I wanted to say no. I wanted to say, "Fuck you." I wanted to fuck her again, properly. I wanted to change back into my old dirty clothes, gather my belongings, and hop into my rental car. I wanted to get the hell out of Northern California before it killed me. But, alas, I was hungry. Once I ate, I told myself, my energy and curiosity, and maybe even five cents of courage, would return.

"Sure," I said, "feed me."

Roadkill Bacon and Eggs

"I can make you a three-egg omelet. There's a very nice Gruyère here, with a side of wild boar bacon. Blossom and I had some of that yesterday morning. One of their friends brought them a hunk of smoked roadkill boar. It's really good."

"Sure, knock yourself out."

I sat down at the kitchen table and flipped off my huaraches.

Quince smiled at me. "You know, you look more like Bobby in those clothes than he does."

That comment struck us as funny and we both laughed a little sheepishly.

A moment later, Quince brought me a cup of coffee. "Milk? Sugar?"

"Just milk."

"There is no milk. Well, just one baby bottle left for Milosz."

"Then why did you ask?"

"So I'd know how you liked it."

I sipped at the black coffee and watched how deftly Quince handled the small knife, paring and dicing the shallots, cutting wafer-thin slices of the Gruyère for the omelet.

I found the smell of the gamey, roadkill bacon a bit repellent, but it didn't discourage my appetite when the plate was set in front of me.

Quince sat down across the table with nothing but coffee. I ate a moment in silence. The born-again wife popped up to pull a couple of slices of rye toast from the toaster. I watched her butter them on a small, chipped Fiesta Ware plate.

"You want jam?"

"If I say yes, is there going to be any?"

"There's orange marmalade."

"Fine."

Quince, digging in the fridge, stuck her arm out to show me another jar of preserves. "Fig," she called.

"Yeah, bring that one, please."

Even though Quince was playing my wife/slave, I still felt like the indentured one. I had to hand it to her, she was master of quite the range of personas—Appalachian ex-con, hired wife, kleptomaniac corporate witch, sexual adventurer, and now some sort of bohemian sophisticate. For all I knew, she was barely scratching the surface. The frightening part was that she appeared to be totally in control.

"How's the omelet?"

"Good."

"The bacon?"

I left the question open and watched Quince corral a nervous smile. Which role was she in? I winked at her. "How come you're not having anything to eat?"

"I thought I'd serve you first. But you haven't told me what you think of the bacon."

"It's surprisingly palatable."

"You're damning with faint praise."

"Well, I'm not exactly an expert on roadkill bacon, but from what I can tell, it doesn't taste like it's been poisoned." I smiled at her.

"Are you trying to make some sort of point, Augie?"

I nibbled on my toast and then pushed my plate aside and faced Quince. "Who the fuck are you?"

Quince left her mouth open a second so I could see her pretty white teeth and the bright tip of her tongue. "Or as we used to ask," she said, "how well do you need to know a person you fuck?"

"That was quite an accidental fuck."

Quince put a hand to her crotch. "That's what they all say."

I felt myself go hard again and Quince could tell. At first I crossed my legs and then rearranged myself in my chair.

Milosz, a country not heard from for some time, dropped a Matchbox car out of the playpen and started squawking.

"Would you mind getting that for him, Augie?" Quince asked, knowing that in order to oblige, I'd have to aim my hard dick into the middle of the big room. I demurred and Milosz kept screaming. Quince flashed me a lascivious smile and then hustled over and picked up the little car.

Of God and Love

Once Milosz was purring again, Quince turned to me. "You remember what Rumi said about God and making love?"

"No, I've forgotten."

Quince made little quote marks with her fingers. "'The way you make love, is the way God will be with you.'"

"That's quite a theory."

"I subscribe to it thoroughly."

"I'm in no position to doubt it."

Quince came over and planted her full lips on mine. In a lick, she was down to her panties and began peeling off my Sufi pants. I sat on a wicker chair and Quince climbed atop me. To my amazement, she was already swampy damp.

"You don't go in for a whole lot of foreplay, do you?"

She nodded. "I guess I won't be getting a lot of foreplay from God."

"Pity."

Off we went. I closed my eyes and opened my senses to the pleasure. Then a rogue thought wandered through my craw.

"I take it you're clean," I said, a fuck and a half too late.

"Clean as you are."

"Good," I said, "I'd hate to think of God giving you the clap."

At one point I opened my eyes and was surprised to see Quince's eyes opened wide, even as she worked vigorously to get over the mountain. There was no love lost in this fuck; we were cruising simply on the power of lust. I had a desire to hurt Quince. When she stuck her fingers in my open mouth, I bit them. When she stuck them back in, I bit them harder. I yanked hard on her hair, which each time seemed to send her into fresh rapture. I took hold of her narrow waist and hauled her up and down on my cock. She seemed to be going out of her head but still hadn't come, as far as I could tell.

I'd been well trained not to finish before my mate, but with Quince I didn't really give a damn, and, with a few more long, hard strokes, I let go, and made a point of groaning directly into Quince's left ear.

The wife was not going to be left behind, and rallied mightily to reach the summit. Her come scream was earsplitting. Not only did it set off Milosz on a crying jag, but it raised Blossom from her slumber. She came running in in her nightie, her chestnut hair mussed into a wild ring of fire.

"What the fuck are you two doing?" she hollered.

"Three guesses," said Quince, rising and falling a final time on what was left of me.

I looked at the large orbs of Blossom's breasts through her sheer nightie, the nipples hard as bullets. She shook her head, angrily, and hustled to the playpen to collect her baby boy. "You guys were supposed to be babysitting."

"Isn't this what you did when you babysat, Blossom?" Quince asked.

"What are you talking about?" the true mother and wife shouted.

"I always brought my boyfriend along."

"Yeah," Blossom agreed, "but not in the same room with the baby."

"Do you think he's been scarred for life?" Quince asked.

"Fuck you, Quince," Blossom said.

As she climbed off me, Quince whispered in my ear, "Good thing you didn't finish without me, or God would come quick whenever he fucked you."

Plenty of Milk

Blossom took Milosz into her bedroom to allow us a little space to pull ourselves together. I counted that as an act of kindness and hurried to get dressed as Quince dawdled.

"You in a rush?" she asked.

I shrugged and watched Quince pull on her tight jeans. That done, she put on water for another pot of coffee. I followed her to the stove. It was strange to walk behind her because I could feel my body gravitating toward her. I wanted to put an arm around her shoulder, to hold her close for a moment. Somehow, I kept myself from doing that. I opened the refrigerator and stared at a door filled with nutritional supplements, shelves of covered Tupperware containers, and two large glass bottles of organic milk.

"Something you want?" Quince asked.

"Nothing in here," I said, closing the door.

"It's not a very sexy display, is it?"

I didn't bother to answer, but turned toward Quince, whose lips formed a sexy pout.

"I'm curious why you told me there was no milk."

Quince closed her eyes for a moment. "I don't know. I guess I wanted to deny you something. Lord knows, I couldn't keep from giving my body to you."

As we sipped our coffees, the phone rang. I jumped to answer it. It was Sabbatini. I heard Blossom pick it up in the bedroom and hung up. A moment later, Blossom came out of the bedroom dressed, with Milosz in tow.

"That was Bobby," she said. "I'm going over to pick him up at the hospital. Can I trust you two with Milosz?"

"Absolutely," Quince said. She leapt up and grabbed Milosz by the hand.

"No more hanky-panky?"

Quince smiled like a Girl Scout. "No, I think we've got that out of our system."

"He'll want another bottle soon."

"There's plenty of milk," I said.

Blossom regarded me quizzically.

As she went out the door, Quince led Milosz to the far corner of the big room and tipped over a tin filled with Brio trains and tracks.

Quince turned toward me. "Are you going to play trains with us, Augie? Or is such an activity beneath you?"

CHAPTER TWENTY-TWO

Talking Murder

AFTER MY THIRD cup of coffee, I snapped to and tried to get some useful information from Quince. I sat cross-legged on the floor next to Milosz, as Thomas the Tank Engine and a small trail of freight trains made the rounds of the figure eight that Quince had deftly constructed from the straight and curved pieces of track. She hovered like the God of wooden cars, readjusting track that had gone wayward, rescuing dangling cars, lifting the drawbridge, and blowing a clay whistle that sounded surprisingly close to an actual train's. From time to time, Milosz made a high-pitched, birdlike sound, imitating the clay whistle. It was a tough climate for talking murder.

"I have some questions for you," I said, after Quince fitted a long tunnel in place.

"I expect you do." Quince raised her chin and looked directly at me.

"Did you and Coolican discuss Ruthie's murder?"

"A little bit."

"Has he got any theories?"

"Well, he's got this cockeyed notion that it's linked to Red Carpet Casinos."

"How does that play?"

Quince shook her head. "He has the idea that Ruthie was hired as an escort by one of the Russian principals."

"You mean either Dmitri, or . . . who's the other guy?"

"Boris. Yeah, that's what he thinks."

I didn't mention that this squared up with what Sister Everlast had told me. "And you don't buy that?" I asked.

Quince shook her head. "Well, I can imagine either or both of them hiring her to party with, but I can't see either murdering her."

"Things got a little carried away," I suggested.

"Not with these guys. They're good businessmen in an industry that's always under scrutiny."

I wondered about their business savvy after they threw away $50,000 on Sabbatini.

"They both go to great lengths to avoid controversy," Quince continued.

"But with alcohol and drugs and a little passion . . ."

"I don't believe either of those men is capable of passion," Quince said, trying to make a joke of it.

"No? Well, given what Dmitri implied, you speak from experience. So each of the Russians fucked you dispassionately?"

Quince glared at me. "Not entirely."

"So you contradict yourself."

"All I'm saying is that I don't believe either of them is capable of murder triggered by passion."

"And you base this on the way each of them fucked you?"

"You're working very hard to hurt me, aren't you, Augie?"

"Am I succeeding?"

Quince picked up the train whistle and blew it in several sharp bursts that got Milosz hooting.

"How about me?" I persisted. "Do you see me as being capable of murder?"

Quince shot me an ominous glance. "It's much more likely that you'll be murdered."

I paused to let her reply sink in. "One more question for you."

"Yes, sir."

"How'd you happen to have the keys to my rental car?"

A sheepish look spread across Quince's face. "I plucked them out of your pocket the night before."

"And what exactly was your reason for doing that?"

"I didn't want you to leave without me, Augie."

"You really expect me to believe that?"

Quince bent down over the trains and guided Thomas the Tank Engine and his followers around the figure eight. Instead of blowing the clay whistle again, she made the sound of an automobile revving, *vroom, vroom.*

Even Milosz seemed to sense that something was awry with that.

"That's not the sound a train makes," I said. "You fail the polygraph test."

"I'm not taking a polygraph."

"Hey, it's good enough for me to believe that you took my keys because you're a thief."

"Well, I suppose I'm only returning to my roots," Quince said. She opened her beautiful green eyes wide and smiled wistfully, in a breathtaking pantomime of innocence.

It Will Flame Out

I bristled with trepidation as I heard a car pulling up the steep dirt road to the cabin. It was too soon for Blossom to have returned with Sabbatini. I peeked out of a corner of the blanket covering the smashed front window and saw a polished white Coupe de Ville chugging our way. It looked to be a woman driving. Milosz waddled over to the window to have a look. I had to hold back his little hands, which wanted to grab the jagged edges of the broken glass.

I turned back toward Quince. "Who drives a shiny Cadillac around here?"

"You got me."

After a loud knock, Quince grabbed Milosz and I went to the door. A tall, pinched-face blonde in her late forties stood at the door. Dressed in striped wool slacks and a frilled blouse, with a large crucifix swinging between her breasts, she pushed right past me through the open door.

"Is that damn casino woman still here?" she asked.

I could hear Quince scurry with Milosz into the back. The mystery woman halted almost immediately and turned back toward me. "Oh, you're not Poesy. I thought you were Poesy. You're dressed just like him."

"Yes, I'm wearing his clothes. I didn't have a change of clothes handy." I extended my hand. "I'm Augie Boyer."

"Of course. Eileen Cust," she said, giving me a light shake with her large, bony hand. I could see her trying to make sense of my black eye and smashed nose. She actually grimaced as she took in the show. I didn't feel compelled to reveal the architect of my new look, at least not yet. But the woman looked familiar to me. A tall, plain-looking lady that I couldn't place.

She had no trouble placing me. "You're the one who took Gordon to the emergency room."

"Right. How's he doing?"

"Terrible. They're talking about organ failure. They have him on dialysis and attached to all sorts of other machines. He may not survive."

"I'm so sorry," I said, as Milosz squawked in one of the back rooms.

"Thank you. Poesy and Blossom aren't here? And that woman Quince, the so-called hired wife, whom we all know is really a casino whore—she's not here?"

"Who?" I asked, as if I hadn't heard.

"The casino whore, pardon my French."

"No . . . no, it's just me and Milosz." Who knows why I concocted this answer.

"Well, somebody poisoned, yes, somebody poisoned Gordon and I think those casino people are responsible. He won't tell me who it was. I heard they got dear Poesy as well. But not so badly. Not so badly."

"Yes, he was lucky. He's supposed to be coming home today."

"So, that's where Blossom is. I see."

"Is Mr. Cust conscious?"

"He goes in and out. I'd run directly to the sheriff if Gordon wasn't so opposed to their involvement, you know, in his business. It makes it all very tricky for me. I'm the county commissioner for District Five, you see, and I feel like I'm married to an outlaw."

With that, Mrs. Cust began to sob, her wiry body shaking back and forth. I wrapped an arm around her shoulder to steady her and peeked into the front room to be sure it was clear.

"Would you care to come in for a cup of tea?" I asked.

"Thank you very much," she said, whimpering. "That'd be very nice. Forgive me. Forgive me. I need to pull myself together."

I led Mrs. Cust to the mohair sofa. "Come have a seat. I'm going to put the water on and then go fetch Milosz. I have him in the back playpen."

I found Milosz and Quince huddled together on the floor beside Blossom and Sabbatini's bed.

"Why did you invite her in?" Quince hissed at me.

I hissed back, "Common decency."

Mrs. Cust was blowing her nose in a handkerchief when I returned to the front room a few moments later. I set a small pot of Earl Grey close to her on a crooked wicker side table.

"No Milosz?"

"No, he seemed content enough in his playpen."

"This is very nice of you," she said.

She took a quick look around the room at the thrift shop furniture and the bright, intense paintings, at the homemade bookcases filled with poetry volumes and the framed photos of poets. The faded wool blanket covering the broken window fluttered, as if to please her.

"It must be strange to stay in such an oddball place."

"Not for me. I'm sort of an oddball myself," I said.

Mrs. Cust smiled over at me and I felt like the pet cat. She sipped her tea. "Well, they always seemed like nice people."

"Absolutely."

"Gordon has great respect for Poesy. Of course, we all do. You wouldn't believe the influence he's had. Every book group in West County is memorizing poems now. And people who've never read a poem in their lives are walking around with books of poetry. We think it's just fine that people are reading all this poetry, just as long as they don't neglect the Good Book."

The woman smiled at me as she said this and her eyes grew steely. That's when I realized where I'd seen her. It was only the night before. She was the tall creature, her head wrapped in a scarf, standing outside First Christ River of Blood, spelling REPENT on the signboard.

"How about you, Mrs. Cust?"

"Me?"

"Do you have a favorite poet?"

"Oh, well. I admire Gerard Manley Hopkins, first and foremost."

And then she began to recite a Hopkins poem called "God's Grandeur" in a brittle, faux British accent.

The world is charged with the grandeur of God.
It will flame out, like shining from shook foil;
It gathers to a greatness, like the ooze of oil
Crushed. Why do men then now not reck his rod?
Generations have trod, have trod, have trod;
And all is seared with trade; bleared, smeared with toil;
And wears man's smudge and shares man's smell: the soil
Is bare now, nor can foot feel, being shod.

At this point, Milosz began to squawk so insistently in the back room that I excused myself. Quince asked me how long the tea party was going to go on, but I only shrugged in response. I returned with the boy in my arms, doing my best to keep him from squeezing my broken nose.

"Hello, Milosz," Mrs. Cust called, as I passed through to the kitchen with the boy. I secured him in his high chair, filled a plastic tub with Cheerios, and warmed a bottle of milk. Once he had his bottle, I returned to Mrs. Cust. Thankfully, she wasn't intent on finishing her Hopkins poem.

"Anyway," she said, "we all have high hopes for Ginsberg's Galley. It could be a genuine treasure in Guerneville. And the idea that Poesy could get Gordon, Gordon of all people, to memorize a poem—I can't tell you how amazing that is."

"Yes, he seemed like he was pretty close to getting that e. e. cummings under his belt."

"Oh, that man. To think of all I've put up with. All the lying and whoring around. All those drugs under my own roof, and me a public servant."

Mrs. Cust, her eyes filled with tears, poured down the rest of her tea. I smiled at her and refilled her cup.

The poor woman leaned toward me across the oak table. "I've told nobody this. Why I'm telling a complete stranger, I don't know. I've told nobody except my sister in Montana—the man used to beat me."

"I'm sorry."

She closed her eyes and the wrinkles on her forehead bunched together. "It would start with him slapping me at first. Of course, we don't like making a lot of public noise with our lives, do we? He'd put on these special gloves that were supposed to leave no scars, but by the time he was finished there were plenty of scars. Believe me."

"Yes, I do," I said. "Your husband managed to do this to me with just one punch."

"Oh, my God."

"He was very efficient."

"The animal. You know, he used to fight Golden Gloves."

"Yes, I heard."

"He was heavyweight champion of the county or the district, I don't know which." Mrs. Cust began sobbing, and her handkerchief was already soggy.

I handed her one of Sabbatini's clean handkerchiefs, which I'd grabbed from his bureau when I dressed in his duds.

"Thank you." Mrs. Cust patted her eyes and blew her nose. "Please accept my apology on behalf of Gordon, Mr. Boyer."

"He did apologize to me after the fact."

She shook her head. "And to think that you were good enough to take him to the emergency room after what he did to you." My tea partner poured down a second cup, and then she shook the teapot, which was all but empty. "Would you mind giving me a little more hot water?"

"Not at all." I filled the teakettle and turned on a front burner of the O'Keefe and Merritt, wondering if I'd ever get rid of the woman. I rather enjoyed thinking of Quince sitting in the back room, cursing me out. I wondered why the faux wife had chosen to go into hiding. Had she some secret history with strange Mrs. Cust? Had she seduced old Gordo along the way? Nothing seemed beyond the realm of possibility at this point.

Once I returned with the boiling water and filled the pot, Mrs. Cust looked like she was ready to start up again. She poured herself a cup of weak tea. "I'm not even going to let it steep. At a time like this, I really need to stay hydrated. Oh, that animal. I should have left him years ago." She dropped her hands over her face. "But what a thing to say, when the man is laying half dead in the hospital."

"I understand."

"Do you . . . do you have any idea who was responsible for this?"

I shook my head.

"They tell me it was marijuana edibles."

I nodded.

"I always said his sweet tooth would be his downfall, but I never expected it to be like this."

The Second Coming

I heard another car driving up the long dirt road. It was Sabbatini and Blossom coming in my rented Neon.

When the car doors slammed, I excused myself and carried Milosz with me out to the car to let them know about our visitor and the fact that Quince was hiding in the back room.

Sabbatini looked good. He seemed to have regained his messianic swagger. When he got a gander at me, dressed in his garb, he threw his head back with a hearty laugh. "Look, Blossom," he said, "at first I thought I was seeing myself, but now I realize that I have my first genuine disciple—Brother Augie."

Blossom took Milosz from me, cooed at him, and then turned toward her husband. "That's just what you need, Bobby, a fucking apostle. Don't encourage him, Augie. This whole episode has given his delusions fresh vitality. He thinks he embodies the second coming."

"Not at all," Sabbatini said, throwing his arms in the air like an Old Testament prophet. "Christ multiplied the fishes and the loaves, but my task is far simpler—to multiply the numbers of the poetry-friendly." With that, Sabbatini winked at me.

"He's mad," Blossom said, "but I love him." She gave both Milosz and Bobby a smooch and they did a little family hug. "I better go in and get rid of Mrs. Cust before Quince has a cow."

Sabbatini and I stayed outside a moment. He looked closely at my ruined face. "Poor Augie. Custard sure did a job on you."

I shrugged. "I've been told it lends my face a little character. So, you okay, man?"

The holy man nodded, "Fine. Lost a couple of pounds, though I wouldn't recommend the method." He couldn't take his eyes off my face. "Wow, Custard did that with his last punch."

"Has he died?"

"Not yet, but I don't think he's going to be throwing any more boilermakers."

Confession

Mrs. Cust was sitting with her head in her lap, crying. Sabbatini went over and gave her a hug. He was about to recite a poem of prayer by William Blake before Blossom stopped him.

"They let me in to see him, Eileen," Sabbatini said, "just before we left the hospital."

Mrs. Cust sat up straight and blew her nose in Sabbatini's hanky.

Blossom whispered into my ear, "Don't let him start reciting," and then excused herself to try and mollify Quince.

"Let me put on some more water," I said, and hid out in the kitchen, freshening the kettle and heating, in a dry frying pan, Sabbatini's favorite Sufi snack, an Afgan-style flatbread stuffed with spinach—the closest thing to a tea biscuit I could come up with.

The kitchen was a nice spot for eavesdropping, even if this was nothing more than a pastoral visit.

"I think he's going to hang on, Eileen. There's something he wants to tell us. I couldn't make out much that he said. He's hooked up to all those damn machines. I know he loves you."

Mrs. Cust was sobbing again. "Thank you, Poesy."

"You just have to take it easy, Eileen. Do you have a poet you're working on now?"

The poor woman sniffled for a moment and then answered, "Gerard Manley Hopkins."

"Who could be better? I couldn't think of a better poet for your needs."

But Mrs. Cust wasn't thinking about Hopkins any longer. "Oh, that damn man," she cried, "he was always trouble. I don't know if you're aware of our history, since you're relatively new to the area. We went out during high school in Sebastopol. I've never kept this a secret, but when I got pregnant, my father forced us to marry. Then I lost the baby. That pretty much says it all about our relationship—it's been a long, lousy ride to nowhere.

"And that man, always running around and, I'm ashamed to tell you this, roughing me up pretty badly. Here I am telling you everything, as if you were my minister."

"It's alright," Sabbatini said, his voice soothing. "At times like this, we must take comfort where we can."

"But then last fall, something snapped. I didn't know what it was. Gordon seemed content for the first time in years. He was gone a lot in the evenings, but when he got home he'd be quite pleasant. Then I realized that the man was in love. I hired somebody to tail him. You understand that in my position, I can't be the last person to discover things. This was about six months ago. It didn't take any time at all to find out whom Gordon was consorting with."

At this point, as I flipped the flat bread in the frying pan, I realized that Sabbatini had truly become the woman's confessor.

"At first I didn't want to believe it," she said, "even though I was handed incontrovertible proof. I suppose I went through all the stages of grief. You know, denial and all the rest. But finally I accepted the fact that my husband had fallen in love with a common whore. Don't get me wrong—I had sympathy for Ruthie Rosenberg when she first went astray. She was such a beautiful child. I knew her father well. A fine Jewish man. He tried so hard to make his little business in Guerneville thrive. He had no luck. He did everything for that child. Look what it got him. He was the one I really had sympathy for. Thank God he died before he saw what became of her."

I was so intent on listening to Mrs. Cust that the teakettle took me by surprise when it started whistling. I cut the spinach flatbread into pieces and put them on a plate, and then broke open a couple of satsuma tangerines and arranged them on another plate with a sliced Bosc pear that I'd given a good squeeze of fresh lime.

Thirteen Epiphanies

Once I walked into the big room with the repast, Mrs. Cust exclaimed, "And look what Gordon did to poor Mr. Boyer."

"Don't worry about Augie," Sabbatini said. "If I've ever known a resilient man, it's Augie Boyer."

"Yes, don't bother worrying about me, Mrs. Cust." I put the plates down and grabbed the teapot. "I'll be right back with some fresh tea."

Before I could retreat to my listening post in the kitchen, Sabbatini grabbed my arm. "And the thing about Augie is, he fully appreciates the healing power of poetry. Who are you reading now, man?"

"Wallace Stevens," I said, hoping to throw Sabbatini a curve.

"Wallace Stevens, what a great find for you, Augie. You know I have a rancher in Petaluma who's reading Stevens. At the Friday morning group a couple of weeks back, this guy claimed he was so affected by Stevens's 'Thirteen Ways of Looking at a Blackbird' that he vowed to stop shooting the wild turkeys that wreak havoc on his property."

I shot Sabbatini as wry a smile as I could manage with a broken face. "But, Bobby, what happens when the wild turkeys return and wreak havoc on his property? Isn't your rancher going to blame it on poetry?"

"No way, Augie. Once a man has really heard a poem—you know this—he's found something he's not going to relinquish. And for this man, Baron Rush, who had never looked at the world in this kind of way, that poem was nothing less than an epiphany. No, thirteen epiphanies."

Although he addressed me, Sabbatini nodded to Mrs. Cust as he spoke. Even in his Sufi-wear, he had the aspect of a born-again minister on good terms with God. Which, of course, was true, if you allow that his God was poetry. Anyway, what was the point of trying to slow down Bobby Sabbatini, the beloved Poesy? I nodded to Mrs. Cust, slipped away with the spent teapot, and was soon joined in the kitchen by Blossom and Milosz.

Food Fight

Blossom stuck Milosz back in his high chair, still littered with half-masticated Cheerios. She scrambled an egg for him and gave him a spoon and a little tub of applesauce with a shake of cinnamon. Meanwhile, I shook some raw almonds into a small bowl and built a little mound of crystallized ginger on a chipped saucer.

"How can we get rid of her," Blossom complained, "if you keep feeding her, and Bobby just stays out there holding her hand? I mean, he's treating her like she's the widow in some 1930s stage play."

"The woman's husband is dying."

"The world will be a better place for it."

"How did you get to be such a cold-blooded creature, Blossom?"

"Worked at it, of course. But, come on, how long does he have to go on with this stage drama?"

"Don't you get it, Blossom? She's talking. She's spilling what she's got and she happens to have a lot. Don't forget, Bobby was a detective for twenty-five years. He needs to enable her."

"Yeah, well, she's already fully enabled."

"He's not," I said, and pointed to Milosz, who couldn't get the little spoon in his mouth, but was doing a hell of a job flinging applesauce all over the room.

Blossom started cheering her boy on. "Isn't he cute?"

"You're encouraging him."

"Why the fuck not? Isn't he doing exactly what he's supposed to do?"

"I thought he was supposed to get some of the applesauce in his mouth."

"Does he look like a boy who's starving? No way. And besides, he's got bigger fish to fry. His curiosity is running rampant and that's the thing he has to satisfy. It's hard to believe you were ever a father, Augie."

"Hey," I said, with a sharper edge of defensiveness than I expected, "I was a good father. I just didn't encourage infant anarchy."

"There is no such thing. Milosz is doing exactly what he should be doing—experimenting with physics, exploring the properties of gravity. Look at him with that spoon; he's invented a fucking missile launcher."

Milosz, impervious to us, was giggling with pleasure. Blossom planted a small bunch of smooches on the top of his head. Then she kicked into baby talk. "Oh, you are so precocious. Yes, you are. Just a year and a half, and you're ready for your first major food fight."

"Very cool," I said, and then played what I thought was my trump card, "but guess who gets to clean it up."

After refilling Milosz's tub of applesauce from the big jar and sprinkling it again with cinnamon, Blossom looked back at me over her shoulder and said, "I'll have the wife clean it up."

"What wife? Is Bobby your wife?"

"No, Quince is back."

I started to get agitated. "What are you talking about? She was never your wife in the first place. That was fiction, Blossom. That was you guys just fucking with my head."

"Well, she wants to do the wife thing now, for real. We had a little powwow back there. You know, she's left the casino company."

"Yeah, but that doesn't mean she's going to stay around here and be your slave."

"Quince said that after being out here for a while, she could see the importance of Bobby's work. She really wants to support it."

"Bullshit."

"I think it was the book of Rumi poems that Bobby laid on her. Yeah, that was the catalyst. And you know what else she said? She said she's really fond of you, smashed-up face and everything."

I wanted to scream, but it was the precocious boy in the high chair who started hollering. He'd tossed his tub of applesauce, and now that it had splattered on the floor, he wanted it back.

I looked over at Blossom. She was beaming. "Did you see how far he threw that, Augie? Oh, I wish Bobby had seen that. I think we have ourselves a ballplayer."

Fly on the Wall

I fled to the main room with the nuts and ginger and was surprised to see Sabbatini sitting beside Mrs. Cust on the mohair couch. When

I put the plates down in front of her, Mrs. Cust nodded to me as if I were a servant.

"I'm sitting here gorging myself," she said, "and he keeps bringing more food."

It was a struggle to behave. I wanted to stick my tongue out at the woman. I was tired of being obsequious, sick of having my mind fucked with by just about everybody in this hallowed community. But I was also curious to hear what else Mrs. Cust had to say. It had gotten cold in the cabin. The fire was down to embers and I took some time rebuilding it. That done, I perched on the stool in front of it.

Mrs. Cust, as I hoped, carried on like I wasn't even there, and I achieved a status I'd always hoped for—fly on the wall. I studied Mrs. Cust for a moment, thinking again that she'd been the woman I'd noticed the night before, spelling REPENT multiple times on the signboard outside First Christ River of Blood. It struck me as such an odd time of night to be changing the sign. Maybe she'd just returned from visiting her dying husband at the hospital in Sebastopol.

The lanky woman pinched her mouth into a knot and then aimed her tongue at a molar, perhaps trying to free a wedged nugget of ginger. "I was told by my private investigator," she said, "that she was working out of a massage joint in Monte Rio called McCluhan's. The county's tried to close the place down a number of times because of reports of prostitution. Anyway my investigator—aren't you at all curious who I hired, Poesy?"

Sabbatini shook his head. "Only if you want me to know, Eileen."

"Well, it's Benjamin Pozniak over in Forestville. To think that I knew him when he was a kid and now he knows all there is to know about my dirty underwear."

"Oh, I know Ben," Sabbatini said. "Not to worry. He's a professional. He comes to my Tuesday morning group. Nice fella. He's working very hard on a long poem by Philip Levine."

"Benjamin tells me that that little harlot was paid by the casino people to work exclusively for Gordon. It's as if he had her on retainer. And you understand why the casino people were picking up the tab?"

"They wanted Gordon to persuade you to support the casino plan."

"Exactly. A man is bribed with a live whore to get his wife to comply. Isn't that rich?"

Mrs. Cust paused to stuff a handful of almonds and a couple of lumps of crystallized ginger into her mouth. Sabbatini took the opportunity to shrug and make a goofy face at me. He seemed ready to have the confession come to a close. I wondered if he had a Poesy version of penance to dish out to his confessees. Instead of Hail Marys and Our Fathers, perhaps he ordered a plum poem by William Carlos Williams and an Elemental Ode by Neruda.

"There's something else, Poesy," Mrs. Cust started up again. "Ben tells me that you were the recipient of a large sum of money from the casino people."

"Yes, that's true."

"And what are you doing in return for that money, if you don't mind my asking?"

"Not at all. Between you and me, Eileen, I'm saying nothing but good things about the casino that will never be built."

"How can you be sure it won't be built?"

"You know, and I know, Eileen, that no environmental impact study will ever support a casino with 180 hotel rooms along the river. The roads are insufficient and the septic system can't support anywhere close to that kind of volume. Furthermore, the community will rally against it, and, you, a very important voice as county commissioner from this district, will surely not support it."

"So, you've taken the money under false pretenses."

"Well, that's one way to look at it. I choose to see it as a gift. It makes Ginsberg's Galley possible, and Red Carpet Casinos has also agreed to build and stock a poetry library in Monte Rio. That building's due to commence very soon, as a goodwill gesture for the community."

"That's very shrewd of you, Poesy."

"Well," Sabbatini said, sucking on a hunk of ginger, "I think it's the community that will benefit in the end."

Mrs. Cust began sobbing again.

"Tell me what you're feeling, Eileen. I'm here to offer comfort."

"Oh, I don't know," the woman cried, before blowing her nose, with a bright honking sound, into Sabbatini's hanky. "It's just dawning on me that the man is going to die. In many ways, he was an awful man, Poesy, but I loved him. Listen to me, I'm talking about him as if he's already dead."

Sabbatini tugged the drawstring tighter on his Sufi pants as he stood, and then he bowed his head. Mrs. Cust rose, without being asked, dropped a hand over her breast, and bowed her head, as if she were pledging holy allegiance. There was no way I was going to stand. I poked a log in the fire and watched the high priest spread out his arms over the penitent in a gesture of benediction. Then he began to recite a section from William Carlos Williams's "Of Asphodel, That Greeny Flower."

As he came to the end of his portion, Sabbatini closed his eyes and brought both urgency and an exquisite tenderness into his voice. I have to admit, the effect was spellbinding.

Of asphodel, that greeny flower,
I come my sweet,
to sing to you!
My heart rouses
thinking to bring you news
of something
that concerns you
and concerns many men. Look at
what passes for the new.
You will not find it there but in
despised poems.
It is difficult

to get the news from poems
yet men die miserably every day
for lack
of what is found there.
Hear me out
for I too am concerned
and every man
who wants to die at peace in his bed
besides.

I turned away as the tears streamed down Mrs. Cust's face, not so much in deference to the woman's modesty but because I was afraid that I, too, might start bawling. The effect of Sabbatini's delivery was that cathartic. The man himself stood absolutely still, for a moment, like a conductor through whom the last chord of a major symphony was still resonating.

CHAPTER TWENTY-THREE

Children, Be Nice Now

"YOU MUST FEEL like you got some revenge," Quince said, standing at the fireplace. "Keeping me like a hostage in the back room."

"You could have come out any time," I said, winking at Sabbatini, who sat cross-legged in front of the fire.

Quince shook her head and her hair fell free from its loose braiding. "No way I was coming out here and listening to that madwoman rant about the casino."

"Don't you think she had the right to?"

"Why, because my former bosses paid for her husband's prostitute?"

"So what's your history with Mrs. Cust?"

"We have no history."

"But you slept with her husband?"

"The fuck I did. I wouldn't sleep with that creep."

"So why the backroom bit?"

Quince shrugged. "I just had a feeling."

"A likely story." I gazed over at Sabbatini, who, staring at the fire, had a beatific expression on his face. I expected him to say something like, *children, be nice now*, but he said nothing.

"You should have been out here to listen to Father Sabbatini comfort the soon-to-be widowed."

"I was listening by the open door. Even from a distance it was inspiring. My boss, Dmitri, couldn't get over Bobby's preaching."

"It's not preaching," Sabbatini corrected. "It's poetry."

"Dmitri came out to do some preliminary work on a possible site and to kick off a feasibility study. He ended up going to both Bobby's Tuesday- and Wednesday-morning groups. When he got back he told us that getting the poetry priest as an advocate was our first goal. You should know that Dmitri Lermantov is not the kind of man to sit around and read poetry."

Sabbatini looked up. "After the last year, I've come to believe that any man can find poetry." With that, the poetry priest unfolded himself from his squat and stood up. "I think I need a little rest. I'll leave you two to your own devices."

The phrase struck me as funny and it must have hit Quince in a similar way, because as soon as Sabbatini left the room, we both started laughing.

"You're afraid of my devices, aren't you?" Quince asked.

"I don't know what your game is. I don't know who you are."

"You keep saying that. Maybe you should take some time to find out."

"Who has time for such things?"

Quince aimed a hard look at me.

"What are you staring at?"

"A man who's afraid of his feelings."

Infiltrator

I grabbed my car keys from Blossom and decided to take a drive to try to clear my head. The last thing I wanted to think about was Quince. I stopped in Cazadero, parking in front of First Christ River of Blood.

I wanted to study Mrs. Cust's REPENT sign in the light of day. What did it mean? Who did she mean it for? All of us sinners? Was it a personal command I should take seriously?

As I sat there musing, a late-model Chevy pulled up beside me and a thin, fortyish man with a minister's collar climbed out. He wore a gray gabardine suit that looked older than he was. Locking his door with a click, he noticed me in the Neon and gave a little wave. I waved back. Apparently, that wasn't enough for him. He came over to the driver's side window and I lowered it.

"Can I help you?" he asked.

"No, I'm good."

"Oh, you're good. I'm glad to hear you're good," he said with a wry smile. "So you're not sitting here repenting."

I chuckled. "No, not particularly."

He turned and looked at the signboard. "It's a new message today. Someone must have changed it in the night. I like to allow the members of my parish the opportunity to express themselves. You're welcome to come in for a cup of coffee."

The reverend, I figured, might have more to offer me than a cup of coffee. "Thank you."

I followed him into a small office that featured a metal desk and bookshelf. A large crucifix with a bleeding Christ, appropriate for First Christ River of Blood, adorned the far wall.

"I'm Cecil Hyde," the minister said.

"Augie Boyer."

The man didn't seem to recognize my name. We shook hands and I watched Reverend Hyde drop a pre-measured packet into his coffee machine.

"So, are you just passing through, Mr. Boyer?"

"Yes, on vacation."

The reverend looked at me directly. "That looks like it must hurt," he said, indicating my nose.

"It's not as bad as it looks."

Reverend Hyde poured me a cup of coffee, even though the

coffeemaker wasn't quite finished and continued to drip sizzling drops on the base. "So, what's on your mind?" he asked.

I took his bait. "Well, everywhere I go, people are talking about this tavern that's opening next week in Guerneville."

The reverend grimaced. "Yes, it's called Ginsberg's Galley. A poetry karaoke bar, whatever that is." He poured himself a cup of coffee. "It sounds innocuous enough, even silly on the face of it. But the man who runs the place is a threat."

"Why's that?"

"I see him as a rabble-rouser. The man comes in here with the intention of shaking up the community."

"How so?"

"Well, he has a grand design."

"What is it?"

"To get everybody out here to memorize poetry. 'What's the problem there?' you ask. Well, I'll tell you what the problem is. He's putting ideas into people's heads."

"How does that make him any different than a minister like yourself?"

"That's just the thing. He's not a minister, he's not a messenger of God. He patterns himself after the Messiah, but all he is is the Antichrist. He's using the poetry, don't you see, to practice a form of mind control."

"Aren't you giving the man a little more power than he deserves?" I asked.

"'Poetry,' you say, 'who could be afraid of poetry?'" The reverend nodded rhythmically a few times. "I say, along with Matthew, 'Beware of false prophets who come in sheep's clothing, but inwardly they are ravening wolves.' Poetry. That's just this man's scam, his trick to draw them in. He's misleading people. Like sheep, they follow him. Where is he leading them? He's leading them away from God."

The reverend looked at me with a sneer and then nodded meaningfully, as if he'd just recognized a grave truth. "You're with his church, aren't you? Look at you, you're dressed just like him. You're one of his disciples, for God's sake. Wasting my time. Trying to trick me. You probably have a mouthful of poetry. You're ready to deceive. Get the hell out of here. Do not try and infiltrate my church. Do you hear me? I can see through your poetry. I can see the devil!"

Consolidation

As I drove out of Cazadero, a gray mist hung over the redwoods—the atmosphere was a decent reflection of my brain's condition. I almost pulled the car over at the intersection with Highway 116, the point at which a decision was required. But with no traffic at the stop sign, I sat there a moment and considered my choices. Turning right aimed me toward Jenner and the ocean, left toward Guerneville and the possibility of actual civilization beyond.

Still dressed in Sabbatini's Sufi-wear, as the miserable Reverend Hyde had reminded me, I decided to drive by Coolican's place in Guerneville to retrieve my bag of clothes. I doubted there'd be any sign of the deputy. When I had spoken with him the night before, he'd claimed to be in hiding, and Quince had corroborated his story. Once upon a time I'd had decent breaking-and-entering skills, but by age fifty I'd lost most of my nerve.

I saw no sign of Coolican at his place, and a rabid-sounding dog prowling the inside of the deputy's cottage, discouraged any idea of heroics on my part. There'd been no sign of a dog at Coolican's place when I was last there, but since then the world had changed.

I grabbed a latte at Coffee Bazaar and pondered the possibility of leaving everything behind in Sonoma County. My longtime friendships with Sabbatini and Blossom. Quince, the born-again wife, whom I'd fallen for hard before her rebirth. My spiffy new Swiss Army suitcase, a gift from Rose, filled with the best of my humble wardrobe. It was a lot to give up, but that motley collection of people and stuff hadn't left me with much besides a broken nose and the gaggle of grief and gloom that seemed to follow me everywhere.

Before I arrived at a decision, a tall, sketchy-looking character, perhaps in his early sixties, approached my table. His hair was tied back in a long, rusty-gray ponytail and he had a yellow pencil planted over his left ear. Rising out of one of his back pockets were a pair of drumsticks. Most remarkably, the man had small seashells braided into distinct strands of his kinky red beard.

"I'm taking predictions," he said, in such a matter-of-fact way that I played along with him.

"Predictions for what?"

"How long it's going to take me."

"Take you to do what?"

"To raise enough money to buy some edibles at Marvin's Gardens."

"What's Marvin's Gardens?" I asked.

"That's the dispensary in Guerneville. The good news is I'm legal. I've got my papers. I can purchase cannabis in all of its many forms at any dispensary in the state of California. You're probably like everybody else and don't want to hear the bad news. It's not just that I have insufficient funds, I also have a hole in my pocket."

I looked into the man's face. His expression was soft and tender and mad. He pulled a little notepad from his shirt pocket. "Care to make a prediction?"

"No, thanks," I said, but reached into my pocket and fished out a dollar for him.

"Cool," he said, clearly delighted, "that brings me 20 percent up the road to a Gypsy Gooball."

"Take care not to lose it."

"Exactly my thought." He opened his shirt to reveal a drawstring pouch hanging on a string around his neck. He opened it and stuffed the dollar in. "God bless you," he said. The man bowed to me before moving to the next table.

How nice, I thought, to have all of one's desires reduced to a Gypsy Gooball. It reminded me of a jazz trumpeter I met years ago during an investigation. In the course of an hour's interview, the trumpeter explained the true glory of being a heroin addict. "It's like you take all the problems you got, you know, problems making the rent, pussy problems, problems with your kids, problems with your gig, or your no-gig, and you roll them all together so you only have the one problem—getting yourself right. And that takes care of all of them. That's what we call consolidation."

Things as They Are

I picked up a couple of papers from an empty table. The *Press Democrat* from Santa Rosa had a story about Ruthie Rosenberg's murder. Although the sheriff's department had some fresh leads, everything pointed to the same assailant who'd killed the two kids, execution-style, north of Jenner. It seemed like it was going down pretty much as Coolican had expected. The report made no mention of the pair of small footprints at the probable murder site. The crossbow attacks in Guerneville and Cazadero also managed to fly under the radar.

The local weekly, the *North Bay Bohemian,* had a feature on Bobby Sabbatini and the impending opening of Ginsberg's Galley. The article talked about Sabbatini's far-reaching influence across West County, how poetry groups had sprouted up everywhere, encouraging their members to memorize fresh poems. A shop in Forestville was selling towels embroidered with lines from Emily Dickinson poems, and a Sebastopol healer talked about the holy bell the right poem rings in our bodies. In Sonoma, a dentist befriended by Sabbatini had started piping spoken poems into his office instead of music. "The patients are all positive about it," he said. "I find if they open up to it, poetry makes them wonderfully docile patients."

The article featured a sidebar in which local luminaries talked about the poets they were memorizing. Dorothy Allison was in love with Marianne Moore, while Tom Waits was doing Wallace Stevens, just like me. The singer-songwriter had far more ambition than I did.

He planned to memorize all thirty-three sections of "The Man with the Blue Guitar." The very idea of it made me ache to hear Waits bellow:

Things as they are
Are changed upon the blue guitar.

Have a Purpose

Without spending much time deliberating, I decided to drive east toward Santa Rosa and the interstate. I could get down to San Francisco in little more than an hour and, with any luck, hop a plane back to Minneapolis, chalk up my California vacation as a bust, and say the hell with it.

Just before I turned right to cross the river bridge, heading out of town, I saw my old buddy with the seashells braided in his beard, standing by the side of the road. He was hitchhiking, though, in a different direction than the dispensary he mentioned. Had he given up his ambition for a gooball? I pulled over and cleared the front seat for him.

"Thanks, man," he said, pulling his drumsticks out of his back pocket before sitting down. You heading to Sebastopol?"

"It's on my way. What about the Gypsy Gooball?"

"Ah, man, my fund-raising went dry. I figure I'll pan for gold outside the Whole Foods in Sebastopol. And the dispensary in Sebastopol has a very nice compassionate giving program."

"But do they have gooballs?"

My companion regarded me for a moment. "I must say that for a total stranger, you have a good feel for the contradictions and dilemmas that riddle my life. If I go in the direction I want to go, I starve. I go the other way and I thrive."

"It's the human condition."

"If you say so." The man stuck out his hand toward me. "I'm Redbone."

"Augie Boyer."

"Augie Boyer. Augie Boyer," he said, chewing on my name as if it were a gooball. "You're not from around here, are you?"

I shook my head.

"Whereabouts are you staying?"

"Cazadero."

"In town or off the grid?"

"I guess you'd say off the grid."

Redbone nodded his head approvingly. "Whereabouts?"

I took a long look at my interrogator and told myself to chill, to not get irritated with the questions, that this was probably the only time in my life I'd be grilled by a hitchhiker with seashells braided into his beard. "You know Poesy?" I asked.

"Of course, I know Poesy. I love Poesy. Poesy treated me to a whole gooball a couple of months ago."

Suddenly my one-dollar contribution to the Gypsy Gooball fund seemed awfully cheap.

"Yeah, Poesy got me to memorize a Theodore Roethke poem right on the spot. He told me I had a rare facility. But last time I saw him, he handed me a Robert Lowell poem." Redbone got an embarrassed look on his face. "I haven't learned it yet. It's not that I've got anything against the confessional school, per se, but Lowell's blue-blood weepiness just kind of rubs me the wrong way. How about you, Augie Boyer, how do you relate to the angst of blue bloods?"

I had to pause before answering. That was one of the more curious questions of a curious week. "I think angst in general is overrated," I said.

"No kidding," Redbone agreed. "You'd think it had some particular nutrient, that you could build a diet around it."

"The Angst and Gooball Diet," I suggested.

"No, thank you. Where there are gooballs, there's no need for angst."

I gazed over at my wild hitchhiker, not quite believing I was having this conversation.

"Funny thing," Redbone said, "you kind of remind me of Poesy. Maybe it's the clothes. So, you're staying with Poesy?"

I nodded.

"Wow. Staying with Poesy. That must be intense."

"You don't know the half of it."

"So what happened to your nose?"

"I kind of bumped into a redneck."

"You've got to be careful, Augie, they're the mad dogs of West County."

I nodded. "Tell me something, Redbone, did you know a woman named Ruthie Rosenberg?"

Redbone bunched his lips together as if to say, *mum's the word.* Then he hung his head. "I knew who she was, but I didn't know her. The sheriff had me over in Santa Rosa for four hours of questioning. They weren't very friendly."

I thought about Coolican's idea that the sheriff's department would be out trolling for drifters to pin the murder on. Redbone fit the bill, though he didn't seem capable of hurting a flea.

"They kept asking me where I lived and I kept answering, no place in particular. That didn't seem to satisfy them. They asked how I knew Ruthie Rosenberg, and when I said I never met her, they asked the same question over and over again. They asked how often I frequented prostitutes and when I said I'd never been to one in my life, which is the truth, they wanted to know how I got my sexual satisfaction. That's when I made the mistake of saying, 'That's none of your business.' We went round and round like that for hours. I think in the end they just got bored with me."

When I smiled at Redbone, I could see that he was already off somewhere else, clicking a rhythm with his tongue on his palate and gripping his drumsticks as if he were getting ready to attack a drum kit.

"Are you a drummer?"

"Yep, a drummer without skins at the moment. But the cool thing I've discovered is that the world is filled with surfaces to drum on. Mind?"

Before, I could respond, he'd executed a perfectly controlled drumroll on the padded dashboard.

"You're good, man."

"Yeah, I try not to let it go to my head."

I watched him drum for a while. He settled into a nice, medium tempo, four-four. You could see his left foot working an imaginary bass drum pedal.

"Jazz you're playing, isn't it?" I asked.

Redbone winked at me as he doubled time, and then clattered a roll on the door handle, as if he were attacking the hi-hat. Once we drove through Forestville, he started really driving the beat and scatting a brisk bebop tune.

"Sounds like the band was falling behind a little there," I suggested.

"It's my job to keep them honest," he said. "Sometimes that feels like my only purpose in life."

In Sebastopol, Redbone directed me to the Whole Foods in a small strip mall. "It's the best spot in town for fund-raising," he confided. "Maybe I'll load up like a squirrel in winter. Hit the dispensary like a fully leveraged trust fund bambino. Chow down on a Sesame Smoke Cookie and take a River Rust Rugala for the road."

As he was getting out of the car, Redbone paused and regarded me with so penetrating a glance, I was forced to look away. He shook my hand and said, "You look a little lost, Augie Boyer. Have a purpose, little brother. Have a purpose."

The mad drifter suggests
that, perhaps, it's me
who's drifted across the center line.

Interfacing with Spud

After parking in downtown Sebastopol, I realized that I needed to take a whiz. As I strolled up Main Street, I still felt stunned by Redbone's admonition. I lacked a sense of purpose. Nearly fifty-five years old and I didn't know what I was doing with my life. I was, however, alive, which distinguished me from Gordon Cust, who I figured by now had gone off to sample edibles on the other side.

It must have been the siren I heard, followed by the sight of the ambulance stuck in Main Street traffic, that made me realize that Palm Drive, the hospital where I'd taken Custard and Sabbatini, was only blocks away. It was worth a shot.

It turned out that Custard had not yet died. He was in intensive care, however, and visitors were not allowed. I'd been to the emergency room but hadn't seen the rest of the small hospital, so I made my way up and down a couple of hallways, surprised by the relative dearth of staff. At the end of the second hallway, I discovered the tiny intensive care unit. A pair of sheriff's deputies stood outside the room and I was happy to see that Spud, of the great red Idaho-shaped birthmark, was one of them.

"Hey, Spud, Augie Boyer."

"Augie."

We shook hands.

"What the hell happened to you, man?"

"Gordon Cust showed me why he was once a Golden Gloves champ."

"Ah, that's right, and you're the guy who brought Custard and Poesy into the emergency room. Isn't it just like Poesy to walk out the next day, while Custard hangs on by a thread?"

"Yeah, it's his luck that he only had one of the toxic bonbons. Custard must have chowed down on a dozen."

"He loved his edibles. You didn't eat any of them, huh, Augie?"

"No, Sabbatini had got me so ripped on Sea Ranch Tsunami that I wasn't looking for anything to top it off. I'm not in shape like you folks out here, so I have to pace myself."

"And look at you," Spud said, "you're dressed just like Poesy."

I didn't bother to explain.

"Tell me something," Spud said. "How come you and Custard interfaced?"

Spud's choice of verb amused me. But Custard had clearly interfaced with my nose.

"We were at the River Rose," I said, "and I must have bugged Custard with the questions I was asking."

"What kind of questions?" Spud wondered.

"I was asking about his relationship with Ruthie Rosenberg. And I kept asking after he told me to stop. I hadn't realized he'd been a boxer."

"So you were doing a little sleuthing on behalf of Coolican?"

"I guess you could say I was freelancing."

"So after Custard does this to you, you go joyriding with him?"

"Well, Sabbatini shows up and does his peacemaker thing. You know how he is. And Custard is really contrite. Doesn't stop apologizing. And before you know it, we're cruising around together and reciting poems."

"Did Custard say where he got the bonbons?"

"No, he wasn't telling."

"Coolican thinks he picked them up in Mendocino. He'd been up there, apparently, the day before."

The other deputy gave Spud a sideways frown. Apparently, he didn't like the information sharing.

I shrugged, trying to appear indifferent. "I wouldn't know. So you guys are standing out here to protect Custard in case anybody comes along to finish him off."

"Like you," the other deputy said.

Laughing, Spud said, "Hey, Augie, this is my partner Neil Wince."

Wince, who must have been in his early forties, was smiling now. We nodded to each other.

"He's a P.I. from Minnesota, a good friend of Poesy's. But get this, he's also Minnesota Rose's father," Spud added, as if that explained everything.

Deputy Wince drew a blank.

Spud shrugged. "The only music he listens to is baseball. So have you talked to Rose lately?"

"No, not since I've been out here. But I'll work on the autographed photos."

"Great."

I nodded toward intensive care. "So how's he doing in there?"

"Barely."

"Conscious?"

"He groans a little. One of the nurses said he was mumbling early this morning."

"Any way I can get in there to try to talk with him?"

Spud shook his head. "No can do. Naw, we can't let you in there, Augie."

"How about one of you comes in there with me? Custard and I went through a lot together yesterday. You know I did my damnedest to save his life. It might be good for the man's spirit to see what a right hand he still has, or at least had."

The two deputies stepped aside and conferred for a moment. I knew I was blowing smoke. At this point, Custard was probably brain-dead, but I had a hunch I wanted a chance to play. A doctor came out of Custard's room and the two deputies approached him, presumably asking about my request.

Rain or Hail

A minute later Spud and I were inside the intensive care suite. The room was lit so brightly I worried about radiation exposure. What a place to die. A male nurse, name-tagged LANCE, was bent over the patient, reinserting an IV. Custard had hoses and tubes coming out everywhere. A machine attached to him clicked every half second. Custard's eyes looked as if they were stitched closed. Oxygen streamed in through his nostrils, and his lips formed an *O*, as if, like every other redneck and tax-averse creep in the country, he was intent on cursing President Obama. Perhaps his dying word would be *Obamacare.* I doubted he was musing on *Occupy.*

"Custard," I called, "it's Augie."

Nurse Lance looked up at me as if I were as mad as a man trying to make conversation with an eggplant.

I persisted. "You got to open your eyes, man, to see the damage you did with that one shot to the nose."

"Yeah?" came a soft, hoarse, but unmistakable wheeze from the patient.

All three of us looked up in wonder. The shape of Custard's mouth had changed.

"No kidding, man. I'm like a walking Ripley's Believe It or Not. As soon as I tell people that it was just one punch that did this, they all shake their heads. Really. It seems like everybody in the county remembers you as a Golden Gloves champ even if they weren't alive during your glory years."

Custard still hadn't opened his eyes, but he managed to push out a few words. "Is Poesy here?"

Maybe that was Custard's way of asking for a priest. "No, he's not here. Just me and Deputy Spud."

The male nurse looked up at me as if he wanted to be acknowledged. I granted his wish. "Nurse Lance is here as well."

"Hey, Spud," the patient mumbled.

"Custard, how you feel?"

"I don't feel anything. Where's Poesy?"

"He's coming," I lied.

"The only thing in my head is that poem," Custard said. He went quiet for a long moment and I was afraid we'd heard the last from him. I kept chattering with him because I didn't want him to become an eggplant. Not yet.

"You know, it's only a week until Poesy opens the Galley," I said. "You got to get your poem down and recite it."

Spud and Nurse Lance each looked at me as if I were daft.

"Impossible," Custard muttered.

"What would Poesy say?"

"But I still can't remember it." After another silence, Custard began to say the poem in a creepy singsong. It was like listening to a dead man talking.

rain or hail
sam done
the best he kin
till they digged his hole

:sam was a man

stout as a bridge
rugged as a bear
slickern a weasel
how be you

"Damn," he whispered, "that's as far as I get anymore. I used to go further."

"I'll tell Poesy you've been working on it. You can be a man now, like Sam."

"How?"

"Tell us what you did with Ruthie Rosenberg."

Custard issued a sad, hoarse laugh. "I fucked her."

Spud looked at me like I was pushing things further than I should. Nurse Lance's head jerked up from a monitor. It seemed like he had nothing more to do but didn't want to go anywhere.

"And what else did you do with Ruthie?"

Custard made a long grunting sound, opened his mouth creakily wide, and sucked for a breath. I thought he was going to die right then before he could make himself useful.

"I loved her," he said, gasping.

"Yes."

"Never love a whore, Augie."

"I'm sure that's good advice."

"I thought she loved me. She didn't . . . love me. I found her . . . I found her with that Russian. She was . . . still with that Russian."

"Yevtushenko?"

"Yeah."

"So what did you do, Custard?"

"What did I do?"

"Yeah, what did you do to Ruthie?"

Custard finally lifted his eyelids. Two little slits. He looked around until he found me.

I met his eyes. "What did you do with Ruthie, Custard?"

His eyes opened wider. "She lied to me. She cheated me . . . She was the worst whore . . . She made you love her . . . A whore's not supposed . . . a whore's not supposed to do that."

I looked at Spud, whose eyes had grown large. I wished we had some sort of recording device but did not want to break the flow, if that's what you would call it.

"So you took her out to the Last Judgment Campground?"

"No, I never brought her out there. . . ." Custard looked around again, but didn't seem to be able to find me.

"I'm right here, Custard."

The man's lips twitched. "She was always stoned . . . stoned out of her mind. Stoned on crack."

"How about you?"

"I'd have my chocolate bars," he said, a dreamy expression on his face as he closed his eyes.

"And they didn't make you sick?"

"No, they were righteous. . . . I got sick if I drank too much Jack Daniel's."

"But not sick like this?"

"No. This is something special." Custard started to laugh, but pretty soon he was choking.

The nurse came over and tried to help Custard, who finally came out of it.

"She was so beautiful," Custard said, his eyes fluttering open again.

"But you killed her," I said.

Custard tried to find me again. "I didn't kill her . . . but they found her dead."

"You had nothing to do with it?"

Custard looked like he was trying to shake his head. His eyes were open but didn't look like they could see anymore. "I loved her," he whispered.

A moment later, Custard yanked the oxygen tubes out of his nostrils. Nurse Lance rushed over to reinsert them.

Custard flailed his arms in agitation. Once he'd settled down, I took hold of the man's large hand, the same right that had smashed me yesterday. "Custard, you would make this community rest a lot easier if you confessed to killing Ruthie."

"But I didn't kill her," he whispered. "I loved her."

I looked away and caught Nurse Lance's glare. Spud had a grimace on his face. Custard closed his eyes and never opened them again. I had more things to ask him, but simply shook my head. I felt like I'd been beaten at my own game. Custard's breaths became shallower, but his lips were moving again. I couldn't hear him and bent my ear down toward his mouth.

rain or hail
sam done
the best he kin
till they digged . . .

Custard's mouth hung open a minute and his head jerked forward. Nurse Lance quickly called a code blue, but before the crew arrived, the bastard was dead.

CHAPTER TWENTY-FOUR

Two Funerals

MY FAILED ATTEMPT to extract a deathbed confession from Custard had the effect of reattaching me to the community. I no longer felt like I could simply drive away. At Bobby and Blossom's, where I now shared a bedroom with "Aunt" Quince, I became Uncle Augie. The reborn wife seemed to be finished with all her tricks, though I had trouble believing that would last. I made a silent pledge to stay through the opening of Ginsberg's Galley. After that, all bets were off.

In the next week there were two funerals, though Custard's was, at the widow's request, a private graveside burial in Forestville. The word from Deputy Spud, who witnessed it, officially, from a respectful distance, was that besides Mrs. Cust and her minister, only a few family members attended.

For some reason, the private burial gave further credence to the widely accepted view that Custard was indeed Ruthie Rosenberg's killer, even if he'd denied it on his deathbed. I wasn't sure how this followed, but it spared the community a bit of soul-searching. People wanted to begin the healing process after Ruthie Rosenberg's murder, and this was the most convenient way of achieving closure.

Of course, the sheriff's department would piddle along with its investigation and Custard would end up the presumed killer, just as the anonymous drifter got all the credit for killing the two Christian campers on Fish Head Beach.

I thought long and hard about whether I should stick my broken nose any further into the matter of Ruthie's Rosenberg's murder and decided, sadly, that I was out of my league. I also realized that wherever I went, my smashed-up face was taken as further proof of Custard's violence. Plenty of questions remained open: Who poisoned Gordon Cust? Who fired arrows at Jesse Coolican? And what about the trails of small footsteps, barefoot and not, at the presumed location of Ruthie Rosenberg's murder?

I posed the last question at different times to Deputies Spud and Coolican. Their answers were eerily in concert—the small footprints were inconclusive and couldn't be definitively tied to the time of Ruthie Rosenberg's murder.

It was as if the community had chosen to put the horror behind it, as if the entire population of West County had buried these dark mysteries with Gordon Cust, as if they'd all chosen to get fuck-faced together.

The memorial for Ruthie Rosenberg was a sad affair. Blossom, Sabbatini, Quince, and I drove out to the ocean together in the sanitized Volvo. Several dozen people gathered at Portuguese Beach, south of Jenner, to say a few words and scatter Ruthie's ashes. It was a bright spring day with a faint breeze, too nice a day for a memorial.

Sabbatini, acting as the chaplain, had us gather in a large circle. I found it touching to see Coolican and Yevtushenko, two of Ruthie's former lovers, standing side by side.

The Russian wore a black fedora and a dark suit that was a size too small. He looked like a cross between a small-time gangster and an immigrant undertaker. "Ruthie," he said, tearing up as soon as he pronounced her name, "she had the demon inside her. I had always hope it would go away, because she is so loving, so beautiful. But then she's smothered by that terrible demon, that monster."

Yevtushenko talked about how much Ruthie loved to dance, how he'd even taken tango lessons in Sebastopol to try and keep up with her. "Still," he said, trying to make a joke, "I step on her toes." But by then the emotion had gotten the better of him and he pulled out a handkerchief and began crying in earnest. At that point Quince grabbed my hand and I could see tears forming in the corners of her eyes.

Coolican, dressed in his deputy's uniform, stepped forward into the mourning circle and took off his hat. "Ruth Ann Rosenberg," the deputy intoned, before bowing his head.

I found myself thinking, *Gosh, the nameless dame actually had three names, but did they give her an identity?*

"Ruth Ann Rosenberg," Coolican repeated. "I used to say her names over and over, as if by repeating them I could somehow make her love me." Coolican pulled out a handkerchief and wiped his eyes.

"I went to school with Ruthie and worked for her father. She ran with the fast kids and I was a slow kid. I minded the books and was pretty much a loner. She was so beautiful, everybody fell in love with her. Of course, I did, too. But I think what got me was her mind. If you knew her, you knew how philosophical she could be. She had so many questions, the kind nobody can answer."

As Coolican spoke, I looked at the faces I knew in the crowd. There was Sister Everlast, muscles bursting in a sleeveless black sheath, while the tears streamed down her cheeks. I nodded to Sky and her friend Patty, and I exchanged sad smiles with Manzy. At first I didn't recognize the tall woman standing behind the circle in a dark suit and veiled hat, but then I realized it was Mrs. Cust paying her respects.

Coolican rocked back and forth like an old Jew in prayer. "I think she relied on drugs to quiet the questions. I remember one time in her early twenties she asked if I thought she'd changed from a girl into a woman. 'I always thought a bell would ring,' she said. 'I imagined a great gong tolling inside me, but I haven't heard anything like that.' I told her that she was most definitely a woman. Then she just stared at me with those big eyes. I didn't know what to tell her; I never knew what to tell her. This was after I went to college, and Ruthie, like a lot of people, thought I actually knew something. I bowed my head. 'You must have missed it, Ruthie,' I said. 'You are already a woman.' I don't know if she believed me, but I'll never forget her smile that day."

Coolican bit his lower lip and nodded rhythmically a few more times. "Ruthie was a woman."

I heard Blossom, standing on the other side of Quince, whisper to her, "Damn, this is an A-1 tearjerker." And even Blossom the Cynical, which is what I sometimes called her when she was in my employ, started sniffling. She tugged on her black velour hat, with its faux rhinestone pin, and shivered, as if a chill of emotion had broken over her.

Bobby Sabbatini spoke last. He told about Ruthie coming to his Thursday-morning group and how, sometimes, it was clear that she hadn't been to bed the night before. "One time she stayed after the group to chat and I asked her how come she never recited a poem like the others. 'Poetry is for good people,' she said, 'I just get to listen.' I told her that she *was* a good woman and that poetry was for everybody. I lent her a fat poetry anthology and talked about poetry being a lifeline, a way for her to save her life. Maybe a week later, I saw her walking on the street in Guerneville. She was excited to see me. She said she's just memorized a tiny poem that she'd recite at the next Thursday group. But she never came back to the group. This is the poem, by Marianne Moore, that she memorized.

I, too, dislike it.
reading it, however, with a perfect contempt for it, one dis-
covers in
it, after all, a place for the genuine.

The Moment in Question

The day before the opening of Ginsberg's Galley, I had a lot on my mind. In thirty-six hours, I was due to head back to Minnesota, a reality that had begun to loom large for Quince and me. She'd even begun to talk nonsense about returning with me to the Twin Cities. It's true, we'd spent some lovely time together in the last week and felt that once we got past the high jinks of our tortured beginning, we actually fit each other well.

Toward the end of the week, Blossom granted Quince a two-day furlough from her wifely duties and we drove up into the not-so-wild wilds of Mendocino. One night we built a fire at Glass Beach, near Fort Bragg, and talked about the possibility of putting our lives together. Much as I liked the sheer madness of the idea, I didn't see it happening. The challenge seemed overwhelming.

In the firelight at Glass Beach, I could make out Quince's face. She seemed both calm and vulnerable. "I'm not saying forever and ever," she said. "And I realize that I can never replace your wife."

I'd made the mistake of confessing the difficulty I had getting over Nina's leaving me. "You don't need to replace anyone," I said.

"Well, you seem like a guy with a big hole to fill and I don't know if I'm the gal for the job."

"Then why do you want to be with me?"

"Are you fishing for compliments?" Quince asked.

I spit into the fire and listened to its brief sizzle. "No, I'm just trying to understand your logic."

"Love and logic don't go together."

"You're very clever," I said. "Aren't you?"

"You don't seem like the kind of man to fall for a dumb woman." She kissed me and whispered, "It doesn't have to be forever. Let's live in the moment."

It was a fine sentiment but, stung in the past, I felt wary of the present and doubtful about the future.

Identity Theft

On the afternoon before the big event, Quince and I drove to Identity Theft, the mask shop in the town of Graton. Sabbatini had been after us for the last week to get over there before we were left with the face of a poet we didn't care for. But it wasn't poet masks I noticed when we first walked into the shop. I saw Lady Gaga in enormous shades, a cherubic Michelle Obama with a Good Housekeeping Seal of Approval plastered on her forehead. Dylan appeared pinched at seventy, with a string tie that made me think of Custard. Had he been buried in his agate string tie?

Then there were the politicos: W. as an infant, Sarah Palin with one eye shut in a perpetual wink, Obama himself as a 1940s hipster in a porkpie hat, a cigarette hanging out of the corner of his mouth. I stopped to admire a lovely grotesque of Newt Gingrich, so pink that it looked as if it had been carved from a ham.

Quince laughed with me in front of Newt. "The historian himself. These are cool and all, but there aren't any poets here."

The proprietor must have overhead her. "Oh, are you guys Poesies?" he asked. "We've got a special gallery of Poesy's poets in the back. We've had Poesies coming in for those masks from all over the county."

I stood with my mouth open for a moment, slowly understanding that the term *Poesies* now referred to Sabbatini's disciples and that the county was crawling with them.

The man extended a hairy hand to me and then to Quince. "I'm Edgar," he said. "We're a little picked over, but I'm sure you'll find someone you like."

He led us into a back gallery filled with the masks of poets. Despite being impressed by Sister Everlast's Ezra Pound, I wasn't prepared for such an array of witty and imaginatively conceived likenesses.

The masks, formed of some sort of high-tech papier-mâché, utilized digital screen prints of the poets' mugs enhanced with bright touches of metallic paint. Some of the masks were adorned with facial hair, others with characteristic hairpieces or hats. This late in the game, there were still a couple of dozen masks left, all placed artfully over the faces of full-size manikins.

I tried on Langston Hughes, T. S. Eliot, and Shakespeare, whose visage Quince raved about. The bard had been given the requisite high forehead and a wispy mustache, crafted of horsehair dyed a dusky brown hue. The lips were a beautifully unnatural magenta, with a good-size mouth hole, allowing the wearer plenty of room for sticking out his tongue.

When I donned the mask, Quince rushed over and planted a big kiss on the gaudy lips, before sliding her tongue through the mouth hole to play with mine.

"Oh, I love you as Willie," she exclaimed. "How about every time I kiss you, you recite a sonnet?"

"Well, here's the rub," I said in my best Elizabethan brogue, "seeing that I have yet to commit a single sonnet to memory, you'll have to keep your kisses to a minimum."

"That won't do," Quince replied.

When I slipped off the mask, Quince was all over me, embracing me as if I'd just returned from a long trip.

Once she got over her disappointment that there were no masks of Rumi, the great Sufi master, Quince became adventurous. We agreed that the Anne Sexton mask was too severe, the Emily Dickinson too spinsterish. Quince tried on a few others. Neither the Denise Levertov or the Sylvia Plath captured her imagination, but she did a little jump after donning Marianne Moore's tricornered hat and mask. I left her sashaying in front of the full-length mirror, the sexiest incarnation of M. M. the world had ever seen.

As we looked around in the gallery a little longer, I spotted Wallace Stevens, the poet whom I most wanted to embody. I slipped on the beautifully stoic mask. The bland businessman's mug had a knotted tie attached below the chin, and each cheek bore rosy moles, uncharacteristic to Stevens, giving Wallace the look of a Pierrot painted by Rouault.

It was as Marianne Moore and Wallace Stevens that we greeted Jesse Coolican, when he strolled into Identity Theft. He seemed a little bit unnerved to discover that it was Quince and me behind the poet masks. I had seen Coolican only once since Ruthie Rosenberg's memorial service, and he'd been rather distant, no longer willing to entertain questions about her possible murderer.

My affectionate greeting, delivered with one of Wallace Stevens's signature lines, "You understand, good Deputy Coolican, that *the only emperor is the emperor of ice cream,*" was greeted with an indifferent smile, and a "How ya doing, Augie?"

"Who you going to go as?" I asked.

"I really don't have a clue," he said. "I've always been a little queasy about masks. I think it's fallout from the Lone Ranger." He offered us a wry smile and then began to make his way around the shop, gazing at the possibilities.

Clearly, Coolican didn't want to be bothered. I chalked it up to the emotional roller coaster the deputy had been on for the last few weeks. I'd seen it before with guys—after rare moments of vulnerability, they tended to close up like clams.

I watched the deputy nod in recognition as he walked past each of the masks. He stood a long time in front of the Robert Creeley mask with a wily eye patch, muttering lines from one of his poems. Then he moved on to William Blake, who managed to look very proper, despite having a detail from the Great Green Dragon tattooed across his forehead.

I realized that Coolican had no intention of choosing a mask until Quince and I left the shop. That was easy to understand. Nobody wanted their identity revealed before the event, and I began to wonder if I should switch from Wallace Stevens. But damn it, I'd already bonded with the Emperor of Ice Cream.

Quince ripped off her Marianne Moore mask. "I can't wear this," she whispered to me. "That's Ruthie Rosenberg's poet. I'm not wearing the dead woman's poet."

A moment later she eased into an Elizabeth Bishop mask. It came with an elaborate rolled bun of a hairpiece. I stood back to gaze at

Quince's fresh aspect and was reminded of my Aunt Dorothea, dead more than twenty years now.

I noticed Coolican, standing now between Randall Jarrell, with a waxed handlebar mustache, and John Berryman, hidden behind giant black specs and a beard that would have been the envy of any Old Testament prophet.

"Who is Elizabeth Bishop?" Quince asked.

"You've got a day to find out."

"Oh my God, the pressure. But I do love her."

"Then you shall be her."

I'd noted with some dismay that there were no prices on the masks, and figured that as objects of art, which they clearly were, the prices would be dear. I was not wrong. Prices for purchase of the masks started at twelve hundred dollars, with the W. S. Merwin and Denise Levertov. Fortunately, the shop had a rental policy. "We understand," Edgar said, "that most of our customers are in no position to purchase our masks. Especially not the Poesies. Normally, we rent them for $100 a week, but, of course, we're always up for a reasonable trade."

It wasn't lost on me that the local version of African trade beads was herbal. I wondered if even edibles had become an acceptable form of currency.

"But," Edgar continued, "we've come up with a special rental price of fifty dollars for the Poesies and for the opening of the Galley."

Quince, perhaps experiencing some retrospective guilt for the cost I paid for the silk scarf, insisted on picking up my rental fee and deposits. I was happy to let her, and the two of us, with friendly nods to Coolican, walked arm in arm from the shop, our personas wrapped in tissue paper and tucked away in exotic, hemp-handled sacks.

Drowning in a Glass of Water

That evening, after we snuck the masks into our back room, Quince made a lovely pasta Bolognese, and the four of us, plus baby Milosz, had a pleasant dinner together. Blossom was in particularly good form.

"I'm so excited for the opening," she said, as she broke off a little hunk of baguette and handed it to Milosz to teethe on. "Bobby's worked so hard on it, and despite all this nasty shit, it's finally going to open. Even if it turns out to be a bust, it's going to be our bust."

"No way it's going to be a bust," I said, and told her about Edgar from the mask shop, mentioning that fifty-seven masks to date had been rented or purchased for the opening.

"Add to that," Blossom said, "the fact that most of the Sisters of Perpetual Indulgence are designing their own masks and costumes."

"It's all very emotional for me," Sabbatini admitted. "I've been trying to get myself into a Zen place with it, but it's not working."

"What do you think the problem is, honey?" Blossom wondered.

Sabbatini shook his head.

"Maybe you should smoke a little Fuck Face," I suggested.

"Yes, when all else fails. *Je croix je noye dans un verre d'eau.*"

"Speak English, Bobby," Blossom cried.

"I feel like I'm drowning in a glass of water."

Poetry Is Blind

After we finished the dishes, Sabbatini asked me to go for a stroll. I figured he wanted someone to smoke the Fuck Face with, but he didn't bother to pull out a joint and we walked a long way down the steep dirt road in relative silence. No poems were recited, no French phrases dropped, in the Sabbatini manner, as fairy dust. I decided to follow the man's lead, and commented on little but the chill of the night and the planet Venus, nudged close to the crescent moon.

I could tell just by the way he held the flashlight that Sabbatini had the weight of the world on his shoulders. It had to be hard work bringing so much faith into a community, even if the faith came in the form of poetry. Although he made more sense to me as a St. Paul police detective than a West County poetry messiah, I'd come to accept that Sabbatini had followed the path he was meant to follow.

A little more than a mile into our walk, Sabbatini finally opened up. “A couple of things I want to talk about. First of all, the business of my taking casino money. I really wrestled with that, Augie.”

“I can’t imagine you endorsing a casino, Bobby.”

“The casino was never going to be built, Augie. Everybody in the know told me that.”

“So, you sold out, Bobby.”

“Is that what you think?”

“Of course. But you’re not the first poetry man to do that and clearly not the first priest.”

“But, Augie, the dough’s small change to Red Carpet Casinos. Like research and development money.”

“Yeah, research and folly, in this case.”

“But don’t you think the good that Ginsberg’s Galley will do for the community justifies my malfeasance?”

I shrugged.

“At least that’s how I’m rationalizing it. But I’m not really sure about it. Have I sold my soul, Augie?”

I gave Sabbatini a slap on the back. “I seriously doubt that. In your position, I may have done the same thing.”

A little farther up the road, Sabbatini stretched out his arm and pointed to the left. “That’s where Custard’s property begins.”

I looked over but could see next to nothing in the dark.

“I really fucked up with Custard,” Sabbatini said.

“What do you mean?”

“I thought he was a changed man. It’s my own arrogance, really. I knew that Custard wasn’t what you’d call a good man. That he’d battered his wife. That he bullied people in business and in his personal life. That he was a selfish bastard. But there he was, memorizing a poem by e. e. cummings.”

“Hey, Bobby, I fear that poetry, like love, is blind.”

“No, poetry is not blind; we are.”

“Well, you can’t be responsible for everybody who comes into your church.”

"I just couldn't imagine that a person who went to the trouble to memorize poetry could murder somebody."

I stopped Sabbatini and put my arm around his shoulder. "Listen, Bobby, I'm not satisfied that Custard's the killer."

"Well, you're the only one around here who isn't."

"I know."

As we walked farther down the road, I told Sabbatini about a Jewish client I once had who wanted me to find out which of his employees was stealing from him. When I discovered it was a fellow named Kornfeld, my client said, "It can't be Kornfeld. Kornfeld keeps kosher."

Sabbatini got my point. "The real issue here is my arrogance."

Again, I shrugged. I didn't want to interfere with Sabbatini's self-flagellation. I found it rather refreshing in a holy man.

"It just calls into question the whole enterprise," he said.

"Why's that?"

"Listen, if I'm given to this degree of folly, then I seriously wonder if I have anything to offer anybody else."

I was of two minds. As much as I wanted to comfort the wounded messiah, I was disturbed that he, like the rest of the community, was settling for easy justice in regard to Ruthie Rosenberg's killing. Nobody seemed curious, in the least, about who poisoned Custard.

It wasn't like I had a plan. But, Christ, the sheriff's department might have shaken down the casino Russians before they left town. And what about cracking open Custard's empire and having a look? Which were they more squeamish about—dishonoring the dastardly dead, or tangling with his widow, the county supervisor? But I wasn't getting paid to worry about this shit, and nobody was interested in what I thought.

Sabbatini and I walked on in silence for another half mile or so, until he circled me like a sheepdog to get me to turn back.

A few steps toward home, Sabbatini exclaimed, "See how insidious evil can be. It even fucks with your brain after the grave." He reached into his coat pocket and pulled out a fat joint. "I think it's time for my medicine. Care for a little Fuck Face?"

I wasn't having any.

CHAPTER TWENTY-FIVE

Mardi Gras on Main Street

QUINCE AND I stood awestruck in the doorway of Ginsberg's Galley. The guests all wore masks or elaborate costumes and promenaded across the long open floor in two broad lanes. Along with a soundtrack of splintered verse—a collage of poets' voices that Sabbatini must have spliced together—a 1960s-style strobe light fractured the visual field. I felt like I'd walked into a vibrant abstraction. If I squinted slightly, I saw Picasso's *Les Demoiselles d'Avignon* or a Max Beckmann triptych of cabaret debauchery.

A few of the "poets" possessed Harpo Marx–style rubber horns and weren't shy about tooting them, punctuating the cacophony with the sound of a traffic jam, circa 1900.

It was hard to know how to penetrate the procession. Finally, I saw a gap between Frank O'Hara, clearly in his cups, and a lively pair of poets—Walt Whitman and Ezra Pound—marching in step together. This Ezra—young and dandyish—had an entirely different look than the old-man version that Sister Everlast presented. Neither Walt or Ezra wore masks, though both were elaborately costumed.

Once Quince and I fell in, the booming-voiced Whitman hollered: "Welcome, fellow poets. 'Every atom belonging to me, as good belongs to you.'"

I turned and caught a glance of the bearded Whitman, who paraded in a top hat and houndstooth overcoat. He winked at me and made a cone of his ear. "Just trying to pick up the blab of the pave," he said.

The poets kept coming toward us. The eye-patched Robert Creeley, with his wry smile, masked the face of a curvy woman in a black sheath with a plunging neckline. Even through the riot of sound, I could hear the Creeley-babe slurping from a tumbler of whisky. Along came C. K. Williams, balancing a martini. His mask featured an attached monocle and a great seam-like vein running down the middle of the neckpiece. Next came Marianne Moore, drinking from a bottle of Lagunitas IPA. She'd fitted a peacock feather in the ribbon of her tricorne hat. Dough-faced Theodore Roethke was a study in sexual ambiguity. He carried no drink but toted a little watering can and wore a codpiece over his gardening pants. It was the pair of gigantic breasts in the sequined bra, with ivy spiraling through the armpits, that threw me.

Quince slipped out of the procession to fetch us a couple of beers. I watched her tease some folding money out of her bra and pay the bartender, a sober-looking Robert Lowell.

It didn't take long to realize that the Sisters of Perpetual Indulgence, the participants not wearing masks made by the masters of Graton, were the true impersonators. Although the Sisters had donned gorgeously honed costumes and made themselves up with Cleopatra-like extravagance, it was the way they moved that made the difference. They weren't operating, like many of the masked poets, simply from the neck up. The sisters' impersonations involved the entire body.

One consequence of the strobe light, intended or not, was that the throbbing beacons made it next to impossible to guess who was behind the disguises. I tried with no luck to spot Sabbatini and Blossom, and wondered if Coolican and Yevtushenko had shown up.

Fifteen or twenty minutes after we arrived, a miraculous personage joined the procession.

"Look," Quince said, "it's Emily."

And, indeed, along came Emily Dickinson, dressed in a black crepe gown with a frilled collar. She sipped a chartreuse daiquiri through a straw. Her face was pancaked in an oval of chalky white, like a cameo. Even more striking was her black hat, shaped like a sailing schooner. A long, bejeweled dildo, with a compellingly realistic head, protruded from the bow.

It had taken one of the Sisters of Perpetual Indulgence to liberate Emily.

Poetry Priest

A few moments later the strobe light was killed and the cacophonous loop of poetic rants faded out. After hushed murmurs, a masked Allen Ginsberg appeared from out of nowhere and climbed to the small stage, leaving the rest of us little time to gawk, in normal light, at the majestic creatures around us.

Ginsberg's mask was a minimalist affair, tapering off below the cheekbones to reveal a dark shaggy beard. Bobby Sabbatini was clearly behind the mask and beard. I recognized his gait as well as the ripple of his violet Sufi pants as he crossed the stage. Some of the poet-revelers began a chant: "Poesy, Poesy, Poesy."

This was the moment my friend had been waiting for. He'd infected an entire community with his love of poetry. Some folks clearly saw Sabbatini as a modern-day prophet. Now they were returning the love by coming out, with far more than bells on, to support his poetry church, Ginsberg's Galley.

Sabbatini/Ginsberg bowed to the crowd amid a tumult of cheering. He flicked on the mike and his voice came through the fabled new sound system in honeyed tones. "We started simply enough, my friends, by coming to early morning meetings and sharing poems. But look where we've gotten to."

As the cheering revelers crowded close to the stage, I felt a tug of trepidation, an amorphous sense of doom, a shortness of breath that made it difficult to swallow. At my side, Quince sensed that something was up.

She shook me by the arm. "What's going on?"

"Nada."

"This is so much more than I could have imagined," Sabbatini continued. "I doubt that those of us gathered here, to paraphrase our namesake, represent the best minds of our generation, but I know that we are among the best souls."

A chorus of Harpo Marx horns quacked and the Sisters of Perpetual Indulgence incited the crowd to shimmy, a quick wave sweeping across the room. When it reached Emily Dickinson, I saw her stick two fingers in her mouth and emit a shrill whistle, the dildo on her hat pivoting from right to left like the long gun atop an armored tank.

Sabbatini held up his hands to quiet the crowd. "I know that this has been a difficult time for our community. Part of the reason that we've gathered tonight is to acknowledge the healing power of poetry. I also know that I have been accused in some quarters of trying to replace God with poetry."

Some in the spectacular crowd greeted that statement with hisses. Father Sabbatini held up a hand and smiled broadly, pausing to allow cheers to rise and slowly recede.

"I want you to know that it's not my ambition to lead anyone. We all have minds of our own and unique sensibilities. I mean, look at us," he said, sweeping his hands from left to right to include everyone in the room. Another huge cheer rose. "And I assure you, it's not my intention to mess with anybody's theology or shepherd of choice.

"Now, I invite each of you to come up here and recite a poem of your choosing. If you don't have a favorite already committed to memory, well, that's where our state-of-the-art poetry karaoke machine, with over 3,000 poems, kicks in. I'll be sitting to the right of the stage, manning my little machine. Come by and check in before you mount the stage."

Finally, I noticed Blossom cheering her man behind a rather staid mask of Adrienne Rich. She was below the stage to the right, where Sabbatini had a table with a computer and soundboard. Blossom. I remembered her early days with Sabbatini, when he tried every trick imaginable to get her to love poetry. Once a vocal dissenter, she now was his most devoted disciple. I glanced around at the circle of poets rimming the stage, hoping that other people I knew would become apparent. No luck. How about Sister Everlast? Surely she was here.

"And now, in benediction," Sabbatini continued, "a line from Master Ginsberg."

Follow your inner moonlight; don't hide the madness.

To Touch

I had hoped that after Sabbatini's sermon, people would back away from the stage and I'd be better able to survey the crowd. But folks bunched even closer as several masqueraders lined up in front of Sabbatini's table, anxious to ascend the stage and recite poems. I led Quince toward the hallowed table, not because I was anxious to get onstage, but to meet up with Blossom.

Blossom seemed happy to see us, even if her affect was a bit muted. At first I thought she was trying to stay in character as Adrienne Rich, though I found out later that she shared my growing sense of doom.

"Don't you two look fetching," she said. "Wallace Stevens and . . . ?"

"Elizabeth Bishop," Quince said.

I was about to comment on Blossom's quiet elegance as Adrienne Rich, when Sabbatini kicked his poetry karaoke apparatus into gear. With a couple of keystrokes, he caused a large screen to descend into place behind the podium. It filled quickly with a slideshow of photos of the bear-like poet Charles Olson, followed by a digital broadside of Olson's poem "Maximus to Himself." Then the heavy-breathing voice of the poet himself began reading. I didn't know the poem, save for the marvelous first two lines:

I have had to learn the simplest things
last. Which made for difficulties.

A rousing round of applause followed the poem and Sabbatini's display of technology. Then Charles Olson, the first masked poet to perform, strutted onstage in a sailor suit and recited another of the Maximus poems.

"Do you know who's behind the mask?" I asked.

Blossom shook her head.

I gave her my best Wallace Stevens wink. "Maybe we wandered into the wrong poetry karaoke bar."

A quick procession of poets followed, each reciting a short poem. Blossom didn't recognize anybody behind their masks. She suggested that they were probably among the folks from around the county who came to Sabbatini's morning poetry meetings.

Clearly, Sabbatini was having the time of his life. I'd glance over at him from time to time as he poked at his keyboard with two fingers. The images of master poets popped onto the big screen, followed by their voices, compelling and oddly present, reading favored poems. I realized that if you threw a curtain over Sabbatini, he'd be the Wizard of Oz with a tricked-up Mac.

When the faux poets reached the stage, Sabbatini sat back and enjoyed the spectacle as one disciple after another recited poetry.

Walt Whitman, the bloke we'd met with young Ezra Pound, climbed with a bit of pomp to the stage. He tossed his top hat out into the crowd and did a sexy pirouette, flapping his coat open and shut. What followed was a short section of *Leaves of Grass*, performed as a vaudeville number. Old Walt yanked a host of phallic objects out of the great pockets of his overcoat, bellowing:

Mine is no callous shell.
I have instant conductors all over me whether I pass or stop,
They seize every object and lead it harmlessly through me.

Galley Orgy

Next Ezra Pound climbed the stage and started kissing Walt Whitman. The crowd went crazy. Couples throughout the tavern paired off, dancing and groping each other. Across the room, I saw Robinson Jeffers making out with Sylvia Plath. On the far side of the bar, Emily Dickinson was dry-humping one of the bartenders, Robert Lowell. I wasn't sure what Sabbatini would think of his grand opening turning into a masked orgy. Soon Blossom hustled over toward him and it wasn't long before the two were dancing cheek to cheek in the center of the room with quite a crowd gathered around them.

Quince flipped her mask atop her hairpiece and started kissing me on the neck. I pulled away right before she'd have left me a hickey.

"Don't be shy," she said. "Lift your mask, Wallace."

When I did, we kissed like a pair of high school sweethearts. *What the hell,* I thought, *make a life with this woman. It won't be boring.*

Then a tall creature in white face and a velvet dress approached us. She wore a black felt hat with side tassels and a gorgeous aquiline nose crafted of putty. "How do you do?" she said in an arch British accent. I'd just surfaced for air after necking with Quince, my mask having fallen to the floor behind me. I hadn't a clue who this British diva was meant to be.

"Don't tell me you've already become weary of your persona."

I didn't answer but picked up the mask and pulled it back down over my face.

Then she turned to Quince. "I had no idea you could be so spirited, Ms. Bishop."

"And who are you?" Quince asked, with a bit of hostility.

The woman held out her hand to Quince and then curtsied. "Dame Edith Sitwell, a pleasure."

As she held out her hand to me, I noticed the Everlast *E* appliquéd to her felt hat and gave her a rousing handshake.

"Sister Everlast!"

"No, no, you are mistaken. I'm Dame Edith Sitwell."

But there was no mistaking Sister Everlast now. She'd done a good job of hiding her muscular arms beneath her dress, but I could see the biceps stretching out the velvet.

"I don't mean to sound like a prude," she said, sweeping her hand across the floor to indicate the orgy taking shape, "but don't you think all this kissy-kissy business is detracting from the poetry?"

"It's poetry of another type, Dame Sitwell," Quince said, slipping her mask back on.

"Yes, of course, but I have genuine poetry to recite and I hope you'll support me as I try to bring this place back to order."

With that, Dame Sitwell left us and climbed directly onto the stage, not even allowing Sabbatini to get back to his computer table to perform the requisite preamble. Once up there, she flicked the mike. "Greetings, children. You should know that I enjoy an orgy as much as the next lass, but we have poetry to recite."

Gradually, the room fell back into order and Sister Everlast introduced herself, in high English, as Dame Sitwell, and then recited a poem.

And, with that, Quince nudged me and I noticed a group of Sisters in formation, their hands held together at the center, performing an orchestrated gavotte. Pretty soon folks broke into small groups and the whole room, with Sabbatini and Blossom at the center, gavotted in magical orbits.

Sinners

As we stood at the bar, Quince and I watched an odd-looking man climb up to the small stage. He was dressed like a nineteeth-century undertaker and wore a simple Lone Ranger mask. Sabbatini hadn't yet got back to his station and the undertaker grabbed hold of the mike and said, "Test, test, test."

Quince and I giggled, wondering what kind of dark poetry to expect.

"Yes," the man continued, "this is a test of your faith. Your faithfulness. You understand that you are in the presence of the devil."

"It's Reverend Hyde from First Christ River of Blood," I told Quince.

The reverend, peeling off his Lone Ranger mask, his face a blooming blush, shouted: "I am a messenger of Jesus Christ."

"We don't want your message," someone shouted.

Then, Sabbatini, back up front, called out, "Let him speak."

"Don't you see what you're doing? Don't you see?" the red-faced man continued. "You are practicing blasphemy. Blasphemy in the presence of God. Don't you see that you're following the Antichrist? He looks friendly enough, but he's the devil, tempting you with poetry. Remember Eden. The devil, disguised as a serpent, tempted with an apple. Don't let the devil tempt you with poetry. Do not take another bite."

Meanwhile, the Sisters of Perpetual Indulgence began chanting a rousing chorus: "We don't want your plastic Jesus! We don't want your plastic Jesus! We don't want your plastic Jesus! Fearmonger, fearmonger, fearmonger."

In a flash, a dozen Sisters climbed onto the stage, turned off the mike, and hustled Reverend Hyde off and out of the tavern. It was a striking example of Sister-power. On his way out, the reverend got the last word, hollering "SINNERS" with everything he had.

The Cavalcade

After order was restored, Coolican and Yevtushenko pushed through the swinging doors of the Galley. Neither of them was masked. I wondered why they were tardy. Yevtushenko wore pressed jeans and a

T-shirt with his namesake's mug, while Coolican appeared in a shiny thrift-store suit and moccasins. His knobbed, Yeatsian walking stick gave him away as the Irish master.

Yevtushenko followed a drunken Frank O'Hara. Quince and I moved closer to the stage. The Russian looked around a little nervously at first and fumbled with the mike. "I would put on the face of the poet," he said, "but when I go into the shop, it is gone." He quickly looked around the tavern as if he expected to see an impostor donning the Yevtushenko mask. Others in the room began looking over their shoulders. I realized how brave it was of Yevtushenko to stand up there.

In a moment, he surprised everybody by reciting in Russian from "Babi Yar," the poet's soaring poem about the site of a massacre in which more than 100,000 Jews, Gypsies, and Russian POWs died. I don't know if he intended it as a defiant act, but it clearly felt that way. Even in the tape that Sabbatini played of the genuine Yevtushenko, the poet read in English. The Russian left the stage to a smattering of applause, streams of sweat running off his forehead.

After a drunken Sylvia Plath came up to recite "Daddy," Sabbatini called for a brief break between poets, and Gil Scott-Heron's "The Revolution Will Not Be Televised" came blaring through the system. People went off to refresh their drinks. On my way to get a fresh beer for Quince, I ran into Coolican. He slapped me on the back. "How about Yevtushenko?" he said.

"Yeah, where'd he go? I wanted to congratulate him on his performance."

"I think he ducked out," Coolican said. "He looked a little overcome with emotion. So, I hear we missed a little fire and brimstone, Wallace."

"Yes, the Reverend Cecil Hyde in all his glory. But the Sisters rousted him out of here."

"Thank God for those lasses," Coolican said, with a Yeatsian tremolo to his voice. "Something strange is always happening here in River Town. You turn your back a moment and the Sisters of Perpetual Indulgence have become the Hells Angels."

We stepped up to the bar.

"What will you have, Professor Yeats? Can I stand you to a pint of ale?"

"Wouldn't that be lovely?"

When our beers arrived, we clinked mugs and I said, "You look good as Yeats. The moccasins are a nice touch."

"Thanks. I like to think that Yeats may have donned a pair during one of his U.S. visits."

"Well, he is now." I smiled at the Indian Yeats and realized how fond I was of the man.

Halfway through our beers, a photo of the young Adrienne Rich filled the screen. Then came her voice, reading one of her signature poems, "The Will to Change."

Blossom climbed up to the small stage. Masked as Adrienne Rich, she wore a smart tailored suit with plenty of buttons. Somehow she managed to project both intelligence and soul. Imagine Blossom, the one-time prison girl, now the wife of Poesy, masquerading as Adrienne Rich.

Coolican and I stood side by side to watch her act. She announced "Diving into the Wreck," the perfect poem, I thought, for the nautical tavern we were in, the image of diving into the shipwreck of our own souls. It didn't take Blossom/Adrienne long: as soon as she "put on / the body armor of black rubber," we were going underwater, into the depths with her.

It was the first poem of the night I truly heard. I saw myself descending into the wreck of my own life, wondering if I'd have the moxie to resurface.

By the time she'd finished the poem, Blossom had become Adrienne.

"Damn woman," Coolican said, "she's scarier than her hubby."

"The priest and priestess of the poetry church."

"Indubitably."

Adrienne offered a royal wave to the crowd. Some cheered, while others were still convulsed from their shipwreck experience. It was the loveliest and most sober moment of the evening.

I picked up a beer for Quince and brought Coolican over to say hello.

"Lizzie Bishop, may I introduce William Butler Yeats?"

Quince held out her hand. "Enchanté."

"He's not French, Lizzie, but Irish."

"Oh, I'm charmed," Coolican responded in a dry brogue. He then turned to me. "Would you mind terribly holding my beer? I think I will head up and make my offering."

I took Coolican aside. "You safe up there, man?"

Coolican nodded up at the stage, where Henry Wadsworth Longfellow was reciting "Song of Hiawatha" in a singsong voice.

"No worries, Wallace, the wicked wolf is dead."

Who knows what got into me, but I said, "How about you let me go next?"

"You want to be next, Wallace, be my guest."

Next

After I checked in with Sabbatini, he ran his Wallace Stevens program, a slideshow of photos of the poet and an audio clip of him reading from his poem, "So and So Reclining on Her Couch."

There was a sweet burst of applause when I mounted the stage. As I approached the mike, a number of people called my name, and somebody hollered, "Where's Rose?" That made me smile and I thought fondly of my illustrious daughter.

I looked out into the crowd and noted the few folks I recognized. There were Quince and Blossom and Coolican. Sabbatini, sans his Ginsberg mask, sat at his table beaming. Sister Everlast, still in her Edith Sitwell pose, had an unlit cigar in her mouth. And for the first time that night I noticed Sky, my ambulance-running buddy. Dressed mannishly, she stood near the stage in a handsome Jack Kerouac mask, which she lifted for a moment as she winked at me. I looked out toward the bar where a cluster of Sisters were standing, and searched the back corners of the room. That's where the loners, D. H. Lawrence and Randall Jarrell, were huddled.

After taking a deep breath, I adjusted the mike and spoke directly into it. "I'd like to salute Bobby Sabbatini, or as you know him, Poesy.

I always knew he had a certain greatness about him but had no idea it would take this direction. I knew him in Minnesota when the poetry first hit him. He wouldn't shut up with the stuff, and pretty soon he had cops memorizing W. H. Auden and FBI agents searching for code in obscure poems.

"But now, it's great to see him in a community that's primed to make poetry a centerpiece of its life. Through poetry, Poesy's found a way to bring you closer. It's enough to turn a guy into a convert. We are now all members of Poesy's church, which makes us all Poesies!"

A spontaneous cheer of "Poesies, Poesies, Poesies," went on for a good minute.

"Forgive my speechifying, but I just wanted to salute my buddy, Bobby Sabbatini. The guy really knows how to throw a party."

I hadn't meant to set off a demonstration, but that's what ensued. Various rhythmic chants of "Poesy" played against each other and didn't stop until Sabbatini stood up and bowed. Then he held out his arm to me and I began to recite Part V from Stevens's masterpiece, "The Man with the Blue Guitar."

Do not speak to us of the greatness of poetry,
Of the torches wisping in the underground,

Of the structure of vaults upon a point of light.
There are no shadows in our sun,

Day is desire and night is sleep.
There are no shadows anywhere.

The earth, for us, is flat and bare.
There are no shadows. Poetry

Exceeding music must take the place
Of empty heaven and its hymns.

Ourselves in poetry must take their place,
Even in the chattering of your guitar.

I had the odd sense, as I recited, that a bit of Wallace Stevens was breathing through me. When I'd finished, Sabbatini stood up and bowed to me and mouthed the words, "Thank you."

Sweet and Harsh

When I climbed down from the stage, there were hugs all around. Jesse Coolican was to be next. I patted him on the back, thinking he made a great W. B. Yeats. Sabbatini began a slideshow of Yeats photos and played a recording of the bard reading "The Lake Isle of Innisfree" in a frail, quaking brogue.

Halfway through the great poem, Coolican whispered in my ear, "I got a bad feeling about this. I'm not going up there."

"You sure?" I asked.

Coolican nodded.

I walked over and relayed the message to Sabbatini, back in his Ginsberg disguise, and he turned toward Coolican and mouthed: "No problem." Sabbatini yanked off his Ginsberg mask. Then, audibly, he said, "Coolie, toss me your mask."

The deputy shook his head. "Don't go up there, Poesy," he said.

"Don't be silly, Coolie."

"I mean it."

Sabbatini stood up. I couldn't believe that he was heading to the stage. Coolican bowed his Yeatsian head in shame. I thought of trying to stop Sabbatini but knew he wouldn't have it. Within seconds, the unmasked poetry priest climbed to the stage with the halting step of the poet in old age.

Another wild cheer went up for Poesy, who stepped gingerly to the mike. "What a thrill to pose as W. B. It may take a little imagination on your part. So just squint your eyes if you have to. My first thought was to recite one of the man's signature poems, like 'Sailing to Byzantium,' but who the hell do I think I am? So, here's a twelve-liner called 'Another Song of a Fool.'"

I turned to face Coolican as Sabbatini began reciting. He had peeled off his mask and, now, broke for the stage. Just as Sabbatini read the first two lines of the last stanza—

Like the clangor of a bell,
Sweet and harsh, harsh and sweet,

—Coolican hollered, "Get down, Poesy."

I heard a loud whistle emanating from the rear of the tavern. The crowd gasped as Sabbatini slumped against the podium, a long arrow penetrating his throat. Coolican dashed to his aid.

I turned and saw a person masked as Yevtushenko crouching with a crossbow in the back of the room. Most of the crowd froze before erupting in a frenzy. Some of the masked poets ran around in circles, while others tore off their faux faces, tossing them as they ducked in corners and behind the bar. Before anybody could reach the faux Yevtushenko, he fired again, the arrow whistling over Sabbatini's head as Coolican pulled him to the ground. The next thing I knew, D. H. Lawrence dove from his spot in the corner and pinned the sniper to the floor.

Behind the mask, Eileen Cust lay wild-eyed, foaming at the mouth. Once D. H. Lawrence had pinned her to the ground and Randall Jarrell had stripped off her mask, I could see that she was truly crazed. Even restrained on her back, she projected a fierce and articulate chant: "POESY'S THE ANTICHRIST, POESY'S THE ANTICHRIST, POESY'S THE ANTICHRIST!"

I looked around quickly for Reverend Hyde, but apparently the Sisters had successfully banished him.

Deputy Coolican rushed over and kneeled beside Mrs. Cust as the two men, still masked as Lawrence and Jarrell, held her down. Lawrence spread his large hand over her mouth to quiet her. Coolican was very kind to her. First, he asked Lawrence to lift his hand from the woman's mouth, and then he whispered things I couldn't hear that seemed to calm her.

A man in a Gary Snyder mask hurried over and said, "You should cuff her, Coolie."

Coolican looked up and said, "I left my cuffs in the car, Spud."

"Me too," said the deputy, peeling off his mask to reveal the vast birthmark, shining with sweat. "I'll run out and get mine."

At which point, Sister Everlast, still in Dame Edith Sitwell couture, stepped up and said, "I have a pair of cuffs in my bag." She fished out the cuffs and handed them to Spud.

"Hey," the deputy said, "these are the real deal."

"What did you expect, darling?"

Meanwhile, an ambulance siren sounded, and the small circle surrounding Bobby Sabbatini parted. I hustled to his side. Miraculously, the man was still alive, with the arrow planted in his throat. There was less blood than I expected. A mixture of foam and blood bubbled from his mouth. I wondered how he could breathe. Sabbatini's eyes fluttered open and shut and he looked like he was trying to say something. Quince had her arms around Blossom, who screamed, "DO SOMETHING! DO SOMETHING! LOOK WHAT THEY'VE DONE TO HIM!" The paramedics made no attempt to extract the arrow, but swiftly moved Sabbatini onto a gurney and wheeled him, through a chorus of harrowing wails, out of Ginsberg's Galley.

CHAPTER TWENTY-SIX

What Gives?

FOR SEVERAL WEEKS, it was touch and go. Sabbatini's lead surgeon assured us that he would survive the attack. He rallied at first but then developed an insidious infection with a high fever. I felt that there was no way I could return to Minnesota until Sabbatini was out of the woods. Blossom was a wreck and spent most of her time at the hospital. She needed support and all the help with Milosz that she could get.

Quince and I set up shop together in the spare bedroom. We quit talking about our romance or our future, and just allowed things to unfold at their own pace as we played house in the small Cazadero cabin. Each of us took turns cooking and doing the laundry. Milosz became our borrowed child.

Finally, the swelling in my nose subsided, and I was able to get it reset. For the next two weeks I carried on with it wrapped in white bandages, presenting the only clear amusement around West County. Everybody I ran into felt obliged to recall Jack Nicolson in *Chinatown.*

A strange pall settled over the community—a counterweight, perhaps, to the euphoria experienced at the opening of Ginsberg's Galley. All the masks had been returned to Identity Theft, the early morning poetry meetings were suspended, and everybody was concerned about Sabbatini's condition.

Once his infection subsided and Sabbatini began to heal, what had only been hinted at earlier was now confirmed by his doctors—the man's vocal cords had been irrevocably severed. He would never speak again.

Quince and I visited him every afternoon at the hospital. At first Sabbatini did not accept the news about losing the faculty of speech. He kept opening his mouth to say things, producing nothing but a creaking squeak. Sabbatini would look from one of us to the other as if to say, *What gives?*

Blossom was so relieved that her beloved survived that she became the perfect nurse. She walked him up and down the halls of the hospital, and they played Scrabble for hours. By the time he came home, Sabbatini had a little sign language under his belt that Blossom seemed to understand. He also had an iPad with an app that spoke in jagged, mechanical frequencies whenever he typed.

My humble prayer—
that he who loses one voice
finds another.

Poetry and Prose

The curious saga of the Custards continued as well. Since Mrs. Cust's crossbow attack on Sabbatini, she was being held at the state mental institution in Napa. Meanwhile, the sheriff's department discovered an archery range on the Cust property. And after conversations with a number of former employees, they learned that both husband and wife were sharpshooters and that they were often out on the range in the late afternoons. This was the bond that united them.

When Coolican revealed this information to me, he said, "So, now we'll never know which one took the potshots at me."

A pair of detectives from the sheriff's department visited Mrs. Cust but got nothing from her. I made a case for me and Coolican taking a drive to Napa State Hospital.

"She's not going to talk to us," the deputy said.

"Maybe not. But it will always bug me if we don't give her the chance."

Nearly two months after the attack, Deputy Coolican and I sat in a lounge with Eileen Cust on the fourth floor of Building B. She seemed glad to see us. Her hair had turned almost completely gray since the fateful night, her last peroxide job leaving her only with a few waxy yellow clumps. She was heavily sedated and sat with her hands wrapped around a tall plastic cup, sipping orange juice through a straw.

Coolican had dressed as a civilian in khakis and a vintage bowling shirt, emblazoned on the back with black letters that read SCORPIONS. At first the deputy chattered innocuously with the patient about West County people I didn't know. I gazed at Mrs. Cust and her tall cup of juice, amazed to think that not long ago she was the respected county supervisor for Sonoma County. Now, if she wasn't found mentally incompetent to stand trial, she'd be charged with attempted murder.

Meanwhile, Coolican seamlessly shifted the conversation from the weather along the Russian River to the question he most wanted to ask: "So, Eileen, was it you who shot those arrows at me, or was it your husband?"

Mrs. Cust bit her bottom lip and sipped at her juice. When Coolican repeated the question, she bowed her head. I found myself staring at the curious residue of peroxide in her hair. A long silence followed. I gazed past Mrs. Cust to the light streaming through the grilled windows. Without lifting her head, Mrs. Cust mumbled, "If we wanted to hit you, Jesse, we would have hit you. That's all I'm going to say."

The deputy appeared satisfied that that was all he was going to get.

"So if you had wanted to kill Bobby Sabbatini, Mrs. Cust," I said, "you'd have killed him. You would have, say, shot him through the heart."

The woman lifted her head and stared at me, but she did not answer.

I stared right back at her. "Which one of you killed Ruthie Rosenberg, you or your husband?"

Again, Mrs. Cust dropped her head.

Jesse Coolican glanced at me and shook his head as if I'd gone too far.

I scowled at Coolican, a bit outraged. This wasn't exactly a shoplifting charge we were talking about.

I'm not sure what possessed me, but I caught the woman's eyes and said, "It was *you,* wasn't it, Mrs. Cust, who killed Ruthie Rosenberg?"

Slowly, the former county supervisor lifted her head. Her eyes were bright red like those of someone who'd been staring into a fire for a long time. Her mouth seemed to creak open. "He brought her home to our house. Can you imagine that? He was defiling our home with his whore. I found them in our bed. You can understand, I made quite a fuss. I threw things at them. Anything I could find. I hollered, 'Get your whore out of here.' And that naked little bitch was running around my bedroom like a skinned rabbit. But I kept my wits about me. I did a very good job of keeping my wits about me."

Mrs. Cust nodded her head a few times and then sipped from her juice.

"What did you do next?" I asked.

"Well, I ran out to Gordon's truck and got his rifle."

"Was that the .45 caliber, Mrs. Cust?" Coolican asked.

"It was the rifle he's always had hanging in his rack," she said, irritated by the question.

"What happened next?" I asked.

"Well, I ran into the bedroom and they were both mostly dressed by then, but I saw that whore's panties on my floor."

I glanced over at Coolican. He was having trouble listening to Mrs. Cust's tale.

"I aimed the rifle at Gordon and told that bitch to take off her corduroy slacks and put on her panties. I didn't want them on my floor. That whore was shaking, but she did what I said. And when she started to pull up her corduroys, I said, 'No, no, you leave them on the floor.'" Mrs. Cust chuckled at this point. "I don't know where I got that idea."

Coolican was having a tough time breathing and I told him, in a whisper, that he could leave. But he shook his head and sat there, hard as it must have been to listen.

Mrs. Cust seemed like she enjoyed telling the rest of it. How she locked Custard in the hall closet and said she was going to drive Ruthie home. How she drove her out to Last Judgment and made her run barefoot in her panties up a muddy trail before putting two bullets in the back of her head.

At this point, Jesse Coolican stood up and walked out of the room, but I continued sitting at the table with Mrs. Cust.

"One more question, ma'am."

"Yes."

"Were you the person who poisoned Mr. Cust?"

"Well, yes. If you'd heard what he said to me, you'd understand."

"What did he say?"

Mrs. Cust sipped through her straw, but there was no juice left in her cup. She continued gurgling in the empty cup for a moment. Then she pulled her mouth away and looked directly at me.

"As I was leading his harlot out of the house, Gordon hollered from the closet, 'She's poetry, Eileen, and you're only prose.' That was cruel."

I agreed. "That *was* cruel."

Mrs. Cust raised her voice in outrage. "As if Gordon Cust knew the difference between poetry and prose. It was just a bunch of nonsense Poesy filled his head with. Just a bunch of nonsense," she repeated, and then went back to the straw in her nearly empty glass, gurgling quite madly for the next moment.

In as friendly a way as I could muster, I asked her to write down what she'd just told me.

"I'd be happy to," she said, as if agreeing to share a Bible passage with me.

Since I wasn't law enforcement, I didn't worry about her Miranda rights. I just wanted her confession on paper. I rounded up a couple of sheets and she wrote it down just as she told me, signing her name with an extra flourish. When I asked her to date it, she complied and asked if I could arrange for her to get some more orange juice.

American Poet

On the afternoon that Coolican and I returned from Napa State Hospital, Yevtushenko dropped off a ten-pound Coho salmon he'd caught north of Jenner. Blossom thanked the Russian profusely for his offering and invited Yevtushenko to stay for dinner, but he declined. Coolican and Yevtushenko hugged for a long moment and Sabbatini typed a message on his iPad. A few seconds later the mechanical voice, dialed to peak volume, blasted: "YOU ARE A GENEROUS MAN, MY FRIEND."

Yevtushenko nodded and wiped away the tears running down his flushed cheeks.

Sabbatini did a little more typing. "SO, WHO THE HELL ARE YOU MEMORIZING THESE DAYS?" the machine voice shouted.

The little group of us, save for Yevtushenko and Sabbatini, burst into laughter.

The Russian bowed his head and Sabbatini typed away. "IF THERE EVER WAS A TIME FOR POETRY, IT'S NOW."

Yevtushenko nodded solemnly and then said, "Who do you recommend to be for me my first American poet?"

Without equivocation, Sabbatini typed and the machine blasted: "WALT WHITMAN."

Moses and Aaron

Coolican stayed for supper. Along with the salmon, Quince roasted potatoes and sautéed a medley of Italian eggplant and fennel. Given the enormous salmon, we thought of inviting a bunch of Sabbatini's friends to dine with us, but Blossom decided that it should just be the five of us, and Milosz, so as not to overwhelm the poetry priest.

Sabbatini didn't have much appetite anymore. Along with permanently losing his voice, he seemed different in other ways. He looked a bit pale and drawn now, and yet had a feral look around the eyes.

Once Milosz was put to bed, the five of us made polite conversation. We talked about locals, mostly, and speculated about who lettered the new message, credited to Ezekiel, on the signboard of First Christ River of Blood: NOW LET THEM PUT THEIR HARLOTRY AND THE CARCASSES OF THEIR KINGS FAR AWAY FROM ME.

Coolican joked that Eileen Cust might have a remote device controlling the signboard all the way from Napa State Hospital. Sabbatini got a kick out of that. He perked up even more when Quince brought out the dessert, a glorified rice pudding.

The voiceless poetry man saluted the scalloped soufflé bowl and set to typing on his iPad. I'd guess that the resulting mechanized cackle: "LE GATEAU DU RIZ," was as egregious a corruption of French pronunciation as any of us had ever heard. The monster voice continued: "HOW DID YOU KNOW THAT WAS MY FAVORITE, QUINCE?"

The born-again wife nodded to Sabbatini's actual wife.

As Sabbatini surprised us by feasting on a hearty portion of pudding, Blossom began talking about the film critic Roger Ebert's text-to-voice software. "He sounds almost like himself now. They had all these tapes of old Ebert talking, so they gave the mechanical device his voice. We've got plenty of tapes of Bobby reading poems."

Sabbatini shook his head. Then he went at the iPad. "I HAD PLENTY OF TIME TO THINK WHEN I WAS IN THE HOSPITAL."

"That wasn't thinking," Blossom chimed in, "that was delirium."

Sabbatini smiled at his wife before looking squarely at me and typing away again in a fresh flurry. Quince and I exchanged quizzical glances. My old friend's aspect was so sober, I was tempted to reach across the table and tickle him under the arm.

"I MUST ASK SOMETHING GREAT OF YOU, AUGIE. I NEED YOUR HELP WITH MY WORK."

"What work?" I blurted out.

Sabbatini spread a compassionate smile across his face and then went at the iPad again. "MY WORK AS A POETRY MINISTER. I NEED YOU TO BE MY VOICE, AUGIE."

"You're kidding," I said.

Sabbatini shook his head and laid a benevolent smile on me before typing.

"I NEED YOU TO SPEAK FOR ME AS AARON SPOKE FOR MOSES."

I looked around at the others, expecting them to confirm my sense of the absurdity of this, but Blossom and Coolican and even Quince nodded soberly, as if they were all party to this lunacy.

Suddenly Sabbatini had color back in face. His mechanical rant continued. "THE SCENE IS ESTABLISHED HERE. WITH YOU BESIDE ME, AUGIE, THE MORNING POETRY MEETINGS WILL CONTINUE TO GROW AND GINSBERG'S GALLEY IS BOUND TO BE A SUCCESS."

Coolican let out a hoot of approval while Quince and Blossom smiled. I glared at them all. "This is absolute madness, Bobby. I don't even live in California," I shouted.

Sabbatini typed away like a speed typist and then hit the play button on his app. He stood tall now and spread his arms like a preacher, with the iPad acting as a nasty voicebox in his right hand. "WHO CARES WHERE THE FUCK YOU LIVE? WHAT ARE YOU GOING TO DO, AUGIE, RETURN TO MINNEAPOLIS? AREN'T YOU TIRED OF BEING A SMALL DICK IN A BIG TOWN? HERE YOU'RE ALREADY A LOCAL HERO, AND YOU HAVE A FEELING FOR POETRY LIKE A MAN WITH A CALLING. I SHOULD KNOW, SHOULDN'T I? I MAY HAVE LOST MY VOICE, AUGIE, BUT YOU, MY FRIEND, WILL FINALLY FIND YOURS. LOOK, YOU HAVE A GREAT WOMAN HERE, A WOMAN WHO LOVES YOU. THE POETRY MINISTRY WILL RENT A PLACE FOR YOU IN GUERNEVILLE."

I gazed at Quince, who bowed her head slightly and nodded. Blossom had a fat grin on her face. And Coolican, who seemed to be enjoying this spectacle more than anyone else, said, "I really like the idea of you playing Aaron to Poesy's Moses, Augie. Dig, Aaron was the dude who changed his rod into a snake in Pharaoh's court."

"I don't want him to change his rod into a snake," Quince quipped.

Sabbatini typed a bit more, and then bowed toward Quince and me. "THINK ABOUT IT, YOU TWO. TALK AMONG YOURSELVES. I KNOW YOU'LL MAKE THE RIGHT DECISION."

EPILOGUE

Waiting for Rumi

IT'S BEEN A little more than six months now since I agreed to become Sabbatini's temporary voice, and Quince and I have moved into the town of Guerneville. With the poetry priest's occasional counsel, Quince and I have been running Ginsberg's of Guerneville, and it's going pretty well. We tweaked the name of the establishment with Sabbatini's blessing. For a reason that I couldn't put my finger on, I wanted the name of the town in the tavern's moniker.

"AUGIE," Sabbatini said, when we discussed the name change, "A SENSE OF PLACE IS LAUDABLE. SOME WOULD ARGUE THAT POETRY BEGINS WITH A SENSE OF PLACE."

Surprisingly, the business runs very smoothly. Quince handles the bar, Sister Everlast is our entertainment director, and I host poetry night and keep the morning poetry groups going throughout West County.

For most of the time that Quince and I have been entrenched in Guerneville, the Sabbatinis have been traveling around the country in a pimped-out VW van, meeting with engineers who specialize in text-to-voice software. Sabbatini is very picky and insists he's holding out for a software engineer sensitive to poetry. Not an easy find, or, in Blossom's words, "Software geeks and poetry geeks don't grow from the same tree."

I'm pleased to say that Quince and I are getting along quite nicely. We'd made a point of not talking much about the future until recently. Last month, when we were walking along the beach at Goat Rock, she asked how I'd feel about having a baby.

"You're pregnant?" I gulped.

She shook her head and said, "I was thinking we could adopt."

Neither of us said anything the rest of the way up the beach to the north end, where the river ends and the sea lions beach themselves. The idea was such a surprise to me that I couldn't get it out of my head. By the time we turned back down the beach, I was weighing the pros and cons.

"I'm pretty old for being a new father," I said.

Quince shrugged. "You're not so old."

"We don't make much money," I said.

"How much money do we need?"

"What if you and I split up?"

"What if the sky falls?"

"Don't you have any trepidation?" I asked.

"I wouldn't call it trepidation," Quince said, "but the idea scares me shitless."

"And still?" I asked.

Quince flashed me a wondrous smile. "I can't imagine anything more wonderful, Augie."

"What would you do with a baby, Quince?"

My love bowed her head regally. "Hold it in my arms," she said.

Now, only a few weeks after our walk on the beach, we've begun the adoption process. When the Sabbatinis were home recently, we shared our news. Bobby and Blossom were beside themselves with excitement.

"Do you have names picked out?" Blossom asked.

Quince grinned. "We have a name—Rumi."

"AND WHAT IF IT'S A GIRL?" Sabbatini asked.

"She'll be named Rumi," I announced.

Sabbatini initiated a group hug at the news. Afterward, Milosz ran around the room like a proper dervish.

Blossom nodded with an expression of deep contentment. "Imagine," she said, "someday Milosz will babysit Rumi."

Our hearts already
filled with poetry,
we wait for Rumi.

ACKNOWLEDGMENTS

MANY THANKS TO the early readers of this book, Chester Arnold, Dan Coshnear, Mary Logue, and George Rabasa, who suffered through various drafts and offered useful ideas and encouragement.

Thanks to West County chums Chester Aaron, Marylu Downing, Roger House, Pat Nolan, and Mike Tuggle for their friendship. Please excuse my excesses.

To Mary Mount (Sister Claire Voyante) for sharing her views of Guerneville, West County, and the good works of the Sisters of Perpetual Indulgence.

To Adam Raskin for offering insights from a P.I.'s perspective.

Thanks to Julie Pinkerton, a marvelous editor, for shepherding this baby home.

Finally, a salute à mon amour, Catherine Durand. Quel plaisir.